Amanda looked back over the weeks, past the doubt and fear, to the tears and the panics that had gripped her, and she shook her head.

'Quite frankly, I'm too tired for anything else now.'

'I can imagine. I do know how frightening it can be, you know.'

'You do?'

'Yes,' said Flixe deliberately, 'I was already pregnant with Andrew by the time I married his father.'

Amanda let out a shout of bitter laughter, which troubled Flixe.

'You and my mother both! And people call *this* the "Permissive" age. It seems the only difference is that we're less dishonest about it. How she could be so bloody hypocritical all those years with her little talks about never letting any boy go too far!'

'It's not hypocrisy, Amanda. Both your mother and I were in love when we became pregnant.' Flixe tried not to sound as though she were judging the girl but as Amanda's face closed in Flixe knew she had failed. She got up and went to put her hand lightly on Amanda's smooth dark hair.

'You've a lot of people who care very much what happens to you, Amanda,' she said deliberately. 'Don't be afraid to let them help.'

**NOTRE DAME
PARBOLD**

DAPHNE WRIGHT

The Tightrope Walkers

WARNER BOOKS

A *Warner* Book

First published in Great Britain in 1993
by Little, Brown and Company
This edition published in 1994 by Warner Books

Copyright © Daphne Wright 1993

The moral right of the author has been asserted.

Permission to quote from 'As I Walked Out One Evening'
from *Collected poems by W. H. Auden*,
edited by Edward Mendelson,
granted by Faber & Faber Ltd

*All characters in this publication are fictitious and
any resemblance to real persons, living or dead,
is purely coincidental.*

All rights reserved.
No part of this publication may be reproduced,
stored in a retrieval system or transmitted, in any
form or by any means, without the prior
permission in writing of the publisher, nor be
otherwise circulated in any form of binding or
cover other than that in which it is published and
without a similar condition including this
condition being imposed on the subsequent purchaser.

A CIP catalogue record for this book is
available from the British Library.

ISBN 0 7515 0838 1

Printed in England by Clays Ltd, St Ives plc

Warner Books
A Division of
Little, Brown and Company (UK) Limited
Brettenham House
Lancaster Place
London WC2E 7EN

For Sylvie and Ib Bellew

AUTHOR'S NOTE

As in the other novels in *The Threaded Dances* sequence, all the characters, organisations and houses in this book are figments of the author's imagination and bear no relation to any real organisations, houses or people living or dead.

'Time breaks the threaded dances'

W.H. Auden
'As I Walked Out One Evening'

CHAPTER 1

'Amanda Wallington, the first of our "New Stars", is studying Fine Art at the University of East Anglia. The daughter of David Wallington MP and his wife, Julia, who is a barrister, Amanda spends as much of her vacations as she can in Florence.'

The girl in the photograph was slender and long-legged with a square-chinned, bony face that looked both intelligent and seductively sulky. Her dark hair was long and straight and her eyes, ringed with black make-up and fringed with false lashes, looked enormous. Dressed in a minute skirt of blackberry-coloured wool and a clinging yellow sweater, she was lying along the golden-stone balustrade of a garden overlooking Florence. One of her arms was lifted above her head so that her hand could hold the heavy mass of hair away from her face.

Felicity Suvarov stared down at the photograph of her god-daughter and wondered what she was really thinking as she lay there faintly smiling. She looked languid and sophisti-cated and entirely confident; yet as a child she had been both passionate and angry. Felicity had often thought that Amanda might have been rather lonely as well, but if so she

1

had had far too much pride to tell anyone.

Thinking of her transformation from difficult child to moody adolescent and then to the stunning, self-satisfied beauty of the photograph, Felicity was conscious of sympathy mixed with dislike and even fear, which surprised her. Reluctant to examine the fear, she tried to concentrate on the sympathy, knowing that although Amanda had the world at her feet for the time being, there was a lot that fate could do to her in revenge.

Felicity felt as though she was battling with that revenge herself. For twenty years she had had almost everything anyone could want and had never considered what might happen if it were to be taken away. She dropped the glossy magazine back on her desk and turned to stare out of the window at the leafless trees in the park, trying as so often before to concentrate on the happy past or even the possibly bearable future instead of the grim present.

Her hands clenched as she tried to remember. For a while she could not until, listening to the emptiness of the big house around her, she forced herself to think of it as it had been for so long. What she remembered most clearly was the dark, slender figure of her husband, around whom the whole glorious circus of sound, colour, scent and happiness had revolved.

'Happiness,' she said to herself. 'What a funny little word for something so powerful!'

The house had been so full of it in the old days that it was almost as obvious as the scent of the flowers and pot-pourri she had kept in every room. Their sweetness had been mixed with the spiciness of beeswax polish and the warm smell of yeast lifting sticky dough for the bread she had always made herself because Peter liked it so.

There never seemed to be enough time to make bread any longer, even though three of her four children were away at boarding school and the fourth at university. The food she cooked for herself when she was alone was the quickest and cheapest she could find, and the house seemed to smell of little but dust. Flowers were too expensive a luxury and the pot-pourri had lost its scent long ago.

With an immense effort of will, Felicity stopped herself thinking of the present and went back again to the past. There had been characteristic sounds as well as scents, she reminded herself: the children's music thumping down from their bedrooms, usually punctuated with screams of laughter or rage; and Peter's never-to-be-forgotten voice – slightly drawling, faintly accented, utterly seductive – as he called for her to tell her the latest joke that had tickled his cynical fancy, to arrange another party or, more gently, to tell her how he loved and wanted her even after twenty years of marriage.

In the waves of misery that washed over her, she could not hold on to the past any longer. Her hands gripped the cold iron of the radiator as she tried to force back the useless, rasping tears she hated. Peter was dead. The house was full of dust and loneliness. There were debts to grapple with and work to be done. Refusing to surrender, she straightened her back, tucked her hands inside the sleeves of her fur coat to warm them up again and returned to her desk.

As she was pulling out her chair, she heard the sound of a key in the front door and her lips lifted into a smile. The only person it could possibly be was Andrew, her elder son. Running to the door, she pulled it open, ready to call out. Before she could even say his name, she heard his voice.

'Put it there, Fred. I'll go up and see if my mother's in.'

Her delighted smile died and with it much of the excitement at his unexpected return. She stood for a moment, one hand on the blackened brass door handle and the other at her throat.

'Andrew?' she called when she had got her voice under control. 'Can you come up here a moment?'

Heavy feet pounded up the stairs and then he stood in front of her. For a moment delight resurfaced at the sight of him, tall and slender, dark-haired like his father and with the same flashing eyes and fine bones. Felicity held out her arms and he walked forwards. Bending his head, he kissed her forehead. At the touch of his lips, she smiled and stroked his clean and floppy hair.

As he straightened up, Andrew left his hands on her thin shoulders.

'Hello, Mama,' he said, considering her and noticing that her blonde hair was dishevelled and her dark blue eyes were damp. 'You look slightly worn.'

'I am a bit,' she admitted, almost amused by the understatement. She hugged him again, feeling a moment of pure pleasure as he let her hold on to him. 'Come in here for a minute,' she said as she released him.

'But I've . . .' he was beginning as she seized the ravelled wool of his sloppy jersey and urged him into her study, shutting the door firmly behind them. Before he could say any more, she added as quietly as she could, 'Andrew, I'm sorry but I cannot have any more draft dodgers in the house.'

He stood in the bright winter sun that streamed through the smeared window, squinting slightly against the glare, wondering why she sounded so sharp. Her sympathy with his views on the war in Vietnam had always been a matter of satisfaction and some pride.

'But you agree with us,' he said slowly. 'You always did. What's changed?'

Felicity took a long, slow breath.

'I do agree with you. I hate the war and I have unlimited sympathy for the young men you bring here, but I cannot house any of them any longer.'

She looked at him, seeing the surprise and the hurt in his long, dark eyes.

'It's not just that tripping over their rucksacks in the hall drives me mad,' she said as lightly as possible, 'or that they tend to wear filthy sandals to breakfast and read their books at the table, or . . .'

4

'Mama, you've got this enormous, empty house. Can't you put up with little things like that for something that matters so much?' Andrew's eyes were puzzled and his voice tentative, but the twist of his beautifully cut mouth made him look yet more like his father. Felicity took a grip on herself and made herself say what had to be said.

'I could put up with it easily if I could afford to keep feeding them and letting them have all the hot water they need. The horrible truth is that there is no more money.'

Andrew looked round the elegant room in which his mother had always written her invitations and done her household accounts. The white wallpaper with its fine gold trellis was the same as it had always been and the flat-topped French desk was still there at right-angles to the window, but half the paintings had gone, leaving dust marks on the paper, and it seemed to him that there had once been a gilded clock on the empty chimney-piece. The smears on the window had not struck him before, nor the fact that, despite the sun, the room was bitterly cold. The significance of his mother's wearing her old fur coat and a pair of thick woolly socks in the house began to dawn on him.

'I think we need to talk,' he said, sounding more cautious than he had earlier. 'But I can't leave Fred in the hall.'

'I suppose not. Go and tell him that he's not going to be able to stay here and make him a cup of coffee or something and then come back. He can always go to the youth hostel for tonight and then think again if he's planning to stay in England.'

Andrew left the room and his mother sat down in one of the squashy chairs that stood on either side of the empty fireplace. Her head had started to ache, but it was such a familiar condition that she hardly noticed it.

'Now tell me,' said Andrew a minute later from the doorway.

As he walked towards the other chair, his mother looked carefully at him. She knew that his father's death had

5

affected him badly, but she did not know exactly how. Discussions with her friends had taught her that Andrew told her far more than did their sons, but anything that touched on his feelings seemed to be out of bounds.

Felicity's turmoil of loss and growing anger made her afraid for him, but she was reluctant to force his confidence and perhaps destroy whatever it was that kept him functioning – and affectionate. The knowledge that one day soon she would have to lose him, too, was always with her.

'There's not much to tell, and it's very simple: I do not have enough money to run the house and feed and clothe the children.'

Andrew, thinking of the size of the huge Kensington house, the thickness of his mother's furs, and the lavishness of the life she and his father had always lived, asked simply, 'Why not?'

Felicity, who thought that she had already explained their situation to him, was puzzled.

'Did Papa leave a lot of debts?' Andrew asked when she said nothing.

'No. But all he did leave was a tiny pension that just about clothes the younger ones and pays for a little heat during the school holidays.'

'I don't understand. There always seemed to be stacks of money.' Andrew flushed slightly. 'It used to bother me, actually.'

Felicity raised her eyebrows and managed to smile.

'Well, it needn't bother you any more,' she said drily. 'It turned out to be only a life interest in capital that has reverted to Connie Wroughton. But you knew all this, surely?'

'I don't think I did,' said Andrew slowly. 'Did you tell me? I can't have understood.' He bit the left-hand corner of his lower lip as he had done since babyhood whenever anything worried him. 'Then why are we still living in this vast house?'

'Because there are only fifteen years of the lease left to

6

run,' said his mother patiently. 'I can't afford to buy another fifty years yet and if I tried to sell what's left it would not raise enough to buy anywhere else into which we'd all fit. For the duration of the lease we'll be safe here, if cold, provided that I can earn enough to pay the rates. By the time the lease runs out even Nicky will have left school and you and the girls will be earning your own livings.'

Andrew's face changed and he got up to walk slowly towards the window. Felicity remembered the magazine that still lay open on her desk and hoped that he was too shocked to notice it.

'What about the school fees? And my allowance?'

'Connie pays those, which is remarkably kind of her, given that our only connection with her is that Papa was once married to her sister.'

At that Andrew came back to stare down at his mother. He looked angry and she hoped that he was not going to try to argue with her. She loathed conflict with her family and could never help taking seriously – and personally – anything that was said.

'She says that she's paying them so that I can concentrate on work and ensure that there is at least one more woman in the House of Commons,' Felicity went on. 'But I think it's probably more personal than that.'

'Why didn't you tell me sooner?' asked Andrew, thinking of the times he had taken girls out to dinner instead of eating in hall, and the books he had bought, the clothes and the records. 'There's not much I could have done, but it would have been a bit.'

'Oh, Andrew, darling!' Felicity stretched out her hand. He took it and rubbed his fingers over the roughness of hers.

'Did you know?' he asked, looking down at their hands. 'While he was alive, I mean.'

'Know what?'

'That it was only a life interest?'

'No,' said Felicity, clamping her lips shut so that none of

7

the rage, none of the doubts, should escape.

'Didn't that make you . . . cross with him?'

'Andrew,' she said helplessly, broke off and then decided that the truth might hurt but that it would be less destructive than any kind of lie, however well-intentioned: 'Yes, it did. It does. It's probably unfair of me to say that, but I'm so tired of being fair. And while we're on this horrible subject, Andrew, another thing I can't afford is all those telephone calls to Paris.'

He looked self-conscious and muttered that he was sorry.

'I know you've still a lot of good friends at the Sorbonne, but it would help if you could do most of the keeping in touch by letter.'

'I'm sorry. I didn't realise. Look here, I'll take Fred round to the youth hostel and then come back for lunch.'

'All right,' she said, thinking of the two boiled eggs and lump of cheese that she had planned to eat.

'I won't be long.'

He was back twenty minutes later, by which time she had decided that a tin of soup would make her proposed lunch fit for him. They ate in silence at the scrubbed wooden table in the kitchen until he started to peel his boiled eggs.

'I wish I'd understood all this properly before.'

'Don't think about it now,' said Felicity. 'You've schools at the end of next term and you need to concentrate all your energies on your work.'

She saw a hint of a smile on his lips as he shook his head and her own eyes narrowed in amusement.

'I know your dons have all told you that you're safe for a first, but the last thing you ought to do is let complacency trap you into making a clot of yourself.'

Andrew's lean face creased into a real grin as he watched his mother turn back into the familiar, beautiful, teasing, safe person she had always been.

'I won't do that,' he said. 'I promise. By the way, last week I accepted the BBC traineeship.'

8

'But that's wonderful news,' said Felicity, relieved of one pressing anxiety. 'Darling, I am glad.'

'They don't pay at all well to start with. If I'd known about the money, I could have gone for something more profitable like . . . oh, like accountancy.'

Felicity lost all control of herself and for the first time for ages had to wipe tears of laughter out of her eyes.

'I don't see what's so funny.' Andrew sounded rather dignified and even a little hurt.

'My dearest boy.' Felicity had stopped laughing, but her face was warm with love and amusement. 'Anyone less like an accountant would be hard to imagine. It's not just your grasp of Russian, which Professor Grainger was going on and on about last time we met . . .'

'Glad to hear the old buzzard's noticed it, given that his own grasp of everything is distinctly peculiar.'

'But your politics,' she went on as though he had not spoken, 'and your general . . . oh, I can't think of a word – your excitement. The thought of you sitting at a desk in some dim office adding up columns and columns of figures is just absurd. If that's what you'd have done, I'm glad you didn't know about the money.'

Andrew grinned at her again and, having finished his eggs, took out a packet of cigarettes. He shook one half out and offered it to his mother, who shook her head. She had decided long ago that she simply could not afford the habit. He lit his and she winced slightly at the smell, finding it half unbearably tantalising and half disgusting.

'How are you managing to keep going at all?' he asked, watching her through the pale grey cloud of smoke. 'There may not be an election for another three years and everything you do in the constituency before that must be unpaid, unless Diseholme is giving you something. Is he?'

'He pays my expenses and fees for any research I do for him. Apart from that your aunt Gerry and Julia Wallington have guaranteed my overdraft until the election,' said

Felicity, closing her eyes briefly as she thought of the crushing weight of obligation she carried. Then she opened her eyes again and smiled. 'And I earn useful sums of ready cash from organising these dances and things. It's not too bad and I've not many debts apart from the bank, but there's nothing left over for fripperies.'

'I see,' said Andrew again, frowning as he drew deeply on his cigarette. 'You must have ... I must have seemed horribly selfish.'

At that Felicity reached across the table to touch his bony wrist.

'You've had a lot to cope with this year, too,' she said gently.

Andrew looked away, breathing raggedly, unable to talk even to her about his father's death. After a moment he regained control. Stubbing out his half-smoked cigarette, he said: 'Well, whatever the BBC do pay me can go towards the family pot until the election; that is, if you don't mind my going on living here.'

Felicity closed her eyes for a minute to hide the mixture of relief and anxiety that his offer gave her.

'For a bit it would be lovely, but you ought to move out and build up your own life when you can,' she said doggedly. 'I'll be all right. Everyone says that this is a safe seat and Michael Diseholme is easing me into the constituency very nicely so that when he retires there ought not to be any difficulty.'

'Exploiting you, more like. He just makes you take his surgeries and do all the dreary work in the constituency while he props up the bar in the House of Commons.' Some of Andrew's contempt was caused by his politics, which were the opposite of his mother's, but more came from his personal dislike of the sitting Member of Parliament.

'Well, whatever his motives, the net effect is the same, and I am learning the job.'

'Yes, but you hate it, don't you?'

At that piece of unexpected percipience, Felicity's resolution almost crumbled.

'No,' she said, holding it together as best she could, 'although I do find it difficult. Never mind. All new jobs are hard. I am truly glad about the BBC; I was half afraid that friends of Papa's might try to get you to work for them.'

Andrew lit another cigarette.

'They did actually. I didn't say anything at the time because of all those fearsome injunctions to secrecy, but since you were once involved with them, too, I expect you're a safe confidante.'

'Much as I detest secrets,' said Felicity crisply, 'theirs I do keep. What happened?'

Andrew's eyes were brilliant as he smiled at her.

'I decided to turn them down when they set me a very clumsy test.'

'Oh?' Felicity stood up to switch on the kettle and spoon instant coffee into two cups.

'They gave me a telephone number in case I were ever approached by the other side – as they called it. Two days later a highly dubious Russian appeared with a proposition. Crass, don't you think? I obediently rang the number, reported what had happened and declined their charming offer of employment on the grounds that if they could be so stupid in their dealings with me, it would be far too dangerous to give myself up to them entirely. They were pretty irritated actually.'

'I'll bet they were,' said Felicity, her ready smile surfacing again. 'Well, my darling, I'm dreadfully glad you're not going to be a spy.'

'Me too.'

'Have . . . ?' Felicity bit off the question before she could finish it. If her son had already been reporting to some home-surveillance team on the behaviour of his fellow student activists, he would never tell her, and if he had not the question would be an insult he might not be able to forgive. She made the coffee.

'Did you see those pictures of Amanda?' Andrew asked

casually, as though he were simply changing the subject out of politeness and picking a topic that did not matter to either of them.

'Yes, I did. I thought she looked very glamorous. Have you been in touch since the last vac?'

'Of course. But she's frying some remarkably celestial fish these days and has little time for me.' His voice was light, but not light enough for her to miss his anger.

'Don't let her hurt you, Andrew. She's . . . she's not frightfully careful of people's feelings.'

'Easier said than done.' He drank some coffee, grimaced, and then burst out: 'It's such a waste! All that talent and character being frittered away on being a star of the magazines and the party set. Admiration means more to her at the moment than anything else and she has no time for people who care about the person and not the star.'

'I know,' said his mother, aching for him. 'But it's not really surprising: there she is at just twenty, earning a fortune from the modelling, and apparently just as safe a bet for a first as you.'

'Fine Art,' he said with contempt.

'You're as bad as Julia,' said Felicity, amused. 'It's a perfectly reasonable subject and she seems to do it very well.'

Andrew laughed. 'I must say I never expected to be bracketed with the terrifying Mrs Wallington.'

'Does she frighten you? How interesting!' Felicity thought of her old friend, whose many vulnerabilities she had often tried to protect.

'Goodness, yes. Whenever we meet she fixes me with a basilisk stare and I turn to stone.'

'Amanda will probably be the same,' said Felicity, not averse to warning him off the girl. 'After all, she does look exactly like her mother.'

'God forbid,' said Andrew, laughing again. 'It's good to be home, Mum, even for an hour. Thank you.' He stretched out his hand across the table and she clasped it for a moment.

Andrew got up from the table as soon as he had finished his second cup of coffee to announce that he ought to get back to Oxford. Felicity did not protest, completely faithful to her determination never to cling to him. Out in the hall, he took her in his arms again.

'Don't worry too much, Mama,' he said, patting her back with slightly clumsy tenderness. 'We'll all be all right in the end, you know.'

'I know we will. And you mustn't worry about things like the money. You've enough to do with your own work. How are you getting back?'

'Hitching,' he said briefly, knowing that she disliked the habit but even more determined than usual not to waste any of his grant or allowance on train fares.

'Well, be careful.'

'I shall. But it's okay. We all do it – even the girls. I'll see you at the end of term.'

13

CHAPTER 2

Amanda was examining her latest published photograph with all the critical judgement she applied to her work. The background of Florence did not seem quite clear enough to dispel a possible suspicion that it was merely a photo-montage, which would have detracted from the atmosphere of international success she liked to create around herself, and she thought the details of her several successful careers ought to have been fuller.

She also felt that a more distinguished Christian name would have been desirable for the caption, or perhaps a whimsical nickname like Gibby or Golly or even Toby. Her father occasionally called her Blackberry, but that was wholly unsuitable, and all the possible diminutives of Amanda sounded positively suburban. Once or twice she had considered changing her name to Artemisia, but it seemed too late to do it without arousing snide amusement among her detractors.

Some aspects of the photograph were good, she decided. The colours were interesting and the pose the photographer had chosen was nicely judged: casual, free, young, and yet elegant, too. All the boredom and discomfort of lying on the cold, hard stone, rearranging her limbs to his rudely phrased instructions and then waiting for him to adjust his lenses and his filters seemed worthwhile.

'All in all it's not too bad,' she said aloud as she tucked the magazine's cheque into her bag so that she could take it to the bank. She entered the amount of it neatly into her accounts, adding it to the running total she always kept. That was not bad either.

She put the red account book back among the dictionaries that were stacked on her desk between a pair of antique bronze lions her Italian grandmother had once given her, and riffled through the rest of her letters.

Her room was small and functional, and it had one of the most desirable views on the campus. The leafless trees and distant water were drear in the grey March light, but at least she was spared the sight of loitering undergraduates, bicycles and depressing lines of grey rain-streaked concrete buildings.

To the basic modern furniture supplied by the university Amanda had added only the lions, a variety of Indian bedspreads, a black jar filled with pale yellow tulips and a series of drawings by her godfather, Tibor Smith. She had considered hanging one of his oil portraits of her but decided that the ink drawings of strange towers in violent imaginary landscapes would provide a more subtle statement about herself, and their bleakness fitted better with the grey concrete than would an oil.

The tulips went remarkably well with her yellow velvet trousers and black polo-neck sweater, but that was merely coincidence. Amanda dressed to please herself and not to fit in with anyone or anywhere else.

The first letter in the small pile of post was from her mother, which she slid to one side to reveal a blue envelope addressed in Andrew Suvarov's writing. Pushing that away, too, she found a long, thick white envelope addressed in an eccentrically attractive, black italic hand that she had never seen before. Curiosity banished the slight petulance from her face and she opened the envelope and looked immediately at the signature: Comfort Gillingham.

Amanda stared at the name in surprise. It was familiar, of course. No one, however uninterested in modern painting, could have failed to know of Comfort Gillingham, and art was Amanda's subject. She also knew that her mother had once been married to the painter's brother and she had always been curious about them.

Neither of her parents had ever been willing to answer questions about the Gillinghams, and she had ceased to ask, assuming that there was something about them that was too important to be told. To have received a letter written by one of them gave Amanda a physical thrill. Intrigued by her own reaction, she turned the sheet over to read:

Dear Miss Wallington

Having seen your remarkably interesting face in several magazines lately, I have decided that I should like to paint you. Could you be persuaded to sit for me? The modelling fees I pay could not match anything the magazines offer, but it is possible that you might find other, less obvious, rewards from sitting for me.

Amanda smiled, rather liking the self-conscious conditional Comfort Gillingham had used since the rewards of being painted by so famous a woman were obvious: publicity, the chance to watch one of the most distinguished modern figurative painters at work, and the opportunity of meeting an entirely new circle of useful people. Amanda also approved of the painter's tact in making no mention of the peculiar family connection between them.

I shall be coming to Norwich for the opening of the new exhibition at the Castle Museum next week. I gather that your term ends the previous day, but if you

16

were still to be in the university, I should like to call on you before the show.

Amanda sat at her desk, weaving plans, and for once allowing herself to sink into a series of pleasant fantasies. She had already planned to go to the opening of the exhibition and knew that she would accept Comfort Gillingham's proposition, but she did not want to seem too eager and so she put the letter to the side of her desk to be answered later, when she had read the rest of her post.

Her mother's letter was the usual friendly, dutiful account of her latest case, the dinners she had attended, and interesting things she had seen and heard, but it seemed cool. Sighing, Amanda wrote a quick, careless answer and then opened Andrew's envelope.

She began to smile almost as soon as she started reading. Witty, as most of his letters were, it seemed for once not to be about his feelings for her. She settled back more comfortably to read it in pleasure.

As a child she had believed him to be a bit of a hero, but since he had decided to fall in love with her she had found his company difficult to enjoy. Unsatisfied and searching for something hugely important into which she could fling her considerable energies, she had tried for a time to match his feelings, but it had not worked. The extraordinary, over-mastering something that she felt must be waiting for her only just out of reach remained elusive.

It had eluded her at Norwich, too. She had had expectations of both the city itself and the university that she had discovered to be unrealistic almost as soon as she arrived there, laden with books and luggage on a wet autumn day four terms earlier. The newly built concrete towers, blocks and walkways depressed her, although she had wanted to be impressed with the architecture, and made her think of a nuclear power station or an experimental science laboratory.

As soon as she had unpacked her luggage in the room she had been allocated and reassured her father enough for him to leave her, she had taken a bus into Norwich itself, hoping to find glorious buildings and a welcoming atmosphere that might soothe her unexpected depression.

All she had found was an ordinary, muddled city centre, packed with people, traffic and many of the chain stores that had been familiar all her life. On later visits, she had discovered a few pleasant, quiet, attractive streets, one or two lovely buildings, and the delights of tea in the Georgian Assembly Rooms, but she had never quite got over that first disappointment and had built up an incorrigible prejudice against the place. Her pride had not allowed her even to suggest to anyone else that she was less than content and she did her best to bury her feelings in seeking pleasure.

One of the tutors in another subject had flattered her in her first few weeks by pursuing her quite vigorously and begging her to sleep with him. She enjoyed his attentions more than those of any of her contemporaries and thought that she might well find what she was looking for in sex. Unfortunately, as she explained to him, rather enjoying the misquotation and assuming that she was the first to have thought of it, although her flesh was splendidly willing, her spirit was woefully weak. He seemed to be amused and had spent several evenings talking to her about the astonishing way that sex could illuminate a person's inner life, until eventually Amanda had succumbed hopefully to his blandishments.

The supposedly transfiguring experience had proved to be messy, rather uncomfortable and, as far as she could discover, entirely meaningless. When it was over the tutor had said something to her casually that had hurt her so badly she had refused to listen to any other seductive propositions and had taken immense care to avoid meeting him ever since.

Drugs had been offered to her, too, in words that were almost the same as the concupiscent tutor's and she had accepted the offer of a 'freak pill' from one of the besotted young men she had met on campus.

Swallowing half the violet-coloured tablet, she was told that it was LSD and hoped for Coleridgean visions and insights as well as colour and truth about her self and her identity. All she had achieved were a slight nausea, a sensation that whenever she moved her hand trails of long detached hairs with blobs on the end waved after her fingers, and some interesting pictures of her mind being attached to the rest of her with thick springs covered in tan leather and lying on the surface of a swimming pool.

Later, recovering and admitting the uselessness of the trip, she did wonder whether the springs might be easily detached from their moorings. There could, she decided, have been some kind of message in that, but it did not thrill her.

Giving up interest in what seemed to be the two chief preoccupations of some of her fellows, she had tried to find satisfaction in her work, but there, too, she had been disappointed. She had arrived at the university with a far greater knowledge of both modern British painting and the development of Italian art than any of her fellow under-graduates. Her annual holidays with her grandmother in Fiesole had given her an easy familiarity with the paintings of the Uffizi and the Pitti Palace and the sculpture of the Bargello, and she had taken in a large amount of knowledge about them without even realising that she was doing so.

Unfortunately the first two terms of her course gave her little scope to use her knowledge as the course concentrated on French, German, philosophy and the history of the History of Art. She found the work dull and was upset to discover that her favourite period was not covered in any of the available courses. Having fought her parents so hard to be allowed to read Fine Art at East Anglia, it had been difficult to admit even to herself that she loathed the place, most of the people and the work she had to do.

Once she had admitted it, she gritted her teeth and set to work to extend her horizons beyond the confines of the

university. After several rejections, she managed to get
articles accepted in one or two of the glossy art magazines
and Tibor Smith had introduced her to the editors, journalists and photographers who were beginning to seek her out,
but none of it seemed quite real or important enough.

Vaguely dissatisfied with herself, she reached for the notes
she had written the previous day for an essay on the
increasing feeling that appeared in late Gothic manuscript
painting, and settled down to work.

As she went through the motions of collecting references
and regurgitating what she had read and heard, she let part
of her mind wander over her godfather's possible reactions
to the news that she might sit for Comfort Gillingham. Tibor
had never spoken of her work to Amanda, but they must have
been rivals. For a moment or two it occurred to Amanda to
ask his advice about the Gillingham portrait, but she dismissed the impulse as childish and went back to her essay.
Before she had reached the end of the first page there was a
knock at her door.

'May I come in?'

Opening the door, Amanda grinned at the inquiring face
of her one good friend in Norwich.

'Naturally. Coffee, Iris?'

'Please.'

Iris Fowlins, who had arrived at the university the same
year as Amanda, was reading English and seemed incapable
of being impressed by anything. The daughter of an oil-
company director, she, too, had had a cosmopolitan childhood, and Amanda's tales of Florentine society moved her to
no more than sympathy, which was attractive to someone who
both longed for admiration and yet despised it when it was
offered too easily.

Iris had none of Amanda's glamour; she was plump, had
perennially untidy long hair and dressed badly, and yet there
was a sexiness about her that was appealing. On that day she
was wearing a pair of old black corduroy trousers so loose

20

that they looked as though they might fall off her wide hips and an equally loose tunic made of black jersey splattered with purple flowers. She looked comfortable and quite at ease with her sloppy clothes.

Amanda liked her for her cynicism, her jokes, her refusal to accept anyone's pretentions, and for her enviable emotional sophistication.

'Another letter from your infatuated Oxford admirer?' she asked, pointing to the blue envelope as Amanda handed her a scarlet mug of instant coffee with undissolved crumbs of dried milk clinging to the edge.

'Yes. It's such a pity.'

'What, exactly?' Iris took a mouthful of coffee and grimaced. 'Bugger! You've gone and boiled the kettle again.'

'It's the way I was brought up. You ought to remember that,' said Amanda, who never apologised for anything, even to her friends. 'The pity of poor Andrew is that he writes the most marvellous letters. They're funny, clever, entertaining – and uncomplicated.' Amanda stretched out her long yellow legs and leaned back in her chair.

'Unlike him, you mean? Then that is a pity; not least because he's so good-looking. It seems such a waste.'

'Don't.' Amanda laughed. 'Actually his looks probably strike me less than you because I've known him so long.'

Iris got up and carried her mug to the basin, where she slopped some of the coffee down the drain and refilled her mug with cold water from the tap.

'Some people have all the luck. That's better,' she said, swallowing some coffee. 'What is it about him that turns you off so badly?'

'This and that. How's Benedict?'

Iris looked sideways at her friend and silently accepted her refusal to answer questions. She had her own views on why Amanda found Andrew Suvarov tiresome but had decided to keep them to herself unless she were specifically asked for them.

'Ben's fine,' she said easily. 'He brought me a huge bunch of elegant bare branches yesterday.'

'Lovely!' The sarcasm in Amanda's voice brought a smile to Iris's warm brown eyes.

'They are actually. In that white pot I've got they look terrific against the Klee poster. But I can't imagine where he got them. There just aren't enough trees to have shed that many branches naturally. I'd been moaning about the lack of big, deep, dark woods round here the day before and he must have gone off to get them for me.'

'Romantic.' Amanda sipped some of her hot coffee.

'Yes, but touching too. On the scale I'd say it was well above five, wouldn't you?'

'Perhaps.'

The two of them had worked out their 'acceptability scale' by the second week of their first term as young men, faced with hundreds of available women for the first time in their lives, began to stake out their claims and territories. Very few of their gestures passed the halfway mark of five. Privately, Amanda would have put Andrew Suvarov's letters at about nine and his actual physical presence, despite his looks, at nearer two and a half.

'Do you actually like sex?' she asked abruptly, remembering all his fruitless pleas during the Christmas vacation.

'Depends. Sometimes it's *foie gras* to the sound of trumpets. Usually it's cold porridge to the sound of a Methodist hymn.' Iris wriggled slightly in pleasure at her own joke and drank the remains of her coffee. 'Why?'

'I was just curious. People go on about it so.'

'Wanking's usually better. I've got an essay. I'd better go.'

Amanda watched Iris wave casually from the doorway, thinking admiringly that never in a million years could she have said anything like that. She tried to practise it, imagining herself saying it to her mother. It was not convincing.

She finished her essay, read it through to make certain

22

there were no glaring mistakes or patches of naïvety and then wrote politely to Comfort Gillingham to suggest that they should go to the exhibition together. She would, she wrote, be ready at six o'clock.

In fact she was not ready. Having spent the afternoon fending off the advances of one of her more persistent admirers, she was late getting into the bathrooms. She had to wash her hair, which was so long and thick that it took about three-quarters of an hour to dry. Alternately painting her face and checking her watch, she was still standing in front of the wholly inadequate mirror in her room, making up her face, at six o'clock.

Hurriedly pulling on a new dress, so that she would at least be decent when Comfort Gillingham arrived, she went back to her make-up, carefully sticking on her false eyelashes. When everything was done, she checked each aspect of her appearance in the mirror.

The dress was made of thin black wool printed with maroon swirls and it exaggerated both her height and her slenderness. It had a round-edged collar, a high waist and very tight sleeves, and its hem hung ten inches above her knees. Her dark hair fell, sleek and glossy, over her shoulders and she had made herself up to look very pale to set it off. Almost the only colour in her face was provided by her dark-ringed eyes and the maroon lipstick she had used. She had just decided that all was well when she heard a knock at the door.

Pausing only to spray some Hermès Calèche behind her ears, she opened the door to her visitor.

Comfort Gillingham's extraordinary face, with its bony nose and hooded, glinting, slate-coloured eyes, was familiar from innumerable photographs, but Amanda had expected neither her smallness nor the extraordinary impression of power that she carried with her.

'Do come in,' Amanda said, stepping backwards and feeling unaccountably shy.

'Thank you,' said the painter in a slightly hoarse voice that retained the faintest trace of an American accent. She looked Amanda up and down and laughed.

'What's the matter?' Amanda was slightly affronted.

'I've been watching the development of your face in Tibor's paintings since you were about six. You've now reached the stage where your real individuality is beginning to show at last and yet you get yourself up like any trendy shopgirl. May I sit down?'

Amanda pulled up the only spare chair and gestured to it, unable to think of a suitable answer to a statement that had shocked her, and at the same time titillated, with its mixture of criticism and surprisingly familiar knowledge of her past. Comfort unbuttoned her wide aubergine-coloured coat to reveal emerald silk beneath and sank gracefully down into the chair.

'I didn't know that you knew him,' said Amanda at last. 'He hasn't sold any of the things he's done of me – except to my parents.'

'I've always seen them in his studio as he was working on them. Tibor and I know each other well. Has he never told you that?'

'I don't think he's ever even mentioned you. How bizarre!'

Comfort Gillingham shrugged.

'If I'm to paint you,' she said, watching Amanda, 'I shall strip off all that make-up and have you as you are. Are you prepared to risk that?'

'Is it so dangerous?' Amanda was beginning to relax. She had never met anyone quite like Comfort before, but her peculiar manner was appealing.

Comfort smiled at the question and raised one flying eyebrow.

'If I do my job properly, I'd say it was quite a considerable risk. You may see things you don't expect.'

'Such as?'

'I can't tell yet. Only the preliminary drawings will give us a clue. Well, are you prepared to try?'

'Yes, please.' Amanda could hear an unsuitable eagerness in her voice and damped it down. 'When shall you need me?'

'What plans have you got for the vacation?'

'Nothing except for some scattered modelling jobs in the middle two weeks. I'm not going to Fiesole this vac because I'll be there for most of the summer working on my dissertation.'

'Then I suggest daily sittings for next week,' said Comfort, displaying a most unusual lack of awe in Amanda's plans. 'That will give me time to decide how I'm going to proceed and after that we can fit sittings in with your other work. Shall we go? I have a car waiting downstairs.'

As they walked together from Amanda's room to the windswept car park, Comfort shuddered.

'How can you bear it? It's exactly like a prison.' She waved one long-fingered hand towards the entrance to one of the residential buildings, where labels marked 'Floor 01', 'Floor 02' and so on were the only decoration.

'I find it rather exciting actually,' said Amanda, gesturing gracefully towards the stepped apex of the building that overlooked the lawns and trees. 'The mixture of stark lines and natural curves is rather pleasing.'

Comfort looked amused and changed the subject back to Tibor Smith, whom she appeared to know surprisingly well, until they reached the car she had hired. Amanda thought of the tedious bus ride that would have been her alternative and smiled.

The gallery was already full when they arrived. Comfort stood for a moment at the edge of the noisy throng and then turned, held out her hand and smiled in sudden brilliance as Amanda took it.

'Thank you for saying yes,' Comfort said. 'I think we might both enjoy it. I shall see you at four o'clock the day after tomorrow. It's the same address as on my letter.'

Amanda nodded, feeling the strength of Comfort's hand.

'Thank you for bringing me here,' she said. Comfort nodded and moved into the crowd.

Slightly shaken by the whole episode and by Comfort's strange familiarity with her childhood, Amanda took a glass of champagne and a handful of nuts from a tray and waited for someone to notice her. In the short interval before they did, she watched Comfort Gillingham receiving the homage of a great many important critics, connoisseurs and scholars and for the first time asked herself why such a celebrated painter should have wanted her as a model. The doubts did not persist for long once Amanda's own admirers began to flock round her.

CHAPTER 3

The telephone bell shrilled in Felicity's ear, waking her from a heavy sleep. Blinking and licking her dry lips, she pushed herself up against the pillows and reached for the receiver.

'Hello,' she said, becoming aware that she had woken an hour or so earlier and must have fallen into a second, much deeper, sleep. Her brain felt slow and useless and there was a dryness about her mouth that made forming words uncomfortable.

'Flixe, is that you?' Julia Wallington's voice was urgent enough to wrench Felicity's thoughts from her uncomfortable headache. She remembered going down to the kitchen to make a cup of hot chocolate at about two in the morning and adding a slug of cooking brandy to help her sleep.

'Yes, what's up, Julia?'

'Amanda. She's excelled herself this time. She danced in here yesterday evening to announce triumphantly that Comfort Gillingham of all people has invited her to sit for a portrait, and the wretched child's gone and agreed.'

There was a pause while Flixe tried to make her mind

27

work properly. Memories of the things Julia had said about her first marriage years earlier warned Flixe to take the announcement seriously. She was wryly amused to think of her son's vision of Julia as a terrifying basilisk when she was so ready to ask for help and solace for her various wounds.

'That doesn't sound too disastrous,' Flixe said, her voice warmed by her amusement. 'After all Amanda's quite accustomed to being painted by Tibor. I can see why you're bothered at the idea of the two of them in contact, but I honestly don't think Amanda will get into any kind of trouble. There's nothing Comfort can do to her after all.'

'You don't know her. She could make trouble out of a simple walk in the park. Besides, if she didn't want to get at me, why on earth would she want Amanda?'

Flixe laughed. Back in her familiar role of confidante and adviser, she felt a shadow of the old security.

'Come off it, Julia,' she said easily. 'Amanda's been in the news a lot lately; I suspect your erstwhile sister-in-law merely wants to establish her credentials among the trendy set by painting one of its newest and youngest stars. And she is highly paintable. You must see that.'

As she spoke, Flixe thought with satisfaction that if Amanda were preoccupied with having her portrait painted she would not have much time left in which to torment Andrew, who had arrived back from Oxford the previous day laden with bags of books. With his final schools the following term he needed to work undistracted.

'I suppose you're right,' said Julia slowly, 'but I can't help feeling that something dreadful will come out of it.'

Flixe thought then that she understood what was worrying her old friend. Her headache forgotten, she concentrated on Julia's tricky relations with her daughter.

'Perhaps you're bothered that the two of them will get together to conspire against you?' she suggested. When Julia said nothing, Flixe went on as gently as possible: 'It's not very likely you know. Comfort behaved badly to you twenty-odd years ago, and I know that Amanda is difficult, but I don't think you need worry. Amanda at least is very fond of you.'

'If she is, she never shows it.' Some of the habitual humour was creeping back into Julia's voice. 'You're right, of course, Flixe. I hadn't seen it, but that could well be what's behind my certainty of disaster. I suppose I don't trust Comfort and there's no doubt that Amanda delights in doing things she knows I dislike, whatever she does or doesn't think about me.'

'I think that's because—' Flixe began and then stopped, reluctant to say something that might upset Julia.

'Because what? Come on, Flixe, don't leave me in suspense.'

'I just wondered whether that might be a kind of double-bluff. If you're angry with her – which you often are – then at least she'll know it's because she's done something you disapprove of. D'you see what I mean?'

'Yes,' said Julia after another silence, 'but I think it's a bit over-subtle . . . not something I'd accept in court. I can just imagine opposing counsel's objection: "Supposition, m'lord. There's no corroborative evidence at all for what m'learned friend has just suggested."'

Flixe laughed dutifully, thinking that everyone had a defence against too much difficult emotion. Hers might be other people's problems; Julia's was definitely her work and the success it had brought her.

'Talking of court, I'd better run,' said Julia. 'Thank you, Flixe. You always do manage to cheer me up even when you give me a wigging.'

'And even when I make you cross?'

'Even then. But, Flixe, we've talked enough about me. Before I go, will you tell me how you are – really?'

'Bearing up.' Flixe's voice had changed. While she was consoling Julia it had been warm and backed with affectionate amusement. When their positions were reversed, it seemed to cool and harden in defence. 'Thanks for ringing, Julia. Good-bye.'

'I wish I could do something to help,' said Julia urgently.

'You have, Julia. Without your guarantee at the bank I couldn't have screwed enough of an overdraft out of them to carry on.'

'That's not exactly what I meant.'

'I know, but I don't think anyone can do anything about the rest. Time, no doubt, will help.'

'I hope so, Flixe. You know we all—'

'I know. Thank you, Julia.'

As soon as her friend had rung off, Flixe threw back the blankets and hurried to the adjoining bathroom to run herself a bath. She noticed that her headache had gone completely.

'Why can't I find consoling the constituents as refreshing as doing it for my friends?' she asked herself as she mentally listed the things she had to do that day.

Her three younger children would be breaking up for the holidays in a week's time and then she would need to concentrate on them. Before that she had to complete arrangements for the first of the deb dances she was being paid to organise that season and make sure that all the outstanding constituency matters had been settled. The sitting Member of Parliament had graciously agreed to take all his own surgeries for the school holidays but Flixe knew that he expected her to leave a desk clear of problems.

If his goodwill had not been so important to her future, she thought as she got into her bath and started to wash, she might have been tempted to tell him exactly what she thought of his handing on to her all the work he most disliked but for which he still got the salary.

She was honest enough to recognise that a large measure of her resentment was caused not by the money but by the depressing effect of listening to his constituents' problems. So many of them were insoluble that offering encouragement and comfort seemed hypocritical and yet not to offer anything was worse.

No Member of Parliament, however conscientious and effective, could make the stupid intelligent, the poor rich, the criminal law-abiding, or turn noisy, malicious, difficult people into ideal neighbours. Only when the constituents' difficulties were caused by idle or obstructive officials did Flixe feel she had any chance of sucessfully helping them. Then she pursued their claims with a vigour that Michael Diseholme occasionally mocked but more often applauded, and she even enjoyed doing it. For the rest of the time she felt helpless in the face of the constituents' misery and all too aware of her own.

Trying, as always, to ignore it, she dressed and made up her face carefully so that she would look perfectly in control for her first meeting of the day.

Ann Kirkwaters had been at school with Flixe but they had never been particular friends, and she had been quite surprised when Ann had telephoned a month earlier to ask her to arrange a dance at the very beginning of the season. Ten minutes into their first discussion, Flixe had quickly understood why Ann needed help. She and her daughter Jemima had such different ideas about the ideal dance that they needed an independent umpire. Despite feeling guilty about taking money for something so simple, Flixe had accepted the job at once.

Since then they had managed to agree that the dance would be held in a marquee in the huge garden of the Kirkwaters' house in Berkshire rather than in London. They had chosen the band and the discotheque, the caterers and the florists, but they still had to agree on where the discotheque should be and how it was to be decorated.

Ann wanted another, smaller, tent decorated like a flower garden, but Jemima was determined to have something more unusual. Flixe had produced several ideas, which neither of the two warring Kirkwaters liked, and she had notes and sketches for three more in her briefcase as she drove to the small Knightsbridge house that Ann had rented for the season.

Ann opened the door herself, looking as neat as usual in a short, stiff, scarlet dress, white tights and black patent-leather shoes. Her blonde hair was cut in a short, feathery style that Flixe irreverently thought made her look just like a Pekinese. Her nose was small, her cheekbones prominent and her darting eyes very dark brown, which added to the impression. She was small with fine bones and a once-perfect complexion on which she still lavished enormous care and expense.

Her daughter Jemima was the opposite: large, clumsy and with a greasy skin that tended to break out in spots. Ann despised her looks far too obviously and Flixe felt very sorry for her.

'Flixe, darling,' said Ann, presenting her with a well-powdered cheek to kiss. 'What a relief. We had another scene over the breakfast table this morning. Jemima howled and Simon announced that he was going to stay at his club until she could control herself.'

'Really? How odd!' Flixe followed Ann into the minute drawing room and put her briefcase down on the chintz-covered sofa. 'I thought they got on so well.'

'Usually. But he hates tears and scenes.' Into Ann's face came an odd expression of mixed contempt and satisfaction that Flixe pretended not to see. 'But at least his absence means we can live more easily without his mania for punctuality, and I can telephone my . . . my friends in peace. I only hope he stays away for more than his usual twenty-four-hour sulk.'

'Goodness!' was all Flixe could think of to say in answer.

'Don't look so disapproving,' said Ann, with a conspiratorial smile. 'When he's not here with his mental stopwatch, I can have my breakfast in peace while Jemima lies in bed. She can stumble down as soon as she knows I've finished. That way we can both have a bit of peace before the battles begin.'

'Poor child,' said Flixe before she could stop herself. 'It's all right, Ann, I didn't mean it. Where is she?'

'Sulking in her room. "Stupid child" would be more accurate. Now, what on earth are we going to do about this discotheque?'

'I can't see why she shouldn't have it in the summer-house, Ann. Couldn't you simply give way on that? It would save you money on a second marquee after all.'

'That is a consideration. Honestly, Flixe, you'd have thought she'd be grateful that we're spending thousands on her like this. But she isn't. She talks as though I'm torturing her by forcing her to do things she hates.'

'I expect she will be grateful one day. All right then, can I take it that the summer-house is settled?'

'What if it rains?' Ann flung one perfect leg over the other and looked as satisfied as though she had just said something terribly clever. 'They'll get soaked between the disco and the marquee.'

'Not being God, I can't answer for the weather. But I can make sure there's a host of huge golfing umbrellas at hand in the summer-house just in case. Would that satisfy you?'

Ann wrinkled her nose, looking more than ever like a little dog.

'All right. It would be different, I suppose. Oh, there you are.' Her voice had sharpened into a snap and Flixe looked up to see poor lumpy Jemima standing in the doorway.

'Hello, Jemima,' said Flixe cheerfully. 'I like the new hair.'

'Do you?' The girl went to peer at herself in the large mirror over the fireplace. 'I can't think why. I hate it. Mummy told the man how to cut it.'

Ann drew in a breath, but Flixe glared at her and she said nothing.

'You'll get used to it. Now, your mother has agreed to the summer-house for the discotheque and I thought we could decorate it like the classic orangery: orange and perhaps lemon trees and statues. I've made a drawing.' She took it out of her briefcase and handed it to the girl.

'That sounds appallingly expensive,' said Ann, ignoring the brightening of her daughter's dull grey eyes.

'Not necessarily. We can hire the trees and I thought we could have life-size models made of the statues, either three dimensional or if necessary flat. I've talked to a theatrical-design company who have given me estimates for both sorts and assured me that even the flat ones would look all right. If you agree, we'll work out the details and get a proper quotation for you.'

'It would be nice if we could have something extra,' said Jemima, her eyes gazing yearningly at Flixe, 'something funny that will make people laugh and talk approvingly for once. Couldn't you do something like that, Mrs Suvarov?'

'I can try,' Flixe promised and was rewarded by a smile that made the girl look really pretty. 'Now the caterers: here are their figures, Ann.' Flixe took a sheaf of papers out of her briefcase and handed them over.

Twenty minutes later all the arrangements had been made and the estimates agreed.

'Go and make some coffee, darling,' Ann ordered and, as soon as her daughter was out of earshot, she added: 'Flixe, that was wonderful. You've actually managed to perk her up a bit. I can't tell you how grateful I am.'

A little surprised, because she had actually done very little, Flixe thanked her client.

'And I've been wondering if I could persuade you to come and be part of the house party for the dance. You see, you can do so much more with poor Jemima than I can and I do want her to be reasonably cheerful at her own dance.'

'Well, it would be awfully convenient if I could stay,' said Flixe, 'because then I can keep an eye on everything, but I don't need to be part of the party. It would mess up your numbers for one thing, and for another Simon doesn't really approve of me, does he?'

'Nonsense,' said Ann, looking a little pink. 'He only thinks that I ought to be able to do all that you're doing for us, but I can't. No, do come. I'll find a handy older bachelor to balance you. It won't be hard and it'll do you good, Flixe; you've been in purdah for too long. Do say yes. I'd like you to have some fun for a change. You're looking awful.'

Touched by the idea that her notoriously selfish friend should care enough about her to want to do her good, Flixe accepted the invitation.

'Excellent. Then I've nothing more to worry about,' said Ann with a greater degree of relief than seemed warranted. 'Thank you, darling. That looks lovely.'

Jemima looked surprised at the warmth of her mother's voice as she carried in a heavy tray and set it down on the glass-topped table in front of the sofa.

'Shall I pour?' she said. 'You do have it white, don't you, Mrs Suvarov?'

'Yes, thank you, Jemima. How are you getting on with the tea-parties?'

It was obviously an unlucky question for Jemima flushed and knocked the cup she was holding on the edge of the table. Coffee spilled over the saucer on to the table, splashing Ann's expensive-looking red dress. She glared at her daughter and berated her for the clumsiness.

'Sorry,' said Jemima, obviously near to tears. 'I'll get a cloth.'

As she rushed out of the room, Flixe asked: 'What on earth is the trouble?'

'The silly child went and got herself drunk at the last tea-party and made a fool of herself. She's refusing to go to any more, but she'll have to do it. It's important to meet the girls and get all their addresses – not to speak of making sure she's invited to their parties.'

'Drunk? At a deb's tea-party? It's not possible.'

'Alas it is. Some of them have started having Irish coffee, if you can believe it. Jemima swears she didn't know there was

35

whisky in the coffee and went on drinking it because she was thirsty. She really is too idiotic; she didn't even notice that it tasted of whisky.'

'Poor child,' said Flixe, unaware that she was repeating herself. 'What happened?'

'A very sensible – and nice – girl offered her a lift home and brought her back before she could do any real damage.' Ann leaned forwards to pour the coffee herself. 'A doctor's daughter,' she added airily. 'You'll meet her at the dance. She'll be staying with us, too. She could be a really good influence on Jemima if only the silly girl would stop sulking.'

'I'm not sulking, but I don't like her,' said Jemima from the doorway with a cloth in her hand. She wiped up the coffee that had spilled on to the table. 'She's dull and gives herself ridiculous airs, considering that she's nobody special or particularly glamorous. I can't think why you keep wanting to invite her to things. The chaps don't like her either.'

She took the cloth away to the kitchen and did not reappear. Flixe finished her coffee, refused to listen to Ann's complaints about her daughter and left only half an hour later than she had meant. She was due at her younger sister's house in Holland Park at half past twelve and had wanted to go to the constituency office to sort out her papers before that, but calculated that she would not have time.

Driving round Holland Park, she hoped that Ming had not invited lots of other women. Occasionally she did, but Flixe needed a respite from politeness and conversation. The thought of sinking back into Ming's undemanding company in her remarkably comfortable house was alluring. There were no strange cars outside it when Flixe drew up and she began to feel hopeful.

'Is anyone else coming?' she asked as soon as Ming had kissed her and led the way into the big coral and grey drawing room that set off her collection of modern paintings so well.

'No one except Gerry. I thought it was time we had an orgy of sisterly chat without having to be polite to anyone,' said Ming cheerfully, pouring out two glasses of cold white wine. 'This is one of Mark's discoveries: quite a dry German one. Tell me what you think.'

Flixe drank and raised her eyebrows.

'It's nice. I've always had a bit of a prejudice against German wines, but this is good.'

'I thought so, too. You're looking a bit better, old thing.' Ming always said something like that when they met, although she thought Flixe was still looking exhausted and far too thin.

'Am I? I suppose I must at last be getting used to doing without Peter; and Andrew's home.' Her eyes brightened. 'I try not to use him for solace, but it is lovely having him to chat to at meals.'

'I'm sure it is,' said Ming warmly. 'He's a nice boy, and so like Peter. I don't think you need worry about enjoying having him at home. It's natural.'

'Perhaps.' Flixe fell silent. Ming looked sideways at her, thinking of the luxurious confidence she had had throughout her married life and saddened by the changes in her.

'Don't fight it,' said Ming gently. 'If anything helps, let it. Just because it's helping, you surely don't need to mistrust it.'

Flixe looked startled, having momentarily forgotten her younger sister's ability to understand things without being told about them.

'Do you think I'm hanging on to the misery?' she asked suddenly. 'Out of some kind of loyalty to Peter.'

'I suppose it's possible,' answered Ming. She drank a little more wine as she considered the question. 'I haven't thought about it before. But it wouldn't be surprising; you always were intensely loyal to him when he was alive. Do you remember that evening when he and Mark were arguing about the Cold War?'

Flixe's dark blue eyes looked blank for a moment and then she smiled the old smile. She ran her fingers through her blonde hair and for a little while looked herself again.

'When Mark was objecting to the government's spending so much on spying when he said we rarely learned anything at all interesting and simply laid ourselves open to betrayal? Yes, I do remember.'

'Peter was as nearly angry as I've ever seen him,' said Ming, 'and you waded in and fought on his behalf.'

Flixe laughed, transported back to the past. 'And Peter was so amused that he stopped the battle and then insisted on taking everyone to make pancakes for pudding. We didn't finish clearing up the kitchen until about two in the morning. Yes, I remember. Oh, Mingie, we did have fun, didn't we?'

'Fun and glamour and grandeur. I used to envy you so much.'

'Did you? During all that gloomy time you had before you met Mark?' Flixe's face grew serious again. 'I suppose all this is fair payment for what I had then. Perhaps you did it better having the bad bits first.'

Ming said nothing, wishing she could help.

'How are the children?' asked Flixe conscientiously. Ming had hardly begun to describe the latest antics of her eight-year-old twin sons, who were being educated at a London prep school, when Flixe interrupted her.

'I do envy you having them at home,' she said. 'Nicky loathes going back to school, even though he's in his third year. I wish . . . But I can't and it's probably better for him to be with lots of other boys.'

'Perhaps,' said Ming, who had doggedly fought her husband's assumptions that his sons should be educated exactly as he had been. 'What about the girls?'

'I don't think they mind so much. Sophie's always tearful when she goes back, but her letters are full of excitement, and Fee will be leaving pretty soon anyway.'

The doorbell rang before Ming could answer and she went to let in their elder sister. Gerry had the same delicate bone structure as the other two, as well as the big dark blue eyes that they had all inherited from their mother, but she was far more carelessly dressed in navy corduroy trousers and a thin green jersey, and her hair looked windblown and very grey. Ming brought her into the drawing room, poured her a glass of wine and left her with Flixe, saying: 'I'll go and deal with lunch. It's so unseasonably warm that I thought we could eat outside. Will you both come down in five minutes?'

'Okay,' said Gerry. 'Now, Flixe: how's it going? Have you managed to get Diseholme's agent under control yet?'

'Not entirely,' said Flixe, sounding tired. 'He's intensely against the idea of a female candidate for the constituency, despite Michael's assurances that he chose me himself. But we've time, and Robinson has at least admitted that I'm conscientious and useful. Whenever Michael refuses to open a school fête or talk to the Mothers' Union, Robinson now knows he can rely on me. Provided Wilson doesn't call an election tomorrow, I should manage to bring him round in time to make sure he doesn't scupper my chances of getting elected.'

'I can't think why Robinson's being so difficult. In the old days you could always charm anybody into doing anything for you. It can't just be that you've lost a lot of weight and are a bit mis. Couldn't you flirt with him? That always used to be one of your greatest talents.'

Flixe sighed, recognising that Gerry was trying to do no more than Ming – or indeed Julia – had done. Their techniques of comfort were different, but their intentions were the same. It was simply bad luck that Gerry's was so much more difficult to accept than Ming's.

'I'm afraid I've lost the knack,' said Flixe, trying to smile. 'How's life with you?'

'Not bad. I'm having a bit of a fight with the publishers of this new translation. They've got a most annoying copy-editor who doesn't seem to understand that a translation must faithfully reflect the original text, even if she doesn't like it. I wish she could read Russian – that would solve a lot of the arguments.'

'Lunch!' Ming's voice floated up from the basement kitchen. 'Come on, you two. Stop gassing.'

They walked down the steep stairs into the huge, white kitchen that led through french windows on to a small, sunny terrace, which was edged with pots overflowing with pink, white, dark red and lavender-coloured flowering shrubs. Ming had laid a table there and was waiting for them with a large dish of eggs baked with cream and prawns and another bottle of the cold German wine.

'Golly, Ming, if we drink all that, I'll find myself promising the constituents the earth,' said Flixe. The others laughed and watched as she helped herself to a single egg and a few prawns.

'Have a bit more,' said Gerry, 'or you'll never be able to wear your own clothes again. Ming must be getting bored with lending you the contents of her wardrobe.'

'I don't mind that at all,' said Ming. 'I've got heaps of clothes. Gerry's just jealous of your new figure, Flixe. Don't listen to her.'

'Old habits are hard to break,' said Flixe, smiling at them both. 'I've always listened to Gerry, however bracing she's been.'

'Even though you've never done anything I advised.' There was enough of an edge to her voice to make Ming intervene at once.

'Except taking up politics. By the way, Flixe, do you need any more clothes for anything? Since you're here anyway, it might be a good opportunity to choose some.'

'Actually yes,' Flixe answered. 'I've got to go out to dinner with Michael Diseholme tonight. I'd thought my one new dress would do, but he's just sprung on me the fact that it's to be black tie, so I'll need something tidier. And I've got to appear at one of the dances in early May, so if you've got anything long and floaty, I'd love to borrow that, too.'

'It's lucky we all look so alike,' said Gerry, trying to atone for her earlier mistake. 'I'd offer you some of my clothes, except that they're all such mean rags compared with Ming's.'

'You are good to me. Both of you,' said Flixe, blinking in the bright sunlight. She took a deep draught of the cool wine.

'We've all been through a lot together,' said Ming, 'and you've kept both Gerry and me going through some rough times. It's your turn now. Don't fret about it. How's Julia? I haven't seen her for ages.'

'All right, I think,' said Gerry before Flixe could answer. 'Although she's had some tough cases recently and lost three out of four. She always hates that.'

'And Amanda's being rather tiresome again, although I'm not sure that Julia doesn't exacerbate that problem by expecting her to be difficult and taking all her antics so seriously,' Flixe contributed.

'She's a dreadful little madam,' said Gerry crisply, 'and she needs her bottom spanking. I've never met anyone so vain. I think poor Julia is a monument of patience when it comes to her wretched daughter.'

'Oh, you're a hard woman,' said Ming, amused to remember that it had taken Gerry and Julia some time to break through their mutual jealousy in the days when both of them had wanted to be closest to Flixe. They had done it eventually and in their joint efforts to find work for her, they had become good friends. 'I say, Flixe, don't you think we ought somehow to magic Gerry backwards to Amanda's age and show her what she was like then?'

'Well, I certainly wasn't vain. No one brought up by our mother could have been.'

'No, but you were difficult,' said Flixe, laughing. 'Don't you remember all those fights you had with them both?'

'We all had those, didn't we?'

'I suppose so, Gerry. Ming, that was delicious. I don't want to break up the party, but I really ought to get going soon. Might I go and raid your wardrobe for a little black dress? We could leave the long one until later.'

'You've time for a titchy bit of raspberry sorbet, haven't you? I made it specially, remembering how much you liked the last batch. If greedy Gerry hurries up and finishes her eggs, we can eat it in no time. I'll go and get it out of the freezer.'

'Isn't it strange how tough little Ming can be?' said Gerry, obediently eating up the last of her eggs and prawns.

'At forty-three and the same height as we are, I don't think she qualifies as "little" these days.'

'Perhaps not, but I always think of her as that. Do you remember her at the beginning of the war, so frightened of everything that she could hardly be out of Annie's shadow for a second?'

'Yes,' said Flixe, piling up their plates, 'but I also remember how she gritted her teeth after Annie was killed. I was furious when I found that Peter had sent her to France, but he knew her well enough to see beyond the surface that fooled the rest of us.'

'He knew us all, didn't he?' Gerry's face changed. 'You know, Flixe, I do miss him. It's as though a whole part of our lives has ... God, I'm sorry. I'm always so clumsy when it comes to ... Are you all right?'

'Yes. Don't worry about it. He's dead and I'm a widow and life is bloody. But I am all right.'

'Unbowed in fact,' said Gerry with an uncertain smile. 'Good for you. Ah, that looks glorious, Ming. I'll take the egg debris into the kitchen. Hand it over, Flixe.'

'What was Gerry looking so crushed about?' asked Ming as her eldest sister disappeared.

'She got in a muddle about whether she was comforting me for Peter's death or wanting consolation for it herself and that embarrassed her. She hasn't always got your sensitive touch, you know, Ming.'

'No, but she has other things.'

'I know, and I am truly grateful to her.' Flixe could not help sounding despondent as she thought of the money Gerry had lent her and the strings she had pulled to get her sister the opportunity of a safe parliamentary seat.

Later, when Flixe had gone, carrying an impeccably cut black dress to wear at dinner that night, Ming took Gerry to task.

'She's not up to being teased yet,' she said at one moment.

'Ming,' said Gerry severely, 'if you continually wrap her up in cotton-wool, she'll never snap out of this. Peter's been dead over a year. She's got to start living again and not let herself get into the habit of fragility. There are four children dependent on her.'

'You don't have to tell me: I take the girls out from school twice a term at least and look after them and Nicky whenever Flixe can't,' said Ming crisply, feeling yet again that Gerry did not do her fair share of the more menial tasks involved in supporting their sister. 'But honestly, Flixe will recover more quickly if she's built up now and not chipped away at.'

'Ming, I'm not. I'm just doing my damndest to see that she sticks with Diseholme and the agent long enough to ensure she gets elected to the seat at the first possible opportunity. Once they're convinced she can do the job, Diseholme will probably go at once and let her in at a by-election. Julia and I are both working at that.'

'I know you are, so hard that neither of you has noticed how much Flixe hates it all. You're both impressively important and with wonderful contacts, but the pair of you are just too busy and convinced of your own rightness to look at her properly.'

'Don't be soppy. Flixe has never done a job of work in her life and she'd hate anything at all rigorous. Peter protected her from the world and its costs and brutalities; she floated about in a sea of flowers and furs and lobsters and things, charming all and sundry and never thinking about anything important. Of course it's all been a dreadful shock, but she's strong enough to cope with it, provided she's not softened by too much sentimentality and cosseting.'

Ming banged down the coffee pot she had just picked up and glared at her sister.

'That's not fair. She didn't float at all and she's seen quite as many of life's difficulties as either you or I, and done more cosseting of us than we ever have of her. Don't you remember how no one who asked her for any kind of help went away empty? And she did all that while revolutionising Peter's life and giving him a family and making him happy, besides having the best parties in London and being so tactful with all the men who fell in love with her. Mark has always adored her and he's sure she just needs time to pick herself up.'

'Yes, you're right. She did all that jolly well.' There was something in Gerry's face, some kind of contempt, that made Ming want to drive her point home. It would have been easy to do it by pointing out to Gerry that she had no idea how hard it was to look after four children – or any children at all – but that would have hurt her, and, angry though she was, Ming could never deliberately set out to hurt anyone.

'I sometimes think that people like you and Julia, who are so successful and hard-working, forget that your way of living isn't the only valuable way. Flixe has done very well by those children of hers,' she said at last.

'I know. She's been a wonderful wife and mother. May I have some coffee?' said Gerry in a deliberately conciliatory voice. 'But, Ming, you know as well as I do that none of her quite genuine skills is much good to her now. She has to get some kind of secure, decently paying job for which no qualifications are necessary. There aren't many for anyone, let alone a forty-six-year-old woman with neither degree nor formal skills of any kind.'

'She's quite capable of earning enough from organising functions,' said Ming, 'and if she comes to dislike doing that, she could easily become an interior decorator, or arrange flowers in hotels and casinos, or a hundred other jobs.'

'God forbid!'

'Gerry, the professions are not the only honest way of earning a living.'

After a long pause, Gerry said, frowning: 'Of course they're not, Ming, but they are the most secure. It's perfectly obvious that Flixe could not at this stage become a lawyer or a civil servant or even a teacher. I admit it was a good idea of yours to get her out of the house and earning petty cash by doing these deb dances, but the season is idiotically anachronistic. It's not going to carry on for more than a year or two at the most, and when it goes, Flixe will simply be stuck again and that much older and less employable. Parliament will always be there. The seat is entirely safe. Once she's been elected, she can go on drawing a parliamentary salary until she's carried out of the chamber feet first if necessary.'

Ming sighed and poured herself a cup of black coffee.

'You're right at one level, but she loathes it and it saps all the energy she needs for recovery. She needs to get her confidence back, and dealing with the constituents rubs her nose in her inability to do things. I don't suppose anyone else could do them any better, but she doesn't see that and it's holding her back.'

'She'll get over it. Flixe has always been perfectly capable when she's been forced to do anything, but she takes a lot of forcing. Look at what she did in the war. She ought to have got a proper job years ago and then she'd have been all right when Peter died.'

'Financially perhaps; but I still think she needs gentleness

– and forbearance – more than anything else just now.'

The two sisters sat on opposite sides of the pretty white table, glaring at each other, each convinced that the other was dangerously wrong about Flixe, who had been their prop and stay for years and was now so worryingly weakened.

CHAPTER 4

Amanda presented herself at Comfort Gillingham's house in South Kensington only fifteen minutes late. Comfort opened the door and led the way straight up to her studio, which took up the entire attic floor of the large house. All the internal walls had been knocked down and a row of skylights had been let into the roof on the garden side so that the light from the small dormers over the street was almost irrelevant.

Amanda, accustomed to the welter of canvases, paints, sketches and jumble in her godfather's cavernous studio, was surprised by the tidiness of Comfort's. The spare prepared canvases were neatly stacked in racks beneath a long drawing-table that held an angled board and a series of beautiful ceramic pots full of every kind of pencil, chalk, crayon and paintbrush all as clean as new and arranged in perfect order. Nothing was dirty; nothing out of place.

The walls of the old attic had been painted a clear subtle buff, which Amanda recognised as having been mixed from orange and blue paint, and the simple blinds that rolled over both windows and skylights were of the grey that is achieved by merely adding more blue and a little Chinese white to the mixture. There was an immense looking-glass in an amazingly ornate baroque frame hanging on the end wall opposite the drawing-table.

A shabbily beautiful tapestry screen stood across one corner of the room and there was a lovely worn carpet across half the immense space. A heavy canvas floor-cloth had been spread under the great easel and it was spattered with paint of various colours. Even those blobs seemed half deliberate to Amanda as she gazed about the room.

'Come and take off your jacket,' said Comfort, holding out a padded hanger. 'Would you like a cup of tea or a glass of wine?'

'Some wine would be lovely. Thank you.'

Comfort hung the jacket in a neat cupboard that appeared to be entirely full of clean linen overalls and then poured wine into two slender antique glasses with air-twist stems. She handed one to Amanda and left the other where it stood beside the decanter of claret.

'What I'd like to do this afternoon is sketch you as we talk. I don't want any posing. I need to find out about you and see the things you've been disguising. Look at anything you like, say anything you like, ask anything. Dance. Sing. Waddle. Lie about.'

'Be spontaneous in fact,' said Amanda with a big enough hint of sarcasm to arouse an appreciative smile on Comfort's thin face.

'Precisely.' Comfort reached to the back of her drawing-table for a block of thick drawing-paper, about ten inches by twelve, and a bundle of soft pencils, which she put into the breast pocket of her off-white overall.

Amanda, invited to relax, found herself far more tense than when she had arrived. Looking around the room for something to take her mind off her own constraint, she saw a series of unframed, faded pencil drawings pinned to a board in the corner opposite the tapestry screen. Wandering over to them, she leaned forwards to look, hoping that the artist was appreciating the length and elegance of her legs.

Then she straightened abruptly, forgot about her legs and even her embarrassment. The drawings were quite clearly of her own mother, but not as Amanda had ever seen her.

They had obviously been sketched on the edge of a river, for in one Julia was sitting on the edge of the bank, bare legged, with her skirt rucked up round her thin thighs and her legs dangling in the water. She was not staring contemplatively, as in Tibor's various portraits of her, or accusingly, as she did in court or when talking to her daughter. Instead her face was laughing straight out of the picture.

Comfort, drawing rapidly, said nothing until Amanda turned away.

'She was my dearest friend, you know.'

'I didn't actually,' said Amanda, unexpectedly embarrassed. 'I mean, I knew that she and . . . and your brother had once been married, but I hadn't realised any more than that. She looks awfully young in those drawings.'

'We were at Oxford together. I introduced her to Anthony.'

'I see. At least I don't at all, but I'm not asking disguised questions, I promise.'

'You look rather touching when you're anxious,' was Comfort's only comment as she swapped a sharp pencil for the one she had already blunted. 'Lie down on that sofa, would you, for a moment.'

Obediently Amanda arranged herself elegantly against the cushions, the beautiful old wine glass dangling from one hand, and looked for approval. It was not forthcoming.

'Not as though you're participating in a fashion shoot.' Comfort's voice was acerbic and peremptory. 'Put down the glass and start again. Collapse against the sofa – you've fallen, or been pushed. Better. Push your hands through your hair: it's better tousled. Yes. Good. Hold that for a moment.'

In less time than seemed possible, Comfort had finished that sketch and wanted Amanda sitting up and then leaning over the back of one of the chairs.

'Miss Gillingham,' she began then.

'Call me Comfort. What?' she said, crossing out one of her hasty lines and redrawing it at the side.

'Have you anything of your brother?'

'Anthony? Lots. There's a portfolio in the second drawer of that plan chest.'

Taking that as permission to look, Amanda finished the last of the wine in her glass and fetched the dark green portfolio from the drawer. Conscious only of curiosity, she sat down on a hard chair at the side of the plan chest and started to leaf through the drawings, hooking a swathe of hair behind her ear with one hand. Some of the drawings were obviously recent; others must have dated from the same time as the series of Julia. Amanda looked through them all in silence, trying to imagine her mother married to him.

'He's awfully like you, isn't he?' she said at one moment, holding up a drawing of him in a white coat with a stethoscope hanging round his neck. 'I didn't know that he was a doctor.'

'Didn't she tell you even that?' There was something in Comfort's voice that made Amanda flush as though with shame. She said nothing. After a moment's silence, Comfort added: 'Yes he is like me, although the nose is better on him than me.'

Amanda said nothing.

'That'll do for the moment. Now I need tea.'

'May I make it?' Amanda put down the portfolio and realised that Comfort was looking tired.

'That would be kind. There's a kettle and stuff behind the screen.'

When Amanda came back with a pot of tea, jug of milk and two bone-china cups, she saw that Comfort had taken her place with the portfolio. She looked up at the sound of Amanda's step.

'You know, I hadn't looked at these for ages – or added to them. I ought to do more, especially now that he's not quite so busy at the hospital.'

Amanda poured the tea, wondering whether she could ask the questions that filled her mind. Remembering Comfort's earlier instruction to do, look at or say anything, she risked the first.

'Has he married again?'

Comfort's face seemed to shrink. She folded the portfolio and put it away in the drawer. At last she looked at Amanda again.

'No. When Julia left him something in him was broken, I think. He's never been able to trust anyone again.' She looked at Amanda and smiled with an obvious effort. 'Don't think I'm saying your mother should never have gone to David – if she had to, she had to – but it did something dreadful to Anthony.' Her voice was quiet and the smile on her thin lips wistful. She seemed quite unlike the figure of a celebrated artist.

Amanda wanted to do something to help, but there was nothing. It had all happened years ago. She felt that she ought to apologise, but it was hardly her fault. It was also extraordinary to hear her father described so familiarly by a woman he had never mentioned.

Comfort shook her thin body suddenly as though she were rousing herself from her melancholy memories.

'It's ancient history, my dear. Drink your tea. Do you want to see the sketches?'

'Yes please. Tibor never lets me look at anything until he's finished.'

Comfort handed her the block and retreated to the softness of the sofa, putting up her trousered legs and leaning her head against the arm. She closed her eyes. Amanda walked past her on the way to a chair, noticing that Comfort's hair, which had seemed palely blonde, was actually three-quarters silver.

The drawings made Amanda smile. Slight though they were, each one no more than a few lines and the occasional blur of shading, they seemed remarkably like her. She waited

51

until Comfort had opened her slaty eyes.

'I think they're very clever,' Amanda said. Comfort smiled.

'They're only notes.' She sat up and peered at Amanda through half-closed eyes. She looked, Amanda thought suddenly, like some pre-Raphaelite painting of Lamia: jewelled, fascinating and malevolent. Then her eyes ceased to glitter as she opened them fully again and her smile widened. The only actual jewels about her were a magnificent square-cut emerald ring on the second finger of her left hand and a narrow gold chain that could be seen disappearing down the neck of her dark blue shirt. The impression of malevolence had gone, too.

'I'm still not quite certain how the portrait should be. In some ways I wish that I knew you better.'

'Why only in some ways?' Amanda was interested. She was always glad to hear about herself from a new source.

Comfort looked at her unsmiling.

'Because there are some advantages in approaching you without preconceptions: peeling off your disguises as we work; finding out what there is beneath that admired surface.'

'Do you think there are disguises?'

'There must be, although you seem so confident that some people might assume there are none. What do you think?'

For the first time Amanda was tempted to tell someone about the huge power that she could feel just out of reach and the overmastering sense of something waiting for her if she could only understand what it was.

'More tea, Amanda?' She shook her head, her impulse to confide stopped by the almost auntly invitation. A buzzer sounded on the wall behind her. Comfort got off the sofa with a slight hint of stiffness and went to a white telephone on the wall.

'Yes?'

Amanda could hear the crackle of a voice through the intercom but no more than that.

'She'll come down.' Comfort put back the receiver and

turned to Amanda. 'It seems to be for you. Did you order a taxi?'

Amanda was about to explain Andrew Suvarov's presence when she caught a gleam of curiosity in Comfort's dark grey eyes and merely smiled.

'Thank you. I'd better go then, unless you need me some more?'

'Not today. Can you come earlier tomorrow? Say two o'clock.'

'Certainly.'

'And don't wear any make-up or I'll forcibly take it off you. I meant what I said in Norwich.'

Amanda, who had already opened the door of the studio, turned back, her face surprised and slightly angry.

'It is you who interests me – not the fashion of the moment,' said Comfort. Without another word, she went to her easel and removed the sheet that covered it. Shaken, but also intrigued, Amanda hurried down the stairs.

All the doors on each floor were firmly closed and there were no sounds from the rooms they hid. As she went down, she wondered whether the brother might be behind one of the doors, nursing his hopeless, defeated love for her mother and his anger at her betrayal. It was a discomfiting thought.

Reaching the heavy front door breathless, Amanda wrenched it open and found Andrew Suvarov shivering on the doorstep. He was wearing only a thin sweater under his old donkey jacket.

'I assumed that even a famous painter would let one wait in her hall,' he said, leaning forward to kiss Amanda's warm cheek. 'You feel nice.'

Amanda felt for his hands and held them between her own. Andrew seemed suddenly very safe. She looked around and noticed that it was already dark.

'Are you all right?' he asked, surprised.

'Oh yes, but she's a strange woman. I felt . . . I felt almost as though I was escaping just now.' Amanda shook her head violently and felt better. 'Idiotic. It must be the effect of sitting still all afternoon. I hadn't realised I'd been up there so long. What about a drink?'

'Let's have it with supper,' he said, urging her towards the bus stop. 'There's a bus.'

Amanda, accustomed to the attentions of suitors with cars or at least plenty of money for taxis, was rather insulted, but she still felt too odd to protest about anything and let him bundle her on to the slowly moving, swaying bus. Andrew bought tickets for them both and sat beside her with his hand heavily covering hers on the rough material of the seat.

'What did you talk about all afternoon?' he asked. 'Was it difficult?'

'No, I don't think so. We talked about me and a bit about her brother and my mother, and painting, I think. It didn't seem to last nearly as long as it actually did. Perhaps there were long patches of silence.'

'Here we are.' Andrew stood up, rang the bell and held out a hand to steady her.

Five minutes later they were inside the warm, steamy, dimly lit restaurant. Once again Amanda felt the contrast between the elegancies of the life she preferred and the coarseness of Andrew's. When they had ordered their food and drinks, he started to talk to her about the iniquities and inequities of life in the British Isles, and she let her attention wander, giving him just enough automatic words of encouragement to make him think that she was listening.

'Really?' she would murmur, or 'Goodness me!' depending on the tone of his remarks. He was quite happy, assuming that her relative silence was caused by interest in his ideas and his plans for overturning the horrible system that condemned vast numbers of citizens to a life of humiliation, frustration and hopelessness.

'It is wonderful to be with someone really intelligent,' he said as their main courses were put in front of them, making

54

her smile at his simplicity. 'I can't think why you're wasting your time on history of art.'

Amanda took a large mouthful of casserole and if she had not worried about her dignity would have spat it out as it burned her mouth. She followed it with a swig of wine, which helped a bit.

'That's the sort of thing my mother says, and I'm afraid that it simply betokens a narrow mind.'

He turned and looked at her in the light of the guttering candle. It caught the whites of his eyes, making them gleam. He looked very handsome and Amanda smiled at him. His own rather severe mouth relaxed.

'I was afraid I'd made you angry.'

'Would that matter?' said Amanda idly.

His face grew serious again and she castigated herself for having asked such a stupid question. It had been an automatic response, the kind of light-hearted teasing thing she would have said to anyone, but she could see that he was about to launch into yet another declaration.

'You know it would, Amanda. Listen, darling, I can't play the kind of games your smart friends no doubt get up to. I love you. It's not your face or your famous parents or your glamour or your publicity: it's the you that hides and fears.'

Touched, and revolted too, Amanda looked at him, slowly shaking her head.

'There is no such me,' she said. 'What you see is what there is. You must be putting on to me what you think about yourself. There may be bits of you that – what was it? – hide, but there aren't in me.'

His face tightened and he moved back from her. He looked angry and much tougher than usual. Amanda smiled slightly. Toughness was so much easier to deal with than the demanding protestations of devotion. She finished her casserole and her wine.

'I ought to get back soon,' she said, thinking, Why does

everyone want to turn me into something I'm not? Why can't I be me?

'I've offended you,' said Andrew coldly. 'It wasn't my intention and I ought to apologise.' He signalled to the busy waitress for a bill.

'There's no need for that,' Amanda said, pleased enough to have extracted it from him not to insist on a specific apology. 'Do you suppose they'd telephone for a taxi for me?'

'You don't need a taxi. I'll take you home.'

'Kennington's miles away and in quite the wrong direction for you.'

Andrew said no more. The bill arrived and he paid it in cash before pushing back his chair.

'I was hoping that you'd come back and have some coffee with me,' he said sternly, waiting for her to stand up too. 'My mother's gone out to dinner and she said she wouldn't be using her car tonight so that I could drive you home. It's early yet.'

Thinking that if she were to go straight home she would only have to account for her day to her mother, Amanda eventually agreed. She had not yet reconstructed the events in Comfort's studio in her mind and was not ready to describe them to anyone else.

Andrew walked beside her through the cold streets to Sloane Square tube station and they caught a Circle Line tube to Kensington High Street. Their train was stuck in the last tunnel for five minutes before their stop, during which all the lights in the carriage were extinguished. Amanda sat waiting for Andrew to take her hand again, but he did not. It seemed rather insulting after all the things he had said to her and his insistence that she return to his mother's house for coffee. She moved closer to him in the warm darkness, hearing the breathing of all the other passengers and the occasional embarrassed whisper as they conversed with each other.

Andrew's own breathing deepened and grew faster as Amanda pressed her thigh against his. Gratified, she casually moved her right hand, first to her own face, as though to brush away some of her loose, glossy hair, and then to his leg. His muscles tautened and his breathing grew louder in the silence. There was something remarkably exciting in knowing that there were people all around them who had no idea what was happening. Andrew's hand came down on hers and pressed it hard against his thigh just as the noise from the tube's engine changed and warned them that they were about to be exposed.

When the lights came up again they were sitting several inches apart, their hands in their own laps. Neither looked at the other or said anything until they had emerged from the station into the High Street.

'Did you mean that?' Andrew asked when they were away from the crowds.

'What?' she said, almost genuinely puzzled.

He stopped and turned to face her.

'Are you playing games again? If so, I'm not interested.'

Irritated herself, and determined not to miss her lift to Kennington now that he had persuaded her to come so far in the wrong direction, Amanda said coldly: 'I'm not playing any kind of game. I felt close to you then and I wanted to touch you.'

Andrew's face was lit by a smile that made him look transfigured.

'Did you? I'm so glad.'

He slung an arm around her shoulders and hugged her in so friendly a fashion that she smiled herself and leaned closer to him.

'Hang on a minute. My shoes are horribly tight,' she said, leaning down to take them off.

With his arm around her shoulders still, and her shoes dangling from her free hand, they walked along the street, turning right to climb the hill to his home. He unlocked the door and ushered her in with some ceremony.

'Sorry it's so cold,' he said with a casualness that made her think his mind must be on other things. 'Something seems to have gone wrong with the heating. Come on up to my room.'

They walked up three flights of stairs to the room he had always had in the holidays since he had been sent away to prep school. It had changed since she had last been there several years earlier. The model aeroplanes and cars that had once clogged the shelves were gone. In their place were books, files, boxes of paper and a red portable typewriter. A poster of Che Guevara in a beret adorned one wall and a black-power fist another. The only pictures were three black-and-white photographs of desperate-looking men and women sitting hopelessly amid run-down slums, which had been framed with clear perspex attached to the backing boards with simple steel clips.

Andrew put a match to the joss-sticks in a small brass bowl filled with sand, and to the gas fire, which lit with a small explosion and then settled into a cosy rhythm of pops and splutters. There were two red candles in simple holders on the plain white mantelpiece, and he lit those, too, before turning off the main light. He pulled two immense cushions covered in dark red rep off the bed and arranged them before the fire. Amanda sank down gracefully.

'Coffee?' he said, gesturing to a tray that stood on a chest of drawers beside the basin. It contained an electric kettle, two mugs and several jars. 'Or would you rather have something else?'

'I don't know that I want anything actually,' said Amanda.

'Good,' he answered, folding his long legs under him as he joined her on the dusty cushions.

Each was about four feet square and they were both soft and resilient. He leaned forward, putting a hand under her square chin and tilting it towards him. He seemed wonderfully confident for once. Something of the tingling pleasure she had felt on the tube returned and she let him kiss her, obediently opening her lips as she felt his tongue pushing forwards.

Her back began to ache from the twisted way she was sitting and she slid down on to the cushions to ease it.

'Darling,' murmured Andrew, stroking her neck and moving beside her. 'May I?'

It seemed to her then that it would be dreadfully churlish to refuse as well as marking her as less sophisticated than Andrew, which would be unendurable. After all, she told herself, he had stopped talking about the self that he knew and she did not; he had stopped frightening her with talk of his need of her and the love she did not want. And she liked his stroking. The two of them fitted neatly together on the cushions. It was warm, the scent of joss-sticks tickled the back of her throat, and it was just possible that she might discover the transcendental experience that she wanted. She lay back, saying nothing and doing nothing, which he correctly took to be permission.

'Is this all right?' he asked at one moment. 'Or is this better?'

Amanda, feeling embarrassed, uncomfortable and humiliatingly ignorant, did not know how to say that neither was particularly pleasant and she did not know what 'better' would be, and merely made an uncomplicated noise in her throat. He kissed her again, which was better or at least more familiar, and continued with what he was doing.

When he had finished it, Amanda had to acknowledge that transcendence had eluded her once more. She lay patiently in the warm, glowing dimness, waiting for him to hug her and say something gentle. But he went to sleep, lying heavily across her breasts and adding to the other discomforts.

She woke him, after fifteen minutes of frustrated patience, by stretching her cramped muscles. He moved back and gazed at her.

'Wasn't that wonderful?' he said with a smile of such open,

trusting affection that she found she could not disabuse him.

Still longing to be hugged, Amanda smiled back and held out her arms. He touched one hand.

'We haven't really got time for more,' he said, watching her tenderly. 'I'll run you a bath and then I'd better drive you home. It's after ten.'

Realising that if she protested she was no schoolgirl who had to report home by any particular time he would assume that she was asking for more lovemaking, Amanda went silently to the bathroom and, having carefully locked the door, proceeded to wash vigorously before making up her face again.

Andrew sang as he drove her home. She had never heard him sing before and was amazed at the depth and richness of his bass voice, singing in what she assumed was Russian. The songs sounded sad, and she was touched to think of him yearning for his ancestral certainties. When he pulled up outside her parents' big, Georgian house in Kennington, she leaned across the gear lever to kiss him.

'Thank you, darling,' he said. 'It's wonderful to know that we've really got there at last; I was beginning to be afraid we never would. I'll collect you from Miss Gillingham's at the same time tomorrow.'

'No,' she said, before she thought. 'No, don't do that. I'm not sure what time she'll finish with me tomorrow. She wants me to start earlier. I'll ring you when I get home.'

'Oh, all right,' said Andrew, obviously hurt. 'I must work anyway.' He deliberately smiled again. 'Good-night. Sleep well.'

'Oh, I will,' she said. 'Good-night.'

She waited on the top step, waving to him until he had driven off, and then turned and let herself into the house. With her heart sinking, she heard footsteps behind the kitchen door. It opened and her mother looked out, still dressed in one of the black suits she wore to court.

Tall and severe, she stood there like the prosecuting counsel she often was. Her face, so like Amanda's in shape, was lined and beginning to slacken, the skin firmly attached only to two points on either side of her chin and loosening elsewhere. She had once been as slender as her daughter, although she had always thought of herself as gawky, but she had grown slightly heavier since her fiftieth birthday. Her dark eyes looked paler than they had and somehow sunk into their sockets.

'I can't think why you don't wear eyeliner or at least something on your lashes,' said Amanda pettishly.

'Are you all right?' Julia's voice was sharp with concern.

'Of course I'm all right,' said Amanda, thoroughly irritated and also disturbed by the sharpness. 'Why shouldn't I be?'

'Well, but darling, you've been ages. I was beginning to worry.'

Amanda walked towards the brightly lit, green-and-white kitchen and her mother made way for her.

'Why? You've never worried before.'

Julia, hearing the familiar mixture of resentment, anger and impatience, deliberately relaxed herself, smiled and poured out a cup of tea from the pot she had just made. She offered the cup to her daughter.

'Thanks.'

'It's just that I knew you were going to Comfort Gillingham's studio early this afternoon.' Julia pulled out one of the green chairs and sat down. 'I couldn't imagine that she would keep you so long and I wondered if something had happened. That's all.'

Thinking to herself that something had definitely happened, but that it would be absurd to let it assume any significance, Amanda shook her long hair back from her face.

'I don't know what you're making such a fuss about. I had supper with Andrew Suvarov at the Chelsea Kitchen.'

Julia's face cleared.

'Oh, was that all? Darling, I am glad.'

'I thought you didn't like Andrew.'

'I've never said that.'

'You didn't have to,' said Amanda drily. 'It's always clear when you don't like my friends.'

Julia's shoulders sagged slightly.

'It's not that I dislike him,' she said slowly. 'It's just that I've felt once or twice that he was demanding from you things you were in no position to give him.'

'Oh?' The monosyllable was abrupt and abruptly delivered. 'Such as going to bed with him perhaps. Would that be so terrible? Even your sacred law admits that I'm over the age of consent.'

'No, it wouldn't be terrible at all,' said Julia with care, 'not if you loved him. But, my darling child, I don't think you do.'

'You mean that you don't think sex before marriage is necessarily wrong?' Amanda was astonished and Julia smiled slightly.

'Not necessarily. I think it's often unwise and frequently leads to quite unexpected misery, but if there really is love . . .'

Amanda looked at her and thought of all the times when Julia had hurt her. She felt like kicking something.

'I don't see what love's got to do with it, and even if it has I don't see why you think I couldn't love Andrew.'

'If you were to tell me you loved him, of course I'd believe it,' said Julia, deliberately making her voice kind and unemphatic and suppressing her instinctive dislike of the idea. 'The two of you are old friends and you're obviously fond of him, but it hadn't occurred to me that it was any more than that.' She smiled. 'When he was here at Christmas he seemed to be trying to turn you into something you're not and I rather thought that would have annoyed you.'

Amanda suppressed a wince at that piece of perception. Julia did not look at her daughter as she went on.

'I suppose I thought that you'd have shared my dislike of the way he automatically dismissed things you said when they didn't correspond with his ideas.'

Surprised that her mother should have seen so much and afraid that the unexpected sympathy was going to make her cry, Amanda said brusquely: 'Well, he's not alone in that. You've always dismissed my ideas.'

Julia dropped her head into her hands for a second.

'I'm rather tired, Amanda,' she said at last, realising there was still nothing she could do to mend whatever had been broken between them. She could not remember a time when it had been whole and felt as though she had spent all of Amanda's life trying to make it so. 'I think I'd better go to bed. I've . . .'

'A case in the morning.' Amanda knew that she was sounding nasty and did not mind because it seemed unfair that on this one night when she really needed something from her, her mother could not have waited until she was ready – or able – to talk. The fact that she did not know exactly what it was she wanted did not seem relevant. 'I know. You always have.'

'Your father's not back yet, so don't bolt the front door,' said Julia, ignoring the last salvo. 'Good-night. Sleep well.'

When she had gone, Amanda sat down at the table, put her elbows on the green-and-white cloth, and wept.

CHAPTER 5

When she had done her hair and her face, Flixe put on Ming's black dress and pinned her own sapphire and diamond brooch on the left shoulder. She sprayed a minute amount of scent behind her ears and on her wrists and then picked up the lavish silver-fox coat that had been one of Peter's last presents before his illness.

Feeling its astonishing softness as she slung it round her shoulders, she could not help wondering all over again why on earth he had never told her about the money. He had known he was dying for the last four or five months; he talked a lot about his love of her, about Russia, about their children, his sister, Natalie, and about the relations he must still have living behind the Iron Curtain. He told her what her love had meant to him throughout their marriage. They had even talked frankly of the illness that was devouring him before her eyes and about his inevitable death. But he had never warned her about the money.

Perhaps, Flixe told herself, he had been in too much pain even to think about such mundane things. But there had been days when the pain was under control and he had had some energy – just a little – to spare.

He had spent lavishly all their married life and it had never occurred to her that either of them might have to worry about money. If she had only known what might happen, she could have urged him not to spend all the income, but to put it in some kind of fund for their children's future. She could have got a job, too, or at least worked for some useful qualification so that she need not have been defenceless after his death.

Flixe reminded herself that if things became desperate she could sell her furs and perhaps even the sapphires. They would not bring much, but it was a small comfort to know that they were available against disaster.

She blotted her darkened eyelashes, carefully checking in the mirror that there were no smudges on her face, and then set out to walk the four hundred yards to the house where John Kinghover and his wife were entertaining their friends.

Flixe had timed her arrival impeccably. She hated walking into an unknown house before any of the other guests. On that evening most of them, including Michael Diseholme, had arrived and her introduction to her unknown host was simple. She smiled at him and shook his hand, thanking him for the invitation. He stood looking down at her and refusing to let go of her hand until she felt uncomfortable. He was a tall, florid man with sparse dark hair and very round dark eyes.

'They will have told you that I disapprove of women Members of Parliament,' he said in a rich, slightly smoky voice, 'and I haven't changed my mind, even when they're as good-looking as you.'

Flixe continued to smile and pulled her hand out of his.

'Why should you indeed?' Trying to achieve an instant synthesis of all the aspects of her character that were supposed to make her suitable to represent the constituency, she added: 'But of course I'm not the first to have to face that sort of opinion.'

'I'm well aware of that.' There was enough irritation in his statement to make the sitting Member flinch and glare at his putative successor.

'And, as someone famous said, "I am striving to take into public life what every man gets from his mother".'

At that Mr Kinghover let out a bellow of laughter and patted Flixe's carefully powdered cheek.

'I've always liked a girl with spirit,' he said, watching as she kept the sweet smile on her lips, 'even though . . .'

'Darling,' called his wife, a slender redhead who was dressed in a long Black Watch tartan skirt and a black silk polo-necked sweater lightened with a silver pendant, 'you must give Mrs Suvarov a drink.'

Despite the imperative words she had chosen, Mrs King-hover looked timidly at her husband, which made Flixe dislike him even more. She accepted an icy glass of gin and tonic from him and was then taken to be introduced to the other guests.

Her tour ended with a middle-aged man who looked as though he worked in the City and a slim, gentle-faced girl wearing a long, green corduroy skirt and a tucked, frilled, white cotton Mexicana blouse. With her long mousy-fair hair simply drawn back from her face in a black-velvet hairband and her unobtrusive make-up, she looked much too young to have been invited to the dinner on her own merits and had presumably come with him. Since he had been introduced as Gerald Markham and she as Georgina Mayford, they could not have been related. Flixe assumed that she was his girlfriend and felt rather sorry for her.

That feeling increased as they talked. Gerald Markham's opinions were of the traditional Tory kind, which might have been bought as a job lot rather as some people buy an entire library of second-hand books, but Georgina's were much more interesting. She proffered them tentatively but with an expression in her eyes that suggested she would defend them if necessary. Flixe liked her and hoped that the slight tension in her face would relax as she came to

66

feel more at ease with the adults all round her.

There was a flurry of activity at the door as the last of the guests arrived. Georgina looked up and a free smile banished the anxiety from her grey-green eyes.

'Are you all right?' Flixe asked quietly. The girl turned to her at once with the same open smile.

'Goodness yes. Thank you. It was just that I was getting a bit worried about my father. We were supposed to come together tonight, but he was called out to an emergency and I've been slightly worried about what might have been happening.'

'Oh, I see.' Flixe was not quite sure why she was so relieved. 'Is he a doctor?'

'That's right.'

By then her father had been introduced to everyone else in the room and had been brought to stand in front of them. He stroked his daughter's hair briefly and smiled at Flixe.

'Mrs Suvarov,' said Mrs Kinghover, 'this is Doctor Mayford, Georgina's father.'

'How do you do?' said Flixe warmly. She liked the easy affectionate way he had greeted his daughter.

They were obviously very fond of each other and they looked alike, too, although the doctor's hair was much blonder than his daughter's and his eyes were greener. It was partly the shape of their faces that made them seem so similar, with their broad foreheads, full mouths and firm chins, and partly their shared expression of amused and tolerant interest in what was going on around them. They were both tall, although the doctor topped his daughter by at least six inches, and their shoulders were broad and square. They looked lightly tanned as though they had recently been skiing, fit, interested and, above all, content. It was, Flixe thought, a remarkably attractive combination.

George Mayford shook Flixe's hand, saying: 'Suvarov. That's an unusual name. Are you Russian?'

'No, but my husband was,' she said, wishing that she could

prevent the constraint that most people felt when they discovered she was a widow. She saw Doctor Mayford registering her slight withdrawal, but he did not comment. He merely smiled, crinkling up his eyes, in wordless apology.

'Daddy,' said Georgina, who had been ignoring a tentative signal from Mrs Kinghover, 'can I just ask what happened before we get separated?'

'Nothing much,' he said, turning towards his daughter. 'You could say that it was a false alarm. All's well.'

'Thank goodness!' She quickly explained to Flixe that he had been called out to someone who had been threatening suicide. 'You see, I had to know.'

'I do understand that,' said Flixe, wondering what part Georgina's mother played in their obviously close-knit relationship and why she was not at the dinner.

'Shall we all go in and dine?' said Mrs Kinghover brightly before Flixe had a chance to find out.

She followed her hostess into the big, gloomy dining room, where she discovered that she had been seated between the doctor and Gerald Markham, which seemed like a calculated insult since Michael Diseholme had been placed on their hostess's right. Flixe knew that she ought to have minded, but was merely relieved that she would not have to parry John Kinghover's insulting compliments – or direct insults. His City colleague had seemed harmless if dull, and the doctor positively to be welcomed.

She turned to him first as a hot crab soufflé was offered to each guest in turn, saying: 'If you were called to a possible suicide does that mean you are a psychiatrist?'

He shook out his napkin and laid it across his knees.

'Yes. I used to be in general practice, but so many of my patients seemed distressed rather than more conventionally ill that I turned to psychiatry some years ago and by chance I've built a speciality in exogenous depression.'

'That sounds remarkably impressive, but what does it mean?' It was her turn to help herself to soufflé and she spooned some on to her heavily gilded, dark-blue-and-white plate.

'Some people call it reactive depression. Technically exogenous means "of external origin". I believe that there are two main sorts of depression: exogenous, which is caused by some event that impinged on the patient, and endogenous, which is usually the result of some biochemical deficiency.'

'How do you tell the difference?'

He looked at her, as though to check whether she was really interested or merely being polite.

'It can be extremely difficult,' he said when he was sure. 'After all, the symptoms are the same: early waking, loss of appetite, inability to make decisions, terrible emptiness and so on. I'm sure you know what I'm talking about.'

'Why should you think that?' Flixe did not want to think that the battle against misery that she hoped one day to win was visible to casual acquaintances, even ones like the Mayfords whom she immediately liked.

'Most human beings have come across it at some time in their lives.'

'Perhaps,' said Flixe seriously and then, relieved that she had not been exuding sadness, she turned to him with a twinkling smile. 'I think it's awfully brave of you to talk about your expertise at dinner.'

His smooth, slightly tanned face creased as his lips lifted and his greenish grey eyes narrowed into a smile that suggested he knew exactly what she was about to say. Even so, she said it.

'Don't you find that people tend to tell you their sorrows over the soup? It must get very dull.'

'I suppose it might, but I always find ways of stopping them.'

'Because . . .' Flixe paused, aware that the old easy frivolity was still beyond her range. Despite her own serious interest in the subject, or perhaps because of it, she wanted to tease him, but the right words escaped her and the ones that occurred to her seemed too harsh.

'. . . I don't want to offer my services free over a meal?' George Mayford supplied the words and the right mocking note. 'I have medical colleagues who say they're sometimes tempted to have a meter running on the dinner-table like a taxi so that they can show importunate strangers how much their time ought to be costing, and others who announce that they are gravediggers so that they don't have to listen to long involved accounts of operations that have gone wrong.'

Flixe laughed.

'Yes, that was rather what I meant.'

'I thought so,' he said with an answering smile. 'But that's not why I avoid it. Once people start talking about their distress, they tend to be unable to stop and it often lands them in tears, which embarrasses them and everyone else.'

'That sounds both sensible and kind,' said Flixe, no longer laughing. 'I'm afraid I was being frivolous and you're right to pull me up. It is something that matters a lot.'

'I didn't mean to pull you up,' he said at once. 'I'm all for frivolity. It helps most difficulties. Your soufflé's getting cold.'

Reminded of the purpose of the evening, Flixe finished her soufflé and ate a corner of the thin toast she had been offered, wishing that the psychiatrist her elder sister had found for her after Peter's death had been as sensible as Doctor Mayford seemed. The temptation to ask his advice was severe.

'That seems strange for a psychiatrist,' she said instead. 'I thought you all took everything frightfully seriously.'

'Only ourselves usually,' he said, which made her laugh as it had been meant to do.

For the first time since Peter's death she had recognised real attraction in a man's eyes and felt herself respond to it with pleasure. It was a sensation she had never expected to feel again and she enjoyed it. With her dark blue eyes shining and her lips curving into a wonderful smile, she said: 'You must be truly unassailable in your self-confidence to be able to joke about it. If I weren't afraid of being faced with a ticking taximeter I'd ask how you did it. It seems a far more impressive achievement than any list of medical degrees.'

'It's only a trick. Anyone can learn. Don't tell on me.'

'I won't,' she said, still smiling as she turned to the banker on her other side.

They chatted in a civilised, meaningless way about films, about the generation gap, his children and hers until a pair of fillets of beef in puff pastry had been served and eaten. Flixe turned back to Doctor Mayford with a little spurt of pleasure. He was still talking to the woman on his right and Flixe sat watching him out of the corner of her eyes.

He was listening to his companion with a politely deferential air that amused Flixe when she overheard the woman explaining her servant problems in a voice so plangent that it verged on a whine. Something in his expression suggested he knew that Flixe was watching him. She turned away and caught the eye of his daughter, who smiled as though she shared Flixe's amusement.

When the doctor had disengaged himself from the woman with the servant problems, the first thing Flixe said to him was: 'Your daughter is a very impressive girl.'

His face creased once more into its lively smile and his eyes glittered in the candle-light.

'I'm glad you think so,' he said. 'Sometimes I worry that she's so self-contained: it comes of being so much with adults. I've tried to keep her in touch with her own generation, but there are times when it's been hard.' He looked down at Flixe as though trying to decide something.

She raised her eyebrows but did not speak.

'And she's such a good companion,' he said with a slight frown, 'that I fear I've exploited her these last years.'

'What does she do?'

'She's going up to university next year and in the meantime,'

71

he said, making Flixe realise that she had indeed under-estimated Georgina's age, 'I've persuaded her to do the season.'

'What a rare combination!' The laugh was back in Flixe's eyes.

'I know. There are only one or two others doing it before university, but I'm determined that Gina shan't miss out on anything. Having brought her up without a mother, I'm frighteningly conscious of the things she might lack. She loathes the idea of being a deb incidentally, thinks it's an appalling waste of time and so on, but she has capitulated to please me – which was never really the point.'

'She'll probably enjoy it once it's started. They usually do, even if they've found the girls' tea-parties dull. I wonder . . .'

'What?'

'Someone was talking the other day about a very sensible doctor's daughter at a deb tea-party. Could it have been Georgina?'

'I expect so. She is sensible. Very.' He lifted his wine glass. 'I do worry about that too.'

Thinking of her own daughters, some of whose exploits at boarding school were quite hair-raising, and of Andrew whose participation in rent strikes, demonstrations and even riots was a source of almost continual anxiety, Flixe said astringently: 'As a seriously worried parent myself, I cannot imagine minding about one of mine being sensible.'

She thought that he would make a joke of it, but, after swallowing a mouthful of the fruity white wine in his glass, he said seriously: 'Unless she's missing out – has missed out, I suppose now – on all the irresponsibility and freedom that never come again.'

'Universities just at the moment seem to be hotbeds of irresponsibility and freedom. She'll probably let go once she's there.'

'You're right, of course, and paradoxically that's a worry too. Isn't it difficult being a parent?'

72

'Fiendishly,' said Flixe with such fervour that he laughed once more.

They had finished their chocolate and orange mousse by then and as Flixe started to get up, obedient to another signal from Mrs Kinghover, he leaned towards her and murmured: 'I'd expected to be ferociously bored tonight. It's been a great pleasure finding myself beside you.'

Flixe smiled and when she reached the doorway looked back at him. She felt as though she had known him for ages. He inclined his head slightly, acknowledging her unspoken message, just before she turned away to follow the other women up to their hostess's bedroom.

There she made herself agreeable to Mrs Kinghover, re-powdered her face and dealt with her hair. It amused her to see some of the other guests patronising Georgina Mayford and finding themselves at a loss when she made it perfectly clear that she needed no help from them.

As the women were politely herded into the yellow-and-blue drawing room for coffee, Flixe complimented her. Georgina smiled.

'It's easy. They mean to be kind and so it doesn't matter what they actually say.'

'I'm not absolutely sure that they do,' said Flixe, thinking that no girl as sensible and good-natured as Georgina should be hoodwinked by a group of middle-aged harpies. 'Some of them sounded quite bitchy in their offers of advice.'

'They did, didn't they?' Georgina still managed to be tolerant. 'But I've noticed that women of that age often do. Quite a lot of them – or their friends – have been in love with my father at one time or another and they know that I have all the cards in that suit.'

'I'm not sure that I understand.' Flixe accepted a cup of coffee from Mrs Kinghover and shook her head at the chocolates. As soon as they were alone again, Georgina explained.

'My mother died when I was born and, as he's never

73

married again, my father . . .' She stopped and looked a trifle self-conscious. 'Well, he's been a target for any woman on her own or anyone with a divorced friend,' she added carefully.

'I can imagine,' said Flixe, thinking of his looks and his easy charm. 'That must have been difficult for you as you grew up.'

'Not really. I'm not sure how to put this delicately, but he's always been very discreet and I've never known which of them – if any – have been more than friends.' Georgina looked at Flixe and obviously saw sympathetic comprehension in her face for she added: 'I think he probably is a bit of a rake although he takes great care to conceal it from me.'

'I think you might be right.' Flixe thought that there had been something about the way he moved and about the pleasure with which he had accepted more of John King-hover's splendid burgundy that suggested he enjoyed sensual pleasures. 'Do you mind that?'

Georgina smiled and once more looked much older than her years.

'No. He's been so very civilised about it, and never let anything impinge on me. I think he must take them abroad, you see. The only effect on me is that occasionally some women – like these – find it necessary to demonstrate their superiority to me.'

Flixe found herself laughing at the mixture of good sense and kindness in Georgina's account of her father. The girl laughed with her.

'Are you going to read psychiatry at university and follow in his footsteps? It sounds as though you'd be very good at it.'

'Good heavens no! I could never be a doctor. I'm after a nice, useless degree. History.'

'I see. Where?'

'Oxford. Somerville.'

'Oh, what a pity!' Flixe said, adding as she saw the first

uncertainty on the girl's face, 'My elder son is up at Magdalen now, but he's in his final year. If only he'd been there next year as well he could have taken you about a bit.' It struck her forcibly that this intelligent, tolerant, averagely good-looking girl would be far more suitable for Andrew than the self-absorbed beauty who had enthralled him.

'Perhaps he'll do some post-graduate work?'

'Alas no. He's all set up with a traineeship at the BBC. But perhaps I could introduce the two of you after he's done with schools so that he can give you some good advice.'

Remembering that most of Andrew's extra-curricular activities were connected with the overthrow of the established order and the triumph of the working-classes, Flixe almost blushed.

'Do you know Jemima Kirkwaters?' she asked to distract Georgina's attention from her own confusion. A shadow fell over the clear grey-green eyes.

'Slightly,' said Georgina.

'I've been wondering whether it was you who drove her home after the disastrous tea-party. She was telling me about it only this morning.'

The shadow lifted as Georgina smiled again.

'Yes it was. I hadn't realised that you knew her that well. Poor girl; I felt very sorry for her. It was a piece of horrible unkindness on the part of our hostess not to warn Jemima about the whisky.'

The men reappeared, smelling of port and cigars, before Flixe could answer her and they were separated once more. Flixe found herself talking to John Kinghover, whose belligerence seemed only to have increased with the alcohol he had drunk. She dealt with him as well as she could, ignoring his grosser taunts and trying to charm him out of his bad temper. It seemed that she must have succeeded for eventually he patted her shoulder and turned to say to Michael Diseholme, who had been standing behind them, 'She'll do. I don't know how easy she'll find that bear garden you call the House of Commons, but for my money she'll do all right by the constituency.'

Good, thought Flixe, feeling almost impossibly tired, then I can go home now. Showing nothing of her desire for escape, she chatted for a little longer before thanking him and his wife for the dinner. On her way out, Flixe waved good-bye to Georgina Mayford who smiled gaily back, nodded to the rest of the guests and went to fetch her coat. Doctor Mayford stopped her at the door.

'Mrs Suvarov,' he said, with a charming tentativeness in his deep voice, 'would you think it unbecomingly forward if I were to invite you to lunch tomorrow? I would leave a respectable number of days before asking you, but I have an unexpected – and quite rare – free slot in my day tomorrow.'

Flixe was on the point of brushing off his invitation with an easy excuse when she looked at him. A faint, self-conscious smile in his eyes pleased her, as did the tilt of his good-looking head. Georgina's indiscretions returned to her mind and she thought she recognised the kind of man he was. It was a kind she knew and liked, not least because Peter had been one of them, too. She smiled.

'Do you know, I should like that enormously,' she said with a deliberation he could not mistake. He looked pleased.

'I shall telephone you in the morning,' he said, holding out his hand.

'Thank you. I'm in the book.' Flixe shook hands with him.

Walking back through the cold, deserted streets of big white houses, Flixe recognised in herself a faint reflection of the happy frivolity that had once been her familiar. The thought of spending a pleasant, luxurious hour or two flirting with George Mayford made her feel as though she were faced with an unexpected fire in the middle of some winter landscape: diverting and comforting but unimportant. For a little while in his company she would be able to forget her troubles.

She slept better that night, not well enough but better, and was up and dressed by eight. For once she did not confine her breakfast to a mug of Nescafé in her study. Instead, she laid herself a proper place at the scrubbed wooden table in the sunny kitchen, using her French porcelain crockery, and made a pot of real coffee and another of hot milk. Sitting down with *The Times* and the *Guardian*, which she took every day as part of her education in the world of politics, she poured out her coffee and savoured the rich scent of it, which she liked almost more than the taste.

Before she had finished the first cupful, Andrew put in an unexpected appearance. She rarely saw him until lunchtime. Putting down her newspaper at once, she fetched him a cup and plate and laid a place opposite her own.

'Are you hungry? I think there's some bacon left or I could boil you an egg if you'd rather.'

Her son shook his unkempt head. Flixe thought that he looked different from the previous day, less tense and almost at peace for once.

'No, thanks. Just coffee. How was your party?'

'Not too bad at all,' she answered, feeling her lips curving irrepressibly at the memory of that little lift to her spirits as she met George Mayford's eyes. She poured Andrew a cup of coffee. 'There were some unexpectedly pleasant people there. And you? How was Amanda?'

'Remarkably sweet,' he said and hid his face in the huge flowered cup. When Flixe did not comment he swallowed and revealed himself again. 'She made me happy.'

'I'm glad,' said Flixe simply. Not quite sure what his statement actually meant, she wanted to warn him not to rely on whatever Amanda had managed to give him, but she did not think she could afford the cost of taking away the rare, easy happiness from his dark eyes.

'And you don't hate her, do you? Not really?' said Andrew, sounding much less confident than usual.

'I've never hated her,' said Flixe, adding honestly, 'although there have been times when I haven't particularly admired her.'

'I know. But you always would if you knew her properly. Underneath all that silliness, she is worth the most tremendous amount. You'll see.'

Flixe looked at him rather sadly. She wanted to let him have his happiness untrammelled but she did not want to lie to him. Eventually she compromised.

'You may be right. I think she's had too much too easy for too long and it has tended to make her rather unthinking and sometimes unkind. I find that hard to ignore, although I'm really glad she was good to you yesterday. How's the work going?'

'Not too bad. May I have some more coffee?'

Flixe refilled his cup, trying to summon the necessary courage to ask the rest of her questions. He had no father. It was her responsibility.

'Andrew,' she began and then added in a rush, 'it's none of my business whether or not you and Amanda are ... sleeping together, and I don't want to know unless you want to tell me, but if you are I do hope that you are being careful.'

He looked blankly at her for a moment, and then laughed, saying easily, 'I couldn't think what you were talking about for a moment. She's on the Pill. Girls like her always are.'

'Oh good.' Flixe was not certain whether she liked the implications of the answer, but at least it was reassuring. 'What sort of girls?'

'Fashionable, sexy, popular.' He drank some more coffee and made a face. 'Amanda-like.'

'Oh. Would you put a couple of slices of bread in the toaster? I think we both need something to eat.'

Andrew did as she asked. She knew that he wanted to tell her something – or perhaps ask something – but she did not know how to encourage his confidence without seeming to pry. When the toast was ready she buttered her slice carefully and added a smear of Marmite.

'Mum?'

Here it comes, she thought, and smiled encouragingly at him.

'Should you mind awfully if we were to marry? I'd hate you to feel that I was deserting you, particularly now that I know about the money, but . . .'

Her buttery toast sagged between her fingers and dropped on to the plate.

'In the context, that doesn't matter at all,' she said quickly, 'but I'm not sure that this is the right time for you to be thinking about marrying anyone. Have you talked to Amanda about it?'

He shook his head.

'No. But she knows that I'll ask her soon.'

'My darling boy.' Flixe wiped her sticky fingers on her napkin and reached across the table for his hand. He gave it with surprisingly little hesitation. 'I don't want to sound like every stuffy parent, but it's too soon for you to know whether you could possibly be happy with her.'

'We've been friends all my life and I know her quite well enough to be certain that I couldn't be happy with anyone else.'

'I see. Can you be as certain that you know yourself yet?'

There was silence. He slowly pulled his hand away from hers.

'I think so.' He sounded both dignified and hurt.

'If you can, Andrew, try to wait at least until you're working at the BBC. University is a strange world that has no real counterpart outside. Things – and people – may look different to you once you've left it.'

'Not Amanda,' he said, pushing back his chair. He stood up, looking at his mother with his most confident smile lightening his face. 'I love her. And it begins to look as though she's coming to understand that she loves me, too.'

Flixe stood, too, and reached up to kiss his cheek. 'I'm so

glad you're happy,' she said. That at least was true. The problems of Amanda's real feelings and the unthinking arrogance of what Andrew had said seemed for a moment unimportant compared with his happiness.

He laid his dark head on hers for a moment and then abruptly left her for his books and the clouds of incense that he liked to have around him as he worked.

George Mayford telephoned before Flixe could even begin to consider her son's announcement properly and arranged to meet her at the Etoile in Charlotte Street at half past twelve.

They lunched slowly and well, talking lightly of things that were wholly unimportant and yet interesting to them both. Flixe felt as though the combined stresses that kept her upright like some temporary structure were all relaxed and for the blessed hour and a half they spent together she let herself sag.

George Mayford talked and listened and watched her drawn face soften in the warm dimness of the restaurant. She had amused him at the dinner party and now she touched him. When he had paid the bill and they were standing on the pavement outside the restaurant he took her hand between both of his.

'I enjoyed that hugely, Felicity.'

'And I. Thank you. You've done more for me than you could possibly know.'

'Can we meet again?'

'I hope so. I'd like it a lot.'

'Good. I'll telephone you.' He let go of her hand and she pulled on her gloves. 'Can I be cheeky enough to say one thing?'

She looked up in surprise, her remarkable eyes alert and a slightly mischievous smile on her lips.

'You could always try.'

'I do know what it feels like,' he said seriously. 'After my wife died it was quite literally years before I was back to normal. All you can do is try to go with it – not fight it.'

The mischief disappeared and a slightly bitter expression crossed her face.

'That sounds remarkably like what they say about having a baby, but it still hurts hideously, just as that did.'

'I know,' he said. 'And about childbirth too, even though I'm a man. But the pain does stop in the end.'

Flixe turned her face away. Much of the pleasure of their lunch had been washed away by the returning tide of misery and worry, and it seemed worse than usual because of the slackening of her guy-ropes.

'I'll ring you,' he said abruptly, recognising what he had done. 'Thank you for today.'

He lifted his hat and walked away. Flixe went slowly home and, in defiance of her plans to spend no unnecessary money, telephoned her sister-in-law in Paris.

'Flixe, how are you?' said Natalie. 'Has something happened?'

'I rather think it has, which is why I've rung now. Are you all right?'

'Not so bad. I am very tired and my back keeps aching, but not so bad. What is it that is happening to you, Flixe?'

'I have met someone,' she said simply. 'And it is a strange feeling. I don't quite know what to do about it.'

'Nice?' asked Peter's sister with a kind of tenderness in her voice that made Flixe smile.

'Very, I think.'

'And so?'

'Ah, Natalie, I don't know. Do you think, I can . . . ?'

'Flixe, are you asking my permission to allow this man into your life?' There was amusement mixed with the tenderness in Natalie's question.

'I suppose I must be.' Flixe laughed. 'Silly, isn't it?'

'Yes, but understandable. Peter would have been glad to know that you are not completely alone any more; just as I am glad.'

Flixe was silent, having been given exactly what she had wanted.

'Don't be afraid, Flixe.'

'Natalie, you are the best friend I could have. Without you it would all have been even more impossible.'

'Good. We are together then. But you must ring off now or your bill will be enormous. I love you, Flixe. Good-bye.'

She rang off at once to leave Flixe sitting with the receiver in her hand and a new tranquillity growing in her mind.

CHAPTER 6

When Amanda arrived at the studio she was half afraid that Comfort would look at her and instantly know what had happened. Her brief bout of tears had not marked her skin, but she thought that her eyes looked quite different from the previous day.

'Good, no make-up,' Comfort said, apparently noticing nothing unusual. 'I've decided to paint you as though you've just surfaced from under the sea – a mermaid or a sea nymph; something not really of the earth.'

'Goodness!' said Amanda, surprised and not certain that she liked the idea. 'You don't mean actually wet?'

'Yes, I think so. The nearest bathroom's the first door on the right on the floor immediately below this, and there's a shower attachment to the taps. Will you wet your hair? Or would you rather I did it for you?'

'But . . . ?'

'There are plenty of driers in the house for when we've finished. Don't worry. Oh, and I've hung a towel over the bath for you.'

Taken aback, but intrigued enough to do as she was told without protest, Amanda opened the door of the bathroom and found herself surrounded by more luxury than she would have expected. The walls were covered in what seemed to be cotton damask dyed a peculiarly vibrant blue-red. There was another large looking-glass, this time framed in polished mahogany, covering most of one wall above the mahogany dado rail. The carpet was the colour of blue-black ink and there was a really distinguished mahogany tallboy on the wall opposite the mirror, with gold-framed, nineteenth-century landscapes on either side. The white bath sat regally within its mahogany panelling in the middle of the room, surrounded by small tables carrying soap and shaving materials and a magnifying mirror framed in polished brass. The pleated blind at the window and the comfortable-looking armchair beside it were covered in a red-and-blue paisley print.

Noticing the shaving gear, Amanda decided that the bathroom must be part of Comfort's brother's domain and felt like an interloper. She looked around the room for a bathmat and found it hanging over a heated brass rail. Carefully placing the mat beside the bath, she knelt and with her head hanging over the edge of the bath proceeded to wet her long hair thoroughly. Then she got up, leaving the dampened and crumpled bathmat where it was, wrapped the waiting towel around her head, and went back up the stairs to the studio.

Comfort was waiting there in her loose, creamy overall, draping and looping a long piece of glittering aquamarine silk this way and that about the sofa.

'Good,' she said, looking up. 'Did you bring a brush or comb?'

'Of course.' Amanda rummaged in her bag. Finding the comb, she pulled it gently through her long, wet hair, sprinkling drops of water all round her on the old carpet. After a moment, Comfort came to take the comb out of her hand. With one firm hand on Amanda's forehead, she combed all the hair carefully straight back over her head and behind her ears.

'That's better,' she said, tilting Amanda's chin towards the light, just as firmly as Andrew had done the previous evening.

'I hate my ears.'

'Nonsense!' Comfort turned Amanda's head to the side and inspected one of the offending members. She took out Amanda's plain gold stud earrings and put them on her drawing-table. 'They're perfectly all right. Now, I'd like you to take off your sweater and things so that I can pin this round your shoulders. It'll help give me the illusion of the sea.'

Reminding herself that she was perfectly at ease with her own body, and relieved that she had put on a clean bra that day, Amanda pulled off both her jersey and her shirt.

'I thought you said you preferred my hair fluffed up,' she said, sounding rather offended.

Comfort smiled as she arranged the silk round Amanda's shoulders, pushing her bra straps down out of sight as she did so. The touch of her long, bony fingers was extraordinary and, as she tried to cope with it, Amanda's eyes took on a faraway expression that pleased Comfort.

'If you've just surfaced it would be sleeked back by the pressure of the water. Think of an otter.'

Amanda's face broke into genuine amusement.

'Their hair is usually a bit shorter than mine.'

'I'd never have exected you to be so literal,' said Comfort, bringing a hint of stubbornness back into Amanda's eyes. 'Good, I like that expression. I've turned the sofa round. Go and kneel on it, looking over the back of it at me just like that,' she said. 'You can rest your arms on the back if you get tired.'

Amanda did as she was told, but the position was clearly not quite right for Comfort came back and pulled the silk a little lower.

'It's important that they know you've breasts,' she said briskly as she retreated to her easel. 'No. It still isn't quite right. Will you lie back against the arm of the sofa and drape your arm along the back?'

Amanda rearranged herself again.

'Pull the silk a little lower and hitch yourself up a bit higher. Good. Yes, I think that'll do. Lie like that for a bit.'

Comfort worked quickly, looking up every few seconds and staring quite coldly at Amanda, who soon began to feel seriously uncomfortable. It was partly the pose, which made her arm and shoulders ache after about ten minutes, and partly the masterful way in which the painter had given her orders. Photographers had been giving Amanda orders ever since she started modelling, but all they cared about was producing a telling photograph. This was different. She remembered uncomfortably that Comfort had said she meant to peel away her subject's disguises to reveal the person who hid inside them.

'You can rest now,' said Comfort after what felt like an hour, but was probably not nearly as long. 'Tea?'

'Thank you.' That afternoon Amanda did not offer to make the tea, but sat up on the sofa, feeling genuinely stiff and stretching each aching muscle.

As they drank their tea, Comfort began to talk about the few things she knew about mermaids. Amanda began to feel less tired as her imagination was caught and she smiled as she told Comfort the story of Hans Andersen's Little Mermaid, who, in search of a soul and human love, followed her prince on to dry land.

'And, as they'd warned her, every step she took on her new feet felt as though she were walking on naked sword blades,' she finished.

'Some love!' said Comfort. 'What happened in the end?'

'Do you know, I can't remember. I have a feeling he spurned her despite the bloody footprints, but I think the story ended happily.'

'Did it? As far as I can remember, most fairy tales actually have a rather horrible end.'

86

'You're surely thinking of the Brothers Grimm. Hans Andersen's stories were usually kinder.'

'Perhaps.' Comfort squinted at her model and then walked over to check the canvas, making a small correction. 'I wonder how many people nowadays could relate to such self-sacrifice. No one seems to think it necessary to make any sacrifices at all for love any more. All the old ideas of its being wild and dangerous have gone. Friends of mine talk as though it's more on a par with a laxative than a force for tremendous good – or the reverse. People have made it useful but unimportant now. I think that's rather a pity.'

'Perhaps,' said Amanda, rather enjoying the idea of love as an elemental force. 'But it was only the mermaid who had to make sacrifices; not the prince at all. I don't think I approve of that.'

'You're right, of course,' said Comfort. 'And it is absurd. Most women who are loved have far too much power to have to do that sort of thing, if only they could understand it.'

Considering Andrew's tricky devotion, Amanda was not sure that she agreed. Perhaps what he felt was not love at all. That was an encouraging thought. She finished her tea smiling.

'We've had fifteen minutes,' said Comfort before Amanda could say anything more. 'Back to work.'

She fetched a wet towel from the bathroom to sleek the girl's hair back once more, and returned to her easel. As she worked, they talked more and more easily about mythical women and the changing perceptions of femininity through history.

Amanda, who had been brought up to consider women as human beings whose sex ought to be irrelevant as they fought for a fair deal in an unfair world, found herself surprised and bewitched by Comfort's ideas of women who had not only power but also rights simply because they were female.

It was not until after six that she announced they had done

enough for the day. Amanda, who was feeling both enormously stimulated and very tired, slid down on to the seat of the sofa, stretching her legs over the end and closing her eyes. Before she had recovered enough to think of tidying herself up, she heard the door of the studio click. After a moment's silence, she opened her eyes to see a tall, fair man standing watching her with an extraordinary expression in his eyes.

Amanda recognised him at once from the drawings, but she decided she would have been able to identify him simply from his similarity to Comfort. He was much taller than she, of course, and broader, but he had her dark, slightly bluish grey eyes and her big nose, and his lips had just the same sharply cut elegance. He looked distinguished and yet somehow familiar. Amanda smiled at him, watching his eyes widen with recognition and, she thought, real interest.

'Anthony!' Comfort's voice made him turn away, but he held out a hand towards Amanda as though he did not want to lose contact. She was far too far away from him to do anything about it, but she liked the idea.

'Come on in,' Comfort went on, oblivious to the messages Amanda was reading into Anthony's gesture. 'We've just finished and were about to have a drink. This is . . .'

'The mermaid,' he said, walking towards Amanda at last. 'I know. When I found my bathroom damp, I knew she'd been in there. I hoped I'd be in time to catch sight of her before the waves closed over her head again.'

His smile was warmer than his sister's and his interest seemed much more personal. Amanda took his proffered hand at once and liked the feeling of it grasping hers. It was cool and quite dry. The contrast with his extravagant welcome was piquant and pleasing.

'Did I make a fearful mess in your bathroom?' she asked, trying to test his apparent interest in her.

'Not at all.' He smiled confidingly down at her as though they shared some secret. 'I was honoured.'

'It's his fault in any case,' said Comfort, beginning to clean her brushes. Amanda looked away from Anthony with some difficulty.

'He took one look at the sketches yesterday and said "mermaid".'

'Did you?' Amanda was delighted. 'Why?'

'Something about the grace of your movements, I suppose. Your hair looked sinuous, too, and made me think of mermaids' tails. And the enticing tilt to your lopsided smile suggested mystery.' For a moment his face hardened. Amanda remembered how all her life people had told her that her smile was exactly like her mother's and wondered if that was the only reason that he kept staring at her.

'Will you pour us a glass of wine, Anthony?' Comfort's voice brought distraction to her brother's eyes and he nodded.

'Unless I could inveigle you both to my drawing room?' he said. 'I have plenty of drink down there.'

'Let's stay up here,' said Comfort, disappointing Amanda, who was fascinated by the thought of seeing more of his part of the house. 'Then I can talk to you both while I deal with my brushes. But Anthony, let the child go behind the screen and put her clothes on again.'

Suddenly conscious of her bare neck and cleavage, Amanda smiled brilliantly at Anthony. Getting off the sofa with as much grace as she could manage, she retreated to the tapestry screen and removed the thick silk from her naked shoulders. There was no mirror, so she had no idea what she looked like when she emerged, but her hair still felt damp and she was sure that his vision of her as a mermaid would not be spoiled.

She glanced at the great baroque mirror as she passed it and was pleased to see that her eyes were gleaming and that her half-dried hair was forming wavy curls down her back.

Anthony greeted her with another half-reminiscent smile and held out a glass of wine. Amanda accepted it, glad that

89

she could drink with him without worrying that Andrew might appear and spoil everything.

The three of them finished the first bottle of wine, talking about things Amanda had seen and thought and the Gillinghams had done. Listening to them, Amanda felt as though they must have been everywhere and seen everything. Their casual references to foreign film-makers, painters, writers and scientists excited her and underlined the flattery of their curiosity about her. Searching her mind for a word to describe them and discarding suave, sophisticated and worldly, she eventually came up with debonair, which seemed to suit them both.

After Anthony had described a magnificent performance of *Andromaque* that he and Comfort had recently seen at the Comédie Française in Paris, he turned to his sister, who had been watching him with pleasure in her eyes, and said: 'I think we ought to feed this child, don't you? You've worn her out and she obviously needs nourishment. She looks a bit pale.'

Amanda had stiffened at his description of her as a child and was by then confident enough of his approval to give expression to her crossness.

'I am not a child.'

Anthony laughed and laid one long hand on her knee, letting his thumb stroke gently up and down.

'It's only my way of coping with envy of your youth and all the excitement of the life you've got ahead of you.'

'Comfort called me a child earlier.' Amanda spoke sulkily but she moved her knee nearer to him and had the satisfaction of feeling his hand press down for an instant before he withdrew it altogether.

'She's envious, too, aren't you?'

'I wonder,' said Comfort slowly as though she were genuinely considering the idea. 'I hated being a child – before the war – but perhaps I wouldn't mind being twenty now with all the freedoms you have, Amanda. You could do anything you want without risking your future or your reputation.'

'I wonder if that's true,' she said, finding herself staring at Anthony. Seeing him frown, Amanda quickly turned the conversation away from herself. 'Weren't you free?' she asked Comfort. 'Even in America?'

Comfort's face grew very still.

'Not really,' she said coolly. 'I suppose I had more actual liberty than my English equivalents and I was madly privileged in all material senses, but my mother wrenched me away from my father and Anthony when I was still an infant and so I was never free of the unhappiness of that. I didn't find Anthony again until our father's funeral. I don't think I've managed to forgive my mother yet.'

'Why not?'

Comfort shrugged. Her face was very hard.

'I think forgiveness is a sign of weakness – not of oneself necessarily, but of one's will. If you can't hold to your anger it must have been a pretty poor thing in the beginning, and . . . I suppose would make a mockery of all the misery that had caused it.'

Amanda pushed herself further back into the sofa, running her fingers through her slowly drying hair. She had the feeling that Comfort had told the exact truth and found something in herself responding to it.

'That seems almost wicked,' she said lightly, 'but it makes complete sense, unlike the way I've been brought up – to turn the other cheek.'

'David was always remarkably saintly,' said Anthony suddenly, and Amanda turned to him.

'He is a very rare person,' she said with unaccustomed fervour, really wanting him to understand her father and not to hate him for taking her mother. 'And—' She broke off, unable to imagine her mother with Anthony Gillingham.

'It's all right,' he said with quick, intuitive sympathy. Once more she had the feeling that somehow he knew her well.

'I'm not like Comfort: I can forgive people things.'

'I'm glad. You mustn't hate him. He . . . I couldn't do without him.'

Comfort lounged over to the side-table to fetch the decanter of wine so that she could refill their glasses.

'It's strange that you don't look at all like David,' she said with her back to the others. Amanda looked up and smiled.

'My eyes are quite like his, but it is true that I'm thought to look more like my mother, which is odd, because in character I'm much more like him.'

Anthony had raised his glass to his lips, but he did not drink.

'Are you?'

'Oh, I think so. I've none of my mother's hardness.'

'She never used to be hard,' he said, a slight smile lifting the corners of his lips and his eyes. 'The reverse really. Perhaps she's changed, or perhaps you've misunderstood her.'

His tolerance struck Amanda forcibly and she smiled at him more warmly than before, aware of the complicated contradictions in her feelings for her mother but quite unable to do anything about them.

'But all that is by the way,' he said, his eyes beginning to smile as he watched her. 'Comfort, we are going to take this ch . . . this mermaid out to dinner, aren't we?'

'Naturally. Why don't you book a table somewhere?'

'What about the White Tower?'

'Good idea. I'd better change,' said Comfort. Turning to Amanda, she added: 'Do you want to paint your lovely face? If so, do come and use my bathroom.'

Amanda went, amused that the only compliment Comfort had paid her that day should have been so casual but glad to have had it.

When Amanda eventually parted from them outside the restaurant, Comfort patted her shoulder and reminded her to come to the studio again the next day. Anthony first hailed a taxi for her and then, as the driver waited, took her face between his hands and kissed first one cheek and then the other.

She got into the cab in a daze of happiness, replete not only with wonderful Greek food but also with unstinted admiration. The drive back across the river seemed to take no time at all and she tipped the taxi-driver extravagantly, although Anthony had already paid him in advance.

Seeing a band of light under the kitchen door, Amanda went in, hoping to find her father. Only her mother was there, sitting reading a law journal with a cup of coffee in front of her. She looked up as Amanda came in, her face whiter than usual and more perturbed.

'Andrew rang twice,' she said abruptly. 'He wanted you to ring back, but it's a bit late to disturb poor Flixe now.'

'Thanks,' said Amanda casually, adding: 'The Gillinghams took me out to dinner.'

'How kind!'

'You don't sound as though you think so, but they were very kind to me – both of them. They took me to the White Tower and sent me home in a taxi. It was a lot more luxurious than Andrew's Chelsea Kitchen supper.'

'Oh. Good. Well, I'd better be off to bed now unless you'd like anything.'

'No, no, I don't think so. I'm not sleepy myself and so I may sit up a bit for Daddy. I didn't see him yesterday at all. There isn't a division tonight, is there?'

'Not as far as I know. He oughtn't to be too long.'

'Good-night.'

'Good-night, darling.' Julia washed up her coffee cup and went to the door. With her hand on the knob she turned. 'Are you all right?'

'Why shouldn't I be? I've had a marvellous time and the picture's going to be stunning. D'you want to hear about it?'

The sound of a key in the lock heralded the arrival of

David Wallington and the subject of Amanda's portrait was dropped.

David was glad to see his wife and daughter talking in apparent amity for once and he smiled at them both. He was a tall man, very broad in the shoulder, but reasonably slim still. His hair was greying in distinguished wings at his temples, but it was still thick and smooth. Only his face showed his full age.

To Amanda he looked as he had always looked, but Julia often noticed sadly that his eyes were surrounded by deep lines and seemed guarded where once they had been full of trusting enthusiasm. His mouth still smiled but there was a sardonic twist to it that had not been there when they had married.

Julia, noticing that Amanda wanted her to go to bed so that she could have her father to herself, kissed David casually.

'I'm off to bed. Don't be too late, you two.'

David's hand had automatically gone to Julia's shoulder to hold her close to him, and he stroked her silvering head with his other hand as she spoke.

'All right. I'll come with you.'

'Why not have a quick whisky while I bath?' said Julia, sliding her eyes in Amanda's direction.

'Good idea,' said David after a pause. 'Leave the bath in for me, and I'll follow you up.'

Julia turned to her daughter.

'Good-night, darling,' she said again.

''Night,' said Amanda over her shoulder as she reached for the bottles that were kept on a white tray beside the fridge. 'Johnnie Walker or malt?'

'Whatever's nearest,' he answered, exchanging a commiserating smile with Julia. When she had gone, he turned back to his daughter, who was holding out a heavy cut-glass tumbler. 'You're not very kind to her, are you?'

Amanda looked at him, her lips beginning to quiver. She felt very tired again as she shook her head.

'She doesn't want me to be,' she said at last. 'She's not interested in what I feel like, and she's never been exactly kind to me.'

'She tries to be, Amanda, but you won't let her.'

'Well, she doesn't try hard enough. She doesn't understand anything and she's always criticising me and stopping me doing what I want and . . .'

David's face broke into a smile.

'Come off it, Blackberry,' he said, using the nickname he had bestowed on her in childhood and had rarely used since she left school. 'No one has ever been able to stop you doing anything you want.'

Amanda just shook her head. It seemed to her that her entire life had been spent pushing against unfair restrictions and idiotic rules that had been designed to frustrate every genuine wish she had ever had.

'Look at the way she bludgeoned me about university.' Seeing her father's mouth twist and remembering how much she had found to dislike in Norwich, Amanda hastily added, 'And look at the things she says about my modelling jobs.'

'She's just concerned that you shouldn't waste your time on something that can't last when you might be building up a real career.'

'It's not that at all,' said Amanda coldly. 'She thinks it's degrading and vulgar to show oneself off in magazine photographs – and she's jealous of the way people admire me.'

'Don't say things like that. You know they're not true, but they hurt all the same – and they hurt you, too. All either of us want is for you to find a job that will last and satisfy you for as long as you need it. Standing in front of a camera isn't going to do either of those.'

Amanda shrugged and poured herself a large single malt whisky. She looked over her shoulder, as though challenging David to criticise, but he merely smiled.

'I've never expected it to do that. All I want from it is

enough money to show my sainted mother that I can earn infinitely more than any junior lawyer, doctor or whatever it is she wants me to be before I've even left university.' She drank some whisky and suppressed a shudder. 'And I have done. I've probably got enough to buy myself a house. Perhaps I should do that. At least it might impress her.'

'Do you want to do that?' David's voice was gentle. Amanda looked at him, slightly surprised, and then looked away.

'Yes,' she said and then looked as nearly frightened as he had ever seen her. 'Don't tell her.'

They both listened to the sound of Julia's bathwater running out of the taps in the bathroom above.

'Why not?' When his daughter said nothing, David tried again. 'Why can't you let her know how much you care what she thinks?'

'Because she hates me,' said Amanda, turning away.

David stood up at once and went to stand beside her, his hands on her shoulders. She let her head lean back a little to rest against him. He began to stroke her hair.

'She doesn't, you know. Quite the reverse. She cares dreadfully and it makes her unhappy when you're so aggressive.'

'You don't understand. She may tell you that, but it's only because she knows you mind about me and she wants your approval. But she loathes me.' She closed her eyes and returned to her chair. 'I've never understood why, but I suppose it doesn't matter.'

David followed her and knelt in front of her. Putting his hands on her shoulders again he said urgently: 'It matters a lot. This is too important to get wrong again, Amanda. Your mother doesn't hate you. She loves you just as much as I do. Talk to her honestly for once, darling girl, and be quiet enough to listen to her properly and you'll find out.'

Amanda, who had been gazing at him with love, sat up straighter, her face returning to sullen obstructiveness. She sighed.

'If I do exactly what she wants, you mean. I want her to love me for me,' she added passionately, 'not for being the perfect reflection of her or the answer to all her unsatisfied yearnings or whatever it is she wants. I'm me.'

David let his head droop until his forehead rested on Amanda's knees. He felt tired and, as always, ripped to shreds by the way Julia and Amanda fought each other. He stood up.

'Try, darling, if you can,' he said rather helplessly and went up to his wife.

Julia was drying herself as he came into the room. Wrapping herself in the big white towel, she sat on the edge of the bath and took the pins out of her hair as he undressed and got into the bath. Sitting beside him, with her steam-dampened hair falling down her back, she listened as he talked about his day in Parliament. Neither of them felt strong enough to discuss their daughter then.

After a while Julia heard his voice slowing and smiled to see his eyelids drooping over his eyes. Dabbling her left hand in the bathwater, she realised it was quite cold and leaned forwards to take out the plug. David woke with a start and she held out her hands, smiling widely.

'Come to bed, David. You're all in.'

'Thank God for you, Jules,' he said, levering his long body out of the water and wrapping it in the warm towel she had fetched for him. 'Do I ever tell you how much it means to share this Vale of Tears with you?'

Amanda, passing the door on her way to bed, heard what he said and frowned. Not wanting to hear her mother's answer she went on up the stairs.

Julia rubbed his back dry.

'Is it so sad?' she asked, stroking the back of his dark head. He twisted his head so that he could look at her and leaned back to kiss her stroking hand.

'Good heavens, no! But there are aspects that make one understand whoever it was who christened it that. For myself

– with you – it's hardly ever a matter for tears.'

'Good.'

'And what about you, my only love?'

The question had been frivolously put, but Julia knew that her husband really minded what her answer might be. After a moment's thought, she said slowly and quite seriously: 'When I've had a fight with Amanda or lost an important case it's pretty dreadful, but the rest of the time I'd say I was a happy woman.'

'I'm glad of that,' said David and took her to bed.

CHAPTER 7

'I've been reading more about mermaids,' said Comfort as Amanda settled into her pose on the studio sofa for her second sitting.

'Oh?'

'Yes, and I've discovered some excellent antidotes to Hans Andersen's self-sacrificing version.'

'That sounds promising.' Amanda wriggled her shoulders to set them more comfortably against the sofa arm. 'What are they?'

'Most mermaids seem to have spent their time teasing and tantalising sailors into following them, sidling above the waves with only their female selves showing, and then as soon as they had seduced the men away from safety they would reveal their fishy tails and leave the poor lustful fools to drown in frustration.'

'You sound almost as though you approve,' said Amanda, her eyes gleaming as she tried to see past Comfort's calm face to what she was actually thinking. 'It sounds unnecessarily cruel.'

'Open your eyes properly. Good. I think I do approve – don't you? And is self-protection really cruelty? It's hard to keep power over a man once you've let him seduce you.

Mermaids seem to me to have the best of all possible worlds: enjoyment of their own incredible sexiness as they give themselves to the waves, endless courtship – which you'll discover is always the best bit of any affair – and total power.'

'But no soul,' said Amanda, laughing as she remembered odd pieces of mermaid lore from her childhood. 'Don't forget that it was as much for lack of a soul as for love that Hans Andersen's followed her mortal.'

'Pshaw! Who wants a soul?'

'Well, if not a soul, then what about immortality, Comfort?' Amanda enjoyed the momentary flash in the painter's slate-grey eyes. 'Don't all artists want that?'

'Perhaps,' said Comfort, obviously surprised by Amanda's teasing. 'Oh, blast!' she added as the telephone started to ring. 'I'd better answer that. It must be important. Almost no one has my number here. Rest for a while.'

She picked up the receiver, said her name and then waited in silence, her face growing increasingly worried. At last she said: 'Yes, of course I'll come. Hold on and try not to worry too much.' She put down the receiver and turned back to Amanda. 'I'm going to have to leave you.'

'I hope it's not too serious,' said Amanda, feeling almost as deprived as the drowning sailors. The intensity of her disappointment seemed disproportionate until she realised that it was not the entertaining afternoon with Comfort that she minded missing but the possibility of another dinner with Anthony. Trying to look untroubled, she pulled off the aquamarine silk and reached for her collapsed bra straps. 'I'll get out of your way.'

'I hope so too,' said Comfort, sounding rather vague. 'A friend of mine has had the most frightful shock and I must go to her.' She blinked twice and frowned. 'Look here, I think Anthony's in this afternoon. I'll take you down to him and he can look after you for me.'

Amanda suppressed a sigh of relief and tried to hide her pleasure in a formal protest.

'Please don't worry him. He's sure to be busy and I'm quite capable of looking after myself.'

'Don't be silly. I know you are, but it's a bit much to drag you all the way here, undress you, drench your hair, and then drop you flat. Come on and get dressed.'

Amanda obeyed, smiling to herself, and together they walked down two flights of stairs. Comfort opened one of the panelled doors on the square landing.

'Anthony, I've got to flash off and see to Clemency. There's an emergency. But I've got poor Amanda here; could you give her tea or something and see she gets home all right?'

Amanda could hear the sound of a chair being pushed back and Anthony's slightly husky voice saying: 'It'll be a pleasure. I hope poor Clem will be all right. Will you give her my love?'

Comfort assured him she would, brushed Amanda's damp cheek with one hand, leaving her tingling with surprise, and ran on downstairs. Anthony came to the door.

'Hello,' he said seriously.

'Hello.' Amanda smiled and watched his face relax. His eyes looked much darker grey than she remembered and his whole face even more distinguished.

'Will you come in?' he asked, standing back.

'If you really want me.'

There was a short silence that seemed heavy with meaning. Amanda looked back at Anthony, startled and half intending to qualify what she had said. He put a hand on her shoulder.

'I really want you,' he said deliberately.

She laughed, a high, silly laugh that made her feel a fool, but he slid his hand down her arm to her elbow and urged her into his room.

'I was just thinking how nice it would be to have some tea, but it seemed an unconscionable indulgence to do it on my own. You're heaven-sent.'

At that Amanda laughed properly, feeling better, and walked into the room. She had imagined that it would be full of microscopes and anatomical drawings or even a wax model of a flayed corpse like one she had seen in a hospital museum. Instead she discovered a gracious, if masculine, drawing room decorated with dark green marbled paper and heavy gold-brocade curtains. There were old glazed bookcases filled with books, comfortable chairs, bowls of flowers and sunny paintings of water-filled landscapes. A real fire burned in the brass grate.

'Come and sit by the fire,' Anthony suggested, 'and dry those mermaid locks of yours. I never meant Comfort actually to plunge your head in cold water for her painting.'

'Oh, I don't mind it at all, but I never meant to disturb your work. Comfort seemed to think I needed looking after, but truly I don't.'

'It's not my work you're disturbing.' His voice had grown serious again. She did not look at him, although she could feel him standing very close to her. After a moment he pulled a chair nearer the fire. 'Sit down.'

Amanda obediently sat and felt the soft down cushions billowing up around her. For a moment she thought that she also felt his hand on her head, but a second later could not be certain. She bent nearer the fire and sat combing her fingers through her wet hair.

'You really are like a mermaid, aren't you?'

She turned suddenly and looked at him, thinking of all the things she and Comfort had told each other.

'Not altogether.'

Anthony looked surprised. Rejecting various possible explanations of her cryptic answer, Amanda added lightly: 'They're fish from the waist down and very clammy.'

'And you're not?' Anthony's voice was not light at all.

'No,' she said, slipping her feet out of her shoes and wiggling her toes at him.

Instead of laughing as she had expected, he seemed to breathe more deeply and quickly turned away from her.

'I'm not really working today,' he said almost as though he

were talking at random; 'just writing notes for a paper I'm to give on neurotransmitters in the brain late in July. There's plenty of time yet. I hope you won't be too uncomfortable. Do you want a hairdryer? I think there is one somewhere.'

'It'll soon dry by the fire if I go on combing it.'

'All right. I'd better go and make you some tea. I won't be long.'

Despite his final comment, he seemed to be gone for ages and Amanda sat, her drying hair fluffing about her face, wondering whether she had imagined all the unspoken things he seemed to be telling her. For a while she even wondered whether she had annoyed him so much that he had seized the opportunity to have some peace without her.

Feeling restless and not quite herself, wanting him back and yet not wanting to discover that all the attraction she thought she had seen in him had been imaginary, she got up to walk about his room and examine his books. There were very few medical ones and those there were seemed not just out of date but positively antique. Instead of the expected textbooks there were a great many novels, biographies and, most surprising of all, a shelf of seventeeth-century poets.

She was standing beside the shelves, turning the pages of a volume of Donne's work, when Anthony returned with a large, heavy-looking tray, which he carried to the sofa table.

'I see you've found my secret vice,' he said cheerfully as he put it down. Whether she had imagined some kind of disturbance in him or not, it had gone by then and he was completely in control of himself.

'Vice?' Amanda made herself sound intrigued.

'I started collecting them some time ago and they've run away with a frightening amount of money since. They're first editions.'

'Oh, lord! I've probably dripped over them. I am sorry,' she said, not even noticing that she had made an apology.

'Don't worry. Come and choose what you'll have for tea.'

She carefully replaced the soft leather-bound volume in the shelf and came to his side.

'I thought you might prefer savoury things to cakes,' he said, rearranging the plates on the tray. 'But I don't often entertain people of your age.'

After the way he had been behaving it infuriated Amanda to hear him treating her as a child again. She decided to punish him for it.

'I'm not like anyone else of my age,' she said sharply. 'And I rarely eat tea.'

'No,' he answered, 'I don't suppose you are. But I'm hungry, even if you're not. Come and choose.'

Beside the silver teapot and Meissen milk jug, there were plates of small fingers of toast spread with what looked like Gent's Relish, three-cornered sandwiches filled with smoked salmon, and even a dish of astonishingly early strawberries.

'It looks nice,' she said tepidly, putting two of the small sandwiches on the plate he held out for her. 'Thank you.'

As she took the plate from him she thought of a much better punishment than sulkiness and let her fingers graze his, watching him register the sensation. She smiled a slow, confident smile, forcing him to look properly at her.

'D'you like music?' His voice was abrupt.

The honest answer would have been 'not very much', but Amanda was not very honest and she knew that he had asked the question simply to distract them both from his unmistakable response to her touch.

'Oh yes,' she said eagerly. The eagerness at least was genuine. She wanted him to be pleased with her just as much as she wanted to punish him for his careless patronage.

'What would you like? I've a fairly catholic selection of records.'

'Well, classical anyway,' she said, assuming that that was what he would prefer, 'but beyond that I'd rather leave it to you.'

He flashed her a smile, which made her wonder whether

he knew how little she knew of, or cared for, music and after some thought selected a record and put it carefully on to an elaborate-looking machine. Amanda listened to the automatic clicks and was taken aback to hear the cool purity of a male choir singing what even she recognised as plainsong. Amused, she decided that he must have deliberately chosen the most chaste sound he could.

'It's so simple,' said Anthony, watching her, 'and remarkably peaceful. Like birds but better. Go and sit down again.'

'Rather big birds.'

He smiled at her comment and poured himself a cup of tea, which he brought with him to a chair opposite hers.

'Your hair is drying well.'

'It's probably a bit fluffy. It always is when it's rough dried like this.'

'But it looks soft,' he said and leaned back with his eyes closed, apparently concentrating on the music.

'Yes. Very soft. Feel it.' Amanda put her right hand behind her head, collecting all her hair into one enormous handful and leaned forward to offer it to him.

Anthony opened his eyes and stared at her.

'Feel it,' she said again, keeping her eyes on his. Reluctantly, he moved towards her and put one hand on the dark hair for a moment.

'Yes, it is quite soft,' he said in the voice he must have used to his assistants in the operating theatre. Amanda felt satisfied and sank back in the sumptuous chair, tossing the hair behind her head again and running the fingers of both hands through it. Anthony deliberately shut his eyes.

Smiling at her success in making him touch her when she and not he wanted it, Amanda admitted to herself that he looked magnificent with his shuttered face lying relaxed against a big gold damask cushion. It was many shades darker than his hair, which gleamed in the light of the lamps that stood on tables around the room. She wondered how far she could push him without saying or doing anything overt; and she also wondered how far she wanted to push him and whether her only motive was punishment.

The disciplined rippling sounds of the plainsong abruptly ceased and Anthony opened his eyes without moving his head. He saw that she was looking at him and did not smile.

'That was glorious,' said Amanda when he did not speak either. He passed an impeccably clean hand across his dark grey eyes, and it seemed to her that he shivered.

'Are you all right?' She had made her voice gentle, almost caressing.

'No, I don't think I am,' he said, taking his hand away and looking at her again. 'Are you?'

Pleased with her progress, Amanda slowly shook her head. Anthony got up to turn the record. Amanda put down her cup and plate. With the plainsong filling the sombrely magnificent room again, he returned to his dark-green velvet chair, passing very close to hers but not touching her.

'You look as though you were afraid of me,' she said, pushing at the limits of subtlety. 'I'm no mermaid and I don't think there's any need for fear.'

'No? I feel as though . . . Perhaps you're right.'

Amanda quickly got out of her chair and knelt gracefully by the side of his, looking up at him with eyes full of an expression he could not read.

'Or perhaps I was right all along,' he said, putting his hands on her head and stroking his fingers over the soft dark hair. Suddenly he tilted her face towards him.

Amanda lifted her eyelids again and saw that he was looking at her almost angrily. She shivered a little, slowly licked her lips and then bent her head again in wholly artificial submission. He took his hands away as though her hair had become prickly.

'Why are you doing it?' he asked, his voice abrupt, accusing.

'Why not?' she answered softly and tasted the power that

Comfort had described. Once more she looked at him and her face seemed radiant. He had no idea that what was exciting her most was the knowledge that she had forced him to admit that she was no child, that he did desire her, that she could affect him deeply by simply being herself.

'Oh, God!' Anthony said and kissed her.

Amanda felt fantastically triumphant. She reached up towards him and held his head. His hands gripped her back for an instant before he moved away, pulling against the strength of her hands. When she let him go, he stared down at her. She could see his lips trembling slightly and brushed one finger across them.

'Anthony.'

'I want you so much,' he said through gritted teeth.

'I know you do.'

He got to his feet and pulled her up, wrapping his arms around her when she was standing in front of him.

'Kiss me again,' he commanded. She licked her lips once more as he watched her, gripping his hands round her back again. Then she kissed his chin before letting her lips travel tantalisingly up towards his. Feeling what she was doing to him made her understand something of both his anger and his fear. Knowing that it was within her power to soothe both or let him drown made her feel wonderful.

'You want me, too, don't you? Oh, hell! Amanda, I can't.'

'Yes. You can. We both can,' she said, suddenly aware that it was not only he who was stirred up by what she had been doing. 'What we want, the two of us, is more important than anything else in the world if we have the guts to take it.'

'Come then,' he said, accepting her challenge and issuing his own. He took her hand to lead her through a narrow door in the bookcases. In his bedroom a massive four-poster hung with dark green velvet took up most of the space.

Still undecided, although becoming almost certain of her willingness to drown with him, Amanda let him pull her down on to the dark green counterpane. The bed was firm under her and as he leaned over her his eyes were wild. For a second she felt afraid.

She must have shown some signs of shrinking, for he propped himself up on one elbow, giving her room to move, and made himself smile at her. As she smiled back, he unbuttoned the top of her Biba blouse and let his fingers rest in the hollow of her neck. The softness of his touch banished her fear. He seemed to be in control of himself again.

'I couldn't believe it when I came into the studio and saw you there,' he said, his voice still gratifyingly shaky. 'When you turned and smiled at me as though you'd known me all your life, I felt amazingly welcomed.'

'And I,' she said, wondering if she still had a chance to change her mind. 'You seemed to be terribly familiar and yet exotically strange – and then I discovered that you seemed to know me and understand exactly what I was thinking.'

Amanda felt his fingers stroking her neck and pushing gently down towards her breasts.

'I hoped I did.' A wonderful smile lit his thin face. 'If Comfort hadn't been there, I might not have been able to stop myself asking if I was right.' He leaned forwards to kiss her hair. 'Ah, you smell of woodsmoke now and not damp seaweed. Perhaps I am safe after all.'

As she laughed up at him, he unbuttoned the rest of her blouse and spread it apart with both hands.

'You are terrifyingly beautiful,' he said, leaning forwards to let his lips rest for a moment on her collarbone. As they brushed her skin, she sighed, feeling the familiar, pleasantly tingling sensation and hoping that for once it might last. She thought that she would postpone any change of mind until she had tested it.

The sensations became more complicated as she felt his fingers pushing further down. She thought suddenly that she wanted him almost as much as he seemed to want her and she said his name again, more urgently. He looked at her, leaving his hand on her breast.

'Good,' he said as though he had understood and then he bent his head again.

Neither of them said anything more for a long time as Amanda concentrated on the increasingly unfamiliar sensations he was bestowing on her. At last, full of a yawning need she had never known before, she pulled him to her forcefully and laughed triumphantly.

'You're perfect. Oh, lord, how perfect!' he said, his face alight with a happiness she revelled in. All idea of punishing him had gone and she knew that his happiness and her delight were well worth the sacrifice of all the power she could have had over him by denying them. Then, for a time, she could not think at all, only feel.

Later, when she had recovered from her astonishment and delight, she said: 'You were right when you warned me that the waves would close over my head.'

'What?' he asked, not heavily asleep across her as Andrew had been, but concentrating on her and holding her gently, stroking her hair over and over again.

'You said it the first time I saw you. Was it only yesterday? I feel as though I've known you for ever.' She smiled shyly and added: 'I think you're perfect, too.'

His face changed and some of the happiness and fulfilment seemed to drain away.

'Alas, I'm far from that. Oh, God! Amanda, I should never have done it.'

'You didn't,' she said with a consciously wicked smile, wanting to make him laugh. 'I know you'd already thought of it, but it was I who actually did it. And besides, why not? What harm did it do anyone? It was lovely for me – and you seemed to like it. It doesn't need to mean anything more than that, does it?'

As she spoke she knew that she was lying again. What had happened was of immense importance. But she did not want to frighten him in his newly fragile state.

'I hope not,' he said and started to rearrange her clothes.

'What's the matter?' she asked, holding his hands still against her. He seemed to look quite bleak. 'Why aren't you happy?' she demanded, forgetting everything about punishment. 'I meant you to be happy.'

He moved away and got up from the bed, turning away from her. After a moment's terrible anxiety she heard him say: 'You're right, my dear child, it was lovely and it made me very happy.' He turned back to face her. 'But it was inappropriate. I can't think how I came to let us go so far. I am really sorry.'

'You sound as though you think you took advantage of me.'

'I did,' he said grimly. 'I ought to have known better. God knows I ought.' He came back to stand at the edge of the bed. 'Amanda, I did take advantage of you and there is nothing I can do to mend that except say that I will keep right out of your way from now on. You mustn't be afraid of coming to sit for Comfort: I'll make sure I'm out whenever you're expected. Get dressed, my dear, and I'll send for a taxi.'

'But I don't want you to keep out of my way.' Amanda knew that she was sounding as childish as he seemed to expect her to be, but in her hurt and disappointment she did not know how else to speak. 'I want to be with you again tomorrow. I want to make you happy – and for far longer than a single afternoon.'

Once more his bitter laugh sounded through the room, and Amanda winced, stung suddenly back into reality. It seemed terribly unfair that her moment of power should have been so short after all, and her sacrifice of it spurned.

'Perhaps Comfort was right,' she murmured.

'What?'

'Nothing. But, Anthony, after what we've just shared haven't I the right to try to make you happy?' she asked. 'Haven't I?'

He shook his fair head. She saw that his mouth looked very thin and his eyes hard again. The eager, exciting wanting he had shown so clearly had gone completely. She felt completely rejected and pushed herself back into the pillows as though to hide from what seemed appallingly obvious.

'No, because it is beyond even your generosity to attempt and I don't want to damage you any more than I already have. Ah, don't,' he added as he saw tears gathering in her dark eyes. He moved a little way back towards her again and then stopped.

'I'm not sure that I can help it,' answered Amanda, surprised at how much she was hurting. 'You've made me feel happier than I ever was before and then you take it all away. I just don't think I can help it.'

'I deserve any punishment for what I've done, but this is very hard,' he said, watching her face grow almost plain under the tears. 'Listen to me. It may feel like cruelty to send you away from here now, but it's not. It would be far crueller to let you stay and dig yourself – or let me dig you – deeper into this mess. Amanda, you said you enjoyed what we've just done. Hold on to that. Remember it as a pleasant physical experience, no more. It was no more.'

She lifted her chin and tried to collect some pride so that she did not throw herself on him.

'I'll try if you say I must; but it will be hard.'

There was a deep crease between his eyebrows.

'Thank you. And if you cherish any residual kindness for me,' he said, 'don't tell anyone about this afternoon. It's not that I want to escape from anything, but because that way the damage I've done won't be ... won't be exaggerated by other people's comments.'

'I don't understand why you've changed like this,' said Amanda helplessly. 'Was it no more than "an expense of spirit in a waste of shame"?' She was pleased to see him wince.

'No,' he said after a long time. 'I ought to tell you it was to make you angry so that you'd go more easily. But it wasn't. It was transfiguring.'

111

Amanda's distress was overtaken by relief and she smiled again.

'But it mustn't be repeated. Oh, my darling child, if you knew how much I . . . No. Let's leave it at that. We must. Let's part with grace at least.'

'If we really have to,' she said.

'We must. Try to trust me.' He smiled a little whimsically. 'Although you've no reason to trust me any longer.'

He went back into his sitting room, leaving her to tidy herself. As she followed him, she realised that he was telephoning for a taxi to take her home. When the cab arrived, she made Anthony kiss her. She held him fiercely for a moment and then left him without another word.

She sat in the back of the taxi, seeing nothing through her blurred eyes, wondering how it was possible to discover real love and lose it all in the space of a single afternoon. Nothing that anyone had made her feel before had been a fraction of the emotions Anthony Gillingham had stirred up in her. He needed her, she knew that, and he cared for her too.

Setting her lips in a determined line, she tried to give herself a reason for being so certain of his real feelings. At last, it struck her that if he had not loved her he would not have worried about having sex with her. He would have behaved like the tutor and not cared if he hurt her horribly by a single casual comment when he had done with her.

Anthony had said nothing unkind, even though he had sent her away. He had clearly enjoyed their lovemaking and so if she had meant nothing to him, he would just have repeated the occasion or not as his fancy took him. He must have loved her too.

Perhaps she and Comfort had been wrong, Amanda thought. Perhaps the mermaid had had a good reason to choose to lose her tail and live on earth with her human lover even though the price of fulfilment was those sword blades that dug into her bare feet. Anthony's love would be worth a similar price. Saving him, and the pain it brought her, might be the big thing for which she had waited in such impatience.

Beginning to relax a little and finding the blinding tears drying, Amanda began to think of ways to get round his scruples. Obviously he was worried because he was so much older than she, and because of his connection with her mother, but both those were irrelevant to the reality of what they had discovered. She would not, she decided, force him to see her soon, but she might write to him in a week or two and find some way to reach him again. They had plenty of time. She might even go to his lecture on neurotransmitters and ask some breathtakingly intelligent question from the audience.

A pleasing picture of the occasion coloured itself in her mind and her lips relaxed into a smile just as the taxi drew up outside her parents' big Georgian house in Kennington. Feeling nearly happy again and remarkably healthy, she tried to pay the driver, but discovered that once again Anthony had already done that.

As she let herself into the house, she remembered that it would be blessedly empty. The following week her brother Jonathan would be back from Winchester and the house would be full of noise and mess again, but for a little while it was hers alone. Even the housekeeper was out that afternoon.

Amanda dropped her bag on the hall table and walked slowly upstairs to run herself a bath. There was an envelope addressed to her in her father's writing propped against the door handle of her bedroom. Surprised, she opened it to find a short message:

Andrew Suvarov rang twice this morning before I left for the House. He seems very worried, Amanda, and a bit distressed. Could you ring him as soon as you get in? Even if he's boring you, it's not kind to ignore him. If you don't want to see him, tell him; don't make the poor porpoise flounder about in miserable ignorance.

Smiling at the way David could make even a reprimand amusing, Amanda collected her bathtowel and book and dumped them in the bathroom on her way down to the nearest telephone.

'Auntie Flixe? I'm sorry to have disturbed you,' she said. 'Is Andrew there?'

'He's in his room, Amanda. He'll be glad you rang. Will you hold on while I get him?'

'Yes, thank you.'

Amanda waited, feeling kind to be ringing him and pleasantly superior now that she had discovered how little he knew about her and about making love. With him at least she had lost none of her power. The whole dilemma was clearly more complicated than Comfort had understood.

'Amanda? Darling, whatever happened to you? Are you all right?'

'I'm fine now,' she said, not averse to worrying him just a little more.

'What was it? Did you feel ill? Were you unhappy?'

'Nothing like that. But I did feel a bit . . . shocked isn't right, but I needed time to myself. Can you understand that?'

'Just,' he said with a laugh that reminded her of his father. 'But it was dreadful for me not knowing what was the matter.'

'Poor you. But it's better now.'

'Shall I come and fetch you tonight? What time?'

'Oh, Andrew, I can't come out tonight. I've been sitting in that studio for hours both yesterday and today and my back's gone and my legs ache and I feel completely shagged out.'

'I don't think you quite mean that,' he said, laughing again.

Trying to maintain her dignity, Amanda went on: 'I need an early night. Let's meet tomorrow. What about that French

114

film at the Academy? Shall we see that?'

'If you like. I've got a paper here, hold on. There's a performance at seven-twenty-five. Shall we meet there at quarter past?'

'Okay. I'll see you then.'

'Great. I'll get the tickets.'

Singing tunelessly, Amanda went to have her bath. Afterwards, wrapped in her softest dressing-gown, she lay on the drawing room floor, listening to a selection of sacred music on her parents' old-fashioned gramophone and thinking about what it felt like to have discovered love.

In the security of that knowledge she let herself remember the exact words the tutor had used after he had pulled away from her on his narrow bed at the university.

'It's lovely deflowering virgins: they're always so touchingly grateful.'

'No, they're not,' said Amanda aloud, 'they're puzzled, uncomfortable, shy and completely unaware of what it is they have just been defrauded of. And you were a monster of selfishness and self-delusion.'

Julia arrived home after an exasperating day in court when her client changed the story he had previously told her in chambers and, standing in the witness box, produced a different version that turned her carefully prepared defence of him into nonsense. She stood in the doorway of the drawing room, watching her daughter lying unaware on the floor and thinking instantly, Drugs.

As she pulled off her plain black hat, Julia thought to herself, She does look lovely like that. Could it possibly be true, as everyone says, that she's like I was at that age?

'Hello!' she said aloud.

Amanda opened her eyes and smiled up at her mother, lazily getting off the floor.

'Sorry about this,' she said, gesturing to the dressing-gown and making Julia look at her intently. 'I was so exhausted after today's sitting that I had to bath and then I thought I'd

listen to some music as a way of relaxing. Are you all right?
You look awfully tired.'

'I am a bit.' Julia tried not to let her astonishment show.

'Then you sit here. I'll go and put some clothes on and
make us some tea. How about that?'

'That would be absolutely perfect.' Julia smiled, unable to
think of any drug that would have such a beneficial effect on
her daughter and delighted to see the change in her.

116

CHAPTER 8

George Mayford sent Flixe a dozen Speciosum lilies the next day with a note in what was obviously his own writing and not that of the florist, which said:

I can only apologise for spoiling the jolly time we had.
It seemed an important thing to say before we became
friends. I hope it won't prevent that.

Standing by the front door with the crimson-and-white lilies in her hands, Flixe breathed in their rich scent and closed her eyes. She had always loved flowers and in the old days her house had been full of vases and plants in pots throughout the year. Since the funeral there had been only the occasional jam-jar of primroses or daisies picked by her younger daughter, Sophie, during the school holidays. Even the flowering trees that had once filled her conservatory were gone, killed off by the cold.

She was so flooded with simple gratitude for the flowers and for the apology that she wanted to talk to George at once. She carried the lilies into the kitchen and searched for a suitable pot. Eventually she chose a narrow trumpet-shaped white vase and let the lilies fall casually against its sides without making any attempt to arrange them. Their splendour seemed to need nothing else.

Having filled the vase with water, she carried it up to her study and put it on the deep windowsill beside her desk. Leaning down to pick up the heavy L to R telephone directory from the bottom drawer of her desk, she found the number of his consulting rooms and dialled it. A well-spoken receptionist answered and Flixe asked to speak to Doctor Mayford.

'He's with a patient. May I ask who's calling?'

'Mrs Suvarov. Perhaps I should try later. What would be a good time?'

'I'm not absolutely sure, but if you will give me your number I'm certain he'll ring you when he's free.'

Flixe recited her telephone number and replaced the receiver. She sat at her desk working on the plans for the dances and cocktail parties she was organising, until George rang her back.

'Felicity? You wanted me,' he said, making her feel particularly welcomed, which was strange because only acquaintances used her full name: all her real friends and family called her Flixe.

'Yes,' she said. 'Just to thank you for those glorious lilies – and for your nice note.'

'Oh good, they arrived.' He sounded so brisk that she could not forget he was in the middle of seeing patients and must have had little time for chatting. It jolted her into putting into words something that she was only half-aware of having planned.

'I also wanted to say that since my younger children will be home at the end of next week I'll have to concentrate on them then,' she went on, surprised at her own gaucheness. Taking a grip on her absurd shyness and remembering what Natalie had said, Flixe added directly, as befitted a woman of her age and experience: 'And I don't want to wait until after the school holidays to see you again.'

George laughed at her brisk voice but, before he could suggest a meeting, Flixe said: 'So can I persuade you to come and have a meal here before they get back? You and Georgina.'

'That's extraordinarily kind of you. We'd love it. Have you a particular day in mind?'

'I was wondering about dinner next Monday,' said Flixe, thinking that the evening would provide an excellent opportunity to introduce Andrew to Georgina Mayford without making her hopes for them both too obvious.

'I'm just checking in my diary. Yes, that looks fine for me. I'm not sure about Gina. I'll ask her to telephone you.'

'Thank you, George. About eight o'clock. Not at all smart: just family.'

'I'm very flattered.'

'Good,' said Flixe with a private smile. 'I look forward to it. Good-bye.'

As she put down her receiver she considered who else to invite. It occurred to her that the best way of displaying Georgina's gently intelligent charm might lie in its contrast with Amanda's customary shameless showing-off. As soon as Georgina had rung back to accept the invitation Flixe telephoned the house in Kennington.

'Hello,' she said as her call was answered, 'that sounds like Janice. It's Mrs Suvarov here. How are you? Is Amanda in? Thank you.'

While Julia Wallington's treasured housekeeper went upstairs to fetch Amanda, Flixe decided to invite one of her sisters to assist at what might prove to be a difficult party.

'Hello? Auntie Flixe. What can I do for you?'

There was nothing in Amanda's cheerful voice to suggest that there had been a change in her relations with the Suvarovs, and Flixe was not certain whether to be relieved or sorry.

'I just wondered whether I could persuade you and Jonathan – if he'll be back by then – to come to dinner here on Monday evening. I'm having some new friends, one of whom is a girl of about your age.'

'That's kind of you,' said Amanda, sounding slightly surprised. 'Jon will be back on Friday afternoon and I doubt he has anything fixed. Um. Oh, why not? I've nothing . . . Yes, thank you, I'd like to come.'

'Good,' said Flixe, ignoring her god-daughter's rather graceless acceptance. 'Informal. Eight o'clock. If Jonathan has any other plans, would one of you let me know?'

'Yes, of course. Good-bye.'

Without thinking any more, Flixe then dialled the number of her elder sister's office in London University and asked to speak to her. Gerry also sounded surprised to hear of the invitation, but added: 'It's good to know that you're getting back to normal. Mike and I would love to come. See you then, old thing. Can I bring anything?'

'Some wine would be helpful, if you really mean it.'

'Of course I mean it. Okay, Mike and I will do the wine. What are you going to cook?'

'I haven't decided yet, but it won't be at all elaborate. I expect red would be better than white, because I can't imagine doing fish. There aren't any proper fishmongers round her any more. Yes, red, please, Gerry.'

'Fine. See you at eight on Monday.'

As she was replacing her receiver, Flixe realised with a spurt of amusement that she had chosen her elder sister because she was more likely to argue with George Mayford and force him to respect her than to enchant him. Ming, on the other hand, was so pretty and funny and sweet that most men she met seemed to fall in love with her. Flixe was enjoying George's admiration and flowers too much to be prepared to lose them to her younger sister. The absurdity of reverting to teenage sibling rivalry made her feel young again and she turned to planning her menu with a much lighter heart.

Andrew put his head round the door of her study.

'Hello, Mama,' he said. 'I'm on my way out. Is there anything you need?'

'No, thank you, darling. Come on in for a minute,' she said and then told him about her plans for the dinner party.

He stood looking at her for a moment and then flung his arms round her in an exuberant hug.

'You're wonderful,' he said as he released her. 'You really will see what I meant yesterday morning when you know her better.'

'Good,' said Flixe, suppressing the guilt she felt at her plans to wean him away from Amanda. 'I wish that I could have given you a proper twenty-first party, but . . .'

'Don't be a clot, Mama. We've been through all that long ago and I don't need a party. You've given me my father's cufflinks and that's far more important. This dinner will be a fine substitute.'

Flixe spent much of her free time during the intervening days trying to think what to cook for her party. With the weekend to shop and prepare at least some of the food, she ought to have had plenty of time, but she found it impossible to decide on anything, which was ironic in view of her party-planning work for other people. All her familiar recipes were either far too expensive or smacked too much of healthy nursery food. She read through her huge collection of cookery books in seach of something possible, but she had still been unable to choose by the time the shops shut on Saturday.

By Monday she had decided to make a simple but filling salad of potatoes, hard-boiled eggs and anchovies to be followed by *coq au vin* with rice. For pudding she planned to make a treacle tart, because everyone she had ever met had secretly liked it and it was cheap.

Shopping for the various ingredients late in the afternoon after a tiring day of constituency work, she tried hard to suppress all memories of the dinners she and Peter had given. He had been almost as interested in food as she and they used to discuss possible dishes exhaustively and never considered the expense of anything. All the lobsters they and their guests had eaten, all the truffles and the fillet steak, the asparagus, the out-of-season raspberries and the French cheeses had cost money that could have been saved to protect the children.

'Why?' she said aloud, as she stood in the middle of the supermarket with the heavy bag of potatoes in her hand. Her growing pleasure in her modest plans receded into the approaching misery.

All the efforts she had put into making Peter happy seemed to be mocked by his leaving her not just penniless, but ignorantly penniless. Some of the efforts had been considerable. Whenever he had hurt her, she had worked to rationalise away the pain, reminding herself of what he had suffered in seeing the destruction of the Russia for which he had hoped and worked. She had always tried to ignore his apparently light-hearted – and always brief – infidelities and had never told him how much she disliked them and what they told her about his needs. Everything she had done for years had been designed to make him happy.

Feeling the treacherous tears seeping into her eyes, she put the plastic bag of potatoes into her basket and stared through blurred eyes at her shopping list. It took her ages to find the garlic and when that was safely tucked into the basket she was faced with a search for tinned anchovies, which were not kept with the sardines and pilchards, but miles away with the capers and cocktail biscuits. When she was certain she had everything, she pushed the basket to the cash desk to pay for her purchases and lugged them up the hill.

The clock in the hall seemed to be half an hour fast until she listened to her watch and discovered that it had stopped at five o'clock. The *coq au vin* would take two and half hours to cook once all the preliminary work had been done and with her guests arriving at eight o'clock she had barely enough time.

Dumping the plastic shopping bags on the terracotta tiles of the kitchen floor, she washed her hands at the sink and, without bothering to dry them, pulled an apron over her head and then set to work, trying not to panic.

Twenty minutes later the chickens were simmering in their wine, but she had cut her left hand twice as she chopped the belly of pork into cubes and had set fire to the front of her hair as she flamed the brandy she had poured over the frying chickens. Her eyes were streaming from peeling onions and she had rubbed fat from the pork into them as she brushed away the tears.

Licking the salt blood off her hand, she looked into a small mirror she kept beside the kitchen door to see what damage she had done to her hair. It was not too bad, she decided, as she saw the short curly strands at the right of her forehead. Then she frowned. Once she had been able to cook anything at all without mistakes or panic or even harming herself. It seemed impossible that Peter's death should have robbed her even of that modest and necessary skill. Real tears threatened and she forced them back, angry with her own weaknesses.

Throwing the rinds of the belly of pork into the rubbish bin with unnecessary force, she returned to the kitchen table and began to peel the various vegetables she needed. As she started each new process she had to concentrate really hard before she could think what needed to be done next, and by half past seven she had only just finished and the familiar headache was pinching behind her eyes.

Andrew appeared in the doorway as she was glaring at the kitchen clock yet again.

'Is there anything I can do?'

'Oh, darling! It would be wonderful if you could lay the table while I have a quick bath. Everything's ready, I think. The first course is in a bowl in the fridge and just needs handing round; the chicken will take care of itself. Oh, God! No it won't. I've got to glaze those bloody onions.'

Andrew looked at his mother in surprise. She rarely swore.

'You do the table,' she went on, looking round the kitchen as though she expected to see something dreadful she had to deal with. She shook her head. 'It really is only the onions. I'll deal with them and then I'll have a bath.'

'Calm down, Mum! It's only Amanda and Aunt Gerry. They don't need impressing. Oh, and these Mayfords of yours. You're not frightened of them, are you?'

'Certainly not,' said Flixe firmly as she flung a large lump of butter into a frying pan. She had peeled all forty small onions some time ago but they would take ages to cook. As soon as the butter was melted, she added the onions and put a lid on the pan, turned the gas very low and smiled at her son. It was a shaky smile, but it was real. He grinned back at her.

'No, I'm not afraid of them. It's just that I can't bear not being in control of what I'm doing and I seem to have lost the knack of cooking properly. You'll need cutlery for three courses and wine glasses. Gerry and Mike are bringing the wine. I'm going to leave those while I bath. If you smell burning, let me know.'

She bathed hurriedly in five inches of warm water, determined not to be bright red in the face when her guests came, and dressed in a pair of plain navy woollen trousers and a bright silk tunic that Ming had given her for Christmas. Patterned in navy and emerald with tiny flashes of aquamarine, it suited her fairness. The Russian sapphire brooch seemed out of place for a family evening and so she merely put on the modest earrings that had marked the birth of her elder daughter, brushed her hair and put on her make-up.

The onions were satisfactorily softened by the time she got back to the kitchen and she sprinkled them with sugar and a ladleful of the wine from the cooking chickens, remembering to put on a pan of water for the rice. The treacle tart was complete and already on its plate, which left only the jointing of the chickens and the thickening of their sauce.

She splashed only a little wine and chicken juices on her silken sleeves as she hacked the birds into manageable joints and was able to wash them off before any of the guests came. The wine boiled down to a beautifully glossy syrup and she succeeded in thickening it with *beurre manié* without producing any lumps. But she had done nothing with the pan of merrily boiling water when the front doorbell rang.

'I'll go,' called Andrew, but when she heard him being unnaturally polite, she knew that the first arrivals were the Mayfords. Stripping off her apron, she went out into the hall to introduce them to Andrew. He shook hands with them both and took away their coats. Georgina leaned forwards to kiss Flixe at once, but George merely held out his hand.

'Felicity,' he said as she took it. 'This is such a pleasure.'

'I hope so,' she said with three-quarters of her mind concentrating on her cooking, 'but I was fearfully late starting and there are still . . . What am I thinking of? Come into the drawing room and have a drink.'

'Couldn't I come and help?' asked Georgina with a smile. 'I'm quite a good cook.'

'That would be heaven,' said Flixe, 'but what about your poor father?'

'Can't her poor father come to the kitchen too?' he asked just as Andrew reappeared.

'We'll all come, Mum.'

Flixe decided not to waste energy persuading them to do anything else and led the way into the kitchen.

'What a magnificent room!' George Mayford's deep voice sounded sincere.

'I must say I've always liked it,' said Flixe, looking quickly at the old wooden table, the terracotta floor, the bunches of dessicated herbs that hung from the pulleys over the cooker. The laboriously polished copper pans shone and the simmering wine scented the whole room. She began to relax.

'Georgina, could you weigh out . . . No. I can't get anything right tonight. We're eight so we'll need the whole pound of rice. You'll find the bag in the second cupboard from the right. Thanks.'

Georgina, whose long Liberty-printed cotton dress looked perfectly in place against the old wood of the table and the cupboards, found the rice and handed it over. George pulled out one of the antique Windsor chairs and sat down to watch, while Andrew perched on the edge of the table, swinging one long leg.

Flixe sprinkled the rice into the seething water, watching his reaction to Georgina out of the corner of her eye. He was smiling and asking politely about her plans for Oxford, but there was no sign in his face or voice that he was at all struck with her. Georgina, on the other hand, definitely looked interested in his dark good looks and long, slim figure.

Sighing internally, Flixe poured the finished sauce over the plate of chicken pieces, arranged the glazed onions round the edge, covered the whole thing in aluminium foil and put it in the oven to keep warm. She hoped that she was not going to cause the girl unfair heartache by throwing her in Andrew's way.

'Thank heavens!' she said as she shut the oven door. 'That's it. We can drink peacefully for fifteen minutes. Don't let me forget the rice, Georgina.'

'No, I won't,' she said, turning reluctantly away from Andrew, 'but won't you both call me Gina? Everyone does.'

'All right,' said Flixe. 'It suits you: less Victorian. Come along.'

She tucked her hand in Gina's arm and led her into the pale, elegant drawing room. Anyone who had known it in the old days would have noticed the gaps, where paintings and valuable furniture had gone to the sale-rooms, but it was still an attractive room.

Andrew poured drinks for everyone and answered the door when the others came. Flixe's spirits fell again as he ushered in Jonathan and Amanda ten minutes after Gerry and her husband Mike Endlesham. Amanda was looking particularly glamorous and fashionable in an extraordinary pair of velvet culottes so narrow that they looked like long black shorts, and a virtually transparent white organza shirt with huge pockets tactfully placed over the breasts. Her dark hair had been swept behind her ears and she was wearing enormous black-and-gold earrings and a great deal of black eye make-up. She did not appear to be wearing a bra.

Compared with Gina's pretty sprigged dress and discreet make-up, Amanda's finery was startling. Flixe looked away, depressed, and caught Gerry watching her with sympathy. Both of them usually knew what the other was thinking and Gerry had obviously picked up her sister's fear of Amanda. Flixe grimaced and when she went to refill her sister's sherry glass, she did murmur: 'It was probably always a forlorn hope.'

'Yes, I'm afraid so,' said Gerry, but there was amusement in her voice, which helped Flixe to relax a little more. She stayed talking to Gerry, quite forgetting about the rice until Gina reminded her.

They went into the kitchen together and rescued it just in time.

'I think we'd better eat now,' Flixe said when the rice had been safely drained and put into a warmed dish at the bottom of the oven. 'Will you go and tell them for me while I take in the first course? Andrew will show you the dining room.' She pulled a piece of paper from a cork board next to the fridge. 'This is the placement. You are a dear, Gina. Thank you.'

By the time everyone had eaten the glorified potato salad and Flixe had listened to the apparently genuine compliments on her cooking, she felt a bit better. There were no dreary silences and all of the salad had been finished, but the atmosphere had none of the intense pleasure her old parties had usually created.

The liveliest part of the table centred on Amanda, who was conducting a spirited argument with Mike about the importance of studying Fine Art as an academic subject.

Several of the others were listening to her with varying degrees of amusement. She enjoyed the attention, but disliked the more mocking smiles.

'What on earth does it matter?' Andrew asked as he got to his feet to start collecting the empty plates.

Gina stood up at once and helped him. Flixe saw Amanda look round with a derisive expression in her eyes before she turned back to Mike to say: 'Of course it matters. Man does not live by bread alone – or even Classics or maths. We all need to have our perceptions extended and the fine arts can do that better than almost anything else.'

'I suppose I might be prepared to accept that, but why should the hard-working taxpayer support undergraduates who want to have their perceptions extended? It may be pleasant, it may even be important for your own development, but it's hardly going to help the country pay its way or get back to a position of any influence in the world.'

'It's really time for your generation to get away from that yearning for world power. We once had an empire and Britannia ruled the waves ... so what? We're a small island. We ought to be spending the taxpayers' money on promoting civilisation within our own borders, not laying down the law all over the world.'

'Tricky if there's no money. Civilisation costs a fortune,' said Gerry. Her sympathies were more with Amanda than with her husband, but she had had similiar arguments with him so often that she had come to accept some of his points.

'Precisely,' he said, flashing a smile at her. 'What does need extending, Amanda, is the manufacturing base of this country. We need young people to get industrial productivity up and improve our dismal exports. That's where public money ought to go, not into self-indulgent, soft non-subjects like Fine Art.'

Amanda twisted her body so that she was facing Mike and put her elbows on the table. Flixe wondered what on earth she was going to say. Just as Andrew reappeared with the big hot dish of chicken, Amanda nodded, her face apparently serious. Her forehead crinkled into a frown but there was a gleam in her eyes.

'Yes, I do see that,' she said earnestly. 'I realise that as a civil servant you must feel very strongly about people who don't produce anything for this country to export.'

For a moment Mike looked irritated but then he smiled.

'All right, I'll give you that one,' he said. '*Touché*.'

Gina put a plate in front of Amanda and said over her head: 'Besides, we don't have to export actual things. Skills and knowledge can be just as marketable. If Amanda becomes a world expert on late medieval art and is summoned abroad to give an opinion and paid in foreign currency, isn't that just as useful as if she'd been selling widgets?'

'It's hardly going to increase the sum of human happiness,' said Andrew from the other side of the table as he held the big dish so that his aunt could help herself to chicken.

'Perhaps not.' Amanda held out her glass for Mike to refill with wine. She was not altogther grateful for Gina's convincing championship. 'But it'll certainly increase mine, and that's all I care about.'

There was a moment's silence, into which George Mayford said quietly: 'At your age that's probably quite normal.'

Flixe waited, wondering what Amanda was going to say. Her face looked very cold for a moment but then she tipped her chair back so that her hair hung down behind it in a dark, silky waterfall and laughed.

'What a putdown!' she said and then straightened up again. 'It's much better than mine was. Well done, Doctor Mayford.'

Gina smiled at her father, and Andrew looked at Flixe as if to say: You see, she has a sense of humour; she is intelligent; the selfishness is only a pose. Flixe smiled at him and he moved on to hand the *coq au vin* to George Mayford.

'You haven't lost any of your old skill,' said Mike, switching his attention to Flixe as Amanda turned away from him. Andrew sat down beside her again. 'It's a really good party.'

Flixe smiled ruefully.

'I'm not sure I'd have lost control of all that in the old days,' she said, nodding towards Amanda.

'It was fine. I think we all enjoyed it, especially your doctor. There's more about him than I'd expected.'

'Why?' Flixe was smiling. 'Just because he coped with a potential scene so easily?'

'No. I was talking to him before dinner. There's something remarkably attractive about a man who wears his success so lightly. I've heard quite a bit about him and he's done some good work, but he talks as though he's any old sawbones.' He ate a mouthful of chicken and added: 'This is delicious.'

'You are kind, Mike. I was worried about it because, despite your compliment, I do seem to have lost most of the one genuine talent I ever had. I'm glad it hasn't gone completely.' She smiled down the table at Gina, who was standing with a dish in her hands. 'I don't know what I'd have done without you, Gina, but you don't need to hand the rice round. We can pass it to each other, don't you think?'

'What a good idea,' she said easily, moving back to her chair on Andrew's left without making a fuss. She started talking to Jonathan at once because Andrew was wholly occupied with Amanda.

Jonathan, who was at an awkward stage of mixed shyness and belligerence, blushed and stammered an answer to her question. Under her care, he eventually calmed down and began to talk quite normally about his consuming interest in astrophysics, about which she knew nothing at all.

Later, when the Mayfords had gone and Andrew was driving Amanda and Jonathan back to Kennington in Flixe's car, Gerry poured herself the last of the cooling coffee and said: 'I don't blame you for trying, old thing, but I can't see that delightful Georgina even denting poor Andrew's infatuation.'

'No,' said Flixe sadly, 'although she would obviously be far better for him. I thought she was charming this evening – even standing up for Amanda when you savaged her, Mike.'

'I wonder if she'd really suit him.'

The two sisters stared at him as he refilled his pipe.

'Why not?' asked Gerry with her usual forthrightness. 'She has none of Amanda's selfishness or amazing ability to say the most wounding thing possible. Although I must admit she behaved reasonably well this evening. Perhaps Gina's obvious niceness deterred her.'

'Gina's a sweet girl and she's obviously had plenty of rehearsals for being a good wife to almost any man,' said Mike, 'but I don't think she'd do for Andrew.'

'That sounds remarkably deep, Mike, but I don't quite understand it. By the way, would you both like some brandy? It's only the cooking stuff, but there's plenty,' said Flixe.

'No thanks,' said Gerry. 'It always gives me a ghastly headache next morning, but Mike might.'

'I'd rather have a bit more wine, if there's any left.'

Flixe got up to fetch the last bottle and poured the dregs out into his glass.

'Thanks.' He put his filled but unlit pipe back into the pocket of his suit and sat back in his chair.

'Well?' Flixe perched on the arm and patted his thick grey hair. 'Come on, Mikey. Give.'

'Amanda is a pain in the arse at the moment, but potentially she's far more interesting and she's infinitely sexier. Andrew is so remarkably like Peter that . . .' He paused and looked sideways at Flixe. She shrugged, her face bleak. Gerry directed an angry look at her husband and started to talk about her work until her sister interrupted.

'Don't worry, Gerry,' said Flixe, assuming that her brother-in-law's cavil was something to do with Peter's incorrigible rakishness. She had seen few signs of it in Andrew apart from his remark about girls on the Pill, but was quite prepared to believe that another man might recognise it more easily than she could. 'Let Mike finish. I can take it.'

'That,' he repeated, 'I think anyone as calmly co-operative and basically transparent as Gina Mayford would bore him before long. She'd be fine when he was miserable, warm and comforting, but when he took fire, she'd never be able to match him as you could always match Peter, Flixe.'

At that her dark blue eyes filled with tears far less controllable than the ones that had threatened her in the supermarket. They rolled down her face and she got off the arm of Mike's chair, turning her back on them both.

Seeing Flixe's shoulders shaking and her hand groping under the silk tunic for her trouser pocket, Gerry went to hug her and offer her a handkerchief. Flixe turned in her sister's embrace and laid her head on Gerry's shoulder. She took a deep, shuddering breath.

'I miss him so much.'

CHAPTER 9

Amanda had found the dinner party pretty boring, despite enjoying her own gracious surrender to George Mayford's neat snub, and she was in a bad temper. When Andrew stopped the car outside her parents' house and told her he would collect her from Comfort's studio the next day, she snapped at him.

'For heaven's sake! Stop behaving as though you were my nanny. I am perfectly capable of getting myself home from South Kensington.'

There was a streetlamp shining just in front of the car and in its light she could see him trapping part of his bottom lip between his teeth. Knowing she had hurt him made her feel even more irritable.

'I say, Amanda, steady on,' said her brother tentatively from the back seat, deflecting some of her annoyance to himself.

Amanda ignored him but she did try to sound kinder as she said to Andrew: 'It's just that I never know when Comfort's going to be finished with me and I don't want you hanging about in the cold. I can hardly invite you into her house without permission.'

'Will you ring me when you get in tomorrow then? We could have dinner at least. We must have some time on our own.'

'I'll ring you. I'm not sure about dinner. It's so enervating sitting for one's portrait that I usually just want to go to bed when I get home.'

Andrew turned slightly and jerked his head at Jonathan, who hastily thanked him for the lift and went on into the house. Andrew hung on to Amanda's wrist when she made to follow her brother.

'Listen, darling, what is it? You can't do this. We've made love. We're important to each other. You can't just brush me off like someone you hardly know.'

Amanda pulled her wrist away and hugged it protectively with her other hand. It actually hurt a bit.

'I can do anything I like,' she said coldly. 'I am very fond of you, Andrew, but when you get all wet and clingy and threatening like this I hate it. I am busy at the moment and often very tired. Besides,' she added nastily, 'I thought you were supposed to be working for your first. Or are you so convinced of your brilliance that you don't even need to work?'

'Don't be silly,' he said curtly. 'Of course I'm working.'

'Well, that's all right then. You're working and I'm sitting for my portrait. When we've both got more time we can meet. Good-night. Thank you for bringing us home. I'll ring you when I can see you again.'

Seething with righteous anger at his attempt to bully her, she stalked into the house, ignored the rest of her family and went straight up to bed.

It was a week before she relented enough to talk to him again. Having received some gently elliptical advice from his mother, he managed not to say anything about the un-answered messages he had left for Amanda when she did eventually telephone. Instead, sounding quite casual, he invited her to have dinner with him. Surprised and pleased

134

by his return to normal, she agreed to meet him at a restaurant in the King's Road that evening.

He was more fun than he had been for some time and accepted her unexplained refusal to sleep with him without trying to persuade her to change her mind. She was so relieved not to have to invent excuses that she even agreed to let him collect her from the studio for the next few days.

Andrew did his best to fit in with her expectations of him. He worked all day, while his mother entertained his three younger siblings and kept as much control as possible over her various sorts of work, and then tried to be what Amanda wanted whenever she deigned to bestow her company on him in the evening. He could be amusing and he often tried to sound interested in her work and ideas, but his own enthusiasms were so intense that he could not help talking most about them.

Too often when that happened, Amanda was simply bored and longed for Anthony Gillingham's infinitely more sophisticated company, or even the often thrilling and sometimes waspish conversation of his sister. There seemed to be no end to the causes that aroused Andrew's fury. When he was not inveighing against the iniquities of the British Government's determination to break the trade unions, he was telling her all about the exciting developments in Czechoslovakia or the horrors of the war in Vietnam.

Amanda, who had listened to sophisticated political discussions at home since she could first speak, sometimes felt that if Andrew treated her to one more pedestrian lecture about the consequences of whatever was annoying him at the time she would lose her temper.

'But there's nothing you can do about it,' she said one evening at the end of April, after he had talked for half an hour about the assassination of Martin Luther King and the civil rights movement in America.

'That's not the point. Unless all of us stand up for what we believe, the world has no hope. Don't you even care?' he asked, pushing aside the wine bottle that served as a candlestick and wincing as a small trail of hot wax dribbled on to his hand. As it cooled and hardened, he picked it off in little flakes.

'Yes, I care,' said Amanda with some dignity. 'I do care about a lot of things. I am as horrified as you that King's been shot, but it's thousands of miles away and there's nothing I can do about it. It wouldn't happen here and even if it did . . .'

'How can you be sure? Enoch Powell's just been talking about rivers of blood after all. With that kind of feeling inflaming the country, anything could happen.'

'As you perfectly well know,' she said, picking up her wine glass, 'he was quoting the *Aeneid*; something about the Tiber foaming with much blood. He knows no one's going to be assassinated here; the Thames is certainly not running with blood, nor will it be. There's nothing your bunch of over-earnest students can do about any of the horrors in the world except make people laugh at your naïvety.'

'We're not naïve.' Andrew's voice was incisive and Amanda smiled to hear it, so much more attractive than the reproachful hectoring tones he had been using for most of the evening.

'Perhaps, but it's simply arrogant to think you can alter anything – at all – except your own life and future. And that's what you ought to be doing. Concentrating on yourself. After all there's plenty to get right.'

She drained her wine glass and banged it down on the scrubbed wooden table. A harrassed waitress came scurrying over to remove their smeared plates, thinking that the bang had been a summons. When she had gone, Andrew took one of Amanda's hands and laid it on the table, straightening the long fingers one after the other. She let him do it, curious to know what he was going to say and enjoying the contrast between the dark, rough wood and the whiteness and softness of her fingers. He looked up, his dark eyes sad.

'Amanda, why do we quarrel so much? I wish you'd drop all this pseudo-sophistication and pretended cynicism. It's like a cloak for selfishness. But you're not really selfish, whatever they say. I know you're not. It's as though you put it on just to make me angry. Why, Amanda?'

Amanda removed her hand. Hurt and irritated, she hit back.

'I don't pretend anything and I wouldn't bother to try to make you angry even if I wanted to. The problem's in you. You don't look at anything straight any more. You're just hiding from the realities of life in hopeless causes that make you feel good about yourself instead of tackling your own inadequacies. If you don't stop that, you'll never compensate for them or amount to anything – which would be a waste.'

Stung, Andrew looked away. The waitress offered him a menu, saying: 'Will you have pudding?'

'I don't think so. You don't want anything else, do you, Amanda?'

'No. Just the bill.'

They split it, as they sometimes did, and then Andrew drove her home in silence. Sitting in the parked car outside her house again, she sighed for the days when he had seemed just a part of her life, a good part.

'Andrew, can't we just be friends as we always were? Why do you mind what I think? It's nothing to do with you.'

'Of course it is. I love you. Sometimes I think that you are so afraid of love that you have to keep trying to drive me away by saying things you know will outrage me.' He turned to look at her, but she was staring through the windscreen at the damp road ahead. His voice dropped as he added: 'Or hurt me.'

At that she did look at him and the misery in his face aroused her worst instincts. She thought once again how sad it was that his wonderfully handsome face should hide such a mess of feelings. Looking like that, he ought to have had all his father's sophistication and cool glamour, instead of the mixture of yearning and bullying that annoyed her so badly. She said nothing.

'Why have you changed, Amanda?' he went on after a long silence. 'A few weeks ago you'd come out of your idiotic poses and we were happy together. What happened in between?'

'Nothing.' The knowledge of the immense change wrought in her by her afternoon with Anthony made her voice sharp.

'Then what's different? We made love with each other. I wish I could understand you. Have you met someone else?'

Something of the dreadful unhappiness in his voice made Amanda feel guilty. Irrationally furious with him for that, she turned in her seat to face him.

'I let you make love to me because I was sorry for you,' she said nastily. 'I know that you've been unhappy about your father and I thought that if I slept with you it might help cheer you up. I didn't bargain for your assuming that I'd made a lifetime's commitment by letting you f... do that. I like you and I'd like to be friends, but that's it. No more. Is there no way you can understand that?'

Andrew looked at her for a moment and then got out of the car and walked round it to open her door.

'Good-night,' he said coldly as she walked past him to the front doorsteps of the house.

'Good-night,' she answered. 'Thank you for the lift.'

She woke in the night feeling troubled and unhappy with both herself and Andrew. It seemed monstrously unfair of him to make everything so serious when they could simply have had fun together; and yet part of her recognised his distress and wanted to help. Flinging herself face down on her suddenly lumpy pillow and pushing her fists into the mattress, she thought it would be easier to be what he wanted if he could only ask for it frankly instead of criticising her all the time. If he could just say, Amanda, please be kind to me because I am unhappy and missing my father, she might have been able to do it; but he could not. All he could do was tell her she was selfish and acting a part and lying.

She was uncomfortable on her front and she turned back, staring up at the dark ceiling. It took ages for her to banish all thoughts of him as she tried to get back to sleep, but eventually, just as the faint grey light was appearing at the edges of her bedroom curtains, she did manage to lose consciousness again.

Five hours later, feeling unwell and resentful, she tried to telephone Andrew before she left for Comfort's studio. His mother answered, sounding harrassed, and when Amanda asked for him, Flixe said that he had just left the house on his way to Paris for a few days to stay with his aunt there.

'Thank you,' said Amanda. 'I expect he'll ring me when he gets back.' They said good-bye and then, ignoring Janice's offer of some lunch, Amanda left to go to the studio for the last time.

Comfort took one look at her and said: 'You look like something the cat brought in. What's the matter?'

'I slept badly,' said Amanda, shrugging.

'Well, it's a good thing I only need to tidy up your shoulders. With a face like that . . . Perhaps that's unfair of me. You look as though you're feeling poorly. Take off your shirt and lie on the sofa. I won't be long and then we can have tea and you can tell me all about it.'

Amanda obeyed the first instruction but later, when they were drinking tea, she refused to say anything about the source of her insomnia.

'It's your business,' said Comfort, 'and I'm the last person to try to pry into other people's secrets. But I hope you'll remember me if you want a confidante. Just because the modelling's over, it doesn't mean we need to lose touch.'

'Really?' Amanda's dull face lit up.

'Definitely. We have had some remarkably good talks these last few weeks, haven't we? I've enjoyed your company a great deal more than I'd expected.'

'I'm not sure whether that's a compliment or an insult,'

said Amanda, laughing and feeling much more like herself, 'but I'll take it as the former. Thank you. I've enjoyed it, too. Can I see the painting before I go?'

Comfort smiled and shook her head.

'Not yet. It's at the most tricky stage. I've got you as I want you, but I've yet to paint the sea and the rocks. Until they're there it won't make any sense and I don't want you talking about it until it's finished. If you haven't seen it you can't do any damage.'

'Why should I do damage?'

'If you disliked it or didn't understand it, you might indicate that to anyone who asked even without meaning to. I don't want the people who matter making up their minds about this one before it's exhibited. I want it to be a surprise.'

She smiled at Amanda, who was lazily dressing herself again without bothering to disappear behind the tapestry screen. 'I aim to make quite a splash with this portrait, you know. I'll send you a card for the private view.'

'Goody. When will it be?'

'I'm not precisely sure. But some time this season, probably June. I have a major interest in the gallery and so to some extent I can decide. Shall you be able to escape the East Anglian prison and get yourself to London for the party?'

'I think I can probably manage that,' said Amanda. 'I'd better be off. I've enjoyed these sittings a lot. Will you give my love to Anthony?'

'Surely. As I said, I've enjoyed them too. You're an interesting woman, Amanda.'

Smiling at that, Amanda floated down the stairs and out into the sunny street, convinced that by taking her time and working subtly she might still be able to transform Anthony Gillingham's life. He had not once returned to the studio during her sittings, but with Comfort's vague but apparently permanent welcome, all would probably be well. Amanda felt marvellous.

Her vacation still had two weeks left to run, but she had no more modelling jobs arranged and wanted to enjoy the euphoric feeling well out of the way of criticism from Andrew when he returned from Paris or from her mother. Her departure would also put her out of reach of Anthony, but, since it had become quite clear to her that he was not going to ring her, that would not matter much.

That evening she told her busy parents that she had a lot of reading to do and, being unable to concentrate at home, planned to go back to Norwich early. Slightly to her surprise, Julia and David raised no objections, and she was unable to convince herself that they were not quite pleased at the prospect of seeing her go.

David offered to drive her to Norwich at the weekend with all her books and records and she accepted in delight. There were few times when she had him to herself and she meant to make the most of it.

He was particularly nice to her on the drive, asking no questions and making no remotely critical comments. Instead they discussed an article Amanda was thinking of writing about Comfort Gillingham's work and which of the art journals might be interested in it. Only after they had taken a detour into Cambridge for a really good lunch did David broach any difficult subject.

'Are you having trouble with Andrew Suvarov?' he asked after they had rejoined the main road, apparently concentrating on the heavy traffic ahead of them.

'Not particularly,' said Amanda automatically.

'Come off it, Blackberry.'

Amanda greeted the old nickname with a nostalgic sidelong smile.

'Why Blackberry? I've often wondered.'

'Wild, black-haired and ferociously prickly, but very sweet once you're past the thorns.'

'Pig!'

They both laughed and Amanda added more honestly: 'Yes, I suppose I am having a bit of trouble with him. I like him a lot and he's good company when he's not either banging on about his endless demos and sit-ins or about how much he – you know – loves me.'

'And when he is?'

She shrugged and her mouth thinned.

'Well, quite frankly he's either boring then or sort of threatening. I don't mean that he makes threats, but it ... Oh, I don't know.'

'The fact that he cares so much in itself constitutes a threat, perhaps?'

'Yes, I think it does. Does that make me unnatural?'

David laughed again and let his left hand drop from the steering wheel for a moment to touch hers.

'No. I think it makes you thoroughly normal.'

'Good. That's that over. What shall we talk about next?'

'It's not quite over,' said David gently.

'Bugger! I thought we'd finished.'

'All I wanted to add,' David went on, ignoring his distaste for the expletive she had chosen, 'is that if you can manage to be gentle with him it would be a kindness. I think he's still dreadfully churned up over his father's death and is not in a fit state to be tormented by someone blowing hot and cold over him.'

'I know he is, but I don't blow hot and cold,' she said, suppressing a faint twinge of conscience. Her voice hardened: 'And I don't altogether like your being his mother's messenger boy.'

David, who had dined with Flixe in the House of Commons the previous evening, declined to comment. She had not asked him to talk to Amanda but she had told him enough of her worries for him to want to take on the task.

'I've been very kind to him – kinder than he deserves actually – and if he's gone off to Paris to sulk just because of one argument, that's his own affair. He says worse things to me whenever we meet than I've ever said to him. And he seems to think that his feelings for me mean that he has some kind of rights over me. I haven't given them to him. He's just assumed them, and it makes me cross.'

'All right,' said David, wondering, as he had wondered the previous evening, whether Amanda's kindness had included letting Andrew into her bed. It was a thought that worried him for several reasons.

They said nothing more until they reached the outskirts of Norwich, when Amanda directed him to the university. There he helped her to transfer her innumerable belongings from the windy car park to her little room in the grey concrete block.

It seemed even more bleak than before she had seen the Gillinghams' luxurious house and Amanda half wished that she had stayed in London. She concealed her regrets, kissed her father cheerfully and, when he had gone, caught a bus into Norwich to buy some flowers and a machine for making proper Italian coffee. Comfort Gillingham had shown such horror of the instant version and made such astonishingly delicious real coffee that Amanda had decided to be converted.

Returning, she looked into her pigeon-hole and was surprised but pleased to see a letter and a small flat package. The parcel was addressed in Comfort's writing, while the long white envelope was from Andrew and postmarked in Paris. Amanda stuffed the letter in the pocket of her yellow trousers and unpacked the parcel on her way back to her room. Not looking where she was going, she caught her foot in a crack in the concrete, tripped and, in trying to save herself without dropping the parcel, slipped into a puddle, soaking her yellow velvet trousers, which would need to be expensively dry-cleaned.

'Bloody hell!' she shouted at the top of her voice.

'Oh dear, oh dear! The fallen woman.' The idiotic joke was accompanied by a laugh Amanda remembered with extreme dislike. 'Pride does come before a fall, doesn't it, Amanda?' added the tutor who had seduced her in her first term.

He offered a hand to help her up.

Amanda raised herself out of the puddle without recourse to his assistance and smiled at him, slowly and deliberately. He looked disconcerted, almost, she thought, as though he were wondering whether his paunch was becoming noticeable or the balding patch on the top of his head ceasing to look interestingly like a tonsure and merely looking bald.

'Good heavens, you ought to take care,' she said, feeling suddenly pleased with herself again. 'No one who heard that barrage of clichés would believe that you even knew all those famous writers you claim as such friends, let alone that they were prepared to know you. Nice to run into you. 'Bye.'

She left him without waiting to see how he had taken her insult. Safely back in her own room, with the door firmly locked, she cursed again, changed her velvet trousers for a pair of black corduroys, and sat down at the desk to open her parcel.

It contained a battered leather box with faded gold tooling and a small piece of folded paper. She opened that first.

An antique mermaid for the modern one we found in
the studio.

Love, Comfort and Anthony

P.S. We both miss you, C

With delighted relief welling inside her at the sight of Anthony's signature, Amanda opened the box to find a long gold pin with a small enamelled mermaid at the top, her muscular tail twisting about the pin. It had been made with marvellously precise workmanship. Amanda ran her fingers over the exquisite enamelling, revelling in every detail of the scaly tail and the fine modelling of the mermaid's face before sticking it into the neck of her black jersey and finding a piece of writing paper and her pen.

My dear Comfort and Anthony [she tactfully put

144

Comfort's name first, knowing that Anthony would understand],

Thank you for the ravishing mermaid. She looks very old. Where did you find her? She's so beautiful that I doubt if I shall ever be able to take her off. It's charming of you both to have thought of giving me anything, let alone something as wonderful as this pin.

I truly loved my time in your house and learned so much that I will never forget. I hope that the portrait is going well and that you are pleased with it. I can't wait for the private view.

Love to you both, Amanda

It was not much for the first letter she had written to the man who had shown her the difference between love and sex, but it was all she could allow herself then. She thought of all the things she wanted to write to him and saved them up. Then she opened Andrew's letter.

My darling Amanda,

Missing you is like having had part of me cut away. Forgive me for not making you happier. You sent me into heaven that night we made love, but I am beginning to realise that you might not have felt quite like that. I want to come storming the barricades of Norwich to whisk you away and find a way to let you say those things to me again and show you how much I love you.

I won't quote what it was you said, but I think we both know that it was truer than the words you sent me to Paris with. I wish I had never taken those ones seriously enough to go off and sulk. Oh, Amanda, I do so much want to find the secrets of your real self, the hidden, frightened one, and make it less afraid, not least of me.

But you wouldn't like that and I have schools this term.

Andrew

Amanda, who had been frowning at the presumption of much of what Andrew had written, smiled as she read the last line and wished that he could be as aware and amusing as his letters when they actually met. Skimming over the letter again, she found nothing that needed answering and put it away, deciding that she would wait for the next instalment before she wrote to him. Instead she turned to work.

That term they were to tackle Giotto and she collected all the relevant books from the library to give herself a useful advantage over her lazier colleagues.

She started to read the weightiest of the books and then, finding it unusually dull, switched to another and then another. Eventually she pushed them all to one side of her desk and retreated to bed with her writing paper so that she could write to her grandmother in Fiesole. That did nothing to drive away her dissatisfactions but she finished the letter and stuffed it into an airmail envelope ready for posting. Then she allowed herself to write to Anthony all the things she wanted him to know, aware with each stroke of her pen that she would destroy the letter as soon as it was finished.

Iris returned to Norwich just in time to stop Amanda from falling into a melancholy and the two of them poured out accounts of their vacations to each other. Amanda kept the existence of Anthony and her feelings for him in a separate compartment, which she did not even mention, but her experiences with Andrew became common currency between them.

'So no *foie gras* to the sound of trumpets then?' said Iris, sitting on the floor rolling a joint. 'Want some?'

'No thanks. I just don't like it: makes me feel sick and I hate not being in control. No, there were no trumpets with

Andrew.' She could have added that there hadn't been trumpets with Anthony either, just that staggering moment when she had found extraordinary pleasure in losing control and felt truly at home for the first time in her life. She had been at peace then, and in love at last.

There was a slight smile twitching at her lips and a distant, self-absorbed look in her dark eyes that made Iris privately amused. She was well aware that there was something she had not been told, but she did not press her friend. Instead she lay back, sucking the scented, delirious-making smoke deep into her lungs and letting the future and the past take care of themselves for once.

Amanda looked down at her, uncharacteristically annoyed with her, and then turned back to the desk where Andrew's latest letter lay needing to be answered. The smoke from Iris's joint was making her feel sick.

She ate no supper that night and was surprised to find herself still feeling nauseated the following morning. Flinging open the big, black-edged window and breathing great mouthfuls of damp fresh air, Amanda wondered if she was going to be ill. It was not for several hours that the most obvious – and most terrifying – explanation occurred to her.

When it did, she sat cross-legged on the floor of her room hugging herself and saying the word over and over again to make it seem less important: 'Pregnant. Pregnant. Pregnant.'

The mantra did nothing to take power from the word and she tried to cope with it by telling herself that there was no need to be afraid.

'Everyone has abortions these days,' she said aloud, thanking the Fates that at least she had plenty of money to pay for one and need not involve anyone else in her predicament. There was no need to feel like a Victorian kitchen maid whose only options were an unlikely forced marriage, prostitution, the workhouse or suicide.

If she were truly pregnant her condition need be no more

147

than a mild inconvenience. There was no reason for the instinctive shame she felt. She knew perfectly well that she had done nothing to be ashamed of. Besides, she told herself illogically, no one need know anything about it.

None of her rationalisations could take away the sensation of dread. She felt ill and afraid, and all Andrew's remarks about her hidden self came back to mock her. She did not blame him for her possible pregnancy, but she blamed him completely for her fears. It was almost as though it had been his impertinent invention of a frightened part of her that had led her into trouble.

Pushing away all the absurdities that kept rushing into her mind, Amanda decided that the first thing to do was to find out whether her condition was real. It would be too stupid to work herself into serious anxiety for nothing. After all there were plenty of comforting stories to suggest she might not be pregnant. Mary Tudor, for one, had frequently believed that she was with child, and everyone knew she had died infertile. Even so, Amanda felt utterly convinced that she was pregnant.

She was also completely certain that she did not want the university doctor involved in her life. He was said to be very relaxed about things like the Pill and probably completely reliable and discreet. Amanda had heard nothing to the contrary. But the memory of the tutor's mockery was too strong for her to be able to bear the possibility that people like him might hear that she had been stupid enough to get herself pregnant.

Her parents' doctor would be no good either for the same sort of reason. The only solution seemed to be to go into Norwich, find a private doctor's surgery in some unfrequented part of the city, give a false name and ask for a test for which she could pay cash so that no one need know anything about her.

She did it that afternoon and was surprised to find a young-looking woman in the surgery, who expressed neither surprise nor condemnation at Amanda's stammered

148

explanation of her presence. The doctor was quite matter of fact about her questions and her request for a urine sample. Embarrassed, despite the doctor's attitude, Amanda did as she was told and submitted to a physical examination.

'I can't say for certain until we get the results of the test,' said the doctor while Amanda was putting on her clothes. 'If you come back in three days' time we'll know. It is quite possible, though, that you will have your period by then.'

Amanda looked up, suddenly hopeful and then frowned.

'No, I don't think so,' she said after a moment. 'I'll come back. At the same time?'

'Yes, please. Try not to worry too much. You have more options now than you would have done a few years ago.'

'I know. Thank you.'

Amanda left the surgery, nodded to the receptionist, who smiled pleasantly, and walked aimlessly about the streets. The weather had improved and there was enough warm sunlight to make even Norwich look quite attractive. As she walked down Elm Street, among the crowds of shoppers and tourists, she thought that she was divided from them all by some impervious membrane. The charming, dilapidated medieval and tudor houses still looked pretty, but they could have been part of a stage set for all they meant to her and the busy people could have been marionettes. She felt apart, no longer afraid but quite alone.

Three days later she was back in the surgery, listening with outward coolness to the doctor's announcement of her forthcoming child.

'I see.' Amanda breathed deeply and deliberately relaxed her hands. She was not sure that she liked the sympathy on the doctor's face. 'Thank you for your time. Shall I pay you or the receptionist?'

'There are things to arrange before you go,' said the doctor mildly.

'That's perfectly all right. I shall make my own arrangements. I'm only a visitor to Norwich.'

'You sound as though you've decided on a termination . . .' Before the doctor could finish, Amanda had interrupted.

'That's my business.'

'But as a doctor I have a responsibility to you. Please take time to think before you do anything irreparable. You're very young.'

'Thank you for your advice. Good-bye.'

The doctor sighed.

'Please remember that I am here if you need anything – or if you just want to talk. I . . . It's not a light matter, you know.'

Amanda, who had been calculating that she had until at least October before the twenty-eight-week limit for an abortion expired, managed to smile.

'Thank you for your time,' she said again. 'I'll certainly be in touch with you if I need anything.'

Iris Fowlins greeted Amanda on her return with the news that Comfort had telephoned and wanted Amanda to ring her back as soon as she could.

'Oh thanks, Iris. I'll do that in a minute.'

'Are you all right?' her friend asked, peering at her. There seemed to be no excitement – or even pleasure – in the news that one of the most celebrated painters of the day wanted to talk to her.

'I'm fine.' Amanda switched on the light. 'Cup of tea?'

'Thanks.' Iris, who was wearing a dreadful purple crocheted mini-dress over her tattered green bell-bottomed trousers, curled up on Amanda's bed, crumpling the careful arrangement of different Indian cotton bedspreads she had recently bought to disguise its utilitarian lines. 'I thought you always had milk in yours.'

'Usually, but I've decided I prefer it black and sweet.'

'You're not pregnant are you?' The question was asked in Iris's usual teasing voice and was obviously not meant seriously, but Amanda found that for once she could not lie. She stared at Iris, trying to find the right words. Eventually she realised that her silence had already given Iris the true answer so that the actual words did not matter at all.

'Actually, yes,' she said quite easily. 'But keep it under your hat. No one but you need ever know anything about it.'

'God, Amanda, I'm sorry. I'd never have asked if . . . I've always assumed that you were far too sensible and controlled to let it happen to you. Sorry, I'm making things worse and worse. But why aren't you on the Pill?'

Amanda shrugged.

'I was at one stage in my first term, when I thought . . . But that folded rather soon and the pills made me so spotty and unhappy and I hadn't liked sex anyway; there seemed no point going on.'

'You should have tried a different sort. They all have different dosages and effects. And even spottiness would be better than a disaster like this.'

'It's not such a drama, you know. I can easily afford an abortion and I've got until at least the start of next term before I need have it done. No one need know anything,' she said again, 'unless you betray me.' The upward intonation made her last statement into a question.

'Don't be silly,' said Iris, 'you know I wouldn't do that. Amanda . . .'

'What? You look shocked. It happens to all sorts of people.' She turned away so that she need not watch the unmistakable disapproval in Iris's face. It was not an expression Amanda had ever seen there before and it upset her.

'I know it happens and of course I'm not shocked that it's happened to you. It's just . . . Hell! This is difficult. It's just that I don't think you should charge in and have an abortion without thinking about it.'

Amanda, sipping her boiling tea, looked aghast.

'I rather counted on you, you know,' she said at last. 'It never occurred to me that you'd turn moralistic on me. You haven't suddenly become a Catholic, have you?'

Iris shook her head. 'No, but there are reasons why I don't think you should have a termination. It's not quite as straightforward as "a woman's right to choose", whatever they say. At least it is, but I don't think most of us know enough to make the right choice.'

'You don't have to worry about my not knowing. I've listened to and participated in more abortion debates at home than you've had hot dinners. My father was a firm supporter of David Steel's bill and my mother disapproved of it. That's one reason why I've got to get this sorted out quickly. I don't want her getting wind of my state.'

She stared at Iris, who was looking remarkably uncomfortable.

'I must say that I'd never have expected you to share her views. Why, Iris? I think you owe it to me to explain.'

'I just think that it might . . . damage you,' she said slowly. 'I don't mean physically. Nowadays you can have a perfectly decent doctor instead of a back-street butcher, but I think it might hurt you badly in other ways.' She looked completely serious and quite unlike herself.

'I can't think of anything that could damage me as much as giving birth to an illegitimate baby and struggling to bring it up as an unmarried mother,' Amanda said tartly. 'And if you're about to suggest that I have it adopted at birth, I can't think why that would be less hurtful – more, actually, since I'd have had all the bother of pregnancy and all the pain of delivery, not to speak of everyone's knowing about it. Come on, Iris, it's just not practical. Besides, women still die in childbirth.'

Iris drank her tea and sat with her hands wrapped round the mug, trying to speak.

'What's the matter with you? I've never seen you so suburban.' It had always been their worst insult, but Iris did not rise to it.

'Oh, God. I never meant to tell anyone this,' she said with difficulty, 'but I had an abortion last year.'

Amanda was surprised out of her self-absorption by the sight of tears gathering on Iris's plump cheeks. She had never cried in public before.

'I thought just like you that getting pregnant was a minor inconvenience. I never even told Ben about it. And ever since . . .' Her voice broke completely. Amanda rootled in her top drawer for a clean handkerchief, which she handed to Iris, who scrubbed her eyes with it.

'Ever since I had it done, I've regretted it. I've been through all the arguments about wasting my life on domesticity, ruining my chances of a good job by not finishing here and all the rest. But I can't stop . . . mourning, I suppose.'

Amanda silently fetched Iris's empty mug, washed it out under the tap and poured a stiff measure of whisky from the bottle she kept under the basin.

'Have some of this,' she said, hating to see her friend in such distress. 'I didn't mean to make you so sad. Perhaps it's just the upset to your hormones: something like that must cause a pretty big upset. After all, think of all those women who have dreadful depression after they've had their babies. You're probably just still going through that.'

Iris made an effort to control her voice.

'I don't think so. But it's absurd for me to sob and lean on you when it's you who have the problem now. I didn't tell you for sympathy – I've never told anyone else – only because I care for you too much to let you go through it without a warning. I want you to promise me you'll think before you do it. Nothing will show until well after the end of term and, as you said, you've months before the time limit is up.'

'I can promise you I'll think about it, but I'm not sure how long I'll let it go. It's so much better and less painful in every sense if it's done quickly.'

'You seem to know an awful lot about it.' Iris sipped some whisky, watching Amanda over the rim of the mug.

'I told you, I listened to endless arguments when the bill was going through Parliament. I know all there is to know – including what it does to the women who have them,' said Amanda obscurely. 'Iris, I am sorry that it happened badly for you.'

'What about Andrew? D'you think it's fair to get rid of his child without even letting him know it exists?'

'It doesn't. It's a few cells in my body. Why should he know? It's nothing to do with him.' Amanda's voice shook slightly with anger.

Iris got of the bed and went to stand beside Amanda with an arm around her waist.

'I'm sorry. I didn't mean to sound disapproving. It's none of my business . . .'

'Quite.'

'Except in so far as I've been where you are now and I made a mistake. I'd hate you to go through it without knowing how bad a mistake it was.'

Amanda let her head fall into her friend's shoulder.

'I feel so ill at the moment, it makes me ratty. Sorry, Iris.'

'Come and sit down and drink your tea.'

'But, Iris,' Amanda protested as she obediently returned to her chair, 'if I didn't get rid of it, what on earth would I do with a baby?'

'Well, either look after it like in *The Millstone* or have it adopted if you really can't bear the thought of keeping it. But you must tell the child's father. You must.'

'I couldn't,' she said, but even as she spoke a picture began to assemble itself in her mind. She would not have dreamed of telling Iris, but she knew that it was just as likely that the child was Anthony's, perhaps even more likely.

'What is it? You look quite different.'

Iris's sharp voice brought Amanda back to the present. She shut her mouth hurriedly and smiled as she shook her head.

'I couldn't do that. He's got his final schools this term.'

'Then wait until you can tell him. Amanda, we've been friends for ages.'

'Nearly two years,' she said in agreement.

'Please trust me in this.'

Amanda looked at her impeccable fingernails.

'I have always trusted you – and believed utterly in your

sophistication and your knowledge of the world. By the way, did you say that Comfort Gillingham had telephoned?'

Iris wondered for a moment whether Amanda's innumerable enemies were right in saying that she was completely hard and self-centred.

'Yes,' she said. 'I'd better go. Thanks for the whisky.'

'And thank you for the advice. I'm not . . . I do appreciate your telling me what happened to you.'

Iris's round face relaxed slightly. She nodded.

'If it happened to me again I would go through with it and have the child,' she said before opening the door. 'Whatever it did to my career.'

You must be mad, thought Amanda, watching her go. She was glad to be alone to think about the extra twist to her predicament. Not, she told herself, that it was much of a predicament since she did not intend to have the child or to demand money or any kind of protection from its father, whichever man he was. But the possibility that the father might be Anthony did throw a slightly different light on things.

Amanda walked thoughtfully to the communal telephone, dialled the number of Comfort's studio telephone and thrust a fistful of half-crowns into the machine as soon as she heard Comfort's voice.

'Hello. It's Amanda here. You rang me.'

'Yes. A charming girl answered and promised to find you for me. Amanda, I've finished the portrait and we're planning the party for it. Before finally picking on a date I wanted to ask what the best day would be for you.'

'Ah,' said Amanda, playing for time as she considered her various options. A visit to London would be useful in finding the best doctor and arranging to have the abortion immediately after the end of term; and seeing Anthony again would help, too. 'A Friday evening or Saturday would really be best for me, but perhaps all your people would be going away for the weekend.'

'They'll stay for me,' said Comfort with superb confidence. 'Then we'll plump for the last Friday in May if that's all right with you.'

'Fine.'

'Good and I'd like to buy you a dress. Will you let me?'

'There's absolutely no need. I've plenty of clothes.'

'Humour me in this, Amanda,' said Comfort with a certain amount of steel in her voice. 'I want to point up the mermaidness of my model.'

'Oh, God! Not a coconut-shell bra and a glittery tail.'

'Don't be ridiculous. I take it you're a size ten?'

'Yes. But really . . .'

'Excellent. The party will begin at half past six and so I'd like you here by five-thirty so that you can change. Good-bye, Amanda.'

Determined to take a dress of her own so that if she disliked Comfort's choice or it did not fit she would not be forced to wear it, Amanda returned to her room.

CHAPTER 10

On the morning when Flixe's daughters were due to go back to boarding school, two days after she had taken her younger son to his train in tears, George Mayford rang up to invite her to lunch at the Etoile again.

'I ought not,' she said sadly. 'When I've dropped the girls at Paddington I have to see the agent and go through everything he wants me to do in the constituency before I start attacking the heaps and heaps of paper on my desk at home.'

'But we've only met once since your splendid party,' said George. 'Couldn't duty wait for a couple of hours? You must be so tired after the holidays and I suspect that you need a treat, too.'

It was that small, seductive 'too' which made Flixe smile to herself and decide to yield. Her voice was friendly as well as teasing when she asked: 'Is that the doctor speaking or the friend?'

'Both,' he said firmly and she could hear that he, too, was amused.

'Well, you're both right. A treat would be wonderful,' Flixe admitted, letting her thoughts wander. During the long and tiring interval since they had last met she had missed George enough to think seriously about how she might absorb him into her life without upsetting her children or the various people who were supporting her in one way or another. Loathing self-deception as she did, she had long since admitted to herself that she wanted him as a lover. Her imagination had begun to tantalise her with possibilities one day and then trouble her with their consequences the next until she did not know whether to give in to her instincts or not.

One evening she had telephoned Natalie, whose advice had been quite simple. 'If it will make you even a little happier than you are, you should do it,' Natalie had said. When Flixe had asked whether it might not be disloyal to Peter, his sister had almost snorted. 'It will do him no good wherever he is to think of you losing the possibility of even the smallest piece of fun. Let yourself off for a while, Flixe. All the other things in your life will seem less difficult if you do that sometimes.'

Flixe smiled in retrospect and said firmly: 'And it would be utter bliss to have lunch with you, George. Thank you. Can you manage twelve-thirty? That would give me enough time this afternoon to do some of what needs doing.'

'I'll have to shift a patient,' he said, making her feel a little guilty. 'But she's not too bad. It won't hurt her. Listen: unless you hear from me, I'll book a table for half past twelve.'

Flixe went straight upstairs to her daughters' bedrooms to help with their final packing. Their school trunks had been sent Passenger Luggage in Advance a week earlier, but they had to take night clothes, spongebags, and a change of shirt and underclothes in their overnight cases.

Fiona, at sixteen, was well able to cope, not only with her packing but also with concealing whatever regrets she felt at leaving home once again, but Sophie clung to Flixe and poured out her sorrows about the horrors of the art classes she loathed and the fiendish biology mistress, who apparently hated her and picked on her.

'Oh, grow up!' said Fiona as she listened. 'Anyone would think you were a squit of ten instead of fourteen. You're in the middle-fifth, for goodness' sake. You ought to be able to cope. You've got 'O' levels next year; you can't be such a snivelling baby.'

'Fiona, hush!' Flixe's voice was firm and so was the arm she held around her younger daughter's shoulders. 'You may have felt perfectly happy and sure of yourself in the middle-fifth, but that doesn't mean that Sophie's sadness is either unreal or unjustified. You must try to be gentler.'

'And even if I am a snivelling baby, at least I haven't got disgusting spots and a huge fat bottom,' said Sophie, who suffered from only a few discreet pimples. Flixe waited for a storm of tears or a burst of fury, but none came.

Fiona, who had known perfectly well that she was merely masking her own, different, miseries by lashing out at her weaker sister, shrugged off the insult and turned away. Flixe, her mind divided between the prospect of lunch with George and all the problems of work she had not done during the children's holidays, Andrew's unhappiness and ill-tempered removal to Paris, and the scarlet, tearstained face of twelve-year-old Nicholas, who had gone back to school two days before, wondered how other mothers of big families coped with their children's emotional difficulties.

She had tried several times to talk to them about Peter's death and let them explore and understand their feelings about it as a good mother should, but her own wounds were still so raw that she was clumsy and seemed only to make their unhappiness worse. As they turned away from her, it sometimes seemed as though they blamed her for their father's death.

Flixe ached for them, but there seemed to be nothing she could do to help. It worried her that she used the existence of George and the possibility of making love with him as a plaster for her hurts, but it was so effective even when she could not see him that she ignored her conscience.

159

The thought of lunching with him got her through the painful last two hours of the holidays and helped her to see her daughters off at the station with all the illusion of comforting certainty that they expected of her. Fiona allowed herself to be kissed, which she had rarely done since her father's death, and Sophie hugged her mother so tightly that Flixe begged for mercy.

'You will come and take us out on the first visiting Saturday, won't you? Mummy, please, please.'

Flixe, who hated lies and secrecy even in the interests of peace, put her arms gently round Sophie and said: 'Darling, I can't. Auntie Ming will be coming to take you out that day because I have to organise a dance in Berkshire in the evening. Even if I did come first thing, I'd have to take you back to school straight after lunch, which would be horrid for you.'

Sophie's bottom lip jutted out and tears welled in her blue eyes again.

'It would be better than not seeing you at all.'

'Not really. Ming and Mark always give you the most wonderful time, don't they? You do much more exciting things with them, after all.'

'Yes, but it's not the same. Mummy, please.'

Flixe looked at her, longing to send her off with a comforting half-lie, but she knew that it would lead only to worse misery in the end. She shook her head.

'But there'll be half-term four weeks after that and we'll have a lovely time then. And I promise to keep the second visiting Saturday free for you.'

'Really promise, whatever happens?'

'Really. Time to get on, Sophie.' She kissed her younger daughter and watched her climb into the train. 'Fee, darling, take care of yourself.'

'I thought you were going to say "take care of Sophie",' she said, sounding cross but looking frighteningly vulnerable under the truculence.

Flixe shook her head.

'You matter quite as much, and I know that things are just as difficult for you as they are for her, even though you don't let it show so much. I do understand; and I do love you.'

Fiona checked that there was no one close enough to hear her mother's embarrassing announcement.

'I know,' she said gruffly, looking at her feet. Flixe felt amply rewarded for all the exhausting and emotionally expensive efforts she had made over the last four weeks.

'That's what matters.' She held Fiona's head for a moment, dropped a last kiss on her pimply forehead and went away.

In the tube on the way to Great Portland Street station, she tried to think what more she could do for her children. Connie's blessed paying of their school fees meant that they were safe, cared for, and learning for the next twelve weeks. Flixe knew she ought to write to Connie again and sighed. The thought of the unwritten letters in her head added to the weight of debts she carried with her all the time.

George stood up as soon as she walked through the door of the green-painted restaurant, and when she reached their table he took her hand. For a moment she thought that he was going to kiss it, but either he thought better of the flamboyant gesture or had never even considered it. He merely shook her hand and pulled out her chair.

'I ordered a bottle of Corton Charlemagne,' he said as he gestured towards the ice-bucket. 'Is that all right?'

Flixe, whisked straight back to memories of Peter, sat unable to speak.

'What is it? Do you hate it?'

Understanding that her face must be looking bleak, she managed to smile a little and shake her head.

'No one could hate it,' she said eventually. 'It was my husband's favourite white wine. For a moment I . . .'

'I am sorry. Shall I get them to take it away?'

'Certainly not. I love it too. I always have. Besides,' she added, looking at the bottle and remembering how appallingly expensive it was, 'they've opened it. You couldn't possibly waste a wine like that. Pour me some, please, George.'

Savouring the utterly familiar richness of the wine in her mouth before she swallowed it, Flixe pretended to look at the menu. She felt George's hand on hers and looked up.

'I keep getting things wrong, don't I?'

'You couldn't have known that it used to be our chosen celebration wine,' she said with another tight smile. 'Besides it's not the memory of past celebrations that's distressing me.'

'Oh?' The monosyllable, which might have sounded uninterested, critical or forbidding, seemed genuinely encouraging. Flixe shrugged.

'You probably don't know anything about it, but my husband left us in a slightly parlous state financially, and the memory of things like expensive white burgundy, which we consumed without thinking for twenty years, positively burns these days.'

'I'm sorry,' he said again, looking really upset. 'I ought to have used my imagination a bit.'

'Why on earth should you?' Flixe's voice sounded much warmer. 'You weren't to know.'

He looked at her, thinking how curious her honesty was: not only unexpected but also touching. It made him feel far more protective of her than he had expected, and it also forced him into greater frankness than he had planned.

'I had heard something about the parlous state,' he said gently, 'and it made me want to give you a lavish treat. That's why I ought to have used my imagination to think of how it might seem.'

'People do talk, don't they?'

'I am afraid they do, Felicity. And they always will. It's part of the human condition.'

162

'Not that I mind much,' she went on, smiling at him more easily. 'The real destructiveness happens when people keep secret things that are so explosive that when they are betrayed – as they always are in the end – other people get mortally hurt instead of simply wounded. But I'm sorry you've been involved in my dull story.'

'Felicity.'

'Yes?' she said, surprised by the urgency in his voice.

'Nothing ... No. Let's start again.' His smooth face creased into a smile of self-mockery that almost hurt her. From feeling like a victim, she suddenly became the comforter.

'What's the matter, George?'

'For a psychiatrist I am remarkably bad at dealing with my own emotions.'

'I thought that was part of the job description,' said Flixe, laughing.

'Perhaps. Listen ...'

'Have you decided, sir?'

The waiter stood too close to their table to be ignored.

'Not quite,' said George. 'Give us a few minutes.' Turning back to Flixe, he added, 'Perhaps we ought to choose.'

'Sole for me,' she said when she had read the menu carefully. 'And spinach. Nothing to start.'

'We'll both have sole,' George said to the waiter and ordered a selection of vegetables. They watched the man go. George refilled their glasses.

'I think I must come clean,' he said.

'Yes. That would be a good idea.'

'When I met you at the Kinghovers, I was greatly taken with you,' he began and then stopped.

'I know.' Flixe's face was illuminated by a smile that made her look young and remarkably pretty again. 'I must say it was a delight to see.'

George, slightly taken aback, said: 'I'm glad. And so when I asked you to that first lunch I was following my usual ...

163

technique, I suppose you could call it.' He stopped again and drank some wine. Flixe was puzzled and said so.

'Then, after you had left that evening, I asked Diseholme about you and when he told me about your husband I revised my plans and thought it would be unfair to pursue you at such a time. Besides,' he broke off and after a moment added coolly, 'I realised we would have to try to be ordinary friends, and I'd liked you enough to want that if I could have nothing else.'

'Ah. What a pity.'

George put his big wine glass back on the table. The self-mockery and the warmth had both left his face. His greenish eyes looked alert but worried too.

'Don't look so anxious,' said Flixe with a frank smile as she remembered Natalie's encouragement. 'I just thought that being simply friends might not be enough for either of us. I think we could have given each other quite a lot of pleasure one way and another, and in this bloody world a little pleasure doesn't come amiss.'

There was silence until he said slowly: 'Do you mean what I think you mean?'

'That I would like to go to bed with you? Is that so strange?'

The waiter appeared at his elbow then with two hot plates. Flixe appeared to be quite unconcerned that he might have overheard what she said. When he had arranged the plates and gone to fetch the fish, George answered her.

'It is strange and wonderful. You are a rare woman, Felicity.'

She smiled again, looking confident in a way he had not seen before. As soon as the waiter had laid the fish tenderly on the warmed plate, she started to eat with obvious pleasure.

'Eat up, George,' she said when she saw that he was letting his fish get cold while he gazed at her across the flowers in their silver vase. 'I'm not rare at all, you know: just full of

164

common sense. We are neither of us married and we'd be hurting no one. There's nothing particularly important about sex, but it does – as far as I can remember – considerably enhance one's life.'

He raised his glass in a toast.

'It's not the kind of thing a psychiatrist should say, but that is a very sane way of looking at things.'

'Good. I must say even at my worst I've never felt troubled about my sanity. May I have some more wine?'

He refilled her glass, still clearly in a state of mild shock. Flixe laughed suddenly and apologised.

'Whatever for?' asked George.

'It's just struck me that part of your fun might lie in actual seduction. Have I done you out of a treat?'

He shook his head.

'Not if you mean conquest or persuading someone against her will. I always used to cherish the idea that somewhere in the world might be a woman as free and aware of herself and generous as you.' He smiled. 'But I relegated it long ago to the graveyard of youthful fantasies and pursued my increasingly slick routines of flowers, lunches and what you call seduction.'

There was enough bitterness in his voice to make Flixe wince. Misunderstanding her distaste, he added: 'Never seduction of the young, though. I've always drawn the line at the young or the damaged – or my patients.'

'I should jolly well hope so too. But you don't sound as though you enjoyed the chase: that's what seems so sad.'

George sat back in his chair and allowed the waiter to take away their plates.

'Pudding?'

'No, thank you. Just coffee for me.'

He ordered it and sat twirling his almost empty wine glass between his hands.

'You're right in a way. I always set out telling myself and them that what I wanted was a simple, sexual friendship – and that's what we always had, sometimes simpler and sometimes more sexual than others.'

'But?' Flixe was interested not just in his experiences but also in the light that they might throw on what Peter had really been seeking when he strayed.

'But I suppose that there was something else I wanted,' he said slowly, not looking at her. 'You know, you're having the most extraordinary effect on me. I don't think I'd have admitted that to anyone else.' He looked up, puzzled.

'Do you know what you were looking for?'

'If I said "absolution" would you laugh?' The sound of his voice was frivolous, but Flixe took what he had said seriously.

'Cry more likely,' she said after a long pause. He noticed that her voice was shaking, but he did not interrupt her. 'It's what Peter gave me and what in dying he seems to have taken away.'

There was an expression in George Mayford's eyes then that Flixe could not understand. There seemed to be gratitude in it, but shock and fear as well as other things that she could not decipher, and she did not know which was the most important.

'I have to go to Rome for a long weekend at the beginning of June,' he said abruptly, 'for a medical conference. Would you consider coming too? It's not the half-term weekend for any of your children, because I've checked, and as it's the beginning of the Whitsun recess you presumably won't have any constituency duties either.'

Flixe thought about his proposition and the care he must have taken to find out whether she would be free. She drank the last of the wine in her glass.

'Only if you'll come to bed with me first,' she said frankly. 'Gina told me that she thought you must take your in-amoratas abroad and I don't much fancy taking part in a well-practised routine.'

He laughed.

'Don't worry on that score, Felicity. The things you've said today have smashed my poor routine beyond repair. I'm grateful, you know, and yes, thank you. I'll accept your invitation if you'll accept mine.'

'Excellent. Andrew will be back from Paris tomorrow and he doesn't go up to Oxford until next week.'

'So it must be either tonight or wait for seven days?'

'It does sound rather as though I'm holding a pistol to your head, but it's simply that I don't want to risk upsetting him. He has enough to cope with . . .' Her voice died and she picked up her coffee cup.

'He's a charming boy,' said George, following her lead, 'and it was kind of him to take such trouble with Gina.'

'What?' Flixe's face flushed with pleasure. 'Did he take her out?'

'Yes. Two nights after your dinner party. He rang her up on the spur of the moment, took her to some restaurant in the King's Road and gave her a lot of advice about getting the best out of Oxford. You look surprised. Do you mind that he saw her?'

'To tell you the truth,' said Flixe, when she had drunk her coffee, 'I'm delighted, but I never thought it would happen. He gave me no clues at all, but then perhaps he wouldn't.'

'Were you trying to make a match between them? How salutary! I'd suspected that you wanted to see me when you invited us.'

'I've always been one for economy of effort.' Flixe was delighted with the light-hearted turn their lunch had taken. 'And it crossed my mind that I might achieve both. But my brother-in-law told me I would do no good with Gina.'

'It struck me that your son was violently in love with that other girl, I must say.'

'He does seem to be, and she torments him. That's why he fled to Paris. I thought that Gina's kinder charms might have struck him as forcibly as they struck me. Perhaps they will yet. Who knows?'

'I hope so.' He looked at his watch. 'I must go. Shall I see you this evening?'

'That would be lovely.'

'My last patient is due at six-thirty and so I could be in Kensington by about eight if that's all right.'

'Perfect.' Flixe stood up. 'Thank you for lunch, George, and for . . .'

'Wanting you?' he suggested when she seemed unable to find the right words.

'That too.'

'Good,' he said as he ushered her out of the restaurant. 'May I book you a room in Rome? The decent hotels fill up rather quickly at this time of year.'

Flixe hesitated. It sounded very expensive. His distinguished face went slightly pink.

'I don't know how to put this without your thinking that it's part of the routine, but it would be . . . Hang it! I intend to pay for both of us.'

It was Flixe's turn to blush then, which she did so vividly that he almost hugged her, surrounded though they were by the hurrying denizens of Charlotte Street.

'I feel as though I ought to protest, but we can't argue about it now,' she managed to say. 'So I'd better just say: thank you. That would be lovely.'

That evening he came to her house, bringing neither flowers nor presents, which pleased her. She kissed his cheek when she had shut the door behind him, took his coat and ushered him into the drawing room. Only then was there enough light for her to see his face properly. The golden tan seemed almost grey and the skin around his eyes and mouth looked dragged downwards. The whites of his eyes were reddened.

'Good heavens, you look tired,' she said. 'What about a drink?'

'That would be nice. I am rather. I had a badly distressed patient last thing and however carefully I keep my own emotions out of my work, there are times when I can't help catching a reflection of theirs.'

He sounded not only exhausted but also badly discouraged. Flixe looked at him carefully.

'Come and have some whisky,' she said, putting the rest of her plans aside. It was quite clear to her that if they attempted to make love that evening it could only be a trial of strength for him and a disaster for them both.

As she poured their drinks, she added: 'Do you want to talk about it?'

'Yes,' he said simply, accepting the drink, 'but that would not be professional – or fair on you. After all,' he went on more lightly, 'we're here for some romantic dalliance.'

'I don't think so.' As he frowned, she added quickly: 'I'm not trying to tease you, but you look like a man who needs to go to bed on his own and quite soon. Sit down.'

Looking a little surprised, he sat on one of the two big cream-coloured sofas that stood on either side of the empty fireplace. Flixe sat at the other end of the sofa, pulled two trellised green cushions more comfortably behind her back and smiled at him.

'Was she suffering from exogenous depression?'

He smiled at her question and shook his head.

'He. No, I don't think so, although he is determined to believe that he is, because that seems less irrational and therefore easier to accept. He's been coming to me for months, finding the most ingenious explanations for his continuing trouble, as he calls it, but it's been clear to me for some time that his depression must have a biochemical cause.'

'You sound as though there's nothing you can do in that case. That seems unlikely. What is it that troubles you so much?'

George crossed his legs and drank some more whisky. He looked uncomfortable.

'He used to see one of the interventionist psychiatrists,

who tried him on all sorts of anti-depressants and ECT and got nowhere. He'd improve for a while and then the depression would come crunching back. Then he tried a Freudian analyst, who did not help at all; and so he came to me because I rarely use any of those methods.'

'Then what do you use?'

'I use a mixture of therapeutic techniques and exercises to lead them to listen to their unhappiness so that they can try to change whatever it is in their lives that is causing the trouble. It is exceedingly upsetting to fail – particularly with a man as intelligent and attractive as this patient.'

'Is he still attractive in depression?' Flixe asked, having seen herself becoming less and less able to reach anyone else as the grip of her feelings tightened.

George merely nodded.

'And is your failure with him why you wanted absolution?'

'What? Sorry to sound so rough. No. That's older and much more painful.' He bit his lower lip. 'Although you may be more accurate than I realised. It is possible that this failure has latched on to things from the past and exacerbated them.'

'I've known that happen,' said Flixe gently. 'More whisky?'

'No, thanks. This is plenty.' He sat holding the glass in both hands as though for physical warmth. He even shivered.

'And you?' he said with an obvious effort to get back to normality. 'What is it that you need forgiving for?'

'Lots of things, but you don't want to hear about them. You've had a whole day of other people's miseries and failings.'

'This is different.'

Flixe looked at the blackness of the empty fireplace. Although it was May, the weather was both cold and damp and she would have loved a fire, just as she would have loved the flowers she always used to have in the drawing room whatever the season. She had bought the whisky even though it was an extravagance, knowing they might both find the evening easier with a drink to relax them.

'Being frivolous, a flirt, lazy . . . that sort of thing,' she said seriously. 'It's very uninteresting and I ought to have got over it all long ago. They're adolescent worries.' She looked at him to see if he wanted to hear more and then added carefully: 'The shock of discovering quite how parlous my finances are rather underlined all that, you see; and the fact that my children and I now depend on three women who are quite the opposite of all those things, rubs my face in the fecklessness for which I used to resent being criticised.'

He said nothing and his face was so severe that Flixe felt impelled to explain that she did not expect him to help her. At that he put down his whisky glass and reached across the expanse of down-filled cushions to take both her hands.

'Don't undersell yourself,' he said urgently. 'The most important thing I've learned is that we all have a duty to value ourselves reasonably. If you're concentrating on your weaknesses, make yourself think about the other side – your strengths. Weigh it all up. Don't ignore the good bits of your character just because they're easy for you to get right. Even if you don't have to struggle for them, they are still valuable.'

Flixe sat rather stiffly with her hands in his, her lips slightly parted.

'That makes sense,' she said at last, once more wishing that in her sisters' search for a doctor who could help her they had lighted on George Mayford. Then it struck her that if they had she would never be sitting on the sofa with her hands in his.

He raised them to his lips then and kissed them both, one after the other, turning each one so that he could kiss the palm as well.

'I'm glad. And I'm extraordinarily glad that you let me come here tonight. In a way . . .' His voice tailed off as though he could not bring himself to put words to his thought.

'It meant more than if we had actually made love?'

suggested Flixe. 'Yes, I think it has for me too. Thank you, George. But you ought to get some rest now.'

He got up off the sofa and carried his empty whisky glass to the drinks tray. She joined him there and went with him to the front door. He kissed her then, gently, holding her shoulders.

'If I promise not to try to seduce you, may I ring you up again soon, Felicity?'

'I should be very sad if you didn't,' she answered, 'and when the time is right we will take each other to bed.'

'Indeed we shall. I look forward to it.'

'Now go to bed, George. You look all in.'

He took his coat from her, put it on and left without another word.

As she heated herself a tin of tomato soup, Flixe thought of Andrew and hoped that he might one day be able to find some of the solace that the last, brief, half-hour had given her. She was afraid that if he persisted in believing Amanda to be the only woman he could love, he would have to do without the solace.

CHAPTER 11

Amanda found herself increasingly disturbed by the things Iris had said to her and by her own growing awareness of what was happening to her body. At first it had felt more like an illness than a child, but that sensation was changing.

On Friday she went to the second seminar of term and read her essay on Giotto. She seemed to have lost her power to achieve effortless mastery over her fellow students and one or two produced some remarkably sarcastic criticisms of the main thrust of her argument. Their tutor was clearly as much interested in the disagreements as in Amanda's ideas and probed them all for reasons behind their increasingly personal attacks on each other.

Realising eventually that some hitherto concealed weakness in herself was making her less successful fellows turn on her, Amanda summoned up all her resources and fought back. She won a grudging admission from her main challenger in the end and a commendation from the tutor, but it had been both exhausting and frustrating.

'Trivial,' she muttered to herself as she splashed her way back along the rainy walkway to her room. That, too, seemed stifling in its littleness and when a shy girl from the seminar knocked on the door and wanted to continue the discussion, Amanda decided that she had had quite enough of the university.

'Sorry,' she said, 'I've got to go into Norwich.'

'I'll come in with you. I've got some shopping to do.'

'All right.' Amanda hoped that the lack of enthusiasm in her voice would be enough to make it clear that she wanted no company at all, but it did not seem to have any effect on Monica. 'I'll meet you on the bus.'

Monica ran off to fetch her money and a coat, leaving Amanda to walk to the bus stop as quickly as her dignity would allow in the hope that she would catch a bus before Monica appeared. She was lucky and watched the girl run panting to the stop just as the bus pulled away. Amanda waved and mimed apologies from the back seat and then stared out through the rain-splattered window at the depressing houses they passed during the four-mile journey to Norwich, a surprising number of which seemed to be dentists' surgeries.

She left the bus at the Tombland stop, not at all sure where she was going to go except that it was to be miles away from any shop where she might find herself embroiled with Monica. The rain had stopped and a faint sunlight was escaping through gaps in the grey clouds. Bypassing the gateway into the cathedral close, Amanda walked down Palace Street towards the river.

There seemed to be a muddy path leading along the bank and she turned into it, glad to be quite alone for once. The only people she saw as she walked past shabby red-brick factories, small bridges and mounds of muddy blackberry bushes were a few old men sullenly fishing in the green water. What could their lives be like? she asked herself, watching them as they perched between buildings or on old brick steps in the cold and damp, staring only at the water.

There were plenty of birds, but the old men ignored them, not even wincing at the plaintive yet predatory shrieks of the seagulls that swooped and circled round the factories. Amanda disliked them, preferring the bustling red-beaked black-feathered moorhens and the domestic-looking ducks that nosed among the willow branches on the surface of the water.

She walked on, ignoring the mud that caked her shoes and the brambles that occasionally caught at her clothes, thinking of nothing much until the rain began to fall heavily again. Then she looked round, wondering where the nearest shelter might be and saw the spire of the cathedral to her right. Retracing her steps to the next break in the buildings, she cut up through a narrow street and made her way, with some back-tracking, to the cathedral close and in to the great dark building itself.

Someone was playing the organ and she immediately backed towards the door. A pleasant breezy voice stopped her.

'Can I help?'

Amanda turned her head and saw a friendly-looking elderly man dressed in grey flannels and a tweed jacket.

'I just thought I might be interrupting,' she said in a whisper.

'Oh no. Make yourself at home,' he said in an ordinary voice. 'There'll be choir practice in a few minutes. Find a chair and listen.'

He went off towards the shadowy back of the big church and Amanda was so surprised that she did as he suggested and chose a chair near a pillar. There she sat, looking up with interest. She was pleased in a vague way by the mixture of Norman arches and Gothic vaulting. She liked the bigness and the quietness of the cathedral, too, a quietness that seemed only exaggerated by the organist who was repeating the same little bit of music over and over again until he got it right.

There were quite a lot of people about, she noticed after a while. A young man was polishing chairs further up the nave and there were two women arranging flowers in immense fan shapes at either side of the altar, while another woman was sorting hymn books at a table near the west door.

The choir materialised after a while and Amanda sat peacefully listening to them, glad to be in a place where no one knew her and where no one she knew could get at her. Utterly anonymous and glad to be so, she listened to the choir, singing first hymns, most of which were familiar from her school days, and then what she thought of as more 'churchy' music: psalms and introits and a gloria.

After nearly half an hour the organ stopped, the choir-master said something to his charges, which she did not catch, and a man started to sing unaccompanied, to be joined after a few notes by the others. To Amanda's un-educated and uncomprehending ear the music sounded only vaguely familiar at the beginning, but gradually she pinned it down and knew that it was the piece of plainsong Anthony had played her.

She felt the same pleasure in the disciplined yet sensuous sounds as she had in his room. As she listened to them, she remembered him as he had been before they made love. Thinking of the immediate approval in his eyes as he saw her for the first time and the way he had talked to her that evening, the idea of telling him about her pregnancy began to seem possible.

If she were to present him with their child as well as with her complete love, she might be able to cure his misery, put right the damage her mother had done, win that battle, and achieve the great thing that she had often felt was waiting for her. For a moment she felt powerful again and, for the first time since she had suspected her condition, happy.

The chant ended in a dying trail of perfectly distinct notes and there was silence. Into the happiness the music and her memories had brought her, came a sharp, bitter thought. There was no guarantee that the child did belong to her and Anthony.

Through her mind surged a wave of anger that Andrew should have interfered so disastrously in her life. She knew perfectly well that he had not forced her to sleep with him. In her ignorance of what really mattered she had been more than willing, but he ought not to have been so ignorant. He ought to have been sensible for both of them.

She shrugged, knowing that her petulance was stupid, but the muddle she was in seemed too unfair to be borne. Loving Anthony was the answer to her long yearning to be valued for herself; the thought of bringing him not only fulfilment but also a child seemed to satisfy so many of her longings, and yet she had to face the fact that, because of Andrew's idiotic infatuation and her own weakness in yielding to it, she could not be sure that the gift she wanted to offer Anthony was real.

The soloist started to sing again and gradually the words began to make sense to Amanda as she recognised the magnificat.

Some of the other things Iris had said came back to Amanda and she began to wish that she was a religious believer. That, at least, would have made everything simpler, she thought. Then there would be nothing to decide, merely things to arrange and endure. She put both hands on her stomach and tried to think of what was there as a living child.

It did not seem possible. Instead she tried to imagine what her life might be like if she did allow it to be born. There would be no hardship in giving up her place at Norwich. She could probably get a job with one of the magazines or even one of the major auction houses on the strength of the work she had already done, and if not with them then perhaps with a publisher or a gallery somewhere. Settling more comfortably into the hard chair, with her legs crossed and her hands relaxed again in her lap, Amanda ignored the thought of Andrew Suvarov and started to dream.

The first thing to do would to be spend her accumulated money on a tiny house somewhere so that Anthony felt no pressure to keep her. Then she could leave Norwich, inform him of the baby's existence and her own ability to maintain it, book herself into a London maternity hospital and await its birth. There would of course be fights with her mother. But her father would understand, she knew. Her life might be odd, but it would be entirely feasible.

Anthony could visit her and the child, finding all the simple happiness her mother had denied him and learning to be young again. There would be none of the arguments every married couple had because they would have simply chosen to be together. He could contribute to the wages of a nanny. Amanda would work and the child would grow without any of the pressures she herself had felt all her life. Her child would be free. It would know the meaning of love because it would have been born of nothing but love. It would, she thought, be a happy child. Tears welled in the corners of her eyes as she thought of the differences between what she had had and what she would manage to give her child.

The entire choir was singing again in some glorious, triumphant chorale about joy. Amanda was not sentimental enough to believe that it held a message for her, but she could not help feeling that it was remarkably appropriate. Moved by a diffuse feeling of gratitude, she considered saying a prayer of thanks and pleading for the child, but the thought of looking a fool stopped her. She waited, quiet in her chair, until the end of choir practice and then she left the cathedral.

It was not until she was back in her little room on campus that she faced the fact she would one day have to tell not only Anthony but also Andrew. Even if she did not tell him, he would be sure to find out that she had borne a child and would assume that it was his.

'Blast and damn and bloody hell!' she shouted.

After the happy pictures she had invented of life as the mother of Anthony's baby, the thought of an abortion seemed horrible. But telling Andrew that she had slept with someone else the day after him seemed not so much difficult as impossible. Amanda needed someone to talk to, someone sensible and knowledgeable who would not judge or come to the problem with preconceived ideas about the rights and wrongs of abortion and who would be kind. The only person she knew who might be all those things was her godmother, Flixe Suvarov. That she should also be Andrew's mother and therefore impossible to consult seemed an unfair trick of a malign fate.

CHAPTER 12

Flixe found herself deluged with constituency problems when she got back to work properly after the school holidays. Michael Diseholme seemed to have done very little to sort out the difficulties that had been presented to him during his surgeries, and there was a lot for Flixe to take over. Following up his cases and her own, writing the necessary letters and nagging the relevant government departments seemed to take an infinity of time and distracted her from her other work, which was becoming urgent.

Discussing final arrangements with the florist who was to provide decorations for the Kirkwaters' dance the next day, Flixe kept forgetting things she had meant to say and began to worry that she was muddling the plans with others for later dances, and went over and over her notes to make sure everything was correct.

Leaving at last, and wondering whether she had thoroughly alienated the florist whose services were important to the success of nearly all the dances, Flixe drove quickly to the hairdresser who was to wash and set her hair and then on to Ming's house to collect the dress and jewellery they had chosen together.

Seeing how tired and nervous Flixe was, Ming said: 'Why not stay and have a scratch supper with me? Mark's got one of his client dinners tonight and the boys are in bed, so I'm on my own. Do stay.'

For a moment Flixe looked tempted.

'It would be heaven,' she said at last, 'but I mustn't. If I'm out of reach of all my notes and my own telephone, I'll only worry more.'

'Well, have a drink at least.'

'All right. Yes, it would be nice.'

They went down from Ming's lace-and-silver bedroom to the coral drawing room, where she poured out two glasses of gin and tonic, adding ice from a cork ice-bucket and lemon from a small green pottery dish decorated with clumsily painted orange and blue fish.

'That's nice,' said Flixe with a more natural smile.

'Isn't it? I feel idiotically proud of the boys when they produce anything usable. Michael did this. It's a bit lumpy, but it always makes me smile.'

'I wish I'd had a mother like you.' Flixe looked wistful. 'Sorry, that was idiotic.'

'I don't think it was. Mother had relaxed a bit by the time Annie and I were born, but you and Gerry came in for all the ferocity of her weird ideas about children. It must have been awful. I can vaguely remember some of it.'

'But not as well as the arguments, I suspect.' Some of the old teasing was back in Flixe's voice.

'Don't remind me.' Ming shuddered. 'How I hated them! Hence my feeble, no doubt enraging, efforts to make peace between you all.'

'You still do that a bit. I've noticed. It's touching these days.'

Ming got up to refill their glasses.

'We've all kept some of the old ways,' she said, turning her head to look at her sister. 'Think how angry Gerry still is.'

'I know, and yet both parents liked her best.' Flixe looked

down at her watch. 'Help! I must go, Ming. You've been sweet, but I mustn't have a second drink. Don't let Sophie and Fee be too tiresome tomorrow.'

'I won't. But it won't be difficult: they're always beautifully behaved whenever we take them out from school. If it's decent weather I thought we might go to Oxford and take them on the river for a picnic. My twins always like that. Good luck with the dance.'

Flixe's smile shrank.

'It's absurd to be so worried. I've been organising all kinds of parties quite successfully for years without worrying at all. I suppose it's just that it is so important to get it right now.'

'You'll do fine,' said Ming, touching her arm. 'You always do.'

Flixe kissed her and drove carefully home, thinking yet again of all the things that might go wrong. The most likely cause of failure would be terrible weather and before she went to bed that night Flixe leaned out of her window, peering up at the dark-clouded sky and begging it to clear as earnestly as a child on the eve of her birthday.

When her alarm rang at eight o'clock the next morning, the first thing she did as she got out of bed was to pull back the heavy curtain so that she could look out of the window. Discovering that the sky was a clear blue and that the few clouds were white and as wispy as a chiffon scarf, she smiled and went downstairs to make herself a mug of instant coffee. She took it and a banana back to bed to breakfast in comfort.

There, alternately burning her mouth on the coffee and soothing it with bites of banana, she read through her copy of the careful timetable she had drawn up of the day's activities. With country dances, Flixe's usual practice was to arrive at the house in mid-afternoon to check that everything was as she had planned, but Ann Kirkwaters had begged her to spend the entire day with them, promising to pay an extra twenty-five guineas. Reluctant to sacrifice the money, Flixe had suppressed her instinctive dislike of the proposition and accepted.

As soon as she had finished her simple breakfast, she dressed in a pair of jeans and a comfortably loose blue sweater, packed, and locked up the house.

The drive to the Kirkwaters' house in Berkshire usually took an hour and a half, but there was a traffic jam in Hammersmith and so Flixe was half an hour later than she had planned. As she arrived, she was relieved to see the lorry that had brought the marquee and the florist's van already parked in the drive.

Ann appeared at the front door, obviously upset, as Flixe brought her car to a stop at the foot of the steps. Thinking how much easier it would be to do her job without the clients who made it possible, she still managed to smile cheerfully.

'Hello!' she called brightly through the open window of her little car, hoping to deflect whatever outburst Ann might be contemplating.

'Thank God you're here!'

'What's up? You look distraught,' said Flixe as she got out of her car.

'I am at my wits' end. Stephen is being difficult and Jemima's horse is ill and she's howling upstairs. She'll look ghastly tonight and she's due at the hairdresser's in an hour. She refuses to go with me and she hasn't even passed her driving test. And naturally Stephen won't take her because he's cross with me. They really are so tiresome, the pair of them, and I simply can't bear it.'

'Don't worry, Ann. Just leave Jemima alone and ignore Stephen. We've plenty of time to sort out swollen eyes. Cold tea-bags are marvellous. I can take her to the hairdresser's if you tell me where it is. Calm down. Whatever you do, don't tell her to stop crying. All right?'

'Well, I suppose you know best.' There was considerable doubt in Mrs Kirkwaters' plaintive voice. Flixe found it hard to remember her as the cheerful, excitable schoolgirl she had been when they first knew each other.

'Good. Now I must go and see that the flower people have interpreted my drawings properly. Are they down at the pool?'

'Yes, and that's another thing. Stephen is certain they'll start throwing each other in if we have the discotheque down there. Not the flower girls, I mean, but the children tonight. He's making my life impossible, Flixe.'

'It's too late to worry about the pool now. And they're not exactly children.'

'I suppose not, although Jemima behaves like one all the time. But Stephen wants us to arrange some kind of covering over the pool and I don't know what to do and he doesn't help at all. It's too bad of you not to have thought of it.'

'The discotheque chaps will be disappointed if you decide to cover the pool,' said Flixe in a neutral voice. 'A lot of their lighting effects suggest reflections from the pool even though they're artificial. That's why the decoration of the poolhouse is going to be so simple.'

She saw despair on Ann's face and added impatiently: 'Everyone can swim nowadays. If Stephen is seriously bothered, he can always patrol the pool and fish out anyone who gets into trouble. That'll give him something to do tonight and keep him out of your hair.'

Ann said nothing, but she directed at Flixe a look that was full of coyness, complicity and something else she could not interpret.

'Honestly, Ann,' she said, ignoring whatever unspoken message her client was trying to send her, 'it is too late to do anything about a reliable hard cover for it and anything else would be much more dangerous than the open water. I'll see you later.'

Flixe left her suitcase in the back of the car and walked round the side of the house, down the steps to the lawn where the tent was being put up, through a gap between the magnificent box hedges, and down more of the grey stone

184

steps to the pool. The summer-house was at the far end, but even from where she stood she could see that the plans she had drawn up a month earlier had been carried out precisely.

The three matching pairs of round-headed french windows were all open and the garden furniture had been removed and stored elsewhere. Lavish garlands of shiny evergreens had been strung along the plain white walls and the florist's two assistants were up step-ladders fixing oranges at intervals along the garlands. In each corner of the room stood life-size, mounted cut-out photographs of classical statues and there were large flowering orange trees in artifical stone tubs on either side of the dais where the men running the discotheque would play their records and organise their lights. Twenty of the golfing umbrellas were standing in more tubs on either side of the central french windows.

Everything looked all right there and so Flixe went up into the house to talk to the chief florist who was producing formal vases for the hall and the dining room, before moving on to the marquee. She had no anxieties either, and seemed to bear no malice for the muddles of the previous afternoon, which left Flixe free to take her luggage from the car, hang up Ming's stylish evening dress, and sort out her papers.

She spent the rest of the morning, clipboard in hand, checking that everything was under control. The tent was up and correctly lined with yellow-and-white striped canvas, and the dance floor seemed properly springy. Flixe herself had brought yellow tablecloths for the big round tables that ringed the floor in the marquee, and as soon as she had spread them out the florists transferred their wares into the tent.

They left at half past twelve, having put low vases of yellow and white roses on each of the tables and hung matching arrangements on each of the pillars that supported the tent's roof, as well as assembling a pair of towering pyramid arrangements on each side of the band's platform.

The drink had all been delivered the previous day and Flixe had most of it moved into the caterers' annexe of the marquee, leaving only what was needed for the house party's dinner. She also telephoned the caterers, who confirmed that they would arrive by four o'clock. They were to produce dinner for the ten-strong house party and ten more local guests, serve drinks throughout the dance and then cook and serve breakfast for everyone in the marquee from one o'clock the next morning.

When everything had been checked, Flixe went to pacify Jemima and escort her to the local hairdresser, who put up her long, straight brown hair into lavish ringlets.

They returned in time for a late and very tense picnic lunch, during which Stephen Kirkwaters reiterated his anxieties about drink-crazed debs drowning in the swimming-pool and his dislike of the nude statues in the summer-house, and Ann just managed to restrain herself from commenting on her daughter's swollen eyelids.

It was quite clear to Flixe that they had been quarrelling and she wondered if that was why Ann had insisted that she spend the whole day with them. Watching husband and wife more carefully, she noticed that they never met each other's eyes and, even when they were not actually arguing, they seemed to take pleasure in criticising whatever the other said. Determined not to let their difficulties spoil the dance for their daughter, Flixe insisted that both Ann and Jemima needed to rest.

Flixe herself slept for nearly an hour and woke feeling better than she had done for some time. So restored was she that she was able to offer Ann a mixture of calming and bracing that seemed to keep her angry panic in check. Stephen had disappeared into some private room of his own, which made the task much easier.

By the time the band and the discotheque arrived to set up their equipment, most of the arrangements were complete. The caterers had unpacked and checked all the hired glasses, organised the bars and set out cigarettes on each of the tables in the marquee and in the library of the house, where members of the older generation were to be allowed to play bridge if they could not stand the noise downstairs.

A man from the AA called to announce that he had fixed yellow-and-black signposts at each of the road junctions within a radius of five miles of the house. There were small paraffin lamps lining the drive and the entrance to the field where the cars were to be parked, and the Kirkwaters' gardener had instructions to light them at a quarter to ten.

Flixe surveyed it all with satisfaction and watched the young men rehearsing in the discotheque with a broad and delighted smile. Ignoring the house party guests who drove up at intervals during the late afternoon, Flixe worked on until just before seven, when she went upstairs to help Jemima dress. She found the girl sitting at her dressing-table wearing only underclothes and trying to paint eyeliner on her eyelids.

'I can't get it straight,' she said, turning to Flixe, who only just managed not to laugh at the sight of the panda-like eyes. 'Perhaps Mother's right and I am useless. It's going to be awful, isn't it?'

'No, it isn't. Would you like me to help with your eyes?'

'Oh, please.' Jemima turned back to look at herself. 'I have made rather a mess.'

'Don't worry.' Flixe proceeded to clean off all the smudged make-up, sent Jemima to wash her face and began all over again.

'I hope Mummy's paying you properly for all this,' said Jemima as she examined her painted face when Flixe had finished. 'I can't imagine your service usually includes this kind of thing.'

Flixe smiled at her reflection.

'Don't worry about it. You look lovely. Where's the dress?'

Jemima grimaced and gestured to her wardrobe. Suspended from a padded hanger hooked over one of the doors was a dress of white moiré silk cut on Victorian lines, with a lace-edged yoke and very tight sleeves that puffed out just below the shoulder. There was a stiff belt of black silk with a diamanté buckle.

'I wanted a bright colour, but she wouldn't agree.'

'Don't worry. This is lovely. You'll stand out beautifully in it, and you've plenty of colour in your face. Come on, let's put it on.'

Flixe buttoned up the thirty silk-covered buttons that did up the back and then gently turned Jemima round so that she could look at her.

'It's fine. Don't you worry. You look terrific.' She looked down at her watch.

'I'm going to have to nip off now and change myself or I'll be badly late.'

'Can't I come with you?'

'Why not see if your mother needs any help? I've been rushing about so much this afternoon that I must have a bath,' said Flixe, escaping for a few minutes to the blessed solitude of the remarkably comfortable, blue spare bedroom. It had its own bathroom and she ran herself a deep bath, soaking the tension and the tiredness out of her spine for a few minutes, before hurrying into the dress Ming had lent her.

Her newly set hair needed little doing to it and so it took her only ten minutes to tidy it, make up her face and screw in the pearl drop earrings that Ming had persuaded her to borrow. With the long string of matched pearls twisted into a triple-row choker round her neck, she was ready. The dark blue of the thick silk of her borrowed dress set off her hair and eyes well and the white ruffles that edged the deep V-neck disguised her lack of cleavage. Looking in the mirror, Flixe felt almost as secure in her own attractions as she had done before Peter's death.

She reached the drawing room to find that most of the house party had assembled. The first of them she recognised as she accepted a glass of gin and tonic from Stephen Kirkwaters was Gina Mayford.

'Hello, Mrs Suvarov,' said the girl, coming over to shake hands. 'It is good to see you. Jemima told me you were doing her dance and I hoped we'd have a chance to talk.'

'Gina, how nice! I expected to see you tonight, but I didn't realise that you'd be staying here. I do like your dress.'

Flixe, who would have said something complimentary whatever she thought, was being truthful. Unlike the flowery coventional clothes Gina usually wore, her dance dress was startling. Not only was it remarkably well cut, but it was made of bright pillar-box red silk, which made her mousy hair look blonder and her skin even clearer than usual.

'Do you? I did wonder if it wasn't a bit strong, but I was determined to have something striking for this dance at least.'

'It suits you.'

'I thought so too.' Flixe turned her head at the sound of George Mayford's deep voice.

'Why didn't you tell me you were going to be here?' she asked, unable to help a welcoming smile lighting her face.

He bent to kiss her cheek, momentarily touching her hand as he did so.

'I am not entirely sure,' he said with a smile that was supposed to express whimsical amusement but actually seemed confused and slightly irritable.

Flixe turned to say something casual to Gina to give George a moment to recover and saw that she had moved away to talk to Stephen Kirkwaters, who was looking as sulky as he had done all through lunch. Flixe turned back.

'What's the matter, George?'

Looking up into his face, she was puzzled by his expression, which seemed increasingly withdrawn. After her own surge of pleasure at the sight of him, his coolness was daunting and unexpected.

'Oh, patient problems,' he said abruptly. 'As usual.'

189

'I'm sorry.' Flixe waited for him to say something else and, when he did not, cast about for a suitable topic to raise. Feeling like a shy deb herself, she asked him how he knew the Kirkwaters.

'I met them a while ago,' he said, looking startled, 'and they've been remarkably good to Gina. Ann's promised to keep an eye on her and help her out a bit if she gets into scrapes. It's tricky being a motherless deb.'

'I can imagine. I must say I wish Andrew had been able to be here tonight to see Gina looking so stunning,' said Flixe, thinking it odd that George should imagine that his self-assured, charming daughter could need help from someone as silly as Ann Kirkwaters.

'Your son's not still in Paris, is he?'

Something in George's deep voice had changed. Flixe looked up at him, surprised, to see that he was looking more like himself.

'No. I am glad to say that a consciousness of the importance of his final schools sent him back to Oxford after the demo on the third of May, when the French authorities closed the Sorbonne. Why?'

'There's trouble in Paris. Worse trouble than usual, I mean. I thought you said he'd be back the day after we last met, but I wanted to be sure.'

The slightly upsetting coolness of his greeting had gone completely and Flixe was touched by his obvious concern for her son.

'What sort of trouble?' she asked. 'I've been running about all day here and haven't had a chance to listen to the news.'

'More riots at the Sorbonne. There's something about the French that leads to recurrences of their revolution and . . .'

'Oh, is that all?' Flixe sounded almost cheerful as she interrupted him.

Before George could do more than shake his head, Ann appeared to urge them all into the dining room for dinner. She ushered Flixe to a place on George's right with a coy little smile, whispering: 'Stephen insisted I put you next to George. It's true he's madly eligible, Flixe, but I honestly don't think he's your type. Best I could do, though. Sorry.'

Flixe raised her eyebrows at George, who either had not heard or pretended he had not. As soon as Ann had moved out of earshot, he said frankly: 'I don't know what she said, but whatever it was, please don't let it affect you. I don't think she knows all that much about me, kind though she's being to Gina.'

'I don't intend to,' said Flixe lightly. 'I've been ignoring Ann's advice ever since we first fell out over a midnight feast at school thirty-odd years ago. What's going on in Paris? Another sit-in?'

'It doesn't sound quite like the usual kind,' said George as Flixe moved to one side to allow a waitress to lay a plate of smoked salmon in front of her. 'The students started yesterday by demonstrating peacefully enough for the release of the comrades who were arrested on the third.'

'Yes, I heard that on the wireless yesterday. What happened?'

'They marched to the Sorbonne, collecting large amounts of support from the passers-by, and in the evening started erecting barricades around the university as though they expected a siege. The Communist Party announced their support in the small hours and then the Government seems to have panicked. They sent in the riot police.'

'Well, you can understand that, can't you?' said a bluff voice from the other side of Flixe. She had been sitting in appalled silence at the prospect of pitched battles on the streets of Paris.

'Tanks?' Flixe said, turning towards the man on her left, who had been introduced as Colonel Cooper.

'Not yet, but it may come to that. Good thing, too,' he said.

'It does sound from what Dr Mayford has been saying as though things were getting a bit out of hand,' she said, 'but

191

unleashing the riot police is surely going a bit far. They're ... Haven't they a reputation for sometimes excessive force?'

'Whatever their reputation,' said George, 'they certainly used tear gas last night, and chlorine gas, too, in the end.'

'Quite right, too,' muttered the colonel. 'Whenever the rioters were forced to withdraw from one barricade, they set it on fire. Burning cars, furniture, whatever they laid their hands on. Outrageous!'

'It sounds quite frightful,' said Flixe, inexpressibly relieved that Andrew was safely back in England, but horribly aware of what she would feel if she were Natalie, watching the rioters' fires from her elegant Parisian flat.

'No one's been killed yet, according to what I've heard on the wireless so far,' said George, 'although there've been some fairly horrific beatings – on both sides. The students weren't simply gassed, you see; there were pitched battles for about six hours.'

'It sounds horrible. How did it end?'

'The authorities capitulated and released the student leaders from prison.'

'Should have used rubber bullets,' said the colonel, 'or water cannon. Dam' bad show givin' in like that. It'll only encourage the beggars and lead to the louts over here getting ideas. Foreign agitators and left-wing layabouts – and all the others who do it for fun. Tell me, Mrs Suvarov, what do you think went wrong?'

'With the younger generation?' said Flixe, trying to think of something sensible to say while her mind was occupied almost completely with her son and with Natalie.

'Yes, the long-haired brigade.'

'Goodness knows. It can't simply be that we didn't smack them as babies,' she said vaguely.

George, realising that she was upset, took over the conversation and talked across her to the colonel, eliciting his views about the damaging effects of affluence, the lack of

National Service and the way in which lax morality sapped the strength of young men. Their conversation lasted not only through the smoked salmon and Gewürztraminer but also through the *boeuf bourguignon* and claret. By the time the waitresses had removed the meat plates and handed round the *crème brûlée*, Flixe had remembered that she was at work and could not give in completely to her own concerns.

She smiled at George in gratitude for fielding the colonel. George winked at her and turned belatedly to his other neighbour. Flixe conscientiously started to entertain the colonel by asking about his own children and listening to how their ambitions had been stiffened by his strict discipline. He went on telling her about his views on education and the benefits of military training as he finished his pudding and helped himself to a large mound of stilton.

Flixe, who had declined the cheeses, picked at a small bunch of grapes and let him talk. When the women left the table, Flixe told Ann that she would miss coffee in favour of checking that everything was all right in the marquee and the summer-house.

'Good idea, Flixe,' said Ann, looking much happier now that dinner at least had gone off well. 'I saw you looking very bored with George Mayford. I told Stephen he wasn't your sort, but he won't ever listen to me and made me sit you there. I hope George wasn't too dreary. Never mind: you can dance with all the husbands now and wow them.'

'I'm not in the business of wowing anyone,' said Flixe with a raised eyebrow. 'I'm here to work. It was sweet of you to include me in dinner, but I'd better go and earn my keep now.'

'Oh, you've done that already. Don't worry,' said Ann, surprisingly leaning forward to kiss Flixe's cheek. 'I'll see you later.'

Certain that she would never understand the forces that swung Ann from malice to sweetness, Flixe walked quickly through the covered passage to the marquee, and on to the summer-house to make absolutely certain that there had been no disasters during dinner.

The members of the band and the three young men operating the discotheque all told her that they had been well fed by the caterers and were quite ready for the arrival of the guests at ten o'clock. Adam, the man in charge of the discotheque, complimented her on the decoration of the summer-house, adding: 'Are you available for other dances or is this a one-off?'

'No, no. I'm doing five others this season, but this is the only one for which I've booked you. Why?'

'It's just that we occasionally get asked to supply decoration as well as lights and I wondered if we could call on you?'

'I should be delighted,' said Flixe. 'I haven't a card on me, but if you've a pencil I can give you my telephone number.' She dictated it and went back to the house with a certain satisfaction.

George met her at the entrance to the marquee.

'Everything all right?'

'Fine. I'm sorry I abdicated from my responsibilities at supper.'

'Don't worry about that, so long as you're all right. You looked a bit upset, ill almost, and when you disappeared I was worried.'

'No need. I was just a bit bothered about some relations who live in Paris, but I oughtn't to have let that get in the way of a job.'

'I'm glad. Not that you were worried, but I thought it might have been . . .' He stopped, shut his eyes for a moment and then opened them and smiled at her. 'As I said at lunch: I keep getting things wrong. Will you dance with me later?'

'I'd love to,' she said. He seemed to need comfort and so she laid a hand on his sleeve. 'Once things have begun to take off I can let myself have fun, but I'll be on duty for an hour or so.'

'Right. I'll find you at eleven.' He raised his hand in a kind of salute and walked on into the marquee.

In fact it was half past eleven before Flixe could feel certain that the dance was going to be successful. Until then she refused to stop working. Ann seemed unconcerned to introduce any of her guests to each other and Flixe, who felt sorry for anyone who looked bored or lonely, took on the responsibility. She was particularly worried about Gina, who, despite her striking dress, did not seem to be able to attract young men. Many of the fathers there that evening were anxious to dance with her and talk to her and she obviously enjoyed their company, but Flixe felt that she ought to be helped into her own generation.

'Don't fret about me, please, Mrs Suvarov,' said Gina as Flixe took her away from yet another sexagenarian in order to introduce her to a twenty-year-old student at the Cirencester agricultural college. 'Honestly I do much prefer talking to the grown-ups.'

'I know you do,' said Flixe, 'but you really ought to meet some chaps of your own age. I know your father's anxious for it, too.'

Gina sighed and accepted a glass of champagne from the tray carried past them by a waiter just then. She sipped and looked at Flixe across the edge of the glass.

'But they can't understand me or I them,' she said, not complaining or unhappy but merely announcing a fact. 'I'm out of tune with them. Not just tonight, but always. I simply don't know about the things they care about and so my conversational approaches are laborious. When I make jokes they either don't understand or find them boring. When they're smutty I come over all puritan and when I occasionally venture a mild obscenity they look horrified. When I get lit up with drink in a desperate attempt to enjoy myself and be entertaining, they're completely sober and seem shocked, although most of the time they think I'm intense and dull. I think they're vacuous or snobbish – or frightening. It just never works.'

'Poor Gina,' said Flixe, laughing at the melodramatic sigh with which the young woman ended her explanation, but she could not help remembering Jemima's criticisms and felt sorry for both of them.

'And look at the girls,' Gina added despairingly. 'I bought this red thing because at all the parties I've been to so far my fruit-salady dresses have been far more conventional than anything anyone else has worn. But look at them all tonight: they're all in white or pale blue. It's a disaster.'

'Do you hate doing the season?' Flixe asked gently.

'No, not really.' Gina seemed sincere about that. 'You see, it doesn't matter to me. I'm going up to Oxford next term and so this is an irrelevance – and there are always plenty of parents at these things for me to talk to. I enjoy that – really.'

'I can imagine, but that's not really the point.'

'But they're so much more interesting than the younger lot and infinitely more appreciative,' said Gina with a rueful smile. 'I don't have to try to amuse them or be interesting. They seem to like me as I am.'

At the emphasis in her voice Flixe laughed again.

'I'll bet they do,' she said, thinking that Gina's calm good sense, obvious intelligence and ability to talk happily to the older generation would make most parents contrast her favourably with their own offspring. 'But do come on and talk to this land agent, not for your sake but for his. He really is a bit out of it.'

With that appeal to her generosity, Gina was much happier and went off to set the young man at ease. Flixe sighed. She was afraid that it would be many years before Gina's contemporaries caught up with her and she with them. Flixe hoped that she would not have completely lost her confidence by then.

'Are you up to dancing after all that?' asked George when he eventually found Flixe on her own, 'or do you want to rest your feet?'

'Let's dance,' she said and moved on to the floor as the

band struck up a waltz. 'I love it and I haven't for ages.'

He put his arms round her and and led her into the dance. They moved easily together and were comfortable, so comfortable that Flixe could not help thinking of the evening when they had planned to make love. She moved a little closer to him.

'It's a pity I was so wound up with my patient that evening,' he said, as if reading her thoughts.

Flixe look up in delighted surprise. 'That's rather what I was thinking, too.'

'I thought it might be. We do seem to be in tune, don't we? It's not just my imagination, is it?'

Flixe only smiled and wished that she were young enough to tuck her head under his chin and cling to him as they danced. There was silence between them as they swung neatly round together at the edge of the floor, the skirts of Flixe's borrowed dress flying about her ankles. They passed Ann, who was talking to her husband and looking absolutely furious again. Flixe felt sorry for her, but not sorry enough to forego her own pleasure.

'What's this I've been hearing about the discotheque you've organised in the garden?' George asked her in a voice that was just slightly ragged.

Flixe took a moment to order her thoughts. His hand tightened on her waist for a second.

'Why don't we go down there and see it?' she said at last. 'I ought to keep an eye on things in any case and make certain that Stephen's nightmares of drowned debs are as absurd as I've assumed. It's an hour since I was last there and not many people had found it by then.'

'All right.'

At the end of the waltz they left the floor and Flixe piloted him out of the marquee. As soon as they left it they could hear the sound of the discotheque thudding out through the moonlit garden and saw the lights reflected in the calm blueness of the swimming-pool. George took her hand and she led him down the steps, smelling the heavy sweetness of the early flowers in the borders. They stopped for a moment on the stone-paved edge of the swimming-pool, looking at each other.

Flixe wished once again that the Kirkwaters had wanted a London dance or that she were not in some sense still at work. The music sobbed and howled in front of them and the flowers smelled astonishingly powerful. The very air seemed heavy and when George's hand landed on hers, Flixe had to turn away to stop herself reaching forward to kiss him.

'Felicity,' he said quietly. She swallowed.

'Yes?'

'This is unbearable. Are you all right?'

'A little stirred up,' she said quietly. George gripped her hand.

'What did we come out here for?'

'We came to see the disco,' she said. 'I'm sorry it's horrible for you. Perhaps we ought to ignore each other and be sociable with important strangers.'

He tugged at her hand until she had to look at him again.

'It's far from horrible as you well know. I'm only frustrated by our being . . . surrounded by them all.'

Flixe managed to let out some of her feelings in a sighing laugh as she gestured towards the summer-house. He led her in through the french windows and immediately covered his ears with his hands, laughing at her. Flixe nodded, quite unable to speak against the noise, and waved gracefully towards her two-dimensional nudes of David, the Venus de Milo, Apollo and Daphne.

George nodded his head from side to side as though to express surprise that she was so proud of them and raised his eyebrows. Flixe mouthed 'wait'. They stood by the window, smelling the spiciness of the orange blossom in the tub at their side and watching waves of aquamarine light rising slowly upwards from floor level, covering the walls and the gyrating couples in rhythmic ripples. Just as it reached the chins of the statues, tiny spotlights shone through the holes where their eyes should have been and brilliant white, flexible tongues shot out of their mouths, catching the ultraviolet light from behind the disco and blazing out in the dimness of the room.

'Wonderful!' said George, unable to stop laughing. He grabbed her hand again and took her outside into the relative quiet of the garden. There was a teak bench at the far end of the swimming-pool and he urged her towards it.

'Let's sit down and watch it again from here,' he said, 'where we don't have to have our heads battered in by all that noise.'

The rippling light had reached the dancers' knees again by then, and they watched as it rose like water and saw the statues come to life once more.

'They don't do it every time,' said Flixe, unable to stop smiling at her own joke. 'Jemima and I agreed that it would be more fun if they only performed occasionally.'

'I do think it's funny,' he said, 'and not at all what one expects from a staid deb dance.'

'I'm glad you like it. It seems important to let people laugh, otherwise these thrashes would be too gruesome. Stephen told me that having nude statues is most unsuitable, "putting ideas into their heads, what?" He thinks the whole thing deplorably vulgar.'

George laughed again.

'I don't think it's vulgar at all. They look magnificent and they're funny and puncture pomposity – just like you.'

'I'm glad you like them,' said Flixe, laughing as her faith in his friendship, and his sense of humour, was confirmed. 'And me.'

'That has never been in doubt,' he said, adding: 'I can't think why . . .'

Before he could finish whatever he had been going to say, there was a tremendous crack of thunder at the same time as lightning shot through the dark sky. They were followed almost instantly by rain so heavy that even before George had dragged Flixe into the shelter of a huge oak her dress was soaked and clinging to her skin.

'It's like the monsoon,' he said, staring from their partial shelter at the sheets of water that were falling out of the sky.

'I can't believe you've ever been in a monsoon. Have you?' asked Flixe, who was shivering with a mixture of cold and uncontrollable laughter. Their romantic evening was turning into a farce. 'You do know that the last place to be in a thunderstorm is under a tree, I take it.'

'I know,' he said calmly, 'but I had to get you out of that wet. If it doesn't stop in a minute I'll carry you back to the house.'

'Don't be silly. We'll run for it.'

'You're freezing,' he said as he put his hand against her wet cheek. He pulled off his jacket. 'Come here, Felicity.'

As it hung it round her shoulders, she felt the warmth of his hands through the soaking material of her sleeves, heard the quick intake of breath and then felt him pull her towards him. Held hard against him, she looked up and he kissed her. Her lips parted and for a moment she forgot the cold, the wetness of her clinging clothes, and all her responsibilities as a party-planner and a parent. Rain fell through the oak leaves on to their faces and trickled into their mouths as they kissed each other.

'Why on earth have we waited so long?' George asked as he drew back. Flixe recognised his need to add some frivolity to their overpowering feelings and liked him for it.

'I can't imagine,' she said lightly. 'But we can't discuss it now unless we're prepared to drown. The rain sounds as though it's set in for the night. There are umbrellas by the door of the poolhouse, but those children will probably need them. Let's make a run for the house. I'll have to do something about my clothes.'

Hand in hand they ran through the drenching darkness and Flixe let him in by the back door. They met no one as they splashed up the backstairs to their rooms. At the door of hers they stopped. He looked down at her, saying nothing but clearly feeling everything she felt.

'We can't,' she said at last.

'I know. Think how horribly undignified it would be if anyone came looking for you. Don't fret, Felicity. Despite what I said, we've plenty of time.'

'Yes, we have. Thank you.'

'It does seem . . . I'll see you later. Will you be all right?'

'Yes, but you probably won't see me. My hair's ruined and I haven't brought another long dress, so I'll put on ordinary clothes and waft about the staff regions making sure everything's all right. We can meet for breakfast. Would you tell Ann for me?'

'Certainly. I . . . Felicity.' George seemed unable to complete whatever he had been going to say. Flixe waited and, after a bit, he added: 'As I said, I keep making mistakes. Will you forgive me for them?'

'Don't worry so much, George,' she said, 'unless what you're trying to tell me is that kissing me just now was a mistake?'

'God forbid!' he said with such fervour that she had to laugh.

Laughing with her, looking enormously comforted, he brushed her cheek with one finger and left.

CHAPTER 13

Most of the house party slept late the next morning, but Flixe was up and dressed by half past nine, walking round the marquee, the caterers' annexe, the summer-house and the garden to check for damage or uncleared mess. Everything seemed in order in the big tent, but when she reached the summer-house she discovered that someone had been decorating the statues with lipstick. Amused, but well aware that Stephen Kirkwaters would be appalled by the tasteless graffiti, she fetched a damp cloth from the kitchen and wiped the statues clean.

On her way back through the damp gardens, which were steaming gently in the hot sun, she met Stephen himself.

'Morning, Mrs Suvarov,' he said formally but with a friendlier smile than any she had seen before. 'That was a magnificent job you did last night.'

'I'm glad you're pleased,' she said, surprised. 'I'm sorry that so many of your guests must have got wet in the rainstorm.'

'Did the little blighters good,' he said, 'and none of them fell into the pool. Rain never hurt anyone. I thought it went splendidly and even poor little Jemima was happy by the end. We're very grateful and I've been recommending you to friends all night.'

'How kind!'

'Now, what about a spot of breakfast? I expect they'll have managed to produce something by now.'

Flixe went with him and was relieved to see both the Mayfords and one of the other guests already in the dining room. The thought of sitting alone with Stephen Kirkwaters, even in his remarkably good mood, was not one she welcomed. George got to his feet as soon as he saw her.

'May I get you some coffee, Felicity?'

'That would be lovely. Thank you.'

Stephen held out a chair for her next to George's and she was just sitting down as Ann appeared, looking tense but immaculately made up and very pretty in a pale green linen skirt and green-and-pink shirt with crisp white collar and cuffs.

'Good morning,' she said coldly. 'George, while you're there, pour me some coffee will you.'

'Certainly. How do you like it?'

'Black, as you very well know.'

Stephen, who had poured out his own coffee brought it back to the head of the table and smiled at his wife.

'You must be tired, Ann,' he said kindly. 'How's the head?'

'Perfectly all right, thank you,' she snapped. 'Well, Flixe, all your promises that rain would not spell disaster were wrong. The discotheque was completely cut off and I gather that some pretty frightful scenes went on.'

Flixe was not certain whether Ann had seen the crude lipstick inscriptions and so she merely said: 'I don't suppose it was too bad really. Was anyone's dress ruined?'

'Absolutely not,' said Gina, joining the battle on Flixe's behalf. 'I think everyone enjoyed it. The storm was certainly magnificent to watch from the summer-house and made everything rather exciting.'

Flixe smiled at her and then turned to thank George for the coffee he had put down in front of her. Gina pushed forward a rack of toast then turned to ask Ann about the age of the house. She answered briefly but Stephen elaborated on what she had said and proved to be quite an entertaining talker. Conversation became more general and Flixe began to feel comfortable again, although whenever Ann addressed a word to her it was in a tone of intense annoyance. Flixe could only suppose that she was suffering from a severe hangover.

Stephen continued to be charming to Flixe and insisted later on showing both her and Gina around the small medieval church at the bottom of the garden. Glad to be out of the way of Ann's temper, Flixe went with them willingly.

They returned only just in time for a magnificent cold lunch in the dining room. Ann was still looking irritable and had obviously upset Jemima, who was rather red-eyed. Flixe was directed to a seat between the dull colonel and Stephen, and she did her best to make them laugh.

When everyone had finished coffee and the first guests were talking about trying to miss the bad traffic driving back into London, Gina sidled up to her father to tell him that she had been invited to make a detour on her way back to London and have dinner with some friends.

'I'm sure I could get Mrs Suvarov to give you a lift,' she said, signalling to Flixe. 'If I can, will you lend me the car? You know I'm trustworthy. I promise to be careful driving in the dark.'

Suppressing a smile at what he took to be an attempt to push him closer to Felicity Suvarov, George agreed at once but assured his daughter that he could arrange his own lift back to London. Gina's mouth twitched into something very like a pout, but she was too sophisticated to press her point and merely wished him luck. George waited until she was distracted before talking to Flixe.

As soon as she could extricate herself from Ann's mixture

of strained gratitude and bad temper, Flixe drove him to her house in Kensington.

'Will you come in for a bit?' she said. 'We could have a cup of tea, or . . . '

'Or?' he repeated with a laugh in his voice. 'Yes, please.'

Flixe laughed too and took him straight up to her big, sunny bedroom. There she pulled the curtains across the brilliant light, dimming it to a warm glow and turned to face him. He stroked her hair and then bent to kiss her.

'It seems too good to be true,' he said at last.

'Why?' asked Flixe, worried for the first time since she had met him.

'Oh, I don't know.' George sighed. 'You're so lovely and funny and clever.'

'Clever? Who on earth have you been talking to? That's the last thing I am. You've no need to worry about that. A quick talk to either of my brilliant sisters would soon disillusion you.'

'No. It's true. Perhaps they just can't see it. Ah, Felicity.'

'Are you having second thoughts? We can easily go and have a cup of tea decorously downstairs if you'd rather.'

'No. I suppose I'm just anxious that you shouldn't regret anything. I don't want to lose you by . . . '

'George, what is all this? You're not going to lose me. You'd have to positively push me away. Surely you could tell that last night?' Flixe reached up to brush her hand over his face.

'Don't frown, my dear,' she said. 'Nothing here is that important.'

He took her hand between both of his, turned it over and kissed the palm.

'I suppose I'm anxious because I've never before set out on an affair with someone I've liked so much,' he said at last, sounding acutely uncomfortable.

'Oh, George, that's so sad. Liking must be the only sensible reason for an affair, surely?'

When he did not answer, she said quite briskly: 'Well, I

certainly like you. Are you coming to bed?'

Flixe led him to her big, comfortable bed, and set about banishing his doubts without giving words to any of her own.

'I was right, you know,' he said as he ran his hand tantalisingly down one of her slender thighs. 'You really are a remarkable woman.'

'Thank you,' said Flixe, laughing and kissing his shoulder. He looked much happier. 'You seem pretty wonderful yourself.'

'I do?'

'Definitely.'

'I'm delighted to hear it,' he said, laughing at last. After that everything was all right and they discovered not only furious physical pleasure in each other but also a great deal of fun.

Later, as they were lying together peacefully, Flixe turned her head to look at George and at last considered her own doubts. Despite her longing for the physical solace of making love with him, and the surging desire she had felt in the Kirkwaters' drenched garden, she had been worried that memories of Peter might punish her for her infidelity to him, but they had not. George's fair head on Peter's pillow did not look out of place at all and for the first time in months Flixe found that she could think of her husband without pain.

'Are you all right?' George asked.

'Yes. Did I look otherwise?'

'Slightly forbidding. It made me wonder what you were thinking about.'

'Will you misunderstand if I say my husband?'

George's free hand tightened slightly into a fist beneath the blankets and he tried to make his voice gentle.

'I hope not.'

'I was just thinking,' said Flixe slowly, 'that if there is any kind of afterlife, he must be pleased with us. That sounds very sentimental, but I feel wholly at ease about this, and I was afraid that I might not, if you see what I mean.'

George raised himself up on one elbow so that he could look at her properly, noticing the unusual rosy warmth of her skin and the blackness of her dilated pupils. He stroked the fine blonde hair away from her face, tracing the prominent cheekbones and letting his fingertips run across her lips and down to her pointed chin.

'I'm glad.'

'You sound worried.' Flixe's dark eyebrows contracted slightly. He shook his head, smiling ruefully.

'Not worried, but somehow disturbed. Don't look so upset. Not in a dramatic way. It's just . . . There's something about you that's quite outside my experience. I really like your honesty.' He sounded surprised, as though he was working out what his feelings actually were and was disconcerted by them.

'Good,' said Flixe. 'You must be getting awful pins and needles in your elbow.'

He laughed and dropped back on the bed, putting his hands behind his head.

'Felicity?'

'Mmm?'

'What do you think it means?'

Surprised, she looked sideways at him and saw that he was staring up at the ceiling.

'What does what mean?'

'This extraordinary seriousness I feel about something that ought to be frivolous.'

'It's too soon for that, George.'

'Are you angry with me?'

There was a pause before she leaned over to kiss his firm chin.

'Certainly not, but I suppose I might be slightly afraid. It's not something I had expected or know how to deal with at the moment. Can we just . . . ignore it?'

'The seriousness or the whole thing?' He sounded worried and she kissed him again.

'The seriousness, dear fool. The whole thing is far too good to ignore.'

'Good.' He hugged her and kissed her hair. 'That's all right then. What did you expect when we first met?'

Flixe leaned on him and revelled in the sensation of his skin against hers.

'Flirtation to start with,' she said lightly. 'Then pretty quickly at that gruesome dinner of the Kinghovers it did cross my mind that we might one day end up in bed; and then the more I thought about it all through the children's school holidays, the more lovely I thought it might be – as a kind of treat to make the rest of life easier. Nothing more.'

'Has it been very difficult?' he asked, dropping the teasing note in his voice. 'Life, I mean.'

'Bloody,' said Flixe, muffling her voice in his shoulder. She rolled away from him and stared up at the fringed and ruffled pelmet over the curtains, noticing in horror that there was a new crack in the cornice. If the house were to fall down, she would never be able to afford to do anything about it. She checked the rising panic.

'But if I have occasional blissful treats with you I'll be able to manage.'

'I'd like to be able to help, you know,' he said mildly and she turned to him at once.

'Don't say that. I don't need it. Lots of people are helping me and I can't take on any more debts. I can cope with them at this level. Truly. It is just wonderful to be able to let it all drift for a little while.'

'All right, but will you promise to tell me if you do need help – any sort of help?' Seeing her lovely worn face start to look worried again, he added with a mischievous smile: 'Putting up shelves, changing dripping washers, that sort of thing. I'm quite neat-handed about the house.'

Flixe relaxed again.

'I think that's probably the most romantic offer I've ever had.'

He held her tightly, laughing into her silky hair.

'Good. And if you need anything else – anything – you must promise to tell me. You've got my number. Just ring me.'

As though on cue the telephone beside her bed began to ring. Flixe left it for ten rings, hoping that it would be some casual caller who would be easily put off. Then she said: 'Do you mind if I answer? I always hate the thought that it might be one of the children in distress.'

'Go ahead. I know about telephones. I always have to answer mine.'

'So you do,' she said as she picked up the receiver. Then she recited her number.

'Flixe? Are you all right? I've been ringing for ages,' said her elder sister.

'I'm fine, Gerry; I was in the loo.'

There was a smothered snort of laughter from beside her.

'Have you heard from Natalie?'

'No. I did try to ring the other day, but there was no answer. Why? Gerry, she surely hasn't been involved in any of the fighting? It's all been in the Latin Quarter. Across the river from her.'

'Yes. I mean, yes, it's across the river and no, she wasn't involved, but apparently Bertrand wants to get her away from Paris because it looks as though there's going to be more trouble, and probably some serious strikes. In some ways the obvious place for her to stay is at Ming's because she's got more free time, but I did wonder whether you might like the company?'

'I adore Natalie,' said Flixe truthfully as she wondered why Gerry was acting as an intermediary between them. 'But there's so much on that I'd hardly ever see her. I think it would be better if she went to Ming and Mark. I'll probably see just as much of her there and won't have to worry about her while I'm flogging round my treadmill every day.'

'Okay. I'll fix it. Ming is quite happy to have her. All well with you, old thing?'

'Fine,' said Flixe, increasingly puzzled by her sister's intervention. 'The dance at the Kirkwaters' seems to have gone all right and I had a couple of new enquiries during it, so business may boom. Thanks for ringing, Gerry. Love to Mike. Bye.'

She put the receiver down and turned to George. He thought she looked as though her conscience was feeling most uncomfortable.

'I really ought to telephone my younger sister. I should have done it as soon as we got in. Can you bear it?'

George smiled. 'Why don't I get up and fetch us a drink?' he said.

'Lovely. I think that there's a tiny bit of decent brandy left, which would be nice. It's in the left-hand cupboard in the dining room sideboard. Can you find it?'

'I'm sure I can.'

He collected his clothes and took them into the bathroom so that Flixe could have some privacy. She quickly dialled Ming's number and when her sister answered, said at once: 'Ming, I ought to have rung you first thing this morning.'

There was a laugh at the other end of the line.

'Judging from what I've already heard about the magnificent dance you orchestrated last night I'd have thought you would have been fast asleep. I was going to ring you after supper.'

For a moment Flixe was distracted.

'Have you really heard about the party?'

'Definitely. Three people have rung me up this morning to tell me about my brilliant sister. I'm so pleased it's working, Flixe.'

'Thank you. And it is thanks to you. I'd never have thought of earning money like that if you hadn't suggested those first few clients, and your taking on the girls yesterday really helped. How were they?'

'They were fine.' Ming's voice was warm and sure. 'Sophie was sad when we took them back to school, but no more than any fourteen-year-old would have been. We had a lovely day together.'

'You are the kindest and the best, Ming. I don't know what I'd do without you. I hope Mark doesn't think I'm exploiting you.'

'He's not stupid, you know. And he understands what you're going through.'

'I'm glad. You're lucky with him. It was worth waiting all those years to find him.'

'I've never doubted it,' said Ming, who had not met her husband until she was into her thirties and her sisters had given up hope of her ever finding someone she could love. 'How are you? Really?'

'At this particular moment, Ming, I am floating in bliss. But it may not – probably won't – last.'

'Really?' The word was the same as she had used before but it sounded entirely different. 'If you mean what I think you mean, Flixe, I'm glad. But do take care of yourself.'

'It's all right. I am. When it's . . . when I'm more settled I'll tell you all about it.'

'Only when you want. I hope he's nice enough for you.'

'He's a dear and very kind. But I ought to go in a minute. I hear you're having Natalie to stay.'

'Yes, Bertrand is sending her over tomorrow. Will you drop in? She'll be pining to see you.'

'If I can. Otherwise, I'll telephone. Give her my love.'

'I will. Good-night,'

'Good-night, Mingie.'

Flixe put down the telephone, found her dressing-gown and went in search of George.

The following day Flixe went to the constituency office to write innumerable letters and then drove to Ming's house in

211

Holland Park Avenue. She parked behind her sister's big blue Citroën and went to ring the front doorbell. Ming answered and flung her arms round her sister.

'How heavenly! Natalie and I were just talking about you. Come on in and have tea with us. We've only just started.'

Flixe kissed Ming and together they walked into the drawing room. Natalie was sitting on one of the matching silver-grey sofas. She rose as soon as she saw who the new arrival was and held out her hands.

Flixe took them and clung tightly. She saw that there were tears in Natalie's dark eyes, eyes so like Peter's that her own began to smart.

'I'll fetch another cup,' said Ming, seeing that they needed a little time.

'Andrew is so like him,' said Natalie, releasing her sister-in-law's hands and sitting carefully back on the well-cushioned sofa. 'It's wonderful – and difficult sometimes – just to be with him.'

'I know. It was so good of you to have him. Did he tell you anything? I haven't any idea how he really is but I do know he's hurting.'

Natalie shrugged. Her shoulders looked very thin as they raised the smooth dark blue barathea of her perfect suit.

'That is impossible to say. He was very self-contained, out most of every day and utterly polite when we met. Charming too.'

'I'm glad he was polite. But how are you? It must have been terrible in Paris.'

'It was.' Natalie crossed one slender leg over the other and Flixe silently admired her Ferragamo shoes. It seemed impossible to imagine anyone as exquisite as Natalie being anywhere near rioting students. 'And Bertrand says it will get worse.'

'But what is it all about? I can't understand why students should have got so out of hand in Europe. In America? Yes. They have the draft to contend with and a real campaign

212

about something as important as stopping that awful war, but not here or in Paris.'

'In Paris they have some real problems, too. Not the war, but problems of being a student in a country where everyone has the right to go to university and there is just not enough room. There are not enough professors or even lodgings for the students. It is not strange that they are restive. And then when you find the Government sending in the CRS with gas! What can they expect?'

'Still, it's hardly enough to justify burning cars and causing all that damage. It didn't actually touch you, did it?'

Ming brought in the third cup then, as well as a kettleful of hot water to refill the teapot. While she was pouring out the tea, Flixe pressed Natalie, trying to understand why she had fled to London. Flixe thought that she looked rather frail sitting there and older than her fifty-eight years. Her dark hair was much greyer than it had been at Peter's funeral and her skin looked almost papery with a sinister pale yellow tinge.

'No, but Bertrand is afraid that the students will combine with the workers and stage strikes all over France. As I am not terribly well just now, we thought it better to be here where at least the hospitals will be available if . . . if there should be a crisis.'

Flixe shot a look at Ming, whose expression showed that the news was familiar to her. Suppressing her anger, Flixe put her hand gently on Natalie's and asked about her illness.

'You didn't know?' said Natalie, sounding surprised. Flixe shook her head.

Ming said in dispassionate explanation: 'Gerry wanted to wait until we could give her better news than Bertrand gave us.'

'You shouldn't have kept it from me, Ming.' Flixe let some of her anger out. 'I may be a widow but I am not an idiot. I had a right. Natalie, what is it?'

'It may be nothing, but they think there is perhaps a

213

growth. Perhaps not.' She laid a hand over her left kidney. 'Here. I am to have tests while I am in London.'

'That explains why Bertrand did not telephone me in the first place,' said Flixe. 'It struck me as odd as soon as I heard it. Darling, you . . . you will tell me, won't you, whatever they say?'

'Yes.'

Flixe knew that she had been given a promise. They dropped the subject then and talked of easier things, such as Natalie's daughter, who had recently had her second child. Later Natalie turned to Ming.

'You know about all the painters in London,' she said, 'have you heard about this portrait of Andrew's girlfriend? He seems to have taken a dislike to it, although he could not tell me why and has seen nothing of it.'

'Amanda Wallington? I don't know much about it either, although I gather it's to form the centrepiece of Comfort Gillingham's next show.'

'How do you know that?' asked Flixe, surprised. 'Julia will be horrified if it's given a lot of publicity, though knowing dear little Amanda that's probably inevitable.'

Ming laughed. 'One of the dealers I've occasionally bought things from was telling me about the portrait. It's said to be quite superb, although not yet finished. I rather like some of Miss Gillingham's stuff.'

'I am not sure that I do. There is something sinister in her paintings that I have seen,' said Natalie, shivering. 'But there are not so many in Paris.'

'Really?' Flixe was interested. 'Perhaps I'm not sensitive enough to paintings. Hers seem quite attractive – nice colours – but I can't say I've ever looked particularly carefully.'

'Too loyal to Julia, eh?' said Ming with a smile of rather touching approval on her face. Flixe looked doubtful, but after a moment she nodded.

'In a way, I suppose that's true. Do you know her, Ming?'

'Comfort Gillingham? No. We've been introduced once or twice, but she moves in rather rarefied circles. Is Julia really upset about the portrait?'

'I think she's more bothered by the fact that her daughter has been sucked into the world inhabited by her ex-husband. Quite apart from that, though, she does loathe the way Amanda's life is trumpeted in the press. Julia thinks that it's building up unrealisable expectations and that when Amanda comes a cropper, as she's bound to, it'll hurt her horribly. But you know Julia: beyond expressing a mild distaste for the idea of the painting, she didn't try to stop Amanda sitting for it.'

Natalie laughed. As the skin around her eyes crinkled, Flixe noticed again how dry and sallow it had become.

'From the few things that poor Andrew told me about that young woman, I should think that nothing but a court order could restrain her from doing anything she wanted. Why does he love her, Flixe? She sounds like poison.'

'I'm not certain. She's glamorous and apparently can be fun, although I've seen no signs of it. I've wondered a bit whether it might be her familiarity that makes her seem so important to him.' Flixe looked at her sister-in-law. 'Peter's dying has left Andrew feeling very lost. He's known Amanda since she was born. Perhaps he's just trying to cling on to something from the past.'

'Perhaps,' said Natalie sadly.

She looked desperately tired and Flixe knew that she ought to go. Ming escorted her to the front door.

'Try not to worry too much about Natalie,' Ming said, kissing her sister.

'That's not an easy command to obey.'

'I know,' said Ming, ignoring her sister's acerbic tone. 'But she will have the best care.'

'What's the programme?' asked Flixe more calmly.

'She's going to have a series of outpatient tests starting on Wednesday. If it looks bad, they'll take her in and do a biopsy.

Once they know for sure whether there's a tumour at all, and if so whether it's malignant, they'll decide what to do.'

'You will tell me what happens, won't you? I don't want to badger her, but I have to know. I can't . . .'

Ming merely nodded, saying, 'I love her, too, you know.'

CHAPTER 14

Amanda caught a train to London just before one, planning to fill the boredom of the journey with food. She was relieved to see no one she knew from the university in the dining-car and settled comfortably in a window-seat facing London. A white-jacketed waiter looked slightly surprised to see that she was alone, but he was reasonably polite. Amanda looked disdainfully at the menu, chose the plainest-sounding dish, which was grilled plaice, and ordered herself a half-bottle of Chablis.

She spun out her meal for as long as possible, reading between courses and having several cups of coffee before she eventually paid her bill and allowed the waiter to clear everything from her table except the last glass of wine. The train was due to arrive at Liverpool Street a good deal earlier than her appointment with Comfort, but Amanda wanted to sneak in a meeting alone with Anthony first. She assumed that Comfort would be at the gallery organising – or at least overseeing – the final details of the hanging, so that she could have him to herself.

A taxi from Liverpool Street deposited Amanda outside the Gillinghams' house half an hour earlier than Comfort had stipulated. Anthony answered the front door himself and looked quite taken aback at the sight of the visitor.

'Hello,' she said seriously. 'I hoped you'd be here. Can I come in?'

He stepped aside to allow her into the hall and said: 'Comfort's not here. Was she expecting you now? I'm sure she said half past five to me.'

'I am a little early. I wanted to have a chance to talk to you without her. Shall we go up to your study?'

Anthony opened a door off the hall and gestured with his free hand. Amanda suppressed a sigh and walked into what was obviously the main drawing room, which she had never seen before. Magnificently furnished with an eclectic collection of antiques and modern paintings, it was very simply decorated with the palest of grey walls. Slightly darker heavy linen had been used for the curtains and edged with a two-inch strip the colour of *sang de boeuf* porcelain. The polished parquet floor was partly covered with a thick handmade carpet closely patterned in grey and dark red diamonds. A stunning abstract painted in a mixture of reds, oranges and yellows hung over the empty fireplace and was echoed by two squat vases stuffed to bursting with brightly coloured roses. With great pots of lilies, more abstracts on every wall, a small Barbara Hepworth sculpture on a stone-topped table to the left of the chimney-breast and a Classical mask mounted on a simple stand on its pair, the room was more impressive than welcoming.

'It's spectacular,' Amanda murmured, casually dropping into one corner of a vast grey leather sofa.

'Comfort's taste rather than mine,' said Anthony with a whimsical smile. 'As I expect you can see for yourself.'

'She clearly likes grey,' agreed Amanda, 'and prefers emptier surfaces than you.'

'Amanda, why have you come?' Anthony stood in front of her so that she had to tilt her head on to the soft sofa back to see his face. It looked cold and quite severe.

'Because we've had no direct contact since you made love to me.' She touched the mermaid pin with one hand. 'You sent me this, but that's all. I . . . I've missed you. We need to talk.'

He turned away and pulled forward a French elbow chair covered in grey-striped silk.

'Listen, my dear child.'

'I am not a child,' said Amanda, thinking almost with pride of the one growing inside her.

'Perhaps not, but you are remarkably young – which is perhaps why I allowed myself to behave so stupidly and badly when we last met here.'

Amanda held out both hands.

'Don't be so hard on yourself. You didn't seduce me. We came together as equals.'

'That is my one crumb of comfort,' he said, looking as though he did not find it comforting at all. He stared at Amanda's outstretched hands but did not move towards them. 'I've decided since that day that I was destructively weak, but perhaps not wicked.'

She slid off the deep sofa with some difficulty and once more knelt at his feet, laying her hands supplicatingly on his knees. He covered his face with his own hands, murmuring: 'Please don't.'

'Anthony, you cannot imagine what you did for me then. The only other two people I have made love with were clumsy and allowed me to think that . . . oh, that sex was entirely a matter of their pleasure. You showed me how wrong they were. You showed me that when two people really matter to each other it can be wonderful for both of them.'

She lifted her hands from his knees to grasp his wrists and gently pulled his hands away from his face.

'Look at me. How can you dislike the memory of it so much when it's done so much for me? Don't I look happy?'

A faint smile smoothed some of the bitterness from his lips. He nodded.

'But it's no excuse. Amanda, I don't want retrospectively to spoil whatever pleasure I managed to give you, but the fact that there was pleasure in it for you does not mean that it carried any of the significance you're putting on it.' He looked down at her glowing eyes and sighed. 'Do you understand what I'm telling you?'

She sat back on her heels. There was an impish smile on her face. His own lips twitched.

'You mean you're just better at it than they were?'

Despite his real distress, Anthony could not help laughing.

'I can well believe that,' Amanda went on. 'But it wasn't simply a matter of physical sensations, was it? It did make you happy, too. I know that it did. It couldn't have been simply me that felt like that. It couldn't.'

'Of course I felt things.' He sounded irritable. 'No man of my age could possibly not feel wonderful, and immeasurably grateful, if a young girl as glorious as you wanted him. I felt like a boy again.'

Anthony looked at Amanda as her eyes grew slowly puzzled. Wanting to ensure that she did not build him into a hero and yet desperately wanting not to damage her, he added slowly: 'And you looked so like Julia when I first knew her that it was . . . for a while it was as though all the misery of those years was wiped out.'

Amanda got up at once and turned her back so that he should not see what was in her face.

'Then afterwards,' he went on, 'when I came to my senses again I could not believe that I had been so stupid. She was my wife. You are her child. Quite apart from the ludicrous gap in our ages, you must see that we can't have anything to do with each other. However weak and stupid I am, at least I know that.'

So much, thought Amanda furiously, for my happy fantasies in the cathedral. She was about to turn round and try to tell him about them when they both heard Comfort's key in the lock. Amanda thought that she heard Anthony mutter

'Thank God' as he got out of his chair and went out to greet his sister.

A moment later Comfort came whirling into the drawing room to embrace Amanda.

'Wicked child!' she said, kissing her on both cheeks. 'If I'd known you could get here so soon I'd have sorted everything at the gallery this morning. Your dress is upstairs. Come on up to the spare room to see it. Do you want a bath?'

Looking over Comfort's shoulder directly into Anthony's set face, Amanda tried to show him that she had something important to say. His expression changed to hopeless regret as Comfort swept her upstairs.

'Thank you. I should love a bath,' Amanda said as coolly as possible. 'You know how filthy trains make one.'

'Yes indeed. Here we are.' She opened the door of a conventionally decorated bedroom with matching wallpaper and curtains patterned in green and yellow flowers on white ground. 'The bathroom's through that door there. You get going and I'll lay out your clothes.'

'I left my case in the hall,' said Amanda, obediently heading for the bathroom door. 'It's got all my make-up and things in it.'

Comfort raised her eyebrows slightly, which Amanda did not see, and said coolly that she would fetch the case as well.

Amanda shut the bathroom door and turned on the bath taps, relieved to be alone and wondering when she would get the chance to finish her difficult conversation with Anthony. The evening was obviously going to have to be devoted to Comfort, but there was the rest of the weekend in which to talk to him. She would have to get back to the university in time for her Monday-afternoon seminar, but she had no commitments until then. Testing the temperature of the water, she decided to persuade Anthony to drive her back to Kennington at the end of the party.

That ought not to be too tricky, she thought, since she was adept at eliciting offers of lifts from people at parties. Both her parents had tried to persuade her to learn to drive, but, as she had told them, there was no point in taking on the unnecessary expense of running a car since she could always find someone who wanted to drive her wherever she wanted to go.

Lying in the hot, softened water, she heard Comfort moving about in the bedroom and decided to say nothing. At last the footsteps ceased.

'I'm off to change,' Comfort called through the bathroom door. 'I've brought your bag up and I'll pick you up on my way downstairs. About forty minutes?'

'Fine. Thanks.'

When Amanda had eventually had enough soaking and her fingers and toes were puckered with the effects of the hot water, she let out the bath and wrapped a huge, warm towel around herself before padding out into the bedroom to discover what kind of dress Comfort had produced for her.

Far from the mermaid fancy-dress she had half feared, it was a simply shaped, very short A-line dress. What made it extraordinary was that it was composed entirely of squares of slightly blued aluminium linked together with faceted crystal beads. A pair of flat leather shoes of exactly the same metallic blue were arranged on the floor, and a flesh-coloured bodystocking and a pair of white tights lay beside it on the chintz-covered bed.

Amanda could not help smiling. Comfort's sense of drama had not let either of them down. The dress was strange but wholly fashionable and it ought to show off Amanda's long legs and shining hair to perfection.

She rubbed herself dry, tucked her hair out of the way behind her ears and began to deal with her face. When it was made up to her satisfaction, she shook off the damp towel, leaving it in a heap where it fell, and pulled on the tights and bodystocking before slipping the metal dress over her head.

It was much lighter than she had expected and was not at all scratchy or uncomfortable to wear. She shook herself slightly and heard the plaques chink together, before standing in front of a long mirror between the two windows. The triangular outline of the dress suited her long, straight figure and the dull sheen of the metal seemed to give extra light to her eyes. The beads were like heavy drops of water. She turned and twisted her head so that she could look at her back view.

'It looks well.' Comfort's voice was a shock since Amanda had not noticed her opening the door, but she smiled.

'I think so, too. I can't wait to see the picture.'

'All right. We'll go now. There's a car downstairs. You won't need a coat, because he'll drop us right at the door.'

'And it's pretty warm.'

They went out together without encountering Anthony. When the borrowed chauffeur shut the passenger door on them both and slid into his own seat, Amanda looked behind them at the closed door and said: 'Isn't Anthony coming?'

'He'll be along later. He has some things to do.'

'Oh,' said Amanda and then sat in silence for the rest of the twenty-minute drive to the gallery.

'Good,' said Comfort as they drew up outside it, 'we've ten minutes to ourselves before the hordes are due to start arriving. Come on and look at it.'

Immensely curious to see her portrait and yet still concerned with how she was going to achieve another private talk with Anthony, Amanda followed Comfort into the big modern gallery. There seemed to be no one about at all, although trays of glasses and canapés suggested that the catering staff at least could not be far away.

Amanda recognised Comfort's distinctive style in the portraits and landscapes all round the walls of the first, small room of the gallery, but could see nothing of herself. She wondered for the first time why the painter should have filled her drawing room with abstracts when her own work was so determinedly figurative.

'It's in here. Come along.'

Amanda went and saw a dark canvas six feet by four hanging alone on a plain white wall. She stopped and tried to take it in, but it was too complicated for a single look. Her first impression was of the power of the painting and the second that it was about catastrophe.

Slowly she began to take in the details, deliberately avoiding the figure in the foreground. The most obvious thing about the painting was the storm. The sky was heavy with rain, its darkness relieved only by the few stars and a single streak of vicious lightning that lit the underside of the massed clouds with a greenish silver gleam and shone along the white crests of the waves.

On the left of the painting, in the background, the vague outline of a ship could be seen sinking into the tumultuous sea just under a falling star. Waves pounded against the sharp, seaweedy rocks that took up the remaining two-thirds of the painting.

Lying insouciantly in a gap in the rocks, half-hidden by them, apparently as comfortable as though she were in bed and quite untroubled by the surging, violent sea, was the mermaid. Her scaly silver tail glistened in the unearthly light as it emerged from behind the overhang, its strong muscles suggested by no more than the curve Comfort had given it and the sheen of its skin.

Above the partly concealing rock was Amanda, half smiling, half asleep, and wholly beautiful, the dampness of her long dark hair also catching the weird light. Drops of water lay on her face like jewels and the smoothness of her skin was wonderfully contrasted with the rough, barnacled, sea-blasted rocks. Around her neck, hanging just below her slender collarbone, was a curious wreath of purplish flowers.

'I thought,' she said rather coldly because the picture was so disturbing, 'that you were going to have me bobbing above the surface of the sea.'

'I was,' answered Comfort, looking with critical approval at her own work, 'but this seemed more interesting. I hope you approve of my tact in suggesting nudity while having no more than your neck and shoulders emerging above the rocks.'

'Oh, I do.' Amanda moved closer to examine her painted face. 'And it also prevented you from having to deal with that rather difficult junction of flesh and tail. Clever! Do I really look like that?'

'Sometimes.' Comfort's voice was mildly sarcastic and Amanda turned, suddenly laughing.

'Really? As seductive?'

'Quite as seductive and in just that careless way as though you could not care less how many ships sank or how many people admired you. I did the tail by arranging a big salmon round the leg of a chair. It got fearfully smelly before I'd finished but I think it's worked all right.'

Amanda laughed again, ignoring her less comfortable emotions.

'Oh, my poor Anthony!' she said.

'Why?' Comfort's mouth stiffened.

'Having to smell rotting fish whenever he came home. What does he think of it, by the way?'

Comfort's thin lips relaxed into another smile. She laid a hand on Amanda's metal-clad shoulder.

'He said that it had precisely the right air of mysterious, slightly wicked allure and all your infinite promise.'

Amanda swung round to have another look at herself, trying to see mystery or wickedness in herself. At that moment, apart from the sleepiness and the allure, there seemed to be only slyness in her face and a hint of cruelty. Perhaps that was what he had meant. Mentally shaking off her disagreeable ideas, Amanda said: 'Oh, good. I like "infinite promise".'

'Yes, I thought you might.' Comfort's hand was still on her shoulder and so Amanda turned her head with what she hoped was infinite grace. 'He has every reason to be proud of his daughter.'

Something seemed to sing in Amanda's ears and she felt

herself grow cold and distant. A sense of danger kept her looking politely at Comfort.

'I beg your pardon?' she said formally.

'His daughter,' Comfort repeated. 'Didn't Julia ever tell you? But how extraordinary! You must have thought we were very odd sending you expensive presents and buying you clothes. I am sorry. I ought to have . . .'

Before she could finish, Amanda interrupted her, saying through lips that felt stiff and clumsy: 'What makes you think that?'

'But my dear child,' said Comfort with exaggerated kindness, 'it's perfectly obvious. You were conceived when Julia was living with Anthony in Venice after the war. She didn't divorce him to marry David Wallington for over another year – well after you were born. It was one of the worst of the many cruelties she perpetrated on Anthony: taking his only child from him. I suppose I ought not to be astonished that she never told you, but I am. It's as though she's denied him his fatherhood twice over.'

'I'm not sure that I believe you,' said Amanda, feeling exactly as though she were the damaged ship battered by the storm and not the destroying mermaid after all.

'Don't be silly. It must have occurred to you. You could hardly imagine that Anthony and I would offer unqualified love and rich presents to every little model I use.'

There was now enough cruelty in Comfort's voice to keep Amanda on her feet and smiling with her lips closed to hide her clenched teeth. She wanted to say that she had thought the Gillinghams might have valued her for herself, not because she shared their genes. The discovery that she had been wrong hurt so much that she could feel it even through the effects of the far worse revelation.

In the shock of it all, it did not occur to Amanda that Anthony, knowing her to be his daughter, would never have succumbed to her seductive blandishments. All she could think of was his shame at their moment of shared bliss, his refusal to have anything more to do with her, and his way of addressing her as 'child'.

'It is curious,' she managed to say. 'I think I must have run my bath a bit too hot, I feel slightly dizzy.' With her dignity intact, she hoped, Amanda walked to one of the plain white Saarinen chairs that stood at intervals about the gallery and sat down.

'Poor child,' said Comfort, smiling. 'No wonder you're reeling. I can't think what Julia's been about all these years. I'll fetch you a drink.'

By the time she reappeared with a glass of champagne, the first guests were at the door, and when she went to greet them, Amanda was allowed a blessed few minutes on her own in which to try to control the horror and panic she was feeling. From having been determined to believe that Anthony was the father of her child and Andrew no more than an irrelevance, she was catapulted into longing for someone to assure her of the opposite. Despite all the sophistication and cynicism of which she was so proud, she felt not only appalled but also revolted at the idea that she might be carrying her own father's child.

The next hour was one of horror for Amanda. Trying not to let anyone see that there was anything troubling her, she received compliments with what she hoped was witty charm and responded properly to jokes about mermaids, reasoned criticism and snide leading questions from a journalist who obviously disliked her.

It was not until half past seven that she saw a face that offered any of the protection she so badly wanted. The familiar stocky figure of her godfather, Tibor Smith, stood in the doorway. As untidy and attractive as ever, he kissed Comfort's hand and then her cheek. Amanda, suddenly jealous, wondered what her mother would say if she knew that Tibor was on such friendly terms with her erstwhile sister-in-law.

Comfort took his arm and led him to the portrait. Amanda

moved forwards slightly and the metal plaques of her dress flashed in the light of an overhead spotlight and caught his attention. Turning from the painting and Comfort alike, he looked at Amanda and at once moved through the crowd to put his arms around her.

'What's the matter? You look terrible and terrified,' he whispered into her ear.

Still smiling over his shoulder at the crowd, Amanda whispered back: 'I'm both. Will you take me away without her knowing? Now.'

Tibor pulled back a little way and stared at Amanda's white face. After a moment he nodded and said: 'Wait there. I won't be long.'

He went back to Comfort, looked carefully at the painting for what seemed like ages, said something and then kissed her again. She moved back towards the front door, where more celebrities were appearing. Tibor came back to Amanda, who was standing exactly where he had left her, ignoring a photographer who was trying to attract her attention.

'Come along, my child,' he said, wondering why she winced, and propelled her through the eating, drinking, smoking crowd to a fire door at the back of the building. He pushed it open and they found themselves in a small, greasy, grey alleyway, which led out past back doors, fire escapes, howling cats and dustbins to the main road.

'Turn left. No, wait. Haven't you got a coat?'

'No, it's all right. I'm boiling. And I've left everything in her house. It doesn't matter. Come on. Take me to the studio, please. Have you got a car?'

'No, but there's a taxi.' Tibor hailed it and pushed Amanda in, before giving his address to the driver.

'What is it? Were you feeling faint?' he asked.

Amanda shut her lips tightly together and shook her head. Puzzled, Tibor looked carefully at her, noticing her pallor and the way her hands were clenched on the leather seat of the taxi.

'All right. We'll talk about it later.'

Within ten minutes they were climbing the dusty stairs to Tibor's studio. Amanda reached it and breathed in the familiar smells of cigarette smoke, paint, turpentine, garlic, drink and friendly dust. The large room was as different as possible from Comfort's extraordinarily ordered studio. Amanda had known it well for at least sixteen years. She felt as though she had reached dry land again.

'Thank you,' she said.

Tibor went to the small fridge that shared space under a long table with stacks of stretched canvases and boxes of old brushes he could not bear to throw away or use, and fetched a half-drunk bottle of white wine. He slopped some into a tumbler and handed it to his god-daughter before pouring himself some whisky.

'So,' he said. 'What happened?'

Amanda clutched the tumbler in both hands. She opened her mouth, but said nothing. Increasingly worried, Tibor urged her towards the model's couch that stood, covered in ancient blobs of paint, under a skylight. Amanda sat on it with her back upright and her knees and heels firmly together. Tibor put his glass down on the floor, picked up her feet and swung them round on to the couch. Then he applied gentle pressure to her shoulders. She seemed to come out of whatever trance had been holding her and relaxed against the back, lowering her knees and letting one of her hands leave the glass and flop on to her lap.

'What did Comfort say to you?'

'How do you know she said anything?' asked Amanda.

Tibor shrugged. 'You wanted to escape without her knowing. That in itself suggests she had upset you. Also, I know Comfort well and the sight of your face also suggests that she has been playing her tricks again.'

'Tricks?' Amanda was suddenly hopeful.

'Yes,' said Tibor emphatically. 'She can be very destructive and very tiresome. What has she been saying?'

Amanda took a gulp of the cold, slightly sour wine.

'That A . . . that her brother is my father,' she said. There was enough horror in her voice to make Tibor look at her very carefully. 'That my mother did not marry Daddy until after I was born.'

'Now I know who you have been making me think of all this evening,' he said.

'Oh, Christ! Don't you tell me as well. I know I look just like my bloody mother.'

'Hush, Amanda. There's no need for such rage. You do. You look exactly as she did when she discovered that she was pregnant with you.'

'No wonder she's always hated me,' said Amanda slowly. 'If she wanted to get away from him and then found . . .'

'Stop it.' Tibor's voice was hard and cold enough to make Amanda jump. Seeing that he had her full attention, he went on more softly: 'She did not want to get away from him. She was determined to make her marriage work, although he was not, and Comfort did not help either of them by insisting on being part of what should have been theirs alone. He behaved extremely badly to your mother and it could have been no surprise to anyone who cared for her to see that she turned to David.'

'When did that happen?'

'Earlier in the year she left Anthony. David lived with them in Venice, you see, and while Anthony Gillingham was refusing to sleep with your mother and give her the child she wanted so much, she fell in love with David.'

Amanda was silent while she tried to absorb the significance of what he had said.

'So how do you know so much about it? You weren't in Venice with them too, were you?' She could hear the spite and the anger in her own voice, but there was nothing she could do about either of them.

'No,' said Tibor patiently. 'She left Italy. After she and David had made love, she felt she had to get away and so she came back to London. I was sharing the house with Comfort at the time . . .'

'It's ridiculous!' Amanda interrupted. 'You must be making it all up. There can't have been so many connections between you all.'

Tibor shook his rough, grey head.

'There were: just so many connections and others too. Anyway, I saw that your mother was pregnant and eventually she told me all about it. She did not want to tell David, because she did not understand how much he loved her. He is younger than she and she thought that she would ruin his political career before it even started if she went to him with the child.'

'I see.' Amanda drank some more of the wine and then put the glass on the floor as she grimaced. 'This is disgusting, Tibor.'

'Sorry. It's been open some days now.'

'Why didn't she tell me? It would . . . I would never have gone near the Gillinghams if she'd told me. She just said she didn't want me to have anything to do with them. Why couldn't she have trusted me? I know she doesn't like me, but she must have known I'd understand.'

'Perhaps she has not understood that,' said Tibor casually. He was perched on the side of the couch, holding her hand. 'Now tell me: you are pregnant too, aren't you?'

'How do you know?'

'I have eyes and – as I said – you look just as she did then.'

Amanda did not answer and kept her face away from him.

'You poor child. No wonder you look so ill! It must be very worrying, Amanda. But it is not a disaster. Come, smile.'

At the new gentleness in his voice, she turned back to look at him, gripping his hand between both of hers.

'What shall I do, Tibor?'

'I can't advise you except to say: tell Julia.'

Amanda pulled her hands away. Her flush had gone completely, leaving her face greyish-white. Her eyes looked blank.

231

'I couldn't. She's the last person.'

'She is the person who knows what it feels like, Amanda. She has been where you are now. She can understand. And she cares about you more than you could possibly imagine.'

'She doesn't.' Tears came into Amanda's eyes then, although they did not spill down her face. 'Kind people like you keep trying to persuade me of that, but she doesn't and now I know why. In an odd way, that helps. You see, I thought it was me she disliked, not the facts of my conception.'

'Do you think that you are the only person who comes here to cry on my shoulder?' Tibor asked with a smile. When Amanda only looked puzzled, he added: 'Julia has been here often, hurt – badly hurt – by things you have said to her or things she has tried to say to you that you have not accepted.'

'I don't believe you.'

'Too bad.' Tibor got up then and stood, looking his usual strong, dishevelled self. 'You must get home and you can't go on the streets half-naked like that. Shall I fetch your clothes now or send you home in a taxi and get them later?'

Amanda looked down at the fashionable metal squares that covered the bodystocking. Then she looked back at Tibor, shyer than he had ever seen her.

'Would you really fetch them? I don't much like the idea of going back there.'

'Certainly I will go. I'd better telephone to see if Anthony is still there to let me in. Wait.'

Amanda listened to half the subsequent conversation and heard Tibor say complimentary things about her portrait, adding: 'But she needs her clothes. May I come to fetch them now?'

He listened.

'Yes. It is imperative.'

There was silence again.

'I am afraid that Comfort has been exercising her imagination and her sense of mischief – to put it kindly. What? No.

That's good. I shall see you in ten minutes. Good-bye.'

He turned to smile reassuringly at Amanda.

'I'll be back as soon as I can. Are your parents expecting you at any special time?'

She shook her head.

'Good. Then when you are decent again we can find out where they are and I can take you home. Wait. Are you cold?'

'A bit.'

Tibor ran up the spiral stairs to the gallery where he slept, moving surprisingly lightly for so stocky a man. He was back a moment later with an enormous dark blue eiderdown. It was very old and as he tucked it round Amanda, she smelled the mustiness of it and saw the splits in the silk that covered it.

'This needs cleaning and re-covering,' she said severely.

'Oh, you're so fernickety.'

Amanda smiled, but she did not correct his English.

'It is warm,' he went on, pleased to have made her smile. 'That's all that matters. Go to sleep. The worst is over.'

Tucking her chin over the thickness of the doubled eiderdown, Amanda wondered how he could possibly know that.

'When you see him, you won't tell him about this, will you?' she said, gesturing to her stomach.

'That, no. But it will be difficult to say nothing about what he has allowed Comfort to do to you.'

Amanda was surprised to see that the easy-going, genial man she had known so long could look so ferocious.

'Please don't. It wasn't his fault. He . . .'

'You're right: it wasn't altogether his fault. No one has been able to control Comfort, but he should have stopped her from using you at all. He has always been weak and self-indulgent, hiding that under the arrogance and the brilliance. He and Comfort ruined years of your mother's life and now they have hurt you.' Tibor breathed deeply until he had mastered some of his fury. 'I find it hard to forgive.'

Amanda said nothing. When he had gone, she took off the

metal dress, wrapped the huge eiderdown clumsily around her and waddled across the splintered floor to the messy table that served as Tibor's desk. There she found writing paper and a variety of pens and pencils. Selecting a battered fountain pen that miraculously had ink in it, she wrote a stiff, formal note to Comfort, thanking her for the loan of the dress and making no reference to anything else at all.

That done, Amanda folded the dress with difficulty and laid it on the desk with the letter on top. She knew that Tibor would see that it reached Comfort. Then she returned to the model's couch, rolled herself more comfortably in the eiderdown and obediently closed her eyes. Tibor was in charge, she thought, as she fell into sleep.

She woke two hours later to feel warmer air on her face. For a moment she lay with her eyes closed, letting her memory work. When she had got all the events of the evening straightened out in her mind, she opened her eyes. At the far end of the studio, sitting close together and talking quietly, were Tibor and Julia.

At the sight of her mother, Amanda let out a wordless exclamation. The other two stood up at once and Julia walked across the paint-stained floorboards to the model's couch. There she stood, her face as gentle as Amanda had ever seen it.

'Hello, darling. I've come to take you home.'

Amanda, who had kept her dignity while Comfort tormented her, burst into tears and hated herself for it. She felt her mother's cool hand on her forehead.

'It's all right now. You needn't worry. We can sort everything out. You can relax for a bit.'

Amanda turned her face away, biting her lower lip savagely until the pain of it forced her tears to stop. Then she faced her mother.

'Sorry. For a moment I felt as though I were an ill child and you were taking my temperature. But I'm all right. Did Tibor fetch my things?'

'Yes. They're up in the gallery. Do you want go up now to change?'

Amanda swung her legs off the couch and pulled the massive eiderdown modestly round herself. It was difficult clambering up the narrow spiral staircase with the tattered silk cushioning around her and at one moment she stumbled. Grasping the rail of the stairs as she tripped, she let the eiderdown go and it fell round her ankles. Although the bodystocking was no more revealing than a bathing suit she felt quite naked and utterly humiliated. She pulled the eiderdown round herself again and stumbled on up the stairs. Once dressed in her own clothes, she washed her face in cold water at Tibor's basin before returning to the studio.

'Thank you, Tibor,' she said, putting a hand on his shoulder and leaning forwards to kiss him as she always did. He hugged her with strong arms and she felt the bristles of his chin rubbing against her face. It was a surprisingly comforting sensation.

'You will be all right,' he said. 'Come and see me when you're back in London.'

'I will.' Amanda pulled away from him and picked up her bag. 'Let's go, shall we?'

Julia looked at Tibor for a moment in silent gratitude and then obediently collected her handbag and car keys before following Amanda down the steep wooden stairs to the street door.

They drove in silence until Julia turned off the main road, when Amanda said quietly: 'Does Daddy know?'

'No. He was still at the House when Tibor telephoned and I merely left a note to say I'd gone to collect you. Don't you want him to know?'

'I'm not sure. How much did Tibor tell you?'

'Everything you told him.'

'Oh.' To Amanda's acutely straining ears there seemed to be no criticism or hatred in her mother's voice, but she did not know how to start talking to her.

'You're worn out now. We don't need to talk about anything until you've had a proper sleep.' Julia drew up outside her house and put on the handbrake.

Amanda turned, remembering vividly the night when she had been so horrible to Andrew Suvarov when he parked under just the same streetlight.

'I do want to actually, but it's difficult.'

Julia brushed some of Amanda's hair away from her forehead in a gesture she had used whenever either of the children was ill.

'All right. Let's have a hot drink in the kitchen and try, shall we?'

Amanda nodded and led the way into the house. There was no sign of David. Julia poured some milk into a saucepan and set it on the gas.

'Just hot milk or Horlicks?'

'Hot milk and brandy and brown sugar would be best.'

'What a good idea,' said Julia with a nice laugh. 'Will you fetch the brandy?'

When Amanda brought back the bottle of Courvoisier from the dining room sideboard, Julia was sitting at the green table, stirring sugar into one of the two stoneware mugs. Amanda pulled out a chair a little way away from her mother and sat down, pushing the bottle forwards.

Both of them had difficulty in finding a way to start, but in the end Julia decided that it was her responsibility.

'I know that I disagreed with David about the Abortion Bill, but I must say now that I am delighted it got through,' she said lightly. 'You must have been badly worried, darling, but we can fix it up easily and then you can try and forget the whole worrying business.'

'Why didn't you tell me?' asked Amanda abruptly.

'Tell you what?' Julia thought she knew, but she wanted to be certain before she started talking about the past.

'That I was the result of an affair you had while you were still married to Anthony Gillingham? You can't imagine how unspeakable I felt when Comfort told me I was his daughter.'

'But Tibor explained, didn't he? Amanda, you don't really think that . . . No, of course you don't. Sorry.' Julia sighed. 'It didn't seem important enough to bother you with. You're David's and my daughter, much loved and always wanted; it never seemed necessary to specify that your conception took place before my divorce.'

'But if you'd told me, I'd never had sat for Comfort and I'd never have been put through everything that's happened tonight. Besides, you lied to me. Can't you imagine what that feels like?'

Julia's eyebrows twitched.

'I did ask you not to see the Gillinghams,' she said mildly. 'Couldn't you have trusted that I had a reason?'

'Why should I? You've never trusted me. You just hated me for not measuring up to what you wanted. At least that always seemed to be why you hated me. Now, of course, I understand better. As I said to Tibor that is one positive thing that has come out of all this.'

Julia held her hands tightly together in her lap, trying not to show what she was feeling.

'I have never hated you,' she began, 'and . . .'

'Then why did you behave as though you did?' demanded Amanda passionately. 'All my life you've shown how little you cared.'

Julia shook her head and blinked several times. Trying to pretend that she was in court, explaining a knotty point of law, so that she could keep her emotions properly under control, she said: 'I can understand that as a tiny child you might have thought that my working rather than being here in the house with you all the time meant that I did not care, but once you grew up, you must have understood. You don't lack brains, after all.' As she spoke, Julia realised that she had chosen almost the worst possible words.

Amanda banged down her mug, slopping the sweetened milk over the table.

'And I thought that things might be all right when I saw you at Tibor's and you were kind for once. But trust you to turn it all round and blame me. I am your child. It was your job to explain and teach me – not to blame me for not seeing things as you see them.' She stood up.

To Julia just then, her daughter's face seemed even more poignantly miserable for the smudged make-up that ought to have disguised it. She searched for words that might reach through to that misery and cure it.

'You don't understand, do you?' said Amanda before her mother could open her mouth. 'You never have.'

'Not altogether, but I am trying to understand you, as I have always tried.'

'Not very hard. If you had you'd know . . .' Amanda's voice broke.

She clung on to the edge of the table, unaware that the spilled milk was seeping under her hands, on to the floor. She looked and sounded like a hurt child. If Julia had not been so miserable, she would have smiled at the contrast with her usually immaculate, untouchable daughter.

'You'd know how much I've always wanted you to protect me against the foul things that happen. Mothers are supposed to fit their children for real life and you never have. We've had to learn it all ourselves and it's been bloody painful. And bloody lonely.'

Amanda turned away, her breath tearing out of her chest and her eyes spurting tears. She did not hear Julia's protest but fumbled her way out of the kitchen and fled to the sanctuary of her bedroom.

Julia sat on at the kitchen table, saying aloud but uselessly: 'But I tried. It's my efforts to do precisely that which have always made you so angry. I can't teach you things I don't know. What are the foul things that have happened? What ought I to have done?'

Julia longed for her husband's return. Knowing that he might not be back for hours, she reached for the telephone to ring Felicity Suvarov. It was not until the telephone had rung unanswered for nearly three minutes that she remembered Flixe had disappeared to Rome.

CHAPTER 15

Flixe set off for her weekend with George in Rome in a state of some confusion. She had been plunged into despair by the news that there was indeed a tumour in Natalie's kidney and then enormously encouraged when the doctors announced that it might not be malignant. They were clear that she was very ill and would probably have to lose the entire kidney if the first, risky, operation they planned did not succeed, but they were adamant that one kidney was plenty for anyone.

Flixe had just begun to allow herself to stop worrying about Natalie's health when she received a letter from Ann Kirkwaters, which read:

> Dear Flixe,
>   When I invited you to balance George Mayford at Jemima's dance the last thing I expected was that you would be silly enough to flirt with him. I feel I ought in kindness to warn you that he is notorious for his affairs and that he is no stayer. If you are looking for another meal-ticket, he won't provide it. At most you'll have a couple of months before he's off with the next pretty, available woman. Don't say I didn't warn you.
>
> Ann

The very offensiveness of the letter told Flixe a good deal, but she was reluctant to believe that George, whom she had found to be both sensitive and intelligent as well as gloriously affectionate, could have had a love affair with anyone like Ann Kirkwaters. On the other hand, if he had, it would explain both his stiffness when they met at the dance and his odd mood the following day just before they made love.

Flixe kept telling herself that she was not looking to George for a lifetime's commitment, but the suggestion that he would leave her after only two months bothered her in spite of all her self-protective cynicism. Almost more upsetting was Ann's accusation of gold-digging. That made Flixe feel so dirty that for a while she did not even consider what she would think if she were to discover that George had deliberately concealed a love affair with Ann if not actually lied about it.

'What is it?' he asked after they had eaten a belated dinner in their hotel after a much delayed flight.

'What?'

'Come on, Felicity; don't pretend. Something is worrying you badly. Can't you tell me what it is?'

Flixe, who had always prided herself on not thrusting her own emotions on to other people, gritted her teeth, trying to find a convincing excuse for her mood.

'Is it something I've done – or not done? You're clearly not happy.'

'I'm sorry,' she said at last. 'I must seem like a sulky schoolgirl. I hadn't meant to tell you anything about it, but perhaps I should since I haven't been able to stop its effects. I have had a rather disturbing letter from Ann Kirkwaters. That's all.'

'Ah.' George looked acutely uncomfortable. He drank the last of the wine in his glass and sat up straighter. 'Is it . . . ? I'm not sure what she's told you, but if she suggested that it isn't over, she's . . . This gets worse and worse. Felicity, it

241

is true that for a while she and I were lovers – of a sort – but it's ended.'

'When did it end, George?'

'The day I came to your house so late. Everything I told you about my patient was true, but I had also had a difficult time with Ann. I'd rung her after our lunch, you see, to explain that I couldn't go on. I knew that I couldn't come to you while she was still in my life, as it were.'

'So why did you go to stay with her for the dance?' asked Flixe, frowning as she thought over all the implications of what he was saying.

'Because she begged me to. She said it was the least I could do, and that seemed reason enough. I knew perfectly well that I'd behaved badly to her all along. And I hadn't realised that you would be there.'

'Would that have made so much difference?'

George looked at her and she saw that there was a hint of a smile in his eyes. He nodded.

'I was extremely concerned that neither she nor any of her friends should assume I'd broken with her merely in order to take up in the same sort of way with you.'

'Oh.'

'It's not the same at all, which is why, I suppose, I was so reluctant . . . Felicity, I don't really want to go on talking about this. If it makes you want to stop what we've started, then so be it. Otherwise, can we ignore it for the time being at least?'

'It doesn't make me want to stop,' she said slowly, 'although it does make me ask myself all sorts of questions.' She smiled suddenly. 'But you're right. We can answer them later.'

'Thank you. You look very tired. Do you want to go on up?'

'I think I will,' she said, wondering how their romantic weekend would turn out after such an unpromising start. It was quite clear that only she could ruin or save it.

'I must telephone a couple of colleagues who'll be

attending the conference tomorrow,' said George. 'I'll follow you in due course.'

Flixe nodded again and left him. She had unpacked, had a long bath and got into bed by the time he appeared. He came to stand at the edge of her side of the bed, looking down at her.

'I've checked with the reception desk and there are several vacant rooms on the next floor. Would you rather I had one of them?' he asked.

Flixe smiled up at him. 'No,' she said, having thought it all out in her bath. 'Don't let's make a great drama out of this. I was disconcerted when I realised what had been going on because I was surprised that anyone who had liked Ann should . . .' She broke off, afraid that she was displaying unconscionable vanity.

George sat down on the edge of the bed and held out his right hand. Flixe put hers into it without any reluctance at all.

'I didn't like her,' he said, examining each of Flixe's fingernails in turn so that he did not have to let her see the expression in his eyes. 'That is what is making me feel such a heel at the moment. After what I've discovered it is possible to feel with you, the whole Ann episode – and the others before that – makes me feel dreadful.'

He did look up then and Flixe remembered what he had said to her in her bedroom on the day after the dance. She had thought it sad then, when she knew nothing of any of the women in his life. Now she thought it even worse.

'I suppose the only saving grace is that she didn't like me either,' he said. 'She wanted sensation and a chance to distract herself from a husband who bores her, a daughter who irritates her and a life that doesn't satisfy her. She couldn't have been less interested in me for myself, and, for what it's worth, she was no reluctant conquest.'

'And you? What did you want from her, George? Not that I've any right to ask.'

'Actually I think you have the right. I suppose I wanted sex, a chance to prove I am still attractive to women, some kind of recreation that squash and dinner parties don't provide. It sounds pathetic, doesn't it?'

'Different,' said Flixe, thinking of her own past and Peter's difficult escapades. 'Poor Ann.'

'Yes.' George released her hand and stood up. 'I'd better have a bath. Will I disturb you?'

'No. I'll read a bit and then probably sleep.'

'Fine,' he said. It seemed that her assessment of his brains and sensitivity had not been altogether wrong. 'Sleep well.'

In fact, she did not sleep at all well. Strange beds and travelling always combined to rob her of rest even when she was alone and had nothing to worry about.

Feeling physically shaky the following morning, she found that she was also absurdly nervous of the prospect of wandering about Rome on her own while George attended his conference. Having been a wife for so many years, she had quite lost the ability to feel at ease on her own in a strange place.

She and George breakfasted together at eight so that he could get to the Palazzo Corsini – where the conference was to be held – in time for the first session of the morning and in time to allow her to do some sightseeing before the heat became unbearable.

The first cup of strong black coffee began to revive her and by the time she had eaten a sweet croissant and drunk two more cups of coffee she felt as though she could face the day. She returned to their room after breakfast to collect her shady hat, guidebook and sunglasses and shared George's taxi as far as the Forum. He kissed her hand there, saying urgently: 'You will take care of yourself, won't you?'

'Don't worry about me,' she said firmly, having persuaded herself that she felt perfectly all right again. 'I have a tightly planned schedule of things to see.' Flixe smiled with what she hoped was an air of confidence.

'All right, but don't overdo it and don't go anywhere near the university.'

'Very well, Doctor Mayford,' said Flixe demurely, which made him laugh.

'I know; you're quite capable of looking after yourself. And there's no reason why Roman students should build barricades and set cars on fire just because the French did, but who knows? They are demonstrating here as well, and anything might happen. I wonder...'

'Don't worry so much, George. I'm sure they won't infect the tourist bits of the city. I'll be fine and I'll see you this evening. Good-bye.'

The yellow taxi drove off and Flixe took a deep breath before plunging into the ancient ruins. Having squeezed enough time out of her busy days to read several guidebooks before she left London, she had planned a careful course of self-improvement for her three days in Rome. The first day would be devoted to the Classical ruins, the second to the progress of Christianity, and the third to the secular monuments of the Renaissance and later, taking in buildings, statues and paintings. No major museum would remain unvisited, she had decided, and even if she had to choose among the churches, she would try to cover the most important.

Opening the most pocketable of her guides, she reread the section on the Forum and conscientiously looked at all the ruined temples, houses and basilicas that were mentioned. It was only when heat and exhaustion persuaded her to sit on a broken column base in a patch of shade two and a half hours later that she admitted to boredom. The acres of marble detritus that surrounded her seemed meaningless. It occurred to her that if she had known more she might have been able to exercise her imagination and feel something of the lives that had been spent there, but she could not do it. Even the Colosseum itself seemed no more than a massive, rather ugly, dirty heap of brick. Despite the guidebook's anecdotes of this vestal virgin or that emperor, there was nothing to spark Flixe's imagination. Nothing in her mind or experience met anything in that sea of broken building.

Imagining how Gerry would have revelled in the sights and known everything without needing a guidebook, Flixe felt inadequate and rather stupid. As soon as she had cooled enough to face the walk back through the plain to the modern city, she opened her guidebook again, deciding to break her self-imposed plan and look at something that might engage her.

St Peter's seemed too far to walk and, speaking no Italian at all, she was disinclined to cope with a taxi or bus. The Pantheon looked much nearer, but that was ancient, too. Eventually, having searched through the list of starred sights and checked them with the maps at the back of the book, she decided to walk to the Piazza Navona and find somewhere to sit down in the shade and have an ice or perhaps some lunch.

It was much better there when she eventually found it – a long oval space surrounded by nice old red and ochre houses with a big grey church in the centre of one side and three fountains splashing coolly in the heat. Pigeons flapped about on the smooth pavement and the usual ill-looking cats slunk around the chairs that stood outside each of the bars and restaurants.

Flixe chose one and sat heavily in a red plastic chair under a large parasol, sighing with relief as she took the weight off her aching feet. When a waiter came to ask her pleasure, she managed to explain that she wanted a glass of white wine and a sandwich. The wine was fine, crisp and very cold, but the sandwich was rather a failure, made of a hard roll filled with cold spinach and a tough, cold omelette. Later she ordered a dish of mixed ice-cream, which turned out better.

The square was pleasant, not too crowded despite the artists daubing canvases obviously designed for unwary tourists, and the waiter seemed quite unworried about the amount of time Flixe was taking to eat her simple meal. So she sat on there, dreaming idly in the shady warmth and beginning to think that she might quite like Rome after all. Her head, which had been aching, began to feel better and she stretched her sore feet out in front of her and closed her eyes.

Into her warm, relaxed mind came a picture of Peter so vivid that she almost gasped. It was an image not of the emaciated man dying in pain, nor of the careless husband who had so inexplicably left her in such trouble, but of the man with whom she had fallen in love so long before.

Nearly twenty years her senior, he had seemed the acme of glamour and sophistication to the eighteen-year-old girl who had been seconded to work for him at the beginning of the war. Despite his wicked reputation and his undeniable sexiness he had never made advances to Flixe, and as the years of war passed in terror, boredom and excitement she had come to terms with the fact that her extreme love for him would always be unrequited. At times she had almost enjoyed it. Not until the fighting was almost over, when only the Japanese had yet to surrender, did Peter tell her that he loved her too.

Looking back to the end of the war, Flixe could remember how terrifying her feelings had become then. There had even been times when she had almost longed for the cosiness of the days before she knew that he loved her. Once they were married everything she did or said seemed to take on an appalling importance. She dreaded hurting him or – perhaps worse – falling short of his expectations. It seemed inevitable that he, so fascinating, so experienced, so knowledgeable, should become bored with her.

Having given up to him every shred of self-protection, she could not bear the prospect that he might cease to love her. Life mattered so much that it took all her strength and energy to keep up with it. But it was worth it. The reality of his love and the excitement of being with him made her happier than she had ever expected to be, and she had always had high expectations.

Flixe opened her eyes, blinking in the sharp sunlight, remembering and feeling and coming alive. The memories still hurt, but there was pleasure in them, too. Peter had loved her and that was what mattered. She had been able to give him something that he needed, unbelievable though it had seemed at first, and slowly, as she went on giving it, he, too, had been able to shed some of his layers of protection until the two of them knew each other better than anyone else had ever done.

The intensity had lessened at times, although there were other times when, for no apparent reason, it returned to grip her again, and although she had known he must die she had never even thought of life without him.

'*Signora?*'

The waiter was back. Flixe sent him away by asking for another glass of wine, but his interruption had banished Peter again and the memories she conjured up now were the same ones that had been with her since he died. She drank her wine, paid the bill and decided that St Peter's did not look too far away after all.

It took her half an hour to walk there and her feet were hurting again by the time she reached the entrance to Bernini's magnificent piazza.

'This is better too,' she muttered to herself, avoiding the line of waiting horse-drawn cabs that smelled so strongly and the postcard sellers and the groups of pilgrims and tourists. She liked the curve of the colonnade and the grace of its pillars and spent some time standing in the sun looking at it before walking up the incline to the vast basilica itself.

Inside she was once more struck with a mixture of boredom and distaste. The heavy grandiosity of the interior left her cold and she disliked both its brownness and the appalling power that it represented. Her elder sister had often said that Flixe was too lazy and comfortable ever to be angry, but some things had always roused her ire: tyranny, waste and hypocrisy. In the echoing, gilded, marble-lined basilica, remembering what she had read of the history of the Catholic Church, she felt surrounded by all three.

Distressed and feeling as though she had been discourteous by standing in someone else's church criticising it, however silently, she turned to leave, only looking to her left by chance. There, with a ring of people nine deep in front of it, she saw Michelangelo's Pietà. Someone she had talked to years before in London had sneered at the statue and told her that it was derivative and devoid of any genuine creativity, but she had always found photographs of it desperately moving. Joining the rest of the tourists, she thought that the statue expressed precisely what she wished the vast church might have done. There was pain in it and most terrible sorrow, but there were sacrifice and tenderness and forgiveness, too.

Flixe must have spent longer in St Peter's than she realised, for the sun was much less hot when she emerged and it no longer made the pale stone pavement dazzle. Walking painfully back across the Tiber to her hotel, she decided to buy some postcards for her children. She had heard that the Italian post was terribly erratic and although there seemed little point in sending things that might arrive long after her own return to England, she wanted some contact with them.

She found a shop and spent some time picking the most appropriate cards. For Andrew she chose one of a Bernini statue of David she had not yet seen. Unlike Michelangelo's version, Bernini's was not languidly confident, but furiously determined. The curve of his compact, muscular body as he drew back his sling was masterfully achieved, and the intense frown on his angry young face reminded her of her son. For Fiona the Pietà seemed best and for Sophie a bulging-cheeked angel from a painted ceiling in a Renaissance palace

249

somewhere in Rome. For Nicholas, her youngest and most vulnerable, she chose an endearing picture of a monkey reaching up for some fruit, which was apparently a detail from one of the wall paintings in the Palazzo Borghese.

Having bought them, she took them to a small café, where she ordered a cup of coffee and sat down at a small table to write to her children. The coffee came in a tiny cup and the first mouthful was so strong that it gave her an almost physical jolt. Her eyes widened and she sat awhile tasting the richness before picking up her pen.

By the time she reached the hotel she was limping, aware that there was a growing blister on her right heel, and very tired. At the reception desk they said something to her in Italian, which she did not understand, but she managed to ask for the key to the room, and let herself in to its welcoming coolness in relief.

Having partly opened the shutters to let in some light, she ran herself a tepid bath, added some scented oil, undressed and lay down in it, too tired even to wash. Memories of Peter came flooding back and she let them do with her what they would as she fell asleep.

She opened her eyes to see George sitting on a stool watching her. Dressed in a loose tropical suit of buff linen and a cream shirt with an olive green tie, he looked like the archetypal Englishman abroad, both distinguished and detached. He was smoking and as he saw her eyes opening he smiled, his well-shaped mouth widening and his clear greygreen eyes crinkling at the corners.

Flixe's mind had been so full of Peter and the children all afternoon that the sight of George was a shock. Pushing herself up, she wiped a wet hand over her eyes.

'Have I been asleep?' she asked, the words slurring slightly.

'Yes. You must have worn yourself out, you poor thing.'

'How long?'

'I've been here about ten minutes. I was going to wake you

when I'd finished this.' He stubbed the cigarette out in a glass ashtray that stood beside the basin. 'Are you all right? You look . . . what's that word of yours? Ah yes, bothered.'

'I'm fine,' she said, swallowing and wanting to brush her teeth, 'just a bit startled. I felt as though I'd shut my eyes for a minute and then there you were, as though you'd dropped from heaven.' She shivered suddenly, aware that the water, which had been pleasantly cool, was now uncomfortably cold, and saw that the skin of her fingers was puckered into squashy ridges. 'Ugh. I'd better get out.'

George collected one of the bathtowels, which were more like tablecloths than towels, and stood by the side of the bath holding it out. Flixe got out and he wrapped the towel around her, hugging her. It felt so comforting that she pushed aside the shock she had felt at his presence and put her arms around his neck. He bent to kiss her ear.

'Sorry,' she murmured a little later. 'I must be making you all wet.'

'I love water trickling down my back,' he said, laughing, as he kissed her lips.

Flixe took her arms away and rubbed them on the towel.

'You must be cold,' he said, 'I should have thought. It was just so lovely holding you that I forgot I was meant to be drying you.'

'I'm glad,' said Flixe, touching his face. 'You've lost your tan.'

'Some time ago. Do you mind?'

'No, although it suited you – made your eyes look paler and more dazzling. But I was just thinking what a pity it is that you have to be stuffing away indoors in this lovely weather.'

'It's worse that I'm stuffing away indoors when I could be with you,' he said, making a face of exaggerated regret. 'All day I kept finding that my concentration on the learned papers was slipping as I thought of you. Did you have a good time?'

'It was odd,' said Flixe, vigorously rubbing her chilled body on the towel, 'and faintly disturbing.'

'Oh, my dear.' He brushed the damp hair away from her face and looked carefully at her. 'Are you all right?'

'Yes, but a bit . . . strange. I don't feel quite myself.'

'You don't seem it either. I'd put it down to your sleeping in the bath. Come and lie down for a moment.' He reached for the other towel and swapped it for the damp one, wrapping it round her carefully.

Together they walked through to the bedroom, which seemed warm to Flixe after her cold bath. George whisked the heavy silk counterpane off the bed and urged her to lie down.

She was afraid that he wanted to make love and she did not want to be ungenerous enough to refuse and yet it was the last thing she wanted just then. They lay down together.

'You're going to crumple your smart tropical suit,' said Flixe as he put his arms around her again.

'That doesn't matter. Lie still.' He stroked her hair and occasionally brushed her forehead with his lips and she quite quickly realised that he was making no demands of her at all. She said nothing and allowed herself to relax into the peace of his gentleness.

'Thank you,' she said much later when the strangeness of her mood had passed and neither the contrasts between him and Peter nor his dealings with Ann Kirkwaters seemed important any longer. 'That was remarkably kind.'

'You've nothing to thank me for at all,' he said, kissing her lips briefly. 'But you must be getting hungry. I'll have a quick bath and change out of these and then we'll find somewhere to sup. All right?'

'Lovely,' she said, rolling on to her back and pushing the hair away from her face. 'I'll tidy myself up.'

He disappeared into the bathroom, leaving her to wonder how much he had understood or guessed and whether he had minded her withdrawal from him.

They chose a simple-looking restaurant close to their hotel

and ate remarkably well. As the mixed antipasto was followed by veal cooked with sage and wine, Flixe began to revive and by the time they were sipping a sickly wormwood-flavoured liqueur with their coffee, she was laughing at George's stories and capping them with some of her own. Eventually as they walked back to the hotel arm in arm, he said: 'Do you regret coming here?'

'No. It's good to be away from everything – and here with you.'

He laughed at the polite afterthought, but his amusement seemed kind and Flixe walked closer to him, feeling his fingers tightening slightly on her arm.

'That's all that matters,' he said and asked her no more questions. As soon as they were safely inside their room, he took her in his arms again. This time it was not comfort Flixe felt as he kissed her but pleasure. A moment later George lifted his head and laughed.

'You are the most adorable woman to kiss,' he said. 'Would you like to come to bed?'

'I should like it enormously,' she said with truth. He escorted her to the big bed with some ceremony and kissed her as he laid down against the pillows.

Much later Flixe said: 'I feel extraordinarily equal making love with you. It's a delight.'

'I'm glad, Felicity.' He let his head drop on to her shoulder. 'You make me feel very . . . very privileged.'

She stroked his hair, feeling the soft fineness of it beneath her fingers. He pushed his head nearer her neck and let his eyelids close.

'I trust you,' he murmured. A moment later his breathing changed and Flixe realised that he was asleep.

CHAPTER 16

Flixe woke the following morning in a state of happiness that seemed like a reward for the months of endurance. Despite the big blister on her heel and a strange aching stiffness in her calves from the long walk, she felt physically healthier than she had been for a long time, with her skin sleek and smooth and her head absolutely clear. She had managed to ignore the part George had played in Ann's life and she in his, and found herself simply enjoying the sensation of his long body in the bed beside her. Dangerous though she knew it was, she could not help thinking that life would never again seem unendurable.

That day she dropped her sightseeing plan completely and, as she tasted the variety that Rome offered, solitude, which had frightened her in the months immediately after Peter's death, came to seem almost attractive against the background of George's certain friendship.

Ignoring the important sights and letting herself absorb the charms of simply wandering about the streets of old Rome, Flixe sat down in the sun for an ice or a drink whenever she felt like it. Without any more agonising she let herself walk at whim, frivolously enjoying all sorts of things, from the wonderful open colourfulness of the Quirinale to the rougher charms of the narrow red streets of Trastevere, looking sometimes, at others simply sitting and feeling. The sun shone all day. A certain power that had been missing returned to her and she began to think about her London life with a new, almost detached, resolve.

Her loathing of the political work she had been doing no longer seemed a failing and the possibility of giving up the safe seat that Gerry and Julia had found for her became increasingly alluring as the day went on.

It was only after lunch that Flixe realised that if she threw away everything they had done for her they might be angry enough to withdraw the financial support that had made her life just manageable. Thinking of what it could be like without their help, Flixe shivered, but even that prospect was not as terrible as the thought of struggling on in the constituency, working to become something she simply did not want to be. Even the thought of the freedom she might achieve was enough to make her walk more lightly and smile more easily as she wandered about the city.

In the early evening, she returned to the hotel to bath and change her cornflower-coloured skirt and paler blue shirt for a short, simple, lime green linen dress edged with white piqué that Ming had lent her. Her hair seemed to have become even more blonde in the sun and her skin had begun to tan. With a little make-up to enhance its new colour and a pair of big dark glasses worn on the top of her head to keep her hair out of her eyes, she decided that she looked both attractive and fashionable. Taking pleasure in her own appearance again was new and she walked cheerfully across the river to meet George as he emerged from his conference.

His eyes crinkled into the smile she was coming to know well and he told her that she looked ravishing. When he had introduced her to a few of his fellow Englishmen at the conference, he took her across the road to the small, exquisite, Renaissance Villa Farnesina, which stood just opposite the imposing bulk of the Corsini palace and had been specially opened for the conferees.

As they wandered through the painted rooms, admiring the ceiling that Raphael had designed, laughing at the distorted perspective of the *trompe-l'oeil* frescoes in the Salone delle Prospettive upstairs, and wondering how anyone could have gone to bed in a room so closely decorated as Alessandro Chigi's, Flixe realised that George was not concentrating.

'You seem abstracted,' she said, leaning out of the window and looking out at the formal garden with its dark-leaved orange trees heavy with fruit. 'Is there some trouble?'

'No trouble,' he answered, 'but I keep thinking about something that one of the delegates raised this afternoon.'

'Oh?'

'Yes. I'd like to talk to you about it if it wouldn't bore you.'

Flixe turned, her face warm with pleasure. 'Me? Really?'

'Very much. You're so sensible and . . . so knowledgeable about the things that matter.'

After the previous day's sense of failure at her inability to appreciate the great and famous sights of the eternal city, Flixe was delighted.

'Shall we discuss it over a drink?' she asked and, when he agreed, suggested that since they were so close they should find somewhere to sit in the square outside Santa Maria in Trastevere.

It was a charming place, perhaps even pleasanter than the Piazza Navona, which she had liked so much. They ordered a bottle of cool white Fiorano, a wine that the guidebook informed them was made just outside Rome and rarely drunk anywhere else. With it they were offered dishes of fat green olives and small salty biscuits.

Flixe tasted the wine and leaned back in her chair, enjoying the way the evening sun caught the gilded mosaics above the entrance to the church and the easiness of a world in which you could sit and drink on a pavement out of doors at the end of a day.

'You do look increasingly wonderful each day.' The slight surprise in George's deep voice made her smile.

'I'm relaxing,' she said, 'and my face has always looked better when it's a bit sunburned. But you wanted to talk about something more important than my face.'

He looked for a moment as though he were going to make some extravagant compliment, but then he wrinkled his nose and grinned instead, which pleased her. For Flixe one of George Mayford's great charms was the casualness with which he treated their affair. There was no lack of concern or generosity in him, but he did not load their cheerful, friendly sensuality with any weight of demanding emotion. The fact that he had had plenty of practice no longer seemed distressing. He had made it clear that it had been important for him to free himself from his other commitments before entangling himself with Flixe and that was enough for her.

'It is simply,' he said, wondering why she was smiling in that vague, inward-looking way, 'that one of my colleagues raised the old question of the differences in men's and women's brains.'

Flixe's gaze focussed and the dreamy smile was overtaken by something different, tarter.

'Oh yes?' Her voice was cold. 'That old chestnut. I think their different habits might be a more fruitful topic than their brains.'

'And he asked again,' said George, acknowledging her dig with the slightest of smiles, 'why there have been no great women painters, musicians or poets. It's all right: you don't have to look so furious. I know perfectly well that there have been some, but there are very few and it cannot just be that they are judged more harshly. Have you any idea why women are generally less creative than men?'

Flixe, who had been amused by his defensiveness, had to

257

suppress her immediate irritation at his last question. She tried to control her crossness as she remembered the way her elder sister's furious feminist tirades had always raised her hackles and made her want to dismiss ideas with which she actually agreed.

'I think,' she began with polite tentativeness, 'that there's nothing fundamental . . . no, it is fundamental; there's nothing congenital that prevents women from creating great poetry, music or painting. Without wanting to sound as though I'm whining, I'd say that it's because we have so many different things to do.'

Seeing a slight film of withdrawal glazing over George's eyes, Flixe smiled to herself.

'Listen: you have only to watch a man – or perhaps a woman like my sister Gerry – in the kitchen. They can wash up perfectly well, they can be brilliant cooks, but they can only do one thing at once. Any mother has had to learn to cook meals for each different section of her family while she listens for the baby crying, pays attention to the school-children's account of their day and makes appropriate comments while still thinking of ways to give her husband the attention he needs when he comes back from the office wound up to a pitch of tension that makes him snap at the children and look as though he hates her.'

'What a nightmare!' George's eyes were no longer glazed, but laughing.

'It is sometimes, and people like my sister Gerry or even Julia Wallington, whom you haven't yet met but who's my greatest friend, are so successful in their work partly because they refuse to do it. And because they refuse, people criticise them for disloyalty to their families. They can concentrate so intensely in the middle of ordinary life that they simply do not hear a question addressed to them. Whereas the rest of us are like . . . oh, like an advent calendar.'

Flixe was becoming excited as she talked and her eyes were shining and her cheeks beginning to flush.

'D'you see what I mean?' she asked when George said nothing.

He poured some more wine into their glasses and offered Flixe the little glass dish of olives. Surprised at the interruption, she took one, enjoying the firm, slippery saltiness as she bit into it.

'I'm pursuing you, but I'm a little way behind. Explain about the calendar.'

'An advent calendar. You know, the ones children have so that they can open a door on each day of advent?'

George nodded.

'Catholic things, aren't they? Gina never had one.'

Flixe's eyebrows twitched. 'Well, mothers – and motherly secretaries, friends, sisters, and wives – are like an advent calendar on Christmas Day. All the doors are open. All the energy they might have put into the one thing has been allowed to leak out through the doors.'

'Illuminating.'

Flixe wondered whether George was mocking her. On the assumption that he was too affectionate and sensible for that, she went on, thinking out her idea as she described it.

'Then a hideous difficulty comes when all those open doors aren't needed any more,' she added sadly. 'When your husband dies or your children cease to want to tell you everything they've done that day, you're left with all your doors open and only a cold wind blowing through them. You have to learn to haul them shut.'

She stopped, thinking back over the last months.

'And kind people bung wedges in the way,' she went on, 'trying to keep the doors open because they don't realise how badly one needs to shut them – some of them at least.' She looked up, knowing that her eyes were bright and hoping that George would not notice the tears that she was just managing to keep under control.

He was leaning back in his hard chair, drinking the white wine and watching her.

'I think I see what you mean, although your metaphors are getting a bit mixed.'

'Too bad,' she said robustly, feeling better. She blew her nose. 'Where was I? Oh yes, you can't support yourself emotionally any more from giving through the open doors and no one's putting anything back. You have to shut them and build up reserves. Then, perhaps, you can begin to let some out – highly concentrated – through a single door.'

George sat absorbing what she had said. At last he took a flat, black leather notebook out of his pocket.

'May I write that down?'

'What a compliment! Are you going to use it?'

'With due acknowledgement of course.' He bobbed his head in a continental kind of bow, made a note, and then sat watching her, his notebook forgotten on the darned, white tablecloth. After a while she looked at him quizzically, her head on one side and her eyebrows raised.

'Am I staring? Sorry. I suppose I'm just trying to fix this evening in my mind.'

'It's nice, isn't it?' said Flixe at once. 'Simple, friendly, interesting.'

'Yes, but there are other aspects, too.' He sat up straighter and his voice had grown almost abrupt as he added: 'I appear to be falling in love with you. It's not something I'd allowed for and I'm not certain quite what to do about it.'

Flixe looked at him, her dark violet-blue eyes growing more serious and the cheerful warmth in her cheeks cooling visibly.

'Is it so terrible a thought?' he asked, having worried more about its effect on himself than what it might do to her. He had vaguely assumed that she would either ignore his declaration or be pleased by it. That it might upset her had never occurred to him.

Flixe shook her head at once, the immediate generosity of her smile reassuring him. 'The love? No. That's wonderful. It's the falling part that troubles me. I could love you easily,

George,' she said, 'but I could never fall in love again.'

'It's probably too soon, and I do know . . . I do understand how much you loved your husband. I can see that anyone else would seem second best. Besides, I haven't exactly advertised myself as a good proposition after my idiocy with Ann.'

Seeing that he was bothered, Flixe tried to explain that her reservations had nothing to do with his past, however much she disliked the idea of it.

'It's not Ann, and it's nothing to do with my comparing you to Peter. I'm not, although in many ways you are like him.' She reached out to touch George's arm for a moment. 'I suspect that's partly why I liked you so immediately.'

'Then what?'

Flixe looked at him directly, all her memories facing her again.

'I could never again go through that turmoil, that ill-making anxiety, followed by swoops of swooning ecstasy and followed again by yet more terror. When Peter told me he loved me, he gave me the most tremendous confidence and yet at the same time I lost all kinds of self-protection, all sorts of skills I'd built up to get me through life. It took years before I got most of them back and there are some I still haven't regained.' She laughed.

'Looking back, it seems as though I almost had to learn to walk on my own again in the first years after we married. It was wonderful, but terrifying sometimes, and what his death did to me was so appalling that I couldn't risk it again. I'm just not strong enough.'

When George did not speak, she added quietly: 'Is that very ungenerous of me?'

'No, my dear, it's not. It's like everything else about you: sensible, kind, aware and very honest. I've never felt like that, but I think I can understand it. You're telling me, I think, that you will never again open all the doors in the calendar.'

'That's it exactly,' she said, watching happiness slide across his face and lift the corners of his grey-green eyes. Surprised, she added: 'Why? Does that help?'

He nodded, drained his wine glass and said: 'We ought to think about food. Would you like to stay here or go somewhere tidier? It's our last night and I chose yesterday. We'll go wherever you like.'

'I'd like to stay here,' she answered, happy to let him ignore her question if he wanted. 'Its lack of pomposity is lovely.'

'Good. I like it too.' He signalled to the waiter and they talked about nothing but food until they had chosen what they were going to eat. When the man had taken their order and disappeared, George planted both elbows on the table, propped his chin on his clasped hands and looked at her.

'To a man like me, there could be nothing more reassuring than what you said just then.'

Flixe watched him for a while, trying to work out what he meant without clumsily demanding explanations that he might find difficult to give.

'Does this have something to do with the reason you want absolution?' she said at last. For a moment he veiled his eyes and then looked back at her and nodded.

'I have never said this to anyone and never even thought of saying it, but there's something about you that makes it possible. When we married, I thought I loved my wife, but there was a lot I didn't understand.'

He stopped and seemed unable to go on.

'Such as?' Flixe said as gently as possible. He sat up straight and smiled, but there was still a lot of sadness in his eyes.

'I didn't realise that she was suppressing all her needs in favour of attending to mine or that she had needs I had no idea how to satisfy. I assumed that she would always feel as I did.'

He stopped talking again and ripped the top off a packet of breadsticks. The little square was very quiet. There were few other diners in the restaurant that early and there was none of the unending roar of traffic they would have heard on the other side of the river. The fountain splashed and a cat whined in the dusk.

'What happened?' asked Flixe just as the waiter brought their plates of *antipasto misto*. They waited until he had gone and then began to eat their way through the mixture of vegetables and fish and cured meats that filled their plates.

'It's such a familiar story to me now that I find it hard to remember how strange it seemed then,' said George as he finished eating a particularly good artichoke. 'I suppose it boils down to the fact that she grew terribly bored and I became more and more absorbed in my work.'

'You must both have been very young,' Flixe said half in consolation, half in criticism, before pushing on to her fork a piece of grilled red pepper filled with fine breadcrumbs that had been fried in olive oil and flavoured with herbs and lemon juice. 'Everybody makes mistakes because being with someone else is the one thing no one ever teaches you how to do,' she went on when she had eaten the piece of pepper. 'We all start falling in love too young and have no idea whatsoever of the traps that lie in wait.'

'Did you find many traps?'

'Some,' she answered honestly, 'and none of them were the ones that people had warned me about when I chose to marry a man twenty years my senior with a wicked reputation.'

George smiled at her energetic but unspecified refutation of her husband's critics.

'What about you? Did you and your wife fall into traps?'

'Lots, and I don't think I was really young enough to excuse what I did. I was twenty-four when we married and she was twenty. I just hadn't realised that it was an idea of her that I loved and not the reality, or that her reality could be so different from mine.'

'What was she really like?' asked Flixe, ignoring the excoriating self-criticism in his voice.

'At this distance it's hard to tell. But different. So different,' he said, clearly reluctant even so many years later to criticise his dead wife. 'Gina was almost a last resort to keep us together and things did seem better just before she was born and then . . .'

Once more his voice failed and Flixe saw bitter shame in his eyes.

'How did she die?' she asked, afraid of what she might hear.

'A haemorrhage and various other post-partum complications.'

'That wasn't your fault.'

'No, that wasn't,' he said. 'I'd seen that she was in good hands and I wouldn't let her have the baby at home as she wanted. It was no one's fault.'

'Then why do you blame yourself so much?'

George started to speak, stopped, looked helpless and then squared his shoulders.

'Because there was a part of me that felt relieved,' he said, forcing himself to keep looking at Flixe. She dropped her eyes first, so sorry for him and for the girl he had married and for their daughter that for a moment she could not speak.

'It's understandable, George,' she said gently as soon as she could. 'Yet you've hated yourself for it ever since, haven't you? And made certain that no one would ever depend on you again.'

'Except for Gina.'

'That's different,' said Flixe, thinking of what she had told him about motherly wives and friends and rather wishing that she had added daughters to the list.

'And the patients, though they're different too in another way.'

'Were they your attempt at expiation?' Flixe was relieved when he smiled in his old self-mocking way.

'Presumably. Having failed to cure or even understand my wife's unhappiness I tried to cure everyone else by helping them to realise themselves and not try to be – or expect to be

– transformed by other people's expectations.'

'So that's what you meant by "listening to their unhappiness". I've wondered about it ever since that first lunch.'

He looked down at the multi-coloured vegetables that still filled almost half of his plate and picked up his fork again.

'Yes,' he said, spearing a piece of artichoke and a black olive. 'Listening to it and not blaming anyone for it. Neither the people around them nor – more importantly perhaps – themselves. But it doesn't always work. There are depths of depression that I can't even begin to touch. Terrifying and terrible. No one ought to make light of them.'

'I don't suppose anyone does,' said Flixe, noticing the way he pushed his own past and feelings behind the authority of his work. She wondered where Ann Kirkwaters had fitted into the pattern of his life.

He ate for a while and then looked at her with eyes that seemed clearer and more revealing than before.

'I never expected to talk to anyone about my wife's death. I don't need to ask you not to pass it on to Gina, do I?'

Flixe merely looked at him and he nodded.

'Sorry. Of course I don't.'

The waiter appeared to take away their plates.

'Don't let him take it away yet. You've missed those peppers, which are almost the best bit.' When the waiter had been waved away, Flixe went on: 'Do you regret having told me?'

'No. Oddly enough. I feel immeasurably better,' George said, laughing and obediently eating his food. 'The talking cure, perhaps.'

'Good.' Flixe smiled at him and watched as he ate most of the rest of his first course before she allowed the waiter to bring their veal. Then she decided to risk everything they had built up between them by asking the question in her mind.

'And were Ann and her predecessors chosen because you did not like them enough to care about their emotions? Or is that too harsh of me?'

265

George flinched but he answered readily enough.

'Perhaps a little. From your point of view I can see how tatty my goings-on must seem. In my defence I could say that none of them wanted any more of me than a little pleasure, that all of them were well rooted in marriages that were not going to break because of me, and that they were all too un . . .' He broke off, looking ashamed.

'Unintelligent?' asked Flixe derisively. 'Even stupid people can be unhappy, you know.'

'Of course I know,' he answered irritably. 'And although none of them was particularly clever, that wasn't what I was going to say. "Unsensitive" or rather insensitive was the word I was about to use, and that was unkind enough.'

'I'm sorry, George.'

'No need. You have every right to say whatever you want on that subject. I'm on very shaky ground there.'

'It's odd to find a doctor so humble,' said Flixe reflectively and did not see him flinch again.

Two hours later they strolled back across the Ponte Sisto towards their hotel, arm in arm and at ease with each other again. That night their lovemaking was different, no less friendly, no less satisfying, but more important, as though the things they had talked about had broken down the last few barriers between them.

CHAPTER 17

On the aeroplane next day, George was reading a newspaper.

'Thank goodness,' he said, 'the French seem to have taken a grip at last. I was getting quite anxious.'

'Really?' Flixe's voice was vague and she seemed far more interested in the way the sun laid its light across the massed clouds than on what he might be reading.

'Yes,' he said, puzzled, 'for a few days it really looked as though the Communists might seize power. Weren't you worried?'

At that she turned to look at him and he saw that her eyes were dark with anxiety. He laid his hand on her wrist.

'But it is all right now. You needn't be afraid for your family there. De Gaulle has taken charge again.'

'Oh good. There just seem to be so many things to worry about now that the Communist threat doesn't seem quite as desperate as it might. How good to know it's all right,' she said, smiling vaguely at him. He knew that her mind was not on France or even on himself, but he asked no questions.

Later, as she was in the middle of eating the gelatinous cold food on her plastic tray, he touched her hand again. She looked up.

'You've gone awfully quiet,' he said. 'Are you worried about something in particular that I could help with? Is it still Ann? Or did I say too much about the past – or the future?'

She shook her head at once and he was relieved to see that her eyes focussed on him properly.

'No. Not a single superfluous word, my dear. If I'm preoccupied, it's because . . . I'm not sure. I shall have to talk to Julia and Gerry as soon as I can, and I can't imagine what they're going to do to me.'

'Your sister Gerry?' asked George, obviously puzzled.

'Yes.'

There was something so forbidding about that mono-syllable that George asked no more questions.

The plane landed at Heathrow on time and once they had struggled to collect their luggage from the carousel and had the suitcases chalked by Customs, it was still only nine o'clock.

An hour and a half later they reached Flixe's house, tired but exalted.

'Will you come in and have some late supper?' she said as George carried her suitcase into the house. 'There are things in the store cupboard I could whip up into a risotto.'

'I'd better not. The taxi's waiting and I've patients stacked up for tomorrow morning. Felicity, that was the happiest few days I've spent for a very long time.'

Her face was lit by a smile he had come to love, teasing yet at the same time comforting and aware and forgiving.

'I'm glad. I loved it. Will you telephone me?'

'Naturally. There are a great many more things I want to tell you, but they can keep.'

'What sort of things?'

'Oh, how much you've done for me, how much I . . . care

for you. That sort of thing. But none of it need worry you. The doors can stay shut.'

'Only some of them.' Flixe reached up to kiss him. 'Thank you for a most wonderful holiday, George.'

'Good-night.'

She stood at the doorway as he got back into the waiting taxi, waved once and was driven away. Shutting the front door with a sigh, she bent down to pick up the pile of envelopes that lay on the mat. There was one from Ming, which she opened at once.

Dearest Flixe,

    This is just to let you know that they are going to operate on Natalie first thing on Monday morning. As soon as there is any news I'll pass it on, but we're not likely to hear anything for several hours. I do hope that Rome was wonderful.

Love, Ming

Flixe sighed, thinking of Natalie waiting in the hospital and probably afraid. As she turned to go upstairs, she caught sight of a square blue envelope, which had obviously been pushed through the letter-box after all the rest and must have been kicked aside either by her or by George. She picked up that too and, turning it over, recognised Julia's handwriting.

A little surprised, Flixe tucked it into her pocket and carried her suitcase and the rest of the post upstairs. Lying on her bed, she opened Julia's letter first to read:

Dear Flixe,

    I know that you're in Rome at the moment, but as far as I can remember you are due back this evening. I must talk to you. It is terribly important. I am in court on Monday morning. If you're not back too late will you ring me tonight? I'll come round and see you in the

269

afternoon on Monday if we don't talk before then.

Julia

Even more surprised, Flixe read the note again. It was most unlike Julia to prefix so many sentences with 'I', and the hysteria of the message was astonishing for someone as professionally calm as she.

Flixe picked up the telephone, thinking that although it was well after ten o'clock, Julia's need was obviously urgent enough to overcome the normal rules of politeness. The telephone was answered after the second ring.

'Julia Wallington.'

Her voice, which was hoarse and rough, quite unlike her usual clear articulation, worried Flixe even more. She decided to say nothing about her own plans.

'Julia? It's Flixe here. What on earth has happened? Are you all right? Is it David? What's happened?'

'It's good of you to ring. Did you have an agreeable trip?'

'Yes, but never mind that now. What's the matter?'

'Amanda is pregnant.'

Flixe felt as though the bed beneath her was tilting. She breathed carefully.

'I am so sorry. It's not . . . I thought . . . Isn't she on the Pill?'

'Certainly not. She's not promiscuous, you know.' Julia sounded angry enough for Flixe to swallow what she had been going to say.

'Are you suggesting that the child is Andrew's?' she asked instead.

There was a sound almost like a groan.

'Of course. Who else's?'

Suppressing both her uncharitable reaction to Julia's certainty and her sharp anxiety for her son, Flixe said gently: 'Does he know yet?'

'No.' A familiar asperity was back in Julia's voice. 'Amanda refuses to let him be told until after his exams in spite of the real urgency. She really ought to have had the abortion already. If she leaves it until the end of term, she'll be just about into the second trimester and it will be that much worse for her, and more dangerous. And there's far more risk of people knowing about it.'

'Oh, the good girl!' Flixe felt a warmth of gratitude towards Amanda that she had never expected. It was the first sign of unselfishness she had ever shown and if she had been in the room, Flixe would have hugged her.

'Didn't you hear anything I said? This delay leaves her in a dreadful position. She's refusing to have an abortion until he knows, and . . .'

'Does she want to marry him?' Flixe could not help remembering Andrew's breakfast-time conversation.

'I don't think so. She's that much sense at least.'

Flixe grimaced as she understood that Julia's anxiety was enough to destroy her usual tact completely.

'But someone who clearly has the most disastrous influence over her has told her that it is not fair for her to get rid of the child until he has had a chance to know about it. She won't tell me who; I rather assumed it was you.'

The telephone felt heavy in Flixe's hand as she absorbed all the implications of what Julia had said. Her hysteria and her anger were understandable at last.

'I haven't spoken to her since she came to dinner here in April,' said Flixe as kindly as possible. Then the injustice of her friend's accusation forced her to add angrily: 'Julia, you surely know me better than that. I could not advise a friend's daughter about something so important behind her back.'

'Quite frankly, I'm beginning to wonder if I know anyone. It would never have occurred to me for one thing that your son could be so irresponsible. Or that Amanda would refuse to do the sensible thing now.'

'Julia, calm down,' said Flixe, deliberately suppressing her rage at Julia's assumption that all the irresponsibility had been Andrew's. 'You don't approve of abortion. You've told me that often. Surely you can see Amanda's point of view?'

'Oh, don't you start. The whole thing is set to ruin her life. She cannot marry simply because Andrew's got her into this state.' Julia's voice warmed slightly as she added: 'I don't wish to be rude, Flixe, but he is the least suitable man for her and in any case she is far too young to marry anyone.'

'I quite agree, Julia. I think they'd be disastrous for each other, although I know he longs for it.'

'Does he? That must be why he's got her pregnant.'

Stung by the wholly unfair criticism of her son, Flixe at last lost control of herself. In a voice of biting intensity that Julia had never heard before, she said: 'He didn't get her into the state on his own. I think he was entitled to believe that if she were willing to sleep with him she would have taken precautions against this happening or at least talked to him about it.'

'But, Flixe, she's a child. It was his responsibility.' There was a plea in Julia's voice that Flixe was too angry to answer.

'If she's a child, so is he. He's not quite a year older, and nowadays girls are adult much earlier than we ever were. Julia, didn't you ever warn her about this?'

The casual question added to the things Amanda had said and acted as a fuse. Julia's anxiety and guilt exploded.

'So it's my fault that your son has seduced my daughter and left her pregnant. God damn you both.' She banged down her receiver, leaving Flixe horrified, with much of the anger draining out of her mind as she forced herself to imagine the way Julia must be feeling.

Flixe redialled the number of the Kennington house and heard the telephone ring and ring without answer. Eventually the ringing stopped and she prepared to speak the soothing words she had rehearsed, but the connection was immediately cut. Knowing that there was nothing more she could do that night, Flixe lay back and tried to regain some of the blissful pleasure in which she had returned to London. It had gone.

The next morning, ignoring her determination to free herself from the demands of her political duties and trying not to think too much about Natalie, Flixe rang Julia's house again. The telephone was answered by Janice and after the usual warm-hearted enquiries about each other's health, Flixe asked to speak to Amanda.

'Well, I'm not sure, Mrs Suvarov. I gather she's not very well at all. She hasn't got up yet.'

'Right. I'll come straight round now, then. If she does get up, could you tell her I rang and ask her to wait for me? I really won't be long.'

'Yes, I'll do that.' The housekeeper sounded surprised.

'Good. Thank you, Janice. See you in about half an hour.'

Flixe put down the telephone, grabbed a mackintosh and her handbag and ran downstairs. As she went she noticed how thickly the dust lay on all the skirting boards and she quailed at the thought of cleaning the whole huge house again. Perhaps, she thought, if I make enough money from the parties to settle the rates and the electricity bills and leave some over, I might spend it on a cleaner for one day a week.

She reached Kennington thirty-five minutes later and was admitted to the house by Janice, looking plumply efficient in a spotless white overall. Flixe thought enviously of Julia's freedom from domestic cares and then remembered the highly skilled work she did to justify that freedom.

'Is she up yet?'

'No, Mrs Suvarov. There's been no sound.'

'Then I'd like to go up. Could I take her a cup of whatever she has for breakfast?'

'What a good idea! Will you come into the kitchen while I make it?'

Flixe followed her and sat down for a moment at the kitchen table. She admired Janice's refusal either to gossip about Amanda or to speculate about the causes of her ailment. After a moment the woman poured a cupful of black coffee and held it out.

'Thanks. Don't look so worried, Janice. I am her god-mother after all.'

'So you are,' said the housekeeper, her broad, lined face clearing. 'And I know you won't wake her if she's still asleep.'

Flixe merely smiled and went upstairs to Amanda's room, knocking gently on the white panelled door.

'Who is it?'

'Flixe.'

The door was quickly opened and Amanda stood there, as fashionably dressed as usual and as smart. Only her eyes showed any sign of distress. The lids were slightly swollen, but it was the eyes themselves that told Flixe Amanda was both unhappy and afraid.

'May I come in?'

Amanda nodded and led the way into a bedroom like a flower garden, with pots of plants in white wicker containers and actual white trellis pinned against the dark green walls. The ivory chintz curtains were printed with graceful tendrils of flowers and the same chintz was used for the counterpane and the cover of a comfortable chair. An old Dutch flower painting that Flixe had given Amanda for her christening hung over the mantelpiece.

Seeing it all, Flixe laughed.

'I'd never imagined you would have kept it like this,' she said. Amanda looked round in surprise.

'I'd forgotten. You designed it for me, didn't you, when my mother couldn't understand what I wanted.'

'You were ten,' said Flixe, 'and she was going to give you something strikingly modern.'

'But I wanted a conservatory like yours.'

Flixe made a face as she thought of all the exotic trees and shrubs that had died once she had had to turn off the heating in her conservatory.

'Amanda, I spoke to your mother last night and she told me . . .'

'That I'm pregnant? She had no right. I specifically didn't want anyone told.'

'She was upset.'

'Does she think I'm not?'

'I'm sure she knows exactly what you feel,' said Flixe pacifically. 'May I sit down? I want to help.'

'Oh, yes. Do sit.' Amanda pushed forward the chair and disposed herself elegantly on the bed. 'You won't tell Andrew, will you?'

Flixe shook her head, touched by the contrast between the girl's façade and the much more vulnerable, kinder, self it seemed to hide.

'No. I think it's remarkably generous of you to have considered his exams. Not many girls in your state would have done that.'

Amanda, unused to praise from her mother's women friends, blushed. She had always liked Flixe and so she decided to be frank.

'It's not purely altruistic. Having this pause will help me to decide what on earth to do.'

'I'm not sure I understand.'

'At first I was determined to get rid of it, but now I don't know.'

'Why not?'

There was no answer and so Flixe asked the question she had meant to suppress: 'Do you love him, Amanda?'

Amanda's eyelids dropped again and she stared at her slender ankles, clad that day in bright yellow tights. She shrugged and eventually looked up.

275

'I don't know. I don't think so. I've been horrible to him, though, and he's forgiven me again and again. He writes me the most lovely letters. I'm fonder of him than most people. It's just when we're together he annoys me so much.'

Flixe could not help smiling as she listened to the ingenuous explanation, although its implications for her besotted son were ominous.

'It doesn't sound to me as though you do. What a pity!'

'Why did you come, Auntie Flixe?'

'To see if I could help and to find out why your mother was so unlike herself when we talked on the telephone.'

Amanda let herself flop back against the pillows and stared up at the ceiling.

'She wants me to have an abortion straight away without waiting to tell Andrew. She thinks that if I do that, I can go back to Norwich and pretend nothing has happened and get on with my life. But something has happened – and it's important.'

Flixe considered for a while, unable to ignore a suspicion that there was something crucial that Amanda was not telling her. The girl was intelligent and practical enough to realise that there would certainly be less trouble and probably less unhappiness for everyone if she were to abort the child. With a fleeting admission that she could not wish any of her own children unborn in order to make her life easier or less painful, Flixe tried to guess what Amanda might be thinking.

'You can see Julia's point of view,' she said mildly. 'It would be much easier for you, although ease isn't everything. What does your father think?'

Amanda smiled.

'He says he'll support me whatever I decide to do and is insistent that I shouldn't let anyone else make the decision for me, but I think he's in favour of her solution too.'

'And you're not?'

276

'I don't know.' The three words came out in a wail. 'At first I thought just as she does, but now I don't know. That's why I want to wait and tell Andrew as soon as I can. Then we can decide together. I can't do it alone.'

Flixe sat, thinking of the effect on her son of knowing Amanda's condition. Since he already longed to marry her, the news might make him yet more insistent. Or it might put him off. His mother realised that, much as she adored him, she simply did not know him – or understand his attraction to Amanda – well enough to judge. She remembered telling George Mayford that one of the chief pillars of her personal philosophy was that secrecy was dangerous, and it was not hard to imagine what Andrew might feel if he were ever to discover that he might have had a child.

'I think you are right to do that,' she said slowly. 'And obviously I won't talk to him about the child until you have. Will you let me know if you want me to do anything?'

'Yes, but I can't think what you could do,' said Amanda with a smile that was more honest and less dazzling than usual. 'It was good of you to come.'

'You sound enviably calm.'

Amanda looked back to the nights of sleepless doubt and fear, to the tears and the panics that had gripped her, and she shook her head.

'Quite frankly, I'm too tired for anything else now.'

'I can imagine. I do know how frightening it can be, you know.'

'You do?'

'Yes,' said Flixe deliberately, 'I was already pregnant with Andrew by the time I married his father.'

Amanda let out a shout of bitter laughter, which troubled Flixe.

'You and my mother both! And people call *this* the "Permissive" age. It seems the only difference is that we're less dishonest about it. How she could be so bloody hypocritical all

277

those years with her little talks about never letting any boy go
too far!'

'It's not hypocrisy, Amanda. Both your mother and I were
in love when we became pregnant.' Flixe tried not to sound
as though she were judging the girl but as Amanda's face
closed in Flixe knew she had failed. She got up and went to
put her hand lightly on Amanda's smooth dark hair.

'You've a lot of people who care very much what happens
to you, Amanda,' she said deliberately. 'Don't be afraid to let
them help.'

'No. All right. I'm going back to Norwich this morning.
Will you tell my mother?'

'Don't you think you ought to tell her yourself? It sounds
as though she's been badly hurt by this. Can't you wait until
you can see her before you go?'

Amanda hunched her shoulders.

'She hurt me. I don't want to see her again for a long, long
time.' She looked at Flixe, saw something almost tragic in her
clear dark blue eyes and then said sulkily: 'Oh well, all right.
I'll leave her a letter.'

'Good. Good-bye. And thank you for sparing Andrew
anxiety now. It's quite a sacrifice. Don't think I don't understand that.' Flixe searched in vain for words that did not sound
either patronising or pompous and added: 'In fact I honour
it.'

As Flixe went out of the room, Amanda sat staring after
her, uncertain whether to be furious at her intervention or
relieved by it. When she had packed her few clothes in the
bag she had brought from Norwich, she sat down at the white
cane desk and wrote to her mother.

Dear Mum,
    I've gone back to Norwich. If I stay here any longer
we'll only say things to each other that neither of us will
be able to forget. I have obviously hurt you and you

done the same to me. That makes us quits. Perhaps we could start again.

I do see why you want me to have an abortion, although if you had had one I wouldn't exist. You see, I can't forget that, and it makes me think of my child as something more than I did before. I don't think I can 'get rid of it' just like that. Once or twice when we've had one of our rows, I've thought (perhaps I've even said) that I wished I'd never been born. Realising how easily I might not have been makes that kind of thing sound very hollow. I wish you'd told me yourself.

Amanda

She folded the single sheet of paper and slid it into an envelope, which she addressed and sealed. On her way out of the house, she left it on her mother's desk in her dark green study and went on to say good-bye to Janice.

'Don't take on so,' said the housekeeper. 'You've always been one to find criticism where it was never meant to be.'

'I don't know what you mean.'

'There you are, sounding as though I'd given you a mortal insult. I don't know why you and your mother are going round looking as though we'd just lost the war, and I'm not prying, mind, but it's likely you've been saying things to each other again. Don't take it too hard.'

'No, I see,' said Amanda, very much on her dignity again. 'Thank you, Janice. When she comes back, will you tell her I've left her a letter on her desk? Thank you. I must get back to university. Good-bye.'

'You're not going without kissing me, are you? You've always kissed me when you've left the house for school or anything.'

Amanda looked at Janice, who, even more than any of the nannies Julia had employed, had been the centre of the house during her childhood. Unlike Julia, Janice had always been there. Amanda dropped her bag on the floor and hugged her, murmuring: 'I'm sorry.'

'I know you are, love. Don't take on. You'll be all right. You're very strong. You always have been. Much more so than your brother.'

Amanda laughed and left the house, feeling a little better. She took the Northern Line tube to Bank station and then changed on to the Central for Liverpool Street, where she caught a slow train back to Norwich.

Julia found the letter waiting when she got back to the house after a gruelling day in court before a judge who clearly hated women barristers even when – or perhaps particularly when – they were QCs, and interrupted her whenever he could. Seeing her daughter's hard-edged writing on the envelope, Julia felt a cowardly impulse to leave it until after she had had a restorative bath and drink. She mocked herself into picking up the envelope.

As she read, her eyebrows rose and her lips began to curve into a smile. She had forgotten her daughter's directness of style, just as she had momentarily forgotten Amanda's knack of reducing any proposition to its crucial elements. It was a talent that had its place, but it had often made Amanda a most uncomfortable companion or dinner guest. She could unerringly light on the most appropriately witty comment, which was an enviable skill, but she could just as precisely pick out what everyone else most wanted to keep untouched.

Wishing that Amanda had chosen a more useful degree, and one that would challenge her and use all her talents in some constructive way instead of merely confirming her already high opinion of herself, Julia sat down to write an answer. After much thought, she produced:

Darling,
　　You are probably right, although I'm sad that you've

had to go back so soon. Yes, let's start again. I am perfectly certain that we can. After all, we're both intelligent women!

Try not to worry too much. Whatever you decide we will support you. Please don't forget one thing I said. I have always loved you. And I am sorry if that has not always been clear.

Mum

It crossed her mind to write to Flixe Suvarov, too, but she was still too angry to be sure she would not make things even worse between them.

CHAPTER 18

As soon as Flixe got back to Kensington she telephoned the private hospital where Natalie was undergoing surgery. The nurse to whom Flixe spoke was reassuring and offered to fetch 'the doctor'.

'Mrs Suvarov? Yes, I have splendid news of Madame Bernardone. We took her into theatre at eight this morning and the growth has been successfully removed. She is very tired and there is some fever, but one could say "so far so good".'

'Thank heavens! Is she up to visitors yet?'

'Not yet. I'd leave it a day or so. She'll sleep for most of the rest of today and would be better undisturbed.'

'I see,' said Flixe, trying to keep the disappointment out of her voice. 'Thank you.'

She cut the connection and sat at her desk with the telephone receiver in her left hand, staring out at the dusty chestnut trees of Holland Park, which cut out so much light and left her house gloomy all summer. The ideas of freedom that had tempted her in Rome began to seem even more rational.

After nearly five minutes, the empty buzzing of the

telephone alerted her out of her dreaminess and she replaced the receiver before pulling out of the bottom drawer all her various account books. She added up her debts first, trying not to let the size of them frighten her out of what she knew she wanted to do, and then the costs of running the house, buying the children's clothes and feeding them during the holidays. Then she made a list of everything she had earned from organising parties during the year. The total sum came to almost exactly seventy-five per cent of her expenses and the year was only six months old.

Flixe looked at the figures, thinking of the dances she had had to turn down because of her political commitments. She was beginning to feel quite hopeful that she might be able to earn enough from the work she actually enjoyed – and could do adequately – when she remembered income tax and had to calculate how much of her earnings would be left once the Inland Revenue had had its share.

Depressing though the sums were becoming as she worked on them, Flixe could not bring herself to despair. Having found out what it felt like to be happy again and having allowed herself to imagine life without the work she detested, she could not bear to shut the prison doors on herself once more. Andrew would be earning something from September and so she would be able to save what she had spent on him, even though she was determined to see that he left home to build his own life and did not fall into the habit of helping her at too great a cost to himself.

Reaching for the telephone again she dialled the number of Constance Wroughton, whose sister had been Peter's first wife. There was no answer for ages and then an unknown country voice recited Connie's number. Flixe asked to speak to her.

'Miss Wroughton's in London this week. I'm her daily.' The voice sounded tense, as though its owner was afraid of the telephone.

'Oh,' said Flixe, unfairly irritated. 'Do you know where she's staying?'

'Well, er . . .'

Flixe almost smiled, imagining the formidable Connie telling her cleaner not to pass on any information over the telephone.

'Is it with Mrs Sudley? She's my sister.'

'Yes it is.' The voice sounded relieved.

'Thank you very much,' said Flixe before ringing up Ming. There again she had no luck. There was little she could do to further her plans unless she could find out whether Connie's astonishingly generous offer to pay the children's school fees would stand even if Flixe gave up politics. On the other hand she felt that it was urgent to make a decision and she itched to do something. The prospect of never having to hold another surgery or sit through one more constituency dinner being polite to someone like John Kinghover was so alluring that she decided to talk to Gerry even without confirmation of Connie's continuing support.

Unlike the others, Gerry did answer her telephone and readily agreed to meet her sister for lunch that day, suggesting an Italian restaurant in Holborn.

Flixe took the tube, because of the impossibility of parking her car within walking distance of the restaurant, and found Gerry already waiting for her with a Campari and soda in her hand.

'Hello, old thing,' she said, slightly raising her glass. 'How are you?'

'Fine. Rome was utter bliss. It's quite set me up.'

'I'm glad. I must say you look more like yourself. Drink?'

'A glass of wine eventually, but there's no hurry. What are you planning to eat?'

'They do a lovely veal piccata with orange, sultanas and almonds. I'm going to have that.'

'Sounds good. I'll have it too and some spinach.' Flixe turned to signal to a waitress, but they were all busy and so she turned back to look at her elder sister.

Gerry had had her hair cut since they last met. It was much shorter than before with sharp inverted V-shapes over her ears and a deep fringe, which emphasised the pointed chin and the dark blue eyes that were so like Flixe's own. Instead of one of her usual corduroy jackets and plain skirts or trousers, Gerry was wearing a crisp dress and jacket made of heavy, cornflower blue linen, trimmed with darker blue braid. A hard-edged, boxy-looking, navy blue handbag lay on the banquette beside her, and she was wearing more make-up than usual.

'You're looking pretty good yourself,' said Flixe, who was used to being much the better dressed of the two of them. 'Very together and tidy. What's happened?'

'Nothing,' said Gerry shortly, but there was a look in her eyes that made Flixe suspect she wanted to be pressed. Obediently, she pressed.

'Well, all right,' said Gerry, 'but you must keep it under your hat.'

'Come on. Tell me,' said Flixe. 'You're being made a professor?'

'No. A baroness, for my "services to education".'

'A what?' There was a mixture of astonishment, amusement and admiration in Flixe's expression as she watched her sister.

'Keep your voice down,' said Gerry, laughing guiltily. 'You sounded as though you were calling for the fire brigade.'

'I daresay. Who wouldn't? I never imagined anything like that. And you're only forty-eight and a supporter of the Opposition. How peculiar! Though, come to think of it, it's very sensible of them and you've worked hard enough for it.'

'It's going to be in the Birthday Honours and so I'll be in the Lords when you get to the Commons. We'll have enormous fun, just like the old days.'

There was a very slightly sardonic note in Flixe's voice as she congratulated Gerry.

'Thank you. But, Flixe, what is it? You're beginning to look almost guilty, rather like that time when you had to confess that you'd taken my pony out and lamed him. What have you done?'

'Absolutely nothing.' Flixe could feel herself blushing and did her best not to sound like the defensive younger sister she had once been. 'But this is perhaps the moment to tell you that I am thinking seriously of withdrawing my candidature.'

'What?'

'Now who's sounding like the fire brigade? Gerry, don't look so horrified. Since I've stopped being so miserable that I can't think straight, I've realised how much I hate all the political stuff. It fills me with a mixture of terror, frustration and shame, which makes me feel stupid and incompetent. And I'm not. I am really not.'

'Flixe, for heaven's sake!' There was a sharpness in Gerry's voice that made her sister grit her teeth, unaware that Gerry had already quarrelled with Ming over the same thing. 'You're not a child bride any longer . . .'

'I was never that, as you very well know.'

'Perhaps not, but Peter treated you as one and you always played up to it. That's what got you into this frightful mess in the first place. Ghastly though his death was – and infinitely as I sympathise with you - it did offer you a chance to grow up properly and face reality at last.'

To Flixe it seemed monstrous that her sister should think of all the agony of Peter's death merely as an opportunity for her development and she could feel her self-control slipping. Her forehead felt tight and the words piling up in her mind seemed to push against it.

'Gerry, that's not fair,' she said, still outwardly calm.

'It may not be fair and I know it's unkind, but this is too important to fudge. You've young children who are wholly dependent on you. You're their mother. You can't drop something simply because you don't like it any more. How are you going to feed them?' Watching her sister, Gerry caught a glimpse of an unfamiliar stubbornness. She added caustically: 'Or perhaps you are expecting us to keep your children.'

'God, you sound bitter,' said Flixe, her newly plucked eyebrows meeting across her nose. 'I am bottomlessly grateful to you and Julia and Connie, not to speak of Ming, and it would never occur to me to ask you for anything more.'

'Then how are you going to live, let alone pay off your overdraft?' Gerry's angry frown disappeared into a sour smile as she added: 'Oh, I see. Why didn't I think of it before? It's this new man of yours. You're going to relax into his arms and be looked after all over again. When will you ever grow up and take some responsibility?'

'Gerry, will you stop it?' Flixe could feel the anger rising in her like a tide of boiling liquid. It had the effect of cooking her doubts into solid certainty. 'You haven't given me any time to explain and you're bullying me. Don't.'

Angry herself at the accusation, Gerry banged down her empty glass.

'You're giving in and marrying the first man who's asked you. What's going to happen to you if he dies too, or leaves you for a younger woman? It does happen, you know. You simply must protect yourself. And the only way you can do it is to get some secure, paying work.'

'George has not asked me to marry him.' Flixe knew she was sounding sulky just as she knew that Gerry was right about the need for financial independence.

'Perhaps not, but that's what you're angling for, isn't it? Using the charm and the sex and the glamour all over again to achieve another protector.'

Cut to the quick, Flixe wondered for a horrible moment if that was what her subconscious had been making her do. All the golden pleasure she had given and received in Rome seemed tarnished until she forced herself to remember precisely what she had felt and said and done on her last night with George.

'After all, you've slept with him.' Gerry's voice sounded almost spiteful and Flixe wondered why she should be so angry. Then a possible explanation struck her.

'How do you know?' she asked to gain time while she tested the new possibility against what she knew of her sister.

'It's been perfectly obvious. You'd spent months looking like a dried-up treestump and then suddenly you started putting out leaves and now refulgent flowers again. You've always thought sex could solve everything, haven't you? Solve everything and get you everything you wanted.'

Flixe thought for a moment of the only time since the war that she had ever tried to use sex for an ulterior motive. In a futile attempt to break herself of minding about one of Peter's affairs, she had slept with an old friend who had often asked her to make love with him. Although he had been enthusiastic and polite, the entire occasion had seemed to her sordid and without any grace of affection to save it. There was no pleasure in it for her and, she suspected, little for him. Afterwards they had thanked each other and separated. Flixe had disliked herself intensely and felt for the only time in her life that she had fallen to the standards her father had often accused her of keeping.

Remembering the way he had always measured her against Gerry, Flixe lost her temper for the first time in years.

'You simply don't want me to stop feeling miserable yet, do you?' she said in a quiet voice that disguised none of her fury. 'I haven't paid enough for the things I had with Peter, and you're going to make sure that I settle the bill in full, aren't you?'

Then she turned away to signal to the waitress for the wine she had meant to order. When she looked back she saw Gerry staring at her, white-faced and appalled.

'How can you say that? I've been trying to help you out of the mess he got you into. I've known how desperate you feel, and I have been wholly on your side. He behaved abominably.' Gerry paused and then added slowly, as though digging the words up from some deep pit in her mind: 'You must really hate me if you can even think I want you to be miserable.'

'I don't hate you, Gerry.' Seeing that her sister did not believe her, Flixe added with difficulty, 'But there have been times when you've hated me, haven't there? Come on, you must at least admit that you disliked me badly when Peter chose me, even though you'd already agreed to marry Mike. It wasn't that you wanted Peter, but wasn't there a bit of you that wanted me not to have him?'

Gerry tried to say something but could not. Flixe looked at her.

'I sometimes wondered why you used to press me to tell you how I felt about his love affairs. Was it because you wanted to know they made me miserable so that you needn't mind so much that he had married me?'

'Flixe, please. You're tearing me apart.' Neither Gerry's protest nor her expression stopped what her sister was determined to tell her.

'Being married to Peter was wonderful. But just to satisfy you, I will tell you that there were times when it cost me, times when I wasn't sure I could go on paying for it, when I did stupid things to make me feel better and found that nothing would. Does that help? I used to think that if I loved him enough he would stop needing the others, but it never worked, and that bloody hurt. Now you know it wasn't unalloyed bliss, will you let me off?'

Flixe felt a singing in her head. She wondered if she might be going to faint from hurt and fury.

'Flixe, don't. Please don't. I know that you're not over his death yet and still easily upset. But whatever you think about me, you mustn't believe there is anything about your unhappiness that I've welcomed.'

'Don't be such a hypocrite!' Flixe found that her anger was refuelled by Gerry's refusal to look frankly at her own feelings. 'Of course you did. Just as there are times when a part of me has welcomed your professional setbacks. Don't look so shocked. I've always welcomed your successes too, but with a different bit of me. Wake up, Gerry! Just because neither of us ever says any of these things it doesn't mean they don't exist. Look, I don't think I can eat anything now. I've made myself feel sick. They still haven't come to take our order. I think I'd better go.'

'No, don't go, Flixe. We must sort this out. How long have you been thinking I wanted to punish you?'

Standing by the table, trying to find her gloves and not being able to see properly, Flixe looked back towards her sister. All the old muddle of devotion and need, jealousy and dependence churned inside her.

'On and off for ages.'

'Oh, Flixe, I'm sorry . . . sorry that you've thought it and desperately sorry that my attempts to get you some kind of real protection have seemed to be rooted in cruelty. They truly haven't. Hell! Here's the waitress. Won't you stay and have something? Even a drink or an avocado or something if you can't face a whole meal? Please?'

Something in the patent sincerity of what Gerry had said made Flixe hesitate and, having hesitated, surrender. She had never been able to hold on to anger for long, and she had to admit that Gerry's determination to see her in a secure and profitable job might not have been wholly punitive. Dropping back on to the hard bench, she picked up the menu again.

'Cheese salad for me, then, and some white wine. The veal sounds too much.'

Looking relieved but still wary, Gerry ordered the same before saying again: 'I'm sorry, Flixie. I must have been very clumsy in what I've tried to do. All I've ever wanted is to make certain that you're never in this ghastly position again. I'm worried by the consequences of an action you might take without thinking it through properly and before you're completely yourself again.'

'Are you?' Flixe had still not entirely forgiven her sister and her voice was cold. 'Maybe. Perhaps we ought to leave the murkier bits of our feelings in decent obscurity. But listen to me for a minute. This is important.'

'All right. What?'

Flixe tried to summon up all her explanatory skills so that she could persuade her sister of the reliability of her feelings about the future. Gerry's face under the fashionable haircut was tense.

'Well?' she said.

'Understudying Michael Diseholme really does seem like a punishment,' said Flixe. 'I'm bad at everything to do with the constituency and it demands so much from me that I'm drained. Even if my other work is unworthy and frivolous, it must be better to do what I can do well and enjoy instead of what takes struggle and endurance. Don't you see that?'

The waitress brought their salads and a carafe of house wine. Gerry poured them each a glassful. Flixe took a huge swallow and remembered the finesse of the Roman wine with regret.

'What led to all this?' Gerry asked instead of answering the question.

'This and that,' said Flixe, pushing a piece of Camembert on her fork and wrapping a torn lettuce leaf around it. She managed to smile again. 'Partly a couple of George's phrases. He said to me very early on, "Don't assume that just because you can do something easily it is necessarily worth less than things that are difficult for you." That made an awful lot of sense.'

'You said a couple,' said Gerry when she had swallowed a mouthful of cheese and tomato. 'What was the other?'

'That one should listen to one's unhappiness and take its advice.'

'Is that what you've been doing since you got here today?'

Flixe looked up, surprised.

'No. Today I was just reacting to an old . . .' She hesitated.

'Wound?' suggested Gerry.

'Not exactly. I could explain it all, but it's ancient history now.'

She ate some more salad and followed it with another huge gulp of wine, not wanting to examine the sickening history of her father's criticism of her sluttishness and tartiness or of his unalterable preference for Gerry.

'Don't go through it all if you don't want to, but one day I'd like to hear,' said Gerry as she tried to think back to what each of them had said. 'At least, I think I would.'

At that Flixe laughed aloud and they both felt better.

'And you're right,' Gerry went on with unaccustomed humility, 'there are times when I have – just occasionally – resented some of the easinesses of your life. I suppose it's a short step from that to finding some kind of . . . never enjoyment, but perhaps comfort from things that haven't gone so well for you.'

'I know you have.'

'But, Flixe, you must know that all I've been trying to do recently is to help get you the kind of protection my work has always given me. You can't think . . . No, that's silly: obviously you have thought it. But I haven't tried to punish you since Peter's death – God forbid!'

Flixe noticed that there were tears on Gerry's darkened eyelashes. For a moment she thought of making a joke about them, but then her own throat tightened and she simply smiled, clamping her lips together when they wobbled.

'I suppose that I haven't ever stopped to think about the easinesses of mine that you don't have.'

'I know that too. Gerry, don't get yourself in a state about it. All sisters must be envious of things the others have. It's no big deal as Andrew says. I can't eat any more of this. Let's get some coffee.'

Later, when they were each sipping the froth from the top of a cappuccino and trying to deal with the aftermath of old resentments, Gerry said: 'Are you sure about the work? A safe parliamentary seat is not something to throw away lightly, you know.'

'I do love this coffee, though even it isn't as good as some we had in Rome.'

Gerry's lips tightened as she recognised once again her sister's incorrigible habit of slipping away from the importances of life into contemplation of the entirely frivolous and unnecessary.

'It's all right,' said Flixe at once. 'I am taking it seriously and I do know how hard it is for most sucking politicians to get a decent seat. Your finding me one that is as safe as the Bank of England was wonderful and I am grateful. But I truly hate the thought of being elected to Parliament.' She drank again and then smiled. 'There. It's out. I haven't said it to anyone before now.'

'Why? I'm seriously looking forward to what I can do in the Lords. Don't look like that. I am.'

'I'm sure you are; but it won't be your whole life and you won't have unhappy constituents wanting things all the time. Think what a backbench MP's life is like: dealing with streams of people who not only want but badly need help and then having to go and be howled down and insulted in the House whenever you try to speak. Have you ever sat in on a Commons debate?'

'Actually, no, I haven't,' said Gerry.

'They behave like schoolboys, drowning the speeches in catcalls and bellows and mockery. Gerry, the thought of standing up surrounded by all that makes me shudder. And there really is so little that any of them can actually do to help their constituents: the odd immigration case, perhaps; occasionally some planning measure can be adapted after pressure from an MP. Otherwise, it's writing endless letters, attending debates, sitting up late at night. And you know how much I hate late nights.'

'Yes, I do. I begin to wonder why we thought it was such a suitable job for you.' Gerry was half laughing, half serious.

'You and Julia started out with the basic idea that since poor Flixe had no qualifications and no degree there was nothing else she could do.' Flixe was relieved to find that her fury had receded. She felt much more like herself as she went on: 'She's forty-six, after all, and too old to pass any exams. But, you know, there are all kinds of jobs outside the professions that you and Julia consider respectable.'

'Ming did tell us to leave you alone and let you find something in your own time,' Gerry admitted. 'But the need seemed so urgent.'

'Did she?' Flixe sounded almost vague. In her mind she was telling her younger sister how much she owed her.

'Have you told Julia yet?' As Flixe's face changed, Gerry quickly added: 'What's the matter?'

'Julia doesn't want to talk to me at the moment. I can't tell you why, but as soon as she can bear it, I'll tell her. I owe both of you a huge debt for guaranteeing me at the bank and doing so much else. Don't think I'm not grateful just because I'm going my own way now.'

'No. All right.' Gerry finished her coffee and then, because she had never shirked anything she thought she ought to do, asked: 'Are you going to marry him?'

'George? No. I shouldn't think so.'

'That sounds as though you might. Do be careful.'

'I am.' Flixe smiled. 'He's a remarkably nice man. I know that's a useless word, but it sums up so much. He's interesting, funny, generous, affectionate. Life is infinitely more pleasant with him in it. But we're neither of us taking it too seriously.' She laughed at herself, knowing that there were aspects of her feelings for George that she was not prepared to admit. 'He certainly hasn't asked me to marry him and I doubt that he will. Why would a man like that want to saddle himself with a widow and four children after all?'

Gerry looked at her sister, noticing the regained confidence and bloom in her face. It seemed cruel to do anything that might damage those and yet to withhold necessary advice would surely be more cruel.

'With his daughter's growing up and about to leave him, he is probably facing loneliness for the first time in his life. A man might well consider a widow with children then,' she said quite gently, not looking at Flixe.

Flixe's face changed infinitesimally. Then she made herself relax.

'You could be right. And if you were, so what, Gerry? It wouldn't be such a bad bargain.'

Gerry slowly shook her head, a reluctant smile lighting her eyes.

'I remember once in the war telling Peter that although you always looked fragile and sensitive you were in fact made of pressed steel and toughened glass. I ought not to have forgotten that.'

'Nor should I. But I did.' Flixe laughed and for the first time that day she actually sounded happy. Then she remembered Amanda's baby.

'What's the matter?' asked Gerry.

'I'm worried about Andrew and there's nothing I can do until after his final schools.'

'He'll be fine,' said Gerry. 'A certain first, they say.' She wondered why her sister looked so stubborn again.

CHAPTER 19

Amanda sat, ignoring the half-written essay in front of her and trying not to give way to the panic she had told her godmother she was too tired to feel. The weeks were sliding past with what seemed to be ever increasing speed. She still felt sick in the mornings and the child inside her was growing steadily.

Having listened to her parents discussing every aspect of pregnancy and its termination during the progress of the Abortion Bill, she knew exactly what was happening. By then, at the end of her eighth week of pregnancy, the foetus she carried was only about one inch long, but its eyes, ears and nostrils had formed and even its fingers and toes were marked out. It was impossible to forget that it was a child, not some malignant disease, that she carried.

However much she might remind herself that abortion was legal for another twenty weeks, Amanda could not help remembering that only for another four was it simple and reasonably safe. She also found it impossible to forget that she, too, had once been an inconvenient bundle of growing cells. That knowledge alone seemed to make the idea of a termination impossible.

There were times when she felt as though she were being pulled apart by two equally strong forces. She hated the idea of an abortion and yet to allow the child to be born and to bring it up without knowing which of the two men was its father would be unbearable. The third option of giving birth to the child and then sending it away for adoption by an unknown family was even worse. Her first happy fantasies of a rich, free life with a beloved child, supported by frequent visits from an Anthony tranformed into a happy man, seemed irresponsibly absurd.

Even though she was convinced that Comfort had lied, Amanda could not bear the thought of either of the Gillinghams any longer and it appalled her to think that Anthony might have been the father of her child. If she could have been certain of that, her decision would have been much easier.

'Perhaps,' she said to herself as she sat staring at her essay but seeing none of it, 'I ought to work on the assumption that he is the father and mind less about what I ought to do.'

As she had done so often before, Amanda reached the bleak conclusion that the only sensible thing was to arrange a termination as soon as possible. And yet, as soon as she had decided that, the thought of Andrew's possible feelings stepped in to prevent her. She could not help thinking about some of the things he had said to her: things about honesty between people, about his feelings for her, even about the importance of freeing people from the unfairnesses of life that forced them into misery and poverty.

Much of what he had said had once seemed irritating or sentimental, but it was beginning to assume a great deal more importance and it made the idea of getting rid of the child without telling him seem almost wicked. Amanda had started several letters to him and torn them all up. It was unfair to leave him in ignorance of what was happening to her and yet equally unfair to load her troubles on to him at a time when he was faced with crucial exams; and, she had to admit to herself, when she was still not certain what it was she wanted of him.

Andrew had not written to her for nearly ten days, which was unprecedented. She was so surprised by the silence that she wondered whether he was ill. Unable to concentrate on her essay, she looked at her watch to see whether the day's post would have been distributed and shot downstairs to collect her letters.

As usual her pigeon-hole was full, which still, despite her dilemma, gratified her. There was a thin envelope from her mother, two typed ones from the magazines that published her articles, and a fat brown envelope with the label of her press-cuttings agency on it. There was nothing at all from Oxford.

She read her mother's letter on the way back to her room and was touched by its simplicity but also discomfited by the declaration of love. When she got back to her desk she spilled the cuttings out of their envelope and shuffled quickly through them, hoping that they would distract her. Since the party, she had thought that she would never again be able to bear to look at Comfort's painting, but curiosity got the better of her revulsion and once she had read each of the diary paragraphs from the London newspapers, she turned to the reviews, most of which were headed with a black-and-white photograph of her portrait.

One article caught her eye because of its unlikely title: Go AND CATCH A FALLING STAR! The review had been written by a critic whom Amanda had always admired, and she read his piece carefully. When he had discussed the technicalities of the painting, he turned to its subject.

'With its falling star and its mermaid, not to speak of the mandragora flowers cunningly added to her necklace, this painting deliberately reflects John Donne's *Song*, resonating with ideas of seduction and treachery, beauty and death, frailty and desire. Its subtle colouring of black-greens, purple-browns, silver-greens and greys is heavy with menace and yet itself irresistibly seductive.

'All in all this has become a portrait not of the beautiful young model, Amanda Wallington, but of an idea: betrayal. The only thing missing from the painting to underline its bitter menace is the pregnant root of the mandrake flowers. Despite its apparent romanticism, this is Comfort Gillingham's most powerful and disturbing piece of work yet.

'The rest of the exhibition is more characteristic of Miss Gillingham's recent work . . .'

Amanda stopped reading. She could not remember the particular poem that the reviewer had used and she had no copy of Donne's collected works in her room. Iris Fowlins on the other hand would certainly have at least one and so Amanda went straight to her room.

Iris was in, working hard and apparently disinclined for company. For once she looked hostile as Amanda put her head round the door.

'Sorry to interrupt,' said Amanda, shocked by the unusual lack of welcome, 'but I just wondered if you had a collected Donne I could borrow.'

'Yes.' Iris slid off her chair, hitching at the waistband of her flared trousers, and bent down to reach a fat, brown-paper-covered book from the bottom shelf. Her face was red when she stood up again and held it out to Amanda.

'Poetry is a new departure for you, isn't it?'

'Always willing to broaden my mind, you know,' said Amanda casually. 'I say, are you all right?'

'Yes.' Iris blinked and then wet her lips and pushed the long curly hair behind her ears, looking the very picture of indecision.

'Come on, out with it. What I have done?'

'You? Nothing at all. Amanda, it's me. I've been feeling so guilty about what I said to you.'

'Why?' Amanda's voice had flattened. 'Wasn't it true? Were you practising for your great novel?'

'God no! Everything I said was true, but I oughtn't to have been so dogmatic at a time when you must have been . . .

have needed comfort.' She could not imagine why Amanda flinched. 'Anyway, I've been wanting to say that I was sorry, but I haven't known quite how to do it. Whatever you do decide to do, I'll be there to hold your hand if you want. Sorry. It's awfully clumsy. I'm not used to talking about things that matter.'

'We none of us are, are we?' Amanda gestured to the bed and, when Iris nodded permission, sat down. 'I tried to build bridges with my mother at the weekend – or rather she tried with me – but it was a disaster. We just haven't had enough practice. She's better at letters. Have you got any tea?'

Iris let out a deep sigh and threw back her head to stare at the ceiling for a moment. Then she went to plug in her electric kettle and dropped tea-bags into two reasonably clean mugs.

'I'd managed to convince myself that I'd thrown away all our chances of being friends. It was . . . pretty ghastly actually.'

'Oh, Iris.' Amanda was touched by the admission.

'So why do you want the Donne?' Clearly Iris had had enough sentimentality for the moment and Amanda was quite ready to drop it.

She held out the press cutting, saying: 'I thought I ought to find out just what he's on about.'

'It's creepy. I've always rather liked the poem although it's so anti-women. I'll read it to you while the kettle boils.'

Iris had a beautiful speaking voice, although she, too, could not sing a single accurate note, and Amanda started to listen in delighted silence.

' "Goe, and catch a falling starre,
    Get with child a mandrake roote,
Tell me where all past yeares are,
    Or who cleft the Divels foot,
Teach me to heare Mermaides singing,
    Or to keep off envies stinging,

And finde
What winde
Serves to advance an honest minde.

' "If thou beest borne to strange sights,
Things invisible to see,
Ride ten thousand daies and nights,
Till age snow white haires on thee,
Thou, when thou retorn'st, will tell mee
All strange wonders that befell thee,
And sweare
No where
Lives a woman true, and faire.

' "If thou findst one, let mee know,
Such a pilgrimage were sweet;
Yet doe not, I would not goe,
Though at next doore wee might meet,
Though shee were true, when you met her,
And last, till you write your letter,
Yet shee
Will bee
False, ere I come, to two, or three." '

As the romantic, singing words hardened into the final
cynical bitterness, Amanda shuddered.

'Ugh! What a pig. But I do see what Robertson meant. I
wonder whether Comfort used Donne's ideas deliberately or
whether she just had a vague memory of the poem, which
trickled up her subconscious.'

'It's the falling star that suggests she wasn't being exactly
casual,' said Iris, silently re-reading the poem. She looked up.
'Have you got a better photograph of the painting anywhere?
Colour. I'd love to see it.'

Instead of answering, Amanda gave her the gallery catalogue and went to sit on the bed, thinking: I must be the
pregnant mandrake root as well as the singing mermaid and

301

the faithless woman. Her face stiffened as she remembered Andrew's frequent and critical descriptions of her as 'the star'. Perhaps Comfort had somehow heard of that and added the falling star as a hint that her model's fame was about to collapse and with it her only source of real money. Amanda tried to laugh herself out of her absurd paranoia, all too aware that if she had no money she would have no hope at all of keeping her child on her own.

'I wonder,' she said aloud as a huge, horrible idea occurred to her for the first time.

'What?'

'Well, if Comfort did that deliberately, then perhaps . . . No. No one could be so manipulative. Besides, why? And how could she have done it, or known?'

'What are you blathering on about?' Iris's face was a great deal more anxious than her casual voice, but Amanda was not looking at her. She had seized the catalogue back from her friend and was staring at the photograph. She looked up as the sense of Iris's question reached through to her brain.

'Nothing,' she said, smiling carefully and trying to forget Anthony's treasured copy of Donne's poems. 'Just blathering. Hasn't that kettle boiled yet?'

Iris made the tea. As she handed a mugful to Amanda, she said: 'The portrait is a remarkable piece of work, but I'm not altogether surprised that you don't like it.'

'Oh? Why?'

Iris drank some tea and then put her mug down on top of her essay, slopping some tea on to the page.

'Bugger!' She pulled a foot or so from a roll of pink lavatory paper she kept on the desk and mopped her essay. 'Now I'll have to write it all out again.'

'Why aren't you surprised I don't like the portrait?'

'It's terrifically cruel, isn't it? I don't mean to you exactly. But the mermaid is cruel and enjoying her cruelty, don't you think?'

'Yes,' agreed Amanda, who was regaining a little of her old assurance, 'I think she is. But no one seems to have commented on the fact that Comfort's using two mutually exclusive interpretations of mermaids.' She handed the catalogue back.

Iris looked down at the colour photograph in front of her and then smiled.

'I see what you mean: Donne's entirely magical singing one and the old sailors' version of the one that lures them to wreck their ships. Good for you.'

Amanda laughed rather bitterly.

'Not really. My entire education has taught me how to sneer. I hadn't really noticed before, but that's the clever thing to do, isn't it? We all look for the flaws, the failures, the weaknesses and sneer at them. Then we feel better. It's neither particularly clever nor constructive.'

'I suppose not, but it does hone one's appreciation of what is good.'

Burning her mouth on her tea, Amanda thought for a while.

'I think it might hone it more,' she said, 'if we all learned to concentrate on the good bits rather than the failures and it might stop life being so . . . so accusatory.'

'God, you sound depressed. I'm not surprised, but . . .'

'Don't worry.' Amanda stood up, leaving her unfinished tea on the bedside table. 'It's not that I'm depressed so much as trying to find my way through it all to something different . . . kinder. See you.'

'Sure.'

Iris watched Amanda leave and then turned back, shrugging, to rewrite her essay, noticing her own sneers but content to keep them and positively liking their cleverness.

Amanda ignored her work for a little longer and, picking out her most cherished postcard, wrote a note to Andrew Suvarov. It was very simple and said merely:

You were right. There are bits of me that are afraid.

                                                                        Love, A

She addressed it and turned it over. Since she was going back
to Florence at the end of term, it would be perfectly easy to
get another card of the Ucello, but she was pleased with the
slight pang she felt at parting with it.

No nearer to a decision about her baby, but feeling slightly
more hopeful that there could be a life in which she and
Andrew might be able to take one together, Amanda returned to her essay.

CHAPTER 20

'Isn't it horrible?'

At the unmistakable sound of Julia Wallington's voice, Flixe turned away from *Portrait of a Mermaid*.

'Hello, Julia,' she said, holding out her hands in welcome and a kind of plea.

Julia took one of them and shook it formally.

'I didn't expect to see you here, but I am glad. We need to talk, Flixe.'

Disturbed by Julia's stiffness, Flixe tried to stop herself tightening up in response and kept the smile on her face.

'I don't think there's much for us to talk about. We simply have to leave it up to our children to decide, and then help them with whatever comes next,' she began. Julia shook her head impatiently.

'I don't mean about that, although you seem to have done your bit to influence my daughter in spite of our previous conversation.'

Flixe closed her eyes and wished she had considered Julia's possible reaction to her visit to Amanda.

'It seemed important to offer her friendliness; that's all,' she said, opening her eyes again. 'I was immensely careful to

305

advise nothing except that she should listen to you.'

'Oh. Well, that wasn't what I wanted to say. What you and I need to talk about is the news Gerry has just given me.'

'Ah, yes,' said Flixe, adding childishly in an attempt to find some way of placating Julia, 'I hope you're not very angry about my giving up politics.'

'Certainly not. It's not for me to comment on any decision you might take.' Julia was clearly extremely angry but whether because of Amanda or Flixe herself she could not be sure. 'The last thing I would want would be to force anyone to do anything against their will. I just can't understand why you haven't said anything about disliking the work before. Both you and Amanda seem to assume I'm some kind of tyrant . . .'

'Julia.' Flixe put her hand on her friend's arm and held it there, despite Julia's flinching. 'What is the matter? You sound angry and upset. It can't simply be because I want to give up politics or that I went to call on Amanda.'

There was an obvious struggle behind Julia's dark eyes.

'I suppose I do dislike the fact that you went charging off to see her behind my back after you'd virtually promised not to do just that and that the two of you seem to be in some kind of alliance against me,' she said.

Flixe was surprised to find how much Julia's coldness hurt. Her accusation was wildly unrealistic, but even so Flixe coloured.

'Far from it,' she said, hoping to sound convincing. She seemed to be driving away the very people she most needed – and most liked. 'I wanted Amanda to know that I sympathise with her, as I genuinely do. And I wanted to point out that there might be less pain all round if she did follow her first instinct to abort the child.'

Julia looked surprised and then frowned.

'She didn't tell me that.' A reluctant smile tweaked at the edges of her wide mouth. 'Actually, she didn't tell me anything, but Janice said you'd been to the house and I rather assumed that with all your maternal instincts . . . Flixe, I think I've been doing you a second injustice. I'm sorry.'

'It's easy enough in such a welter of tricky emotions,' said Flixe, relaxing at once. 'It doesn't matter, so long as you do know that I have not been undermining your authority over your daughter.'

Julia winced and looked much more human. 'It's not my authority I mind about. I just want somehow to persuade her of my . . . that I care about her, which she seems unable to believe. I thought you'd been stymying that and I suppose I went a little mad. Besides being so angry with Andrew that some of it seeped over on to you. Flixe, I'm sorry. Will you forgive me?'

'There's nothing to forgive. The pregnancy bears much harder on Amanda than Andrew and therefore on you. But apportioning blame has always seemed rather a futile exercise to me.'

'You've always been a good friend. David reminded me of that last night.' Julia took both of Flixe's hands in hers for a moment and then let them go. 'Isn't it awful about Robert Kennedy?'

'Ghastly! That poor family and the children . . .'

'I know. Thank heavens politics isn't so appallingly dangerous over here.' Julia turned away to stand in front of the painting of her daughter and after a moment said helplessly: 'But awful though the killing is, I can't help thinking more about this. When I look at it I feel as though bloody Comfort had stripped Amanda naked and put her in a freak show. I really hate it.' The immaculately dressed woman who assisted the gallery's owner came between them and the painting, murmuring: 'Do please excuse me.'

Flixe noticed that her dress was made of almost exactly the same off-white linen that covered the walls, which seemed to be taking devotion to work too far. Smiling, Flixe watched as the woman peeled a small red spot off a sheet and stuck it neatly in the edge of the label that was pinned to the wall beside the painting. Flixe's amusement was overtaken by a curious dread and she took a covert look at Julia to see how she was taking the knowledge that someone had bought the portrait.

'Don't worry so, Flixe. It's mine.' At the bitterness of Julia's voice, Flixe raised her eyebrows in a wordless question.

'It irritates me like anything to think that I've put so much money in Comfort's pocket,' Julia went on, 'but as soon as I read Robertson's review, I knew that I had to keep control of the beastly thing. I tried to make them let me have it taken down at once, but alas I failed in that and since I don't want to provoke a scene that might make Comfort do something even worse I didn't insist.'

'So that's why you came.'

'Yes, I had no idea you'd be here. I was going to ring you later when I'd calmed down.'

'I read the review too,' said Flixe, suppressing her real reason for being in the gallery in the interests of preserving amicable relations with Julia. 'I'm on way to see Natalie Bernardone in hospital, but I thought I'd drop in and have a look and give her plenty of time to get through the ward-rounds and bed-making and all that. You must admit, Julia, that it is a remarkable piece of work. Probably the most interesting painting I've seen in years – if ever.'

Julia looked at it, her head on one side and her eyes intent.

'I can't see that at all . . . just the insult.'

'Oh, it is. Look at the curves and the contrasts of texture and the storm and the menace.'

'All right. All right. I'll admit it, but don't go on.'

Flixe laughed. 'But, Julia, it's beautiful, too. Amanda looks quite ravishing.'

'But it's so unspeakably horrible.' Julia shivered, although the big, light gallery was warm. 'I had rather assumed that Comfort would have forgiven me by now, but clearly she hasn't.'

Flixe's impish smile flashed for a moment. After a moment's deliberate refusal to understand, Julia produced an answering smile.

'I know, I know. You think I'm fearfully self-centred. But if Comfort hadn't wanted to get at me, why should she have taken the trouble to use my daughter in a painting that positively shrieks treachery at you?'

'Would you have thought of that without Robertson's piece?' asked Flixe, looking at Julia with her dark blue eyes full of sceptical curiosity.

'Oh, I think so. Actually, I don't know why I'm so surprised. My relationship with them was completely ended years ago, but I still find the thought of some aspects of it remarkably painful. I hate meeting Comfort, still. Presumably she feels the same.'

'We'd better go, then,' said Flixe, who had turned to see the painter entering the gallery with her brother. 'Is there another way out?'

'Why?'

'She's here, with your ex-husband.'

'Hell! No. We'll have to brazen it out. Coming?'

Together they turned their backs on the painting and walked towards the entrance, talking meaningless nonsense to each other and trying not to appear self-conscious. Flixe noticed that Julia's face was slightly flushed.

Whispering, 'It can't be that bad,' Flixe deliberately smiled at the approaching pair, thinking how handsome they looked with their distinguished faces and wonderful dark clothes.

Comfort graciously inclined her head and then turned to Julia with a glittering smile and triumph in her slaty eyes, which made Flixe look curiously at her friend. Julia nodded slightly, her face expressionless, and walked on. She already had a hand on the door before Anthony spoke.

'Julia? Wait a minute, please.'

She sighed at the sound of her ex-husband's voice, but she turned back.

'Hello, Anthony. I gather you've met my daughter.'

'Yes. She's a sweet girl.'

At that Julia's severity broke into a smile of real amusement mixed with something much less pleasant.

'I wonder what she wanted from you,' she said, apparently enjoying herself. 'Amanda's only ever sweet if she's after something.'

'I think that's a little unjust,' Anthony said, adding coolly: 'She reminded me a lot of you. It was good to run into you, Julia.'

Flixe felt her wrist gripped as Julia urged her to the door. When they were safely out on the busy street, Julia said: 'He always had a clever way with a put-down. I suppose I was being rather cheap. I'm sorry you had to listen to that, Flixe. You're surely not walking to the hospital from here. Shall we share a taxi? I can easily drop you off there and go on to chambers.'

'No, thanks. The walk will do me good and I don't want to take you so far out of your way. Julia, don't let them make you so unhappy still. Your life with them was over so very long ago. You've David now and the children, besides your work. Surely you can simply forget all that.'

'Don't worry about me. I'd forgotten it all completely, but this business of the painting and the way they've hurt Amanda has rather stirred it all up again. It'll soon sink back to the bottom of the pool. I did try to keep her out of Comfort's way, but I probably didn't try hard enough or in the right way; perhaps because I couldn't bear to talk frankly enough about it all.'

'I expect Amanda will cope,' said Flixe, leaning forward to kiss Julia. She was trembling slightly. 'With Comfort as well as with her condition. Don't worry too much. The young are extraordinarily resilient. I'm glad we met.'

'I too. By the way, before you dash off, tell me truthfully: are you serious about what you told Gerry?'

Flixe nodded. 'She probably told you that we quarrelled over it.'

'She didn't tell me that,' answered Julia with a slight, lopsided smile. 'But she did say that she thought our falling-out might have influenced you, and if it did, I am sorry. I'd hate you to throw up something that . . .'

'Balderdash!' Flixe's voice was as robust as Julia had ever heard it and almost drowned the noise of the heavy lorries lumbering along Piccadilly. 'I'd pretty much made up my mind in Rome and, oddly, the final doubts were settled while I was talking to Amanda.'

Seeing that Julia was puzzled as she stood on the dusty pavement, looking so efficiently professional, Flixe suggested that they should have a cup of coffee at the Kardomah café, which was just behind them. Julia shook her head.

'I've a conference in half an hour. I'll have to go in a minute. But tell me what you meant.'

'Just that, as we were talking, I realised how dangerous it is to ignore important things about oneself. That's all. I must follow my own bent, Julia, not yours or Gerry's. It's much better to be a good window cleaner than a bad brain surgeon – and less dangerous to other people, too.'

Julia's face broke into a real laugh.

'That is unanswerable. Your common sense always was of the highest order. Let me know if I can help with the new career. Oh, it has been good to see you, Flixe. I hope Natalie is really all right now.'

'Thanks. 'Bye, Julia.'

Having mentioned the Kardomah to Julia, Flixe realised how badly she wanted some coffee herself. Not wanting to sit alone in the café with no protection, she went to buy a newspaper. She had only glanced at the headlines of the ones delivered to the house, but when she had found a table in the café she read every detail of the assassination of Robert Kennedy, shaking her head at the horror of it all. Her coffee had grown cold before she turned to the rest of the foreign news and discovered that the strikes in Paris appeared to be finally over, just as George had suggested on the aeroplane.

De Gaulle had reasserted both his own authority and that of the state. The anarchy and the nights of rioting and arson had been stopped. Sanity seemed to be returning to Paris.

Flixe absentmindedly stirred a large spoonful of brown sugar into her cool coffee, forgetting that she had long since given up sweetening her drinks. The French Prime Minister's earlier capitulation to the students had been revoked. General de Gaulle's promise of a referendum had been withdrawn on 30 May, but neither the Communists nor the students had reverted to violence. It really did look as though the situation was well enough in hand for Natalie to return home as soon as the doctors released her. There were even articles and letters sympathising with the French students, which seemed to be a sure sign that they were quite powerless again.

When Flixe turned to the rest of the news, she saw that the student demonstration in Rome had been quashed, too, and the university reopened. At the foot of that article was another, headed SCUFFLE AT OXFORD DEMONSTRATION. Unable to stop worrying about Andrew, she read it carefully, but it did not sound too serious and she began to think that perhaps the infection of rebellion and violence that had been seen as far afield as Tokyo and the United States would be cured before it damaged her son. At least if he could get his degree he would be reasonably secure, and once he had left Oxford his desire to protest would probably subside.

Thinking of some of the worst symptoms of the violence, she could not help thanking the fates that Andrew had been constrained by his final exams from joining in as he would have done in any other year.

There was nothing more on Czechoslovakia and in a sudden moment of optimism she thought that perhaps the Czechs too would be all right. Warsaw Pact troops were still on manoeuvres just outside the Czech borders, but there had been no specific threats against the newly liberal regime for some time. Flixe raised her coffee cup in a silent, personal toast and then put down the cup again without tasting the coffee in it.

Of all the cruelties of Peter's death, one she had not expected to feel was that he had died before he could see the flowering of Czechoslovakia. What Alexander Dubček was trying to do in Prague had so many echoes of what Peter had wanted for Russia in 1917 that he might have found several emotional wounds healed by it. Flixe had never quite been able to reconcile the man she had known only as an employee of the British Government with the young Bolshevik who had fought to bring down the Tsar in 1917, but as he battled with his illness he had talked to her a lot about that time. Until then she had not been able to see all the scars Peter carried, but she had known they were there, and during the last few weeks of his life she had learned for the first time how raw some of them had remained.

Knowing that she might cry if she let herself think about those weeks, she quickly drank her coffee and ate at least half of the bun before leaving to catch the tube to the hospital where Natalie was recovering from her operation.

When Flixe found her way to the private rooms, she discovered her sister-in-law lying asleep attached to both a drip and a catheter. There was an electric fan blowing cold air at her. She looked very small, very ill and frighteningly like Peter in the last few days of his life. He too had had that yellow skin, those immense shadows under his long-tailed eyes and lips that looked as though half the blood had been drained out of them. Flixe could not bear the thought that Natalie, too, might be dying.

Gripping the cream-painted bedstead with both hands, Flixe ordered herself not to faint. Eventually the waves of hot and cold that had been frightening her ceased and the buzzing in her head calmed down. She whirled round as she heard the squeaking shoes and crackling apron of a passing nurse.

'Doesn't she need help?' Flixe whispered urgently.

313

'No.' The young nurse spoke in an ordinary voice. 'There's nothing to worry about. She still has a high fever, which is why we've got the fan on. Her temperature will come down soon and once she's recovered properly from the anaesthetic all will be well. She'll probably wake soon.' She hurried on her way, cool, efficient and not unsympathetic.

Flixe sat down on an orange plastic chair beside the bed and waited for the residual panic to subside. If Natalie was likely to wake, Flixe did not want her to be alone.

Determined not to let herself sink back into reliving the weeks of Peter's last illness or worrying fruitlessly, Flixe took a notebook out of her bag and made herself a list of all the things she had to check for the Bronnets' dance, which was the last she was organising that season. It seemed a frivolous thing to be doing in that setting, but it was her work and it had to be done somewhere.

The dance was to be less complicated any of the others, partly because Catherine Bronnet was serenely happy doing the season, but mostly because her dance was to be smaller. After some discussion her mother had agreed to hire a marquee in the centre of one of the grandest of London's garden squares, instead of having the dance in one of the huge, luxurious hotels as she had wanted. Flixe had managed to get permission to rent the square gardens and had spent some time with Jane Bronnet and her daughter selecting the best band and deciding how to decorate the tent.

'Flixe?' Natalie's voice was so faint that Flixe hardly heard it, but as she looked up from her notes she saw that her sister-in-law was awake.

'Hello, Natalie. I'm glad you've woken. You poor darling. It must be horrible.'

'It's not so bad. They warned me that it would be painful and they are very good about the morphine.' A smile illuminated her sallow face. 'And Bertrand is here. The strikes ended in time, *grâce à Dieu*.'

'Oh, I am so pleased. And that everything in Paris is

getting back to normal. I've just been reading about it.'

Natalie's eyelids fluttered and closed. Flixe realised she had simply gone to sleep again, too weak to stay awake and concentrate on anything but her most immediate needs. It was only then that Flixe admitted to herself that she had been longing to tell Natalie all the things she had discovered about George in Rome. It was a shock to discover quite how damaged she was, she who had been Flixe's greatest support over the past year or more.

She turned again to her notes, waiting in case Natalie should wake again and need her. Before that happened, Bertrand returned from whatever had taken him away from the ward.

'How good of you to come,' he said softly, kissing both her cheeks.

'I wanted to come yesterday, but they said today would be better. She seems very tired.' Flixe spoke as quietly as he.

He nodded and walked carefully round the bed to his chair. As he was sitting down, Natalie's eyelids lifted again and a smile of relief widened her lips. She pushed one thin hand out of her bedclothes and he took it in both of his, looking down at her with absolute, unconditional love.

Natalie did not even look at Flixe, who was staring at them both with a mixture of gladness and regret. The sensation of loneliness that had been retreating throughout the last few weeks came back with full force and left her gasping.

She got up abruptly, said good-bye to them both, and went home to write to Connie and then type out formal letters of resignation to Conservative Central Office, Michael Diseholme and his agent. There were other letters to write too and she forced herself to concentrate on them, trying to explain her changed circumstances to her bank manager without sounding either pathetically cringing or intimidatingly arrogant. She had already drafted a business plan to send with a request for patience while she repaid her overdraft.

The telephone rang before she had produced a version of that letter she could bear to send.

'Felicity? George here. How are you?'

'Fine,' she said, lying. 'And you?'

'Rome seems aeons ago and my last sight of you almost lost in the mists of time. Can we meet this evening?'

Flixe sighed in relief.

'Why the sigh? Are you trying to tell me you regret Rome . . . or us?'

'Quite the reverse. I'd been feeling rather cut off and a bit beleaguered. It's lovely that you want to see me. Will you come here?'

'Yes, thank you. Isn't it pleasant to be old enough to let each other know what we want without having to play games?' said George with real feeling.

'I hadn't even thought of it, but I see what you mean.' Flixe added with a laugh: 'It's so long since I had to play those sort of games that I'd forgotten, but now you come to mention it, yes: it is good. I'll see you this evening then.'

'Mm. Shall I pick up some smoked salmon and a bottle on my way so that we can picnic? Or would you rather dine out?'

'A picnic would be heaven. George, you are a very . . . comfortable man.'

He laughed as he said good-bye, and Flixe put down her receiver feeling warm and no longer alone. There was only Gerry's warning about his motives to nag at her pleasure, but Flixe was determined to ignore it on the grounds that whatever George's reason for wanting to see her, the fact remained that he did want to made her life much better than it had been.

He came late and obviously tired again just as Flixe was about to give him up and scramble herself an egg for supper. When she opened the door he looked at her like a sheepish boy who has been caught with a handful of illicit chocolates.

'Will you forgive me? By the time I could get to a

telephone it seemed easier just to come here.'

'Don't be silly,' said Flixe, reaching for the bottle of wine and paper bag that he was carrying. 'What was it? A patient?'

'Actually, no. Gina.'

'Oh?' Flixe led the way into the kitchen, where she slid the long-necked bottle into the ice-making compartment of the fridge. 'What's up?'

'I rather wanted to ask your advice actually,' said George, dropping into a chair by the scrubbed wooden table. 'I was driving her to her dinner party for this evening's dance when she told me she's been invited to join a group of people going to the States for two months this summer.'

Flixe, who was fetching plates, bread and cutlery to lay on the table, stiffened slightly.

'Do you disapprove?'

'Well, I do rather and so we quarrelled. Sitting in the car for ages. It's not a familiar thing for us and I found it remarkably painful.'

'What worries you?' asked Flixe, unwrapping the smoked salmon he had brought and laying it out on a white plate with wedges of lemon. It was an unpleasant thought that he could not bear to let the girl grow up and away from him.

'That they're planning to hire a car in New York and drive to the West Coast. There are three of them, you see, three girls; none of them out of their teens. What happens if they burst a tyre in the middle of the desert and can't unscrew the wheel nuts? I don't like it, Flixe.'

'No boys at all?'

'No. It may be absurd of me, but I'd feel happier if there were.'

'Help yourself to salmon – your own salmon,' said Flixe, pushing the plate forwards. George could not understand why she suddenly looked so happy.

'Well?' he said when he had put about a quarter of the salmon on his plate and cut a slice of brown bread.

Helping herself to three sheets of the succulent pink fish,

Flixe considered aspects of his problem. At last, thinking of the predicament Andrew and Amanda had got themselves into, she decided to join George's side of the battle.

'I think you're right to be worried. They might be perfectly safe and able to get help if something goes wrong with the car, but the number of things that could happen to them is frightening. I suspect Gina is feeling over-debbed and sugared and wants something saltier to do; but there must be safer possibilities. What had you planned for her?'

'I hadn't. While she was still at school we used to go to my house in Dorset with two or three friends of hers to make it more fun for her while I – what is it they say? – let it all hang out. But I'd rather assumed she'd want to go abroad on her own this year.'

Flixe laughed and leaned across the table to ruffle his smooth blond hair. He could hardly have been clearer in his refutation of Gerry's ideas if they had been written on a ten-foot board in front of him.

'I didn't know you had a house in Dorset.'

'Didn't you? It's not special but I'm fond of it. My family comes from round there. I have a pretty simple farmhouse, but it's familiar and comfortable.'

Seeing that he had eaten his salmon, Flixe put some more slices on his plate.

'Thank you.' He looked rather anxiously at her and she wondered what was troubling him. She simply smiled and waited.

'I have been planning to ask whether you'd like to come and bring the children to Dorset for part of August,' he said quickly. 'I can't get away until the second week but I'll probably go for the last three. D'you think you might come too? There's not very much to do, although it's near the sea and there are plenty of people near by who'd let the children ride. It's nice down there and there are some good walks, but you might be awfully bored if the weather should turn bad.'

'I can't think of anything better.' Flixe's voice was definite.

'I've been worrying about how on earth to give the family a holiday this year. But we'd be an awful crowd. George, are you sure?'

He nodded.

'I'd love it. It's a selfish request. I'm extremely fond of the place – it's where I grew up – and I like going there, but for years I've longed for adult company and yet not . . . not been able to find the right sort of friend to take.'

Flixe looked down at the ragged pieces of salmon left on her plate and then back at George.

'You're going to think I'm awfully feeble,' she said, sniffing slightly. 'But I am so touched.'

'Good.' All anxiety had left his face and his eyes were bright. 'And I'll tell Gina that I've asked your opinion and you agree that she shouldn't drive across the States. She'll respect that. She's full of admiration for you.'

'Does she know that you and I are lovers?'

George shook his head. 'I don't think so.' Then he grinned, once more looking like a small boy bent on mischief. 'I don't think she can have any idea because she's always urging me to take you out to dinner and telling me how beautiful you are and funny, clever and kind. She still seems determined to make a match between us.'

'She is the sweetest girl,' said Flixe. 'I wish that Andrew had understood that.'

'He's probably too young to appreciate her. Does he know?'

'About us? I shouldn't think so. There's no reason for him to know. I've taken quite a lot of care not to give him any clues because I don't want him distracted before his exams.'

'He's bound to get a degree and the precise class hardly matters these days.'

Flixe clamped her lips together, looking more stubborn than he had suspected she could be. After a moment, she tried to explain.

'It would matter dreadfully to him. A lot of his identity is

319

bound up with being cleverer than most of his contemporaries and since his father died he's been rather shaky. Loving Amanda Wallington so much and so unhappily hasn't helped. If his belief in his brains went too, I'm not sure what would happen to him.'

George put his right hand across the table so that he could hold hers. He felt remarkably jealous of the son she clearly loved so much and he was determined not to give her any idea of his childishness.

'Don't be afraid, Felicity. Whatever happens, between us we'll be able to help him.'

It was extraordinary, she thought, how comforting that little word 'us' could be.

CHAPTER 21

When Gina Mayford telephoned the following afternoon, Flixe braced herself for a blast of resentment. Instead she received an invitation to dine in Harley Street before the Bronnets' dance.

'Catherine Bronnet has only just told me that it's to be one of yours; otherwise I'd have asked you ages ago. I ought to have realised, because I can't imagine who else would have the imagination to set a dance in a tent in the middle of a London square. And only you could have fixed it.'

Flixe laughed.

'That sounds very flattering, but it really wasn't very difficult. It's central, just the right size for a smallish dance and a bit more fun than a stuffy old hotel . . . I think.'

'All the rest of yours have certainly been more fun than any of the others,' said Gina cheerfully. 'You're not worrying, are you, Mrs Suvarov?'

'Not really. And especially not now that I know you're not furious with me. At least, you're not showing any signs of furiosity.'

There was a half-laugh, followed by a short silence, before Gina said: 'If I were to be truly honest, I'd confess that I was getting a bit frightened of the whole American plan, but I'd got my pride involved and I couldn't just give in to my father. The more he worried and described the ghastly things that might happen to us, the more determined I had to be. Your intervention was heaven sent.'

'Thank you, Gina,' said Flixe, touched – and impressed – by the girl's frankness.

'Now I know you'll have to be at the dance anyway,' Gina went on in a brisker voice, 'and it would make it much more interesting for my father if you'd come to our dinner party first. Do say you will.'

'That's awfully kind of you, but I'd have to leave early to finish off all my last-minute checks, which would mess up your arrangements.'

'That doesn't matter at all so long as you come. Do.'

'Then, thank you. I should love to,' said Flixe, intrigued at the prospect of seeing George's flat. They had become remarkably intimate with few of the ordinary stages of getting to know each other and she wanted to fill in some of the gaps.

'Excellent. Eight o'clock.'

'Fine. May I bring anything or help with anything?'

There was a warm-sounding laugh from the other end of the telephone.

'No, thank you. You must know that I'm quite accustomed to organising dinner parties even though my wheel-changing and engineering skills fill you with such doubts.'

'Ah. So you did mind my intervention a bit.'

'Perhaps a bit, despite my own desperate fears. But don't worry: I've promised my father that we won't go unless we can find some brawny young men to go with us.'

'I'm very glad, Gina. He was seriously afraid for you.'

'I know. We did a deal actually.' The laugh was back in her warm voice.

'Really? What was his side of it?'

'I'm not sure I ought to tell you,' said Gina. Then she

added in a rush, sounding much less assured: 'Actually I made him agree that he would come to the Bronnets' and dance with you and take you out to dinner the next day. Now it's your turn to be cross. Have I been very cheeky?'

Flixe smiled to herself, thinking that it did not sound as though Gina would be too distressed when she discovered the truth. 'No. I think it's sweet.'

'Good. I'm glad. We'll both see you then. Good-bye.'

Flixe said good-bye and put down her receiver, smiling still, and then picked it up to telephone Ming to ask for the loan of yet another dance dress. She was enthusiastically welcoming and suggested that Flixe should drive round straight away.

'Alas, I can't. I've got to dig up a whole lot of facts for Michael Diseholme about housing needs and benefits and then draft a speech for him.'

'Why are you sounding so doomy? Isn't that pretty routine?'

'Yes,' said Flixe gloomily, 'but I'm so longing to be shot of the whole political business that I loathe doing any of it. If it wasn't that I agreed to do this speech before I made up my mind to go, I'd force him to do his own work. But he is paying me a research fee for it.'

'That's something, I suppose. Well, might you be through by lunchtime? I've got to leave at about two to go and see someone who's thinking of commissioning a lovely series of articles about the port families in Opporto. I've been reading them up and . . . but you don't want to hear about that now. If you could get to me by oneish, we could have an egg together.'

Flixe sighed in envy of the work Ming had managed to achieve for herself, acknowledging that it was the result of years of hard effort – and real talent.

'That sounds good. I'll make sure I'm with you well before two. You're an angel, Ming.'

Two hours later they were sitting on either side of Ming's

kitchen table with another dish of baked eggs between them. Ming had opened a bottle of cold white burgundy to cheer her sister up.

'So tell me,' she said cosily, 'what is the man like?'

Flixe, who had been helping herself to three eggs, looked up, her dark blue eyes alight with amusement.

'Nice,' she said and laughed at the useless adjective. 'I'd need your talent with words to do him justice, but I'll try. He's interesting, kind – very kind – quiet, generous, sensible, humane and not above admitting his own mistakes.'

'Oh dear, oh dear.'

'Why?'

'Don't look so cross,' said Ming, smiling. 'It's just that he sounds too good to be true. There must be some things about him that aren't perfect.'

Flixe relaxed and ate a mouthful of egg and prawn.

'Mm, delicious,' she said. 'And so simple. You are clever. I suppose . . . No, of course he's not perfect. He has some odd quirks to do with his marriage. He appears to have had a lot of affairs, which is a bit unappealing, and the latest of them was not a good advertisement for his taste. And the fact that he hasn't remarried in eighteen years, despite knowing that it would be infinitely better for his daughter if he'd given her a stepmother, presumably counts against him. And perhaps the fact that he's built up a wonderful support system of devoted patients to make himself feel powerful and good when inside he is clearly still feeling quite the reverse.'

Ming's face had softened as she listened to her sister.

'You like him a lot, don't you?'

'Yes, I think I do. Is it very disloyal of me?'

Ming refilled their wine glasses, although neither of them had drunk much.

'I don't think it's disloyal to Peter at all, if that's what you mean,' she said firmly. 'You gave him everything you had while he was alive to take it. He loved you. He would have detested the thought that you might shut yourself away mourning yourself into nothingness. You're alive, Flixe. You need to live.'

'And you can be as sure as that even without knowing George or what he's like?'

'Why not? I trust your judgement of people and you've obviously thought a lot about him.'

Thinking of the difference in her two sisters' reactions to the news of her love affair, Flixe asked slowly: 'Have you ever loathed me, Ming?'

After a moment's surprise, Ming put her head on one side and considered Flixe.

'There have definitely been times you've made me utterly furious,' Ming said at last. 'And I'm sure I've driven you potty with rage, too. Don't all sisters?'

'I suppose so. I wouldn't know. Doesn't it matter then?'

'Flixe, what is all this? You know perfectly well it doesn't. It's human nature. It doesn't affect anything that matters.'

'I hope you're right. Gerry and I've had a bit of a fisticuffs – metaphorically speaking.'

Ming laughed and ate the last of her eggs.

'Well, that's nothing new,' she said. 'Will you have some more?'

'No thanks; it was wonderful, but I've had enough. What do you mean, nothing new?'

Ming got up to fetch a plate of French cheeses from the larder. She watched Flixe cut herself a slice of Brie.

'Don't you remember how the whole house used to tremble when we were young and you and Gerry battled over things?'

'Did it? I suppose I have forgotten. Actually I feel awful about it. I said things I . . .'

'Mark's right,' said Ming when she saw that Flixe was not going to finish. 'He says there's no future in argument; people always say things that can't be withdrawn and, even if they mean them at the time, it's always better not to say it.'

'But what are you supposed to do when you're driven to

325

fury? Swallow it? That surely makes you feel even worse.'

'I don't know. I don't seem to have felt anything worse than irritation for years. Perhaps I've let myself become too placid.'

'You've earned it,' said Flixe quickly. 'I think you ought to enjoy it while you can. It's so rare. By the way, I've brought back that silver-grey dress of yours.'

'Thanks. If you've finished, we'd better go up and choose another.'

Flixe stood up, saying: 'Is all this pillage of your wardrobe wicked exploitation of your good nature?'

Ming shook her head and they went up to her bedroom to choose from her apparently inexhaustible selection of clothes.

'Will George be at the dance?' she asked as Flixe tried to choose between the dark blue she had worn at the Kirkwaters' and one she had always rejected before on the grounds that she needed something more substantial-looking than ice green chiffon, trailing from her shoulders like water from The Lady of Shalott.

'Yes,' she said, pulling the dress over her head. 'And I'm dining with him and his daughter first.'

'That's heavenly,' said Ming, standing back to look. 'Have a look in the mirror.'

Flixe shrugged her shoulders into the dress and twitched the floating skirt until it hung correctly and then turned to look at herself in the long pier glass by the window. The cut of the dress made her look taller than usual. When she had first tried it on, it seemed to make her look washed-out and bedraggled, but that afternoon its delicacy seemed flattering after all.

Ming opened the small safe in her bedroom wall and took out a pair of small, diamond drop earrings.

'You need very simple jewellery with it. Try these.'

Flixe hung them in her ears and admitted that they looked exactly right with the dress.

'And they add light to your face. Not that it needs much these days. I am really so glad about George.'

'You are sweet, Ming,' said Flixe. She took off the borrowed finery, packed it up and returned home to work on the speech for Michael Diseholme.

On the night of the Bronnets' dance, she made herself up with care, noticing that she had rather more colour than usual, put money and keys in her evening bag, collected her briefcase of papers and drove herself to Harley Street.

Gina opened the door, wearing her scarlet silk again, and escorted Flixe to the spare bedroom so that she could leave her cloak.

'Do you want to wash or anything? Good. Then come and have a drink,' she said as Flixe tweaked her hair into place.

Gina led the way into a long formal drawing room, decorated with a yellow jaspé wallpaper and hung with curtains of pale blue taffetta. Important-looking eighteenth-century oils hung on the walls in gilded frames and the furniture was antique and immaculately kept. One or two superb pieces of china stood unprotected on tables here and there about the room and made Flixe wonder how old Gina had been before she had been allowed in it and who was trusted to clean it.

'Good evening, Felicity,' said George, appearing through a door at the far end of the room. In his evening clothes he looked the perfect owner of the dauntingly formal room. Flixe made a deliberate effort to remember him wearing his creased, baggy linen jacket in Rome.

'Good evening,' she said, holding out her hand. He shook it, but smiled at her with such a blaze of delighted happiness that her slight discomfort vanished into amusement. If Gina saw her father's expression, Flixe thought, their pantomime of politeness would probably have been redundant.

'Would you like a drink?' Gina asked, giving no sign that she had noticed anything unusual. 'We've a bottle of nice hock in the fridge, although I know it's wickedly un-fashionable, or there are all the ordinary things.'

'Some hock would be lovely. George, you do have a magnificent flat.'

'Thank you,' he said, looking slightly surprised. As Gina disappeared to fetch the wine, he added: 'It's extraordinary to think you've never been here until tonight, Felicity. Do you really like it?'

'Yes. I'm not sure I'd find it easy to be cosy in a room like this, but it is highly elegant.'

George's face creased into the familiar smile.

'I know. I always think it's rather like a very superior hotel or perhaps something done up for government entertaining. I had it done by a quite terrifying woman a couple of years ago so that Gina should not be embarrassed by the old tattiness as she grew up. I hadn't time to see to it myself and I didn't think she could have tackled it on her own at that stage.' He looked round the artfully lit, stylishly conventional room with a trace of regret in his eyes. 'It had got dreadfully shabby, but it was more friendly.'

'I see,' said Flixe, rather relieved. 'But what about the paintings and the china? Surely no decorator supplied those.'

'No. They were all here. Most of them belonged to my mother, but I bought one or two of the pots. The pictures were filthy and none of it looked as glossy as this before the decorator had a go at it.'

The front doorbell rang and he left to answer it. The deb he brought back with him was very shy and it took all Flixe's kindness and experience to encourage her to volunteer a single remark. By the time the rest of the guests had appeared and Gina had ushered everyone into the red-and-mahogany dining room, Flixe was feeling worn out with the effort.

She was also interested. Gina's calmly efficient handling of her large party, of whoever was working silently in the kitchen, and the serving of the lavish food were impressive. Gina seemed infinitely more sophisticated than any of her young guests that night and Flixe realised sadly that it was easy to see why they found her out of tune with them.

George had the shy deb on his left and clearly found her very hard to manage. Flixe came to his rescue with some patient questions and the three of them managed to keep up a stilted conversation about films and travel until Gina brought in a tray of coffee.

Flixe stood up.

'Gina, I really ought to slide out now, if you'll forgive me. I must be there before the hordes.'

'Yes, of course, I'll see you out.'

'Oh no, please don't bother. I can easily manage. Thank you very much for a wonderful dinner. I'll see you a bit later.'

George was standing at her side. He said something to the shy girl and to his daughter and escorted Flixe to the spare bedroom to collect her cloak. There he took her in his arms and laid his head on her newly set hair.

'Sorry,' he said after a moment, removing himself. 'But I thought I might never be able to touch you tonight and having you so close was unbearably tantalising. Are you all right?'

'Yes, I'm fine, George,' she said, laying her hand along his cheek. 'But I must dash. You are coming on to the dance, aren't you?'

'Yes. Gina made me promise.' He frowned. 'Felicity, you are worried about something, aren't you?'

'Nothing I can't cope with,' she said, smiling carefully.

'All right. I don't want to nag you. But please try to remember that I am here and capable and available if you need any help.'

Her face softened into a more genuine smile.

'I know. Thank you, George. I am a bit worried just now, but it's a mixture of lots of things. Andrew and his exams and his girlfriend; my poor sister-in-law and her health; and so on. But I can cope and now I really must go.'

He nodded and kissed her again. She pulled away and ran for the lift.

Everything seemed under control when she reached the marquee except for the mysterious disappearance of the caterers' reserve stocks of ice, which was causing a mixture of anxiety and bitter recrimination that threatened to disrupt the entire team. Flixe questioned the last people to have seen the van storing it, telephoned the local police in case they had removed it for causing an obstruction, and eventually discovered it serenely parked in the next street. The driver had decided that his van might be in the way in the first parking space and so he had told someone that he would move it. Whoever had taken the message had either disappeared or forgotten to pass it on to the caterers.

Calm having been restored, Flixe just had time to make her last-minute checks before the Bronnets' party arrived. The tent was looking good, she decided, with a scarlet-and-white striped lining instead of the more usual pastel colours and great fan-shaped arrangements of red flowers alternating with pyramids of green and white. The dark green poles that held up the marquee had been wrapped in plaited red, green and white ribbons so that they looked like giant maypoles, and on each of the round tables at the edge of the dance floor was a miniature pyramid of flowers studded with brass bells.

As the Bronnets and their dinner guests arrived, the band began to play and the first champagne bottles were opened. Flixe went to report that all was well.

As usual the dance took ages to generate enough enthusiasm and goodwill to feel really successful, but it started to get better soon after eleven. Flixe, who had been circling the tent in order to talk to anyone who looked lost, was being polite to an elderly cousin of Jane Bronnet's when she heard a faint susurrus all round her and looked up to see who or what was creating the interest.

In the entrance to the marquee, surrounded by a group of young men and beautifully posed in front of a mass of brilliant red flowers, was Amanda Wallington, dressed in white with a lot of sumptuous ostrich feathers around the very low-cut neck. Her dark hair was piled up into thick, glossy curls. There was no sign of her pregnancy and she looked magnificent.

Flixe could not help smiling in appreciation of the picture she presented and calculating that she must have only just stopped feeling sick. Flixe herself could remember the immense sense of well-being that had filled her at that blessed moment in her own pregnancies and she was afraid that it might make it even harder for Amanda to decide not to have the child.

'Do you know her?' asked the elderly cousin.

'Amanda Wallington? Yes, she's my god-daughter. I hadn't realised that she came to any of these dances.'

'Catherine knows her, I believe, and wanted her here for a touch of sophistication. She's a world-famous model, you know.'

'I think that may be a slight exaggeration, but she is quite successful.'

Flixe watched Amanda progress into the crowd and wondered why Andrew was so certain that what he called 'the star' was not an important part of the real Amanda. She seemed to revel in the attention all round her and wherever she went in the marquee the atmosphere heightened. People wanted to talk to her, to dance with her, to make her laugh, and she could clearly charm all of them into a mixture of admiration and envy. Flixe thought that she recognised someone supremely at home with what she was doing and thought that Andrew might have made the same disastrous mistake as the one George Mayford had admitted in Rome.

'Flixe? It is you. I thought it was from the other side of the tent.'

She turned at the sound of the petulant voice to see Ann

Kirkwaters at her side, dressed in pale pink, which ought to have looked far too young but actually suited her rather well. Trying to be objective, Flixe thought she could understand why George might have been physically attracted to Ann. Flixe pulled herself together and introduced Ann to the elderly cousin, who chatted for a polite moment or two and then drifted away as it became clear that Ann wanted to get Flixe on her own.

'Who on earth was that whiskery relic?' she demanded pettishly.

'One of Jane Bronnet's relations,' said Flixe, glad to have something impersonal to talk about. 'You weren't frightfully kind, Ann.'

'I haven't come to be kind.' She put up a hand to make certain her pretty tiara was securely fixed to her fluffy hair. 'But to ask you what on earth you thought you were doing?'

'About what?' Flixe asked, although she thought she knew the answer.

'I never dreamed you could be so treacherous,' said Ann. 'I made it perfectly clear to you that George was mine, but you went out of your way to take him away.'

'Ann, you did nothing of the kind and nor did I,' said Flixe, keeping her temper with difficulty and loathing the degrading squabble. 'You did not introduce us. He and I already knew each other before your dance; I knew you were friends and I assumed you'd invited him to be kind to me. That, after all, was what you said you'd done.'

'That was a bit self-centred of you, wasn't it? You ought to have seen that I only wanted you as camouflage, so that Simon wouldn't guess why George was there.'

'And I thought you were being kind!' Flixe tried to sound cheerfully ironical, but she was afraid that she had not succeeded.

'That's the last thing I feel. When it happens to you, spare a thought for what you've put me through.'

'When what happens?'

'When George exchanges you for a new model. And he will. His things never last more than five or six months. It would have happened to me anyway, but you cheated me out of my last three months.' Ann peered forward to look into her old friend's eyes. 'Oh, my poor Flixe, were you telling yourself that this was it? How sad! Your precious lover is famous for never getting seriously involved with anyone. Lots of people wanted to marry him, but he's never got caught.'

Flixe turned aside to take a glass of champagne. She felt she needed strengthening.

'Poor man,' she said with feeling. Ann looked astonished and then furious.

'I hope he hurts you,' she said. When she had gone, Flixe closed her eyes.

'What a waste of energy,' she said aloud, reminding herself of the way Gina had dealt with the anger and patronage of women who had wanted her father.

'What? Fixing dances like this?' asked George, who had come to find her. Flixe opened her eyes and smiled at him, shaking her head.

'No, being angry with silly women.'

He held out his arms.

'Dance?'

'Lovely.'

As they whirled round the floor, Flixe could feel George's heart beating. She wished she had been able to avoid Ann.

'Which was the woman?'

'Ann,' she said with a slight laugh to show that she was not really upset.

'Ah. Yes, I saw you talking to her and stayed away until she'd gone. Felicity, I am really sorry about all that. I can't think how I . . .'

'George, I know you said you didn't want to talk about it, but what did happen with her?'

There was a silence but Flixe could tell how disturbed he was by the way his steps faltered for a moment.

'As I told you, I was an idiot,' he said at last. 'I can't remember how much I told you about it so stop me if you've heard it all before. I've never been able to contemplate marrying again and I've nearly always wanted . . . female company. Ann was, I regret to say, one of a series. But it was a complete disaster. Almost as soon as we'd started, I knew I'd have to finish quickly, but I was too much of a coward. I suppose I was waiting for her to get bored and sack me when I met you. Then I knew I'd have to do any sacking myself and quickly.'

George looked so uncomfortable that Flixe was tempted to tell him that none of it mattered, but just as she was about to say the words, she realised that it did in fact matter a great deal.

'And?' she asked gently.

'I was afraid that she'd not only be hurt but also resentful and from what I'd learned of her, I thought she might take out that resentment on Gina. Oh, Felicity, this is horrible.'

'I'm sorry.'

The humility in her voice immediately made him want to explain why he found telling her the shaming story so hard.

'No, it's all right; I just hate appearing such a fool in front of you. Quite apart from the complication of Gina and the season, I didn't want to hurt Ann. After all it was only discovering you that showed me quite how foolish I'd been to think that she was what I was looking for.'

Flixe looked up to see that there was a slight flush along his cheekbones. Her lips lengthened into a smile of immense tenderness.

'D'you know, my dear,' she said after a while, 'I don't think you're a rake at all. You mind far too much about everyone's feelings to qualify.'

'Aagh,' he said theatrically, swinging her out of the dance to an unfrequented corner of the tent, where a cushioned bench stood under a canopy hung with ribbons and bells. 'My dread secret has been discovered. I've worked so hard to

334

keep it hidden and behave as rakes should. You mustn't tell anyone.'

Flixe laughed and leaned towards him.

'I won't. You can rely on me.'

'I thought you didn't approve,' he said, beginning to look less self-conscious as he teased her.

'Of rakes or secrets?'

'Secrets, dear fool.'

'I disapprove only of those that cause trouble. This seems quite innocuous.'

'And you don't mind too much? I think you once said you particularly liked rakes.'

For a moment she felt flooded with sadness. To admit that there were times when Peter's rakishness had made her despair seemed disloyal to the long and important past. And yet to refuse to admit it to George, who was filling her life with a simple happiness she had begun to rely on, seemed unfair.

'And so,' said a cheerful voice from behind them, 'my deal was quite unnecessary. You two obviously know each other much better than you'd let on, don't you?'

With an effort, Flixe turned to smile at Gina.

'Perhaps a little better. Do you mind?'

The girl looked from one to the other and shook her head.

'No, although I think it was a bit unfair that you didn't tell me, Daddy, when I made the deal. I'd have asked for something more if I'd known.'

Flixe recognised that George too was having to make an effort to appear frivolous and untroubled.

'Aha, but I was always a good negotiator. I'd never give ground by making you a present of an important bargaining counter.'

Gina suddenly leaned forward and kissed Flixe.

'I'm really glad. I've wanted it for months. I'll leave you both to it.' She waved casually and disappeared towards the group surrounding Amanda.

'She really is adorable,' said Flixe.

'Yes. Felicity, tell me whatever it was you were going to say before she came.'

'Just that I loved my husband and he was a rake.'

'I see,' said George and then frowned. 'No, actually I don't think I do see at all.'

'It's horribly complicated. Because . . . No.' She took a deep breath. 'I used to have a particular liking for rakes but it seems to have deserted me. I don't want you to think I'm being disloyal to him.'

George's anxiety melted into relief. 'I don't. You seem to be loyalty personified. Shall we dance to celebrate our two broken secrets?'

Much later, after George had gone to be polite to his hostess, Flixe found herself beside Amanda. At the sound of her greeting, Amanda turned away from her excited court.

'Auntie Flixe, how nice! I saw you were here. Can we talk somewhere for a minute?'

'Yes, if you like. Come over here.' Flixe led her to the cushioned bench nearest the caterers' entrance. 'There's a bit of peace here. How are you, Amanda?'

The girl sat in the shadow of an immense pyramid of green-and-white flowers studded with highly polished Granny Smith apples.

'I feel wonderful physically now. Quite different. Sort of glowing. As for the rest, I'm still trying to suppress the terror and the panic. I've got to do something horribly soon. I've got to. And I haven't . . . Oh, help.' She bit her lip and then asked: 'How have his exams gone, do you know?'

Flixe smiled.

'I think he's quite pleased with them, although he's not pinning his faith to anything. Vivas should be called next week and so we'll know a little more then. Hasn't he written to you?'

Amanda's lovely face twisted.

'Yes, but he hasn't said anything about the exams. He's

336

taking a lot of trouble not to bother me with his own concerns, which is entirely my own fault because I was horrible to him when he would go on and on talking about things that bored me rigid.' She sighed. 'There are so many things I wish I'd never done or said. Besides this.'

Her head drooped.

'You haven't told him anything, have you?'

'No. You asked me not to. But his exams are over now, Amanda. If you are going to tell him, the sooner the better, both for him and for you. It's getting urgent if you are going to decide on a termination.'

'There's the viva first,' Amanda said obstinately. She turned to face her godmother who thought she saw a look of desperation in the girl's eyes. Then Amanda stiffened her back and a dazzling smile lit her face again. No one who had not heard their conversation would know that she was not the happiest, least troubled person in the warm, crowded marquee. Flixe was impressed by the efficiency of the mask but worried by it too.

'On with the dance,' said Amanda and then as though she could not help herself asked: 'Are you furious with me, Auntie Flixe?'

'My dear child, no.' Flixe touched her hand and was surprised to find it trembling slightly. 'In fact since all this I've come to understand why he loves you so much.'

For a moment she was afraid that Amanda might burst into tears, but the mask was twitched back into place just in time.

'I'm not sure that I do,' she said, staring at the multi-coloured, shifting crowd in front of them. 'But perhaps it'll provide the answer.'

'And I always thought you were so confident,' said Flixe lightly, despite being appalled at the prospect of Amanda marrying Andrew simply to provide an answer to her unanswerable questions. Amanda shook her head, but she did not say anything.

'How's your mother?'

Amanda lifted one slim shoulder. The soft, floating feathers blew up and brushed her face. She pushed them back.

'I think she's fine. She's got this big case in the Court of Appeal and she doesn't seem to think of much except that. We're fairly friendly at the moment, and not seeing much of each other helps.'

'She's worth being friends with.'

'That sounds as though you think it's entirely up to me and I'm afraid it's not. I try, but she just doesn't like me enough for it to work. Luckily I'm going back to Norwich for a bit after this and so we'll have less chance to quarrel.'

The brilliant smile was switched on once more as Amanda rose gracefully from the bench to return to her clamouring admirers.

CHAPTER 22

Amanda stayed in Norwich for two weeks after the end of term, telling herself that she was simply keeping out of her mother's way but well aware that she was actually trying to pluck up courage to tell Andrew about the child. When she eventually reached London, it was to find a letter and several telephone messages from him. As soon as she had greeted Janice, drunk some tea with her, and carried her luggage upstairs, Amanda telephoned him from her mother's dark green study.

'Darling!' he said when she had announced herself, clearly delighted to hear her voice. 'Thank you for your letters, especially the little short one about being afraid. It came just in time.'

'You've thanked me for that in several letters already, Andrew,' she said quite gently.

'I know, but it made so much difference. You can't imagine.'

'Good. How were the exams?'

'Not too bad. The class lists won't be published for another couple of weeks or so, but I have had a viva, which either

339

means that I did infinitely worse than I think or that I am in line for a first after all.'

'I've never doubted that.'

'Oh, Amanda, how nice of you! I want to see you.'

'Do you?' His exams were over; there was no longer any reason to put off telling him about the child. Despite all her silent rehearsals, the prospect of actually doing it seemed almost impossible. She began to wonder whether it would be too cowardly to make his mother do it for her. 'I must spend this evening with my parents. They've organised something according to Janice. But we could meet tomorrow.'

'Could we? Good. What time and where?'

'Where would you like?' she asked, prepared to be co-operative.

'Why not come here? It's a better base than Kennington. Or we could go and look at pictures if you'd prefer.'

Amanda laughed, thinking that the release of tension about his exams had made Andrew more sensitive than usual to her possible wishes. Perhaps when she saw him it would seem possible to tell him after all.

'And then perhaps on Sunday you might feel like joining me at the demo,' he went on.

'One for me and one for you, I see,' she said, slightly irritated and yet relieved to be irritated. Anger seemed so much safer than all the other feelings. 'What is it designed to achieve this time?'

'An end to the war in Vietnam, of course. We're to meet in Trafalgar Square and march to the American Embassy. Do come. It'll be an historic moment.'

'Really?' There had been an undercurrent of sardonic amusement in his voice which puzzled her.

'Yes. My last major demonstration. Now that I'm joining the bourgeois world of work at the BBC, I'm going to have to give up political protest, but this will be my final fling.'

'In that case,' said Amanda, amused despite her other feelings, 'I should love to come and I'll do my best to make it worth its significance. What does one wear to a riot?'

There was an impatient-sounding sigh.

'It's not a riot. It's a march and you can wear whatever you like. Something comfortable and not one of your transparent masterpieces. It's quite a long walk and one tends to get frightfully dusty.'

Sighing at the thought of his unreliable sense of humour, Amanda suggested meeting him on the steps of the National Gallery at eleven the following morning, adding: 'The tube to Charing Cross is so much easier from here than all the way to your house.'

'Okay. Don't be late.'

In fact it was Andrew who was late, by nearly half an hour. He came running up the steps to where she was sitting on the balustrade reading, his face red with effort rather than embarrassment.

'Darling, I'm sorry. I got held up talking to my mother and didn't realise how late it was getting.'

'That's all right,' said Amanda sedately as she slid off her stone perch. Andrew shook his head slowly as he watched her. That morning she was dressed in a very short, white culotte-dress, belted low on her hips with a thin scarlet-leather belt, and white plastic boots. Her long dark hair was thick and gleaming, held back from her face by an enormous pair of white-framed dark glasses, and her make-up was less startling than usual. It was a boiling-hot day and yet she looked quite cool and remarkably elegant. There was, however, something about her smile that suggested an enormously encouraging lack of certainty.

'God, you're beautiful,' he whispered. 'I always forget quite how much.'

Enjoying the interested audience of tourists and custodians, Amanda flung both arms around his neck and kissed him on the mouth. She felt Andrew's arms go round her back and clutch at her so tightly that she was afraid for her dress.

341

'What are we going to see?' he asked when she had withdrawn from him. 'And how long have we got before you go to Fiesole?'

'I'm off next Wednesday. It's going to be hideously hot, but I must get there soon, before the Uffizi's print department shuts for the holidays.'

'It's a bugger that you've got to work when it's my last month of freedom. I start at the Beeb at the beginning of September.'

'Poor you,' she said, kissing his chin and leading the way into the gallery.

He followed her obediently and trailed round the galleries, stopping when she did and genuinely trying to get as excited about the paintings as she was, but he found it all a dreadful waste of time. To keep away impatience he looked at her instead of the pictures and even let himself fantasise about what she might say on the day she agreed to marry him and where they might live and, more urgently, when she was going to let him make love to her again.

When Amanda had at last seen enough paintings and suggested going to find some lunch in a little Italian restaurant she knew in St Martin's Lane, Andrew leaned forward to whisper: 'Come back to Kensington with me instead? My mother will have gone out seeing to something and the girls aren't back from school yet. The house would be ours. Darling, it's months and months since we made love. I . . . I need you. Please?'

Amanda pulled back to look at him. There was no censure in his dark eyes for once, just an honest pleading. He had been good to her that day and she was almost ready to tell him. That could not be done anywhere public. Her lips curled into a wavering smile as she nodded. Andrew let out the breath he had been holding.

'Good,' he said, gripping her wrist. 'Oh hell! I can't afford a taxi. I do so hate being poor.'

'I can,' said Amanda, waving her small red quilted

shoulder bag. 'Have this one on me.'

'I fully intend to,' he said, grinning.

Amanda smiled perfunctorily, which troubled him, but then she laid her head briefly on his shoulder and he thought everything would be all right.

'By the way,' he went on, 'what's this I've been hearing about the famous Gillingham portrait? I asked my mother and she simply said she hadn't liked it much although it was brilliantly painted. Darling, what is it?'

Amanda had pulled away from him, surprised for a moment that he had not seen any of the press comments about the painting. Then she realised that he would simply ignore the arts pages of the newspapers he read.

'I hate it,' she said in a clear, hard voice. 'There's a taxi. Get it.'

Andrew obeyed and said no more until they were safely sitting in it.

'Why, darling? Why do you hate it?'

'It was part of a rather cruel joke perpetrated on me by that wretched woman, but I think it was only a joke and quite enough has been said about it. There's no need to fuss.'

'I'm sorry,' said Andrew, squeezing her hand. Grateful that he had asked no questions or precipitated the explanation she was not quite ready to give him, Amanda let her head drop on to his shoulder again. He held her gently, silently promising that this time he would be more careful of her and take more time so that he could be sure she would enjoy it as much as he.

'Are you very hungry?' he asked when she had paid the taxi and they were walking up the steps to his mother's house.

'No. Not really. Why?'

'I don't want to rush you.'

He unlocked the door, ushered her in and then pushed it shut with his foot as he took her in his arms.

'Darling.'

Suddenly Amanda knew that she could not let him go on thinking that she was about to go to bed with him before she had told him about the baby.

'Andrew, we must talk.'

'Not now, Amanda. We can talk all you like later.' He was kissing her neck, pushing the heavy mass of hair away from her head and tipping her head back as his lips travelled over her skin. 'I want you so much. I've missed you so much.'

'Andrew. No.' She pushed hard at his shoulders. 'We must talk first.'

She was released at once. To her consternation he dropped on to his knees in front of her and put his arms about her waist, laying his face against her belly.

'I love you.'

'Do you?'

He leaned away from her and looked up into her face, his own almost angry.

'How can you ask that?' His voice was almost a whisper. 'Amanda, you must know.' He pulled himself together and got to his feet again. 'Good God! No one who didn't love you would put up with the way you've carried on since the spring.'

'Has it been so bad?'

Andrew turned away and sat heavily in one of the two Louis Seize chairs that stood either side of the hall table and which no one ever used. The joints of the chair creaked beneath him.

'I think I have loved you all my life,' he said, staring at his grubby tennis shoes, 'although I didn't begin to understand it properly until last summer. You are the most important thing in my life and watching you flirting with other people, seeing you draped over statues and benches in every magazine I pick up, hearing gossip about you from all and sundry half kills me. When you give your tongue free rein to say the most hurtful things it can, you put me on the rack. But nothing you do can stop me loving you.'

When she said nothing he looked up and saw that her face was completely white and her wide mouth looked pinched, almost as though she were frightened.

'What is it?'

She shook her head, tears coming into her eyes. After a declaration like that how could she tell him that she had slept with someone else? Until she could tell him that, she could not tell him about the baby.

'I didn't want to hurt you,' he said, looking at his feet again. 'I wanted to explain.'

Something stirred in the recesses of Amanda's mind; something that had been so successfully hidden that even she had not known it existed. She walked towards him as slowly as though she were walking through treacle and laid her hand on his head, sliding her fingers down to his neck. Once more he looked at her.

'You didn't hurt me,' she said with difficulty. 'It's just that I never expected anyone to say that to me.' Seeing he was puzzled, she tried to explain, although the tears that she couldn't stop kept making her voice peculiar. 'That they wouldn't stop loving me whatever I did. Do you mean it?'

He got out of the chair at once and with a gentleness she had not yet felt from him pulled her slowly into his arms, cradling her and stroking her head.

'Of course I meant it. You weren't afraid I'd stop, were you? Is that why you've been so . . . ? Darling, I've tried and I am simply unable to stop. Don't be afraid. Don't be afraid.' He felt in his pocket for a handkerchief and mopped her streaming eyes. 'You never used to cry – ever. What's happened?'

She simply shook her head, burying her face in his shoulder, quite unable to say anything.

He took her up to his room, dried her face again, made her lie down on his bed and shut the curtains to shade the bright sunlight. Then he undressed her carefully, having a little trouble with her culottes, which made them both laugh, and started to kiss her.

Exhausted, longing for once to be kind to him after what he had given her, Amanda lay back against the soft cotton bedspread and did nothing at all until he sank forwards on to her breast. She murmured his name as kindly as she could and stroked his hair and slowly became aware that he, too, was in tears.

'I'm sorry,' she said in despair, thinking that he must have felt something different in her and guessed her condition. 'I didn't mean to make you unhappy. I never wanted that.'

He slid closer to her, one of his hands still clasped on her shoulders, the other reaching behind him for a corner of the bedspread. He sniffed without embarrassment and mopped his eyes.

'It's not unhappiness; it's the effect of total bliss. You did like it this time, didn't you?'

'Oh yes,' she said, not altogether lying. The physical sensations had been nothing compared to the fire and lightning of Anthony Gillingham's lovemaking, but the emotions were infinitely pleasanter.

'Good,' said Andrew and went to sleep again.

That evening Amanda found her mother waiting for her in the green-and-white kitchen as usual.

'Hello, Mum,' she said, going to refill the kettle at the sink. 'Dad out?'

'No. He's working. How are you?'

'You sound anxious.' Amanda turned from the sink, looking surprised.

'Of course I'm anxious. I'm terribly concerned for you and I've been afraid of . . . that . . .'

'It's not like you to be stuck for words.' Amanda plugged in the kettle and switched it on. 'Oh, I see. You want to know if I've told Andrew that I'm pregnant and what he said and what we're going to do about it.'

'Broadly, yes.' Julia managed to smile. 'Not out of vulgar curiosity, but in case I can help.'

'I haven't told him.'

'Oh, darling!' Julia sounded angry and Amanda sighed. 'No, really. You are tiresome. You've spent the whole day together. You put off telling him because of his exams, which I can just about understand, but . . . if that was out of concern for him and not something else I haven't understood, why haven't you done it now? It's hardly fair, Amanda, to let him take you out without telling him he's made you pregnant.'

'Perhaps if you weren't so used to listening for false stories in criminals' statements and interrupting them at crucial moments so that you can trip them into telling the truth, you'd be able to wait until I could tell you things and then perhaps you would understand me and then perhaps we wouldn't always hurt each other so much.'

Pulled up short by the justice of her daughter's statement as much as by the cold, adult voice in which it had been delivered, Julia opened her mouth to speak, shut it and then started again.

'I am sorry, Amanda. That's fair. What do you want to tell me?'

'I'm going to have some coffee. D'you want anything?'

'No, thank you. I've got this.' Julia raised her glass of weak whisky and water. She waited while Amanda spooned powdered coffee into a mug and added boiling water. 'Well?'

'He loves me,' said Amanda.

'Yes, I know he does.' Julia tried to be gentle enough to help her daughter produce whatever confidence was coming. 'But that doesn't necessarily mean you love him, does it?'

'I don't know. I hadn't thought so.'

There was a pause while Amanda burned her tongue on the coffee.

'What's making you change your mind?'

'He loves me absolutely and without condition,' she said, putting the mug down on the table and looking at her mother. 'Whatever I do or say he loves me.'

There was silence. Julia, still acutely conscious of Amanda's perceptive criticism of her tactics, said nothing.

'It's worth an awful lot,' said Amanda. Julia could not understand why her hard, difficult daughter had tears in her eyes.

'Is it?' she said carefully and watched the tears fall.

'Yes, it bloody is! It's what...' She clamped her mouth shut.

'I'd have thought that a more selective love would be worth more,' Julia went on slowly, picking her words to make her point more clearly. 'How much could you value a love that would be yours even if, say, you had run over someone in a car and refused to stop and try to help them?'

Amanda turned away.

'Oh, don't. You don't understand. You've never understood.'

Julia came to stand beside her daughter's chair and stroked her head.

'I do understand what you mean, Amanda. I know that longing to be absolutely secure in someone's affection, to feel as though it can never be taken away. But sometimes when you're able to feel that from someone you yourself don't love you can come to despise them.'

Amanda stiffened under her mother's stroking hand.

'And sometimes it's possible to feel that the very safety is stifling when it should be wonderful.'

'But at least it would be safe,' she muttered and pulled back to pick up her mug and drink some coffee. Obediently Julia returned to her chair and sipped her whisky.

'Amanda, loving someone else is a bit like walking a tightrope. If you rush, you'll miss your footing and fall off. If you don't take it seriously enough the rope will slacken and that makes you fall, too. If you take it too seriously, the rope tightens and snaps. It needs a very steady nerve to do it right, and absolute trust and considerable determination. You can't just do it on feeling comfortable.'

'That's probably right,' said Amanda, finishing her coffee, 'despite the slickness of the presentation. I think I'll go to bed.'

'Good idea.' Julia had no idea whether she had said what she had meant or whether Amanda had understood it let alone accepted it. 'Are you seeing him tomorrow?'

'Yes. He's coming to fetch me in the morning.'

'Good-night, darling. Sleep well. Oh, by the way, I bought the painting.'

Amanda whirled round.

'*The Mermaid*?'

'Yes. I thought you might prefer to be able to control it.'

'But it was going to cost two thousand pounds.'

'It did. Nevertheless it seemed important that you should know where it was and who was seeing it.'

Amanda hesitated by the door, looking about fourteen in her short dress with her hair untidy and her eyes reddened. She walked back to the table, put a slightly shaking hand on her mother's shoulder and quickly kissed her, as though hoping that the speed with which she did it would make it almost unnoticeable. Julia said nothing and Amanda escaped.

CHAPTER 23

Marching up Regent Street, with Andrew's hand in hers and protest songs ringing in her ears, Amanda managed to forget the scene in the kitchen that had kept her awake half the night. Her head was aching and her eyes burning from lack of sleep, but the fresh air was helping, and there was a tremendous sense of solidarity in her, not only with Andrew but with all the strangers marching with them. Every so often he dropped her hand so that he could put his arm around her waist and sometimes he even kissed her. She could see the excitement and pleasure in his eyes and was glad that she had come on his last demo with him.

The leaders of the march would swing round at intervals to face their followers and bawl slogans or orders through their megaphones, but they seemed to have as little to do with what really mattered as the fluttering banners and the attendant policemen who strode patiently in their hot blue uniforms at the side of the marchers. Ordinary people on the pavements seemed poor fools for not being part of what Amanda could feel.

'What happens now?' she asked as the first rows of the long trail of marchers wheeled left.

'Grosvenor Square,' muttered Andrew. 'The American Embassy. And then on to Speaker's Corner. I told you.'

'Yes I know, but what do we do when we get to the embassy?'

'Demonstrate.'

She laughed at his short, almost impatient, answer and after a moment he laughed back. Everything seemed all right. When the demonstration was over, she would tell him about the child and the ambiguity of its conception, and Andrew would understand. He had said that nothing she could do or say would stop him loving her. It would be all right.

As their row of the crocodile reached Grosvenor Square Amanda saw a solid phalanx of uniformed police lined up in front of the incongruous concrete embassy building that took up an entire side of the square.

'Aha,' said Andrew. 'They've remembered March.'

'What happened in March?' asked Amanda, who had her own way of ignoring those parts of newspapers she found boring.

'We almost succeeded in rushing the embassy. You must have read about it. Come on.'

'But why? I thought simply demonstrating was the point,' she said as he urged her into the battle line that was forming parallel with the defenders'.

'This is the demonstration,' he said, his eyes glittering. His face changed slightly. 'You're not frightened, are you? We just rush towards them and lean. They lean back and either they give in or we do. It's not like Paris.'

'Oh. Good.'

'Would you rather leave?' He leaned towards her, searching her eyes for signs of withdrawal.

Having come so far with him, Amanda was not about to spoil his last battle.

'Certainly not,' she said, pushing her hair behind her ears

and making sure that the buttons on her checked shirt were securely fastened.

'Good girl. But if you change your mind, tell me and I'll get you away somehow.'

'Okay,' she said, squaring her shoulders and balling her hands into fists. Andrew laughed.

'Don't get too excited. Nothing's going to happen until we've got a bit more weight behind us.'

Amanda grew more and more impatient as the tail of the march reached the square. The shouting and the pulsing songs grew louder. She could feel pressure building up in herself and all around her. At last the order was given and they began to move forwards. She and Andrew were not in the first row, but they were close enough to see the expressions in the eyes of some of the police who barred their way.

Some were stolid, others looked wary, and a few as Amanda was beginning to feel: excited. She could smell hot sweat all around her and felt the pounding of thousands of feet through her own bones.

'Pigs!' someone shouted. Others echoed the cry.

'Pigs,' called Amanda experimentally. It sounded good. Andrew grinned at her. 'Pigs. Fucking pigs.' The words of the song her comrades were singing suddenly seemed familiar and she lifted her cracked voice to join them. Such was the noise that it didn't matter that she was incapable of keeping a note or even judging whether she was singing in tune or not. Alternately croaking and shouting, she joined in and felt wonderful as the first line started to push against the police.

Pressed from behind, Amanda's row was forced forwards.

'We shall overcome!' she bellowed and thrust her whole weight against the man in front of her. She saw the blue line ahead break momentarily and felt tremendous satisfaction.

'We shall overco-ome. Hurray!' Her hand felt dangerously slippery in Andrew's and so she linked arms instead, which gave her a much greater feeling of security, and pressed forwards into the charge again. Far to her right she saw a policeman lose his helmet and strike out. Someone else began to hit and a woman screamed.

Slightly sobered, Amanda looked quickly at Andrew.

'Don't worry. It never escalates into real trouble. If you do no more than push, they do no more than push back.'

'All right. And if they do try to arrest me,' she said, repeating the instructions he had given her, 'I just sit down.'

'That's right, darling. But they won't. Here we go again.'

But they couldn't break the line of police. After repeated charges Amanda had been pushed towards the front line. As the force built up behind her again, she was thrust at the blue serge uniforms ahead. Her hair blew in front of her face, blinding her and getting in her mouth. She could not release her hands in order to push it away and so she tossed her head, saw a red-faced policeman grinning at her in superior mockery and launched herself towards him. Her face reached just below his shoulder and as they met with jarring force, she opened her mouth and gripped all she could between her teeth.

It was only his uniform and it tasted of dust and fluff, but she had it between her teeth and she ground them, butting her forehead hard into his shoulder. At last he wrenched away, making her teeth ache as the material ripped through them. She swore and so did he. Someone pulled her back by the shoulders before she could slip her arms out of her companions' and batter his sneering face with both fists as she wanted.

'Stop it,' she howled.

'Come down, Amanda. Come down.' A hand under her chin forced her face round and she saw Andrew smiling at her with deliberate calm. 'You're too high, darling. Cool it and come down.' He slowly took his hands away from her shoulders. All round them the comrades were pressing forwards once again, eddying round them like waves.

Breathing deeply, she kept her eyes on Andrew's and slowly realised what he meant. Her fingers tingled and sweat dribbled revoltingly from behind her knees, her armpits and the palms of her hands.

'Yes,' she said, dizzy with what she had discovered about herself.

'All right to go on?'

'Yes,' she said again, but it soon became clear that the marchers were going to have to give up. No one in Amanda's immediate area had been hurt, but as the pressure round her eased and the distance between her and the policemen grew, she began to feel tired and also quite badly bruised.

'Do we have to go on to Speaker's Corner straight away?' she asked when her breathing was almost normal again. 'I don't want to be feeble, but couldn't we take a short cut and go and sit in the park to get our breaths back?'

Andrew, who had been boiling with rage at the taunts of some of the police and at the news of some scuffles that had been passed along the line, forced himself to come down as he had helped her to do.

'Why don't we rest a bit and then join in? We'll get away from this lot and sit down.'

With his arm around her shoulders, he shielded her from the mass of frustrated men and women who were surging through the square on their way towards Marble Arch, buffeting them.

'Perhaps it would be easier to go with them,' said Amanda at last, feeling as though she were pinned for eternity in the doorway of some infernal tube train during an everlasting rush hour.

'No. You need to rest. I was being selfish. Hang on. It won't be too long.'

At last the mass of the marchers had gone, leaving the police to begin straightening their tunics and picking up their helmets. The square was a mess of cigarette ends, wastepaper and a few trampled flags and placards. A relatively small group of students was still there as Andrew led Amanda to the doorway of a pompous-looking house and urged her to sit down.

'Oh, darling, you've lost a button.'

Amanda looked down and saw that her shirt was gaping and her breasts bursting out of her shirt.

'Thank God I put on a bra today,' she said, tucking the sides of her shirt together. 'Have I been very weedy?'

'Certainly not!'

'What's the matter?' Andrew was standing between her and the embassy and she could not see what was happening, but she could hear the sound of heavy plate-glass breaking and falling on to concrete.

'They're throwing stones. That's pure stupidity now that they're so outnumbered. Come on, darling, I think I'd better get you out of here before things get ugly.'

Unable to take him seriously, Amanda nevertheless went with him down Upper Grosvenor Street, towards Park Lane. As they went, they heard the sound of real fighting behind them. Andrew turned left into Park Street.

'Wait here,' he said, when they reached the next crossroads. 'I'll find out what's happening.'

'Don't go,' said Amanda, feeling extraordinarily vulnerable. 'Look.'

There was smoke in the distance. Silhouetted against it, two young men in jeans ran towards them, stopping a few yards away to overturn a group of dustbins and drop lighted matches into the highly inflammable rubbish they had released. They crossed the road to do the same thing again and ran on. The smell of burning paper and the acrid smoke released by decaying vegetable matter caught at their throats.

'Oh hell! Amanda, I am sorry. It wasn't supposed to be like this at all. I'm not sure where I'd best take you. We can't go back or the police will assume we're the arsonists. Anyone's likely to get picked up.' He looked round, indecisive and clearly upset.

'It's my fault,' said Amanda, wanting him to take charge. 'If we'd gone with the rest, we'd have been all right.'

'Too bad. Look, I think we'd better make for the park and then we can pretend to be a courting couple and be less conspicuous. Come on. You won't mind kissing me under the trees, will you?'

She laughed at that, happy again and prepared to do anything he told her. Hand in hand they ran, reaching Park Lane just as a straggly group outside the Hilton Hotel started flinging stones at its glass sides. The crashing sound of breaking glass and wild shouts of triumph recreated some of the old excitement in Amanda and she felt a mad temptation to join in. Andrew, with better self-control, saw not only a large black Rolls Royce with its windows shattered but also lines of buses all the way along Park Lane disgorging police reinforcements.

'Come on,' he said, dragging Amanda across the road towards the unpoliced side. 'Can you get over the barrier in that skirt?'

'Yes, of course,' she said, hitching it higher up her thighs.

They ran straight into the sluggish traffic, forcing a taxi to swerve out of their way. The driver leaned out of his window to yell: 'Bloody students. Bloody communists. Bloody wogs.'

Amanda tripped and almost fell, losing a shoe, but Andrew gripped her upper arm so tightly that he kept her on her feet. Then they were faced with a solid line of cars, parked bumper to bumper, barring them from the park.

'Up with you, darling,' said Andrew. Looking at him quickly, Amanda saw that excitement was taking over his remorse. Behind him was a group of demonstrators being chased by two policemen, truncheons in their hands.

Amanda scrambled on to the nearest car, ripping the crotch of her tights and scoring a dreadful scratch in the car's pristine scarlet paintwork with the metal heeltip of her remaining shoe as she swung her body across its bonnet. Andrew followed her and they reached the park.

They soon discovered that it was not safe. Demonstrators from both the main march and the various breakaway groups were battling with furious policemen. Andrew saw a girl go down, her skirt hitched up round her waist, her long hair flying.

'Got you,' said a policeman, lunging for her hair.

'Get over by that tree and don't get involved,' Andrew yelled to Amanda as he went to the rescue.

She waited, horrified as she saw the terror in the girl's face and heard her scream, and then turned, hiding her eyes, and ran towards the tree. Her bare foot caught on a stone and she crashed down, only just able to put her hands out in time to save her face being smashed into a patch of broken glass.

Her hands were badly cut and bleeding as she rolled over, tripping a running policeman. He stumbled, cursed and ran on. Amanda put her bloody hands over her eyes, panic freezing her. What was left of her mind seemed to be telling her that her only safety lay in complete stillness.

A heavy shoe crashed into her side as another man tripped over her and then someone fell on her, forcing the breath out of her lungs. At last some sense of reality returned as a crunching pain ripped through her stomach. Gasping, she got to her knees, pushing her hand in the broken milk bottle again.

'Andrew,' she screamed as more fleeing students and furious, pursuing policemen swerved round her. She got to her feet at last and through the blood that her hands had leaked over her eyes, she saw the tree, a vast oak. Stumbling, crying, she reached it, to double up as the pain came again. She slumped down, her back against the tree and her bloody hands crossed over her waist, gripping her sides.

It seemed hours before Andrew returned, with a black eye and a long scratch down his chest showing through a great tear in his shirt. He fell heavily on to his knees in front of her, appalled by the sight of her face, clay-coloured and smeared in blood and mud.

'What happened?'

'I fell,' she said and then closed her eyes as the pain came again.

'But it's worse than that, isn't it? Oh, God, what have they done to you?'

'I think I'm miscarrying,' she said, tears pouring through the mess on her cheeks. She had not meant to tell him like that.

Hours later, she was lying in a white bed in St George's Hospital, clean, padded, bandaged and sedated. The fragments of glass had been removed from her hands and a gynaecologist had been to see her.

Andrew, who had refused to leave her, was sitting at her side, still wearing his torn shirt and his filthy jeans, but with his face and hands washed and his hair brushed tidily over his head.

The policeman who had questioned them had gone. Since Andrew had convinced him that they had been merely trying to get away from the stone-throwers and arsonists, and Amanda had said honestly that she had no idea whether it was a marcher or one of his colleagues who had kicked her and that she had no intention of making a complaint, he had gone on to more important interviews.

The nurses had gone too and the doctor was not expected back for some time.

'I'm sorry,' she said, unable even to touch Andrew because of the bandages that had made boxing gloves over her cut hands.

'Why didn't you tell me?' he asked, tentatively putting his hand on the white cellular blanket that covered her body.

She rolled her head away and said to the cream-painted wall: 'Because I didn't want to disturb your work before

358

schools and because . . .' She broke off, dreading the hurt that she was going to have to deliver. Gritting her teeth and trying to stop the tears that threatened, she said: 'It might not have been yours.'

'I've realised that,' he said at once, his voice carrying no sound of accusation, 'but it was no reason not to tell me. Amanda, it was only yesterday that I told you I'd love you whatever you did. Didn't you understand what I meant?'

She rolled her head back.

'You mean you knew?'

'Not that there was a child. It never even occurred to me. I thought you were on the Pill. But it was obvious that there'd been some other man. I kept trying to tell you that it didn't matter, that I'd love you anyway.'

'Oh, Andrew. What a mess! It was such a mistake, so silly and it caused such trouble. I didn't know whether to have the baby or not – or if it was yours or his. And now I can't. It ought to have been yours.'

'Hush. There's no point tormenting yourself about that. Who was he? It can't have been the painter. Whatever else she might have done to you, she couldn't have impregnated you.'

His tone made Amanda smile and he ruffled her hair.

'That's better, darling.'

'It was her brother.'

Andrew had imagined all kinds of people trying to seduce Amanda, but that she should have succumbed to a man old enough almost to be her grandfather seemed appalling. The memory of meeting one of his father's mistresses came back to Andrew.

It had been an accident that he had encountered them together in a small restaurant, and all three of them tried to behave as though nothing important had happened. The woman was younger than his mother, only about fifteen years older than he, and remarkably beautiful. Perhaps to ease the constraint she must have felt, she had tried to flirt with

Andrew. He had loathed it then and now, trying to picture himself lying in her arms, he was revolted.

After what he had said to Amanda the previous day, it seemed vitally important not to display any of his disgust and he tried to smile reassuringly at her.

'I can't really explain how it all happened.' She sounded despairing. 'And I don't expect you to understand. It was all dreadfully complicated. But even if I was wanton, I didn't do it lightly. It seemed extremely important.'

'No wonder you hate the portrait so much,' he said, still trying to bury what he really felt in sympathy without actually pretending anything he did not feel. 'I don't really understand, but you don't have to explain. I'm here if you want to talk but I'm not asking you to.'

His kindness as much as the tranquillisers she had been given were making Amanda feel as though she were slightly detached from real life. It was as though all the things that had once seemed so important – like pride and the importance of hiding her real feelings – had disappeared. Slowly she began to tell him everything that had happened in the Gillinghams' house.

Andrew put a question every so often when the story became too complicated to follow, but he made no criticism or even comment. When it was over, Amanda felt as though a vast painful carbuncle had been punctured. She had suffered from boils as a child and well remembered the mixed feelings with which she greeted the pus that poured out from them after the hot kaolin poultices had done their work. It was horrible and smelled foul, but it released an almost intolerable pressure.

When her increasingly fluent explanation was over, Andrew briefly touched her hot face and said: 'You have had a rough time. But it's over now. And I'll take care of you. There's no need to worry. Go to sleep now. It's over. You're safe with me.'

'Will you tell them for me?' she asked, revelling in the

security he was offering her. 'My parents, I mean?'

Andrew gaped at her.

'All right,' she said, seeing his shock. 'I suppose it was too much to ask.'

Pulling himself together with an effort, Andrew said casually: 'No. If that's the dragon I'm required to slay for you, I'll do my best.'

Amanda turned on her side, tucking a bunch of pillow under her chin. Her lips relaxed as her eyelids closed. She trusted him.

Andrew waited until he was sure she had gone to sleep and then blew out an immense breath as he tried to imagine himself relating the story he had just heard to Amanda's terrifying mother. Vivid though his imagination was, it could not encompass anything so unlikely. He tried out first one introductory sentence and then another and another. All of them seemed quite impossible.

Remembering at last that Julia Wallington was his own mother's best friend, Andrew decided to ask her advice. Feeling in the pocket of his jeans for a florin and a handful of sixpences, he left Amanda to find a telephone.

' . . . And so you see, Mama,' he said, having told her exactly what had happened, 'I must stay here, but she wants me to tell her parents and I simply don't know how to do it.'

'They know some of it, my love,' said Flixe. 'Although the extra cruelty of Anthony Gillingham's part is going to come as a shock. Would you like me to tell Julia?'

'Would you? Do you think you could?'

'Yes. And if necessary I'll bring her to the hospital. Don't blame yourself too much.'

'That's a little hard. After all I let her get pregnant and it probably was me. He sounds far too old to be reliably fertile. Then I took her on a march that turned into a war and left her to be kicked into a spontaneous abortion. Pretty tricky stuff to forgive oneself for.'

361

'You must try.' Flixe rarely sounded severe but when she did most of her relations obeyed. 'I'll pick you up at the hospital later. Go back to her, Andrew.'

CHAPTER 24

Flixe turned to George, who was sitting in Peter's favourite chair reading the *Observer*.

'There's been a dreadful disaster.'

George dropped the paper at once, saying simply: 'Tell me what I can do.'

For a moment Flixe could not say anything. It seemed absolutely typical of him not to waste time asking unnecessary questions or plunging into a drama of sympathy. He just wanted to know how he could help her. Blinking a little, she told him all she knew.

'I'm not sure yet. My son took his girlfriend on the anti-Vietnam demonstration this afternoon and it seems to have degenerated into a riot. She was pregnant and has now miscarried. They're at St George's and I'm to tell her mother.'

'Was it his child?' asked George, once again getting straight to the important question.

'We'd all assumed so, but apparently there's some doubt and that leads to ramifications of hideous consequence.'

'Do you want to tell me about them?'

'I think so. But first I must ring Julia. You'll pick up some of it as I talk. I'll fill in the rest later.'

She turned aside to pick up the telephone receiver and dial Julia's number.

'Hello? Is that you, Julia? Flixe here.'

'Thank God! I've been listening to the news on the wireless. Are they all right? Have you got them there?'

'No. They're not here, but yes, they are all right. Not unscathed, but all right.'

'Which police station? I take it that they were at that wretched march. Your son, Flixe! But don't worry too much. I'll get a good solicitor there straight away and we'll probably be able to deal with it quietly.'

'They've not been arrested, Julia. Calm down. They're in St George's. Amanda's miscarried.'

'Oh God!' said Julia. 'Is she all right, Flixe?'

'As all right as possible, from what Andrew's told me. She's asleep now – sedated – but she asked him to tell you all about it and he didn't think he could. I'm to be his deputy. May I come round and see you?'

'To tell me what?'

'Could we meet? It's a bit difficult on the telephone.'

'Flixe, for heaven's sake! Whatever it is, tell me now. Then we can meet.'

'Very well. Apparently it might not have been Andrew's baby. It seems that Amanda was having a simultaneous affair with Anthony Gillingham.' Flixe tried to make her voice completely expressionless. There was complete silence from the other end of the telephone. Flixe waited, not certain what kind of comfort to offer.

'I see,' said Julia at last. 'I'd better get to St George's at once. Thank you for telling me.'

'Don't be too hard on her,' said Flixe, who was puzzled by the lack of expression in her friend's voice. 'She's awfully young.'

'It's all right, Flixe. You wouldn't understand. But I do. Oh hell! For some reason I need to tell you. Bloody Comfort told the child that she was Anthony's daughter. That explains why she was in such a frightful state the day you came and saw her here and why she said such . . . things. Paradoxically it makes things easier.'

'The poor girl! Julia, no wonder she was finding it so difficult to tell Andrew. It doesn't matter. I'll probably be seeing you at the hospital.'

'There's no need for you to go.' There was enough unconscious patronage in Julia's voice to make Flixe angry.

'I also have a vulnerable child there, Julia.'

'Ah yes; so you do. Sorry. Good-bye. Oh, and Flixe . . .'

'Yes?'

'Thank you for telling me.'

Flixe looked at George.

'How much of that did you get?'

'Most of it, I think, except the significance of Anthony Gillingham. I take it he's the painter's brother.'

'Yes,' said Flixe and then explained the rest.

'What a mess for you all! It's no wonder there have been times when you've seemed so abstracted. I've been a bit bothered about that.' He smiled ruefully. 'It shows how self-centred one is. I'd been thinking you were trying to find a tactful way of telling me you'd had enough of me. Shall I drive you to the hospital or would that cause difficulties with your boy?'

Flixe tried to think, but her mind was full of the sadness of George's misunderstanding. When he smiled again, more easily, she managed to concentrate.

'I don't know about the difficulties,' she said eventually. 'I told him about you yesterday and he seemed positively glad, which . . . which . . .'

George put an arm around her shoulders and stroked her blonde head.

'Don't cry, Felicity.'

'No,' she agreed, blowing her nose on the handkerchief she had taken out of his pocket. 'It's silly anyway, because it made me happy that he was pleased. He said he'd liked you straight away and was glad to think of us together.'

'Hm. Pretty mature reaction if it's genuine.'

'It may have been simply kindness. He is very kind when he's not too preoccupied. When anything's pointed out to him, he'll always treat it with the utmost seriousness and gentleness, although sometimes one does have to work quite hard to draw his attention away from his own concerns. But we can't talk about it now. He needs us. Yes, do come with me.'

They drove to Knightsbridge, talking about Amanda's possible reactions to the miscarriage and how she might be helped to cope with them, parked the car and met Julia and David in the front hall. David, his face very white under his grey-and-black hair, came forwards at once to take both Flixe's hands.

'Thank you for telling us.'

'She'll be all right, David,' she said, noticing the dazed hurt in his blue eyes. 'I don't think that this last drama has been the worst of it for her.'

'No,' he said. 'I know it hasn't. Those bloody Gillinghams! Sorry.' He turned to George and held out a hand. 'We haven't met, I think. I'm David Wallington.'

'How do you do? George Mayford. I drove Felicity here, but I'll wait in the car for her. I don't want to be in anyone's way.'

'You won't be. We can't all cluster round my daughter's bedside. We'd better let the women go up.' The two men watched Flixe and Julia talking. Flixe took Julia's arm and led the way upstairs. David turned back to the stranger.

'I take it that Flixe has briefed you, Mayford?'

'To a certain extent. But I'm surprised that you should assume it.'

David patted his arm.

'Don't take it amiss, my dear fellow, but her extended family, which has included my wife for some years now, provides a most effective bush telegraph. I feel almost as though you and I've been acquainted for weeks.'

'Good lord!' George longed to ask what David had been told and what conclusions he had drawn from it.

'Do you mind?'

Assuming that David must be talking to distract himself from the dreadful state of his daughter, George set himself to make conversation on the peculiarly difficult subject David had chosen. He suggested that they sit on one of the vinyl-covered benches that were ranged along the walls of the foyer.

Finding a clear space among the waiting visitors and patients, they sat down. There was an old man in a tartan-wool dressing-gown sitting puffing on a pipe. He had bandages round both feet and he looked very ill. George looked away.

'We're all extremely fond of Flixe,' said David abruptly.

There was enough emphasis in his simple statement to make George realise that there was a hidden message in it and it took him only seconds to work out what it must be. Smiling slightly he said: 'Alas, her intentions seem considerably less serious than mine, if that's what you were asking.'

A nurse appeared, her uniform crackling with starch, and bent over the old man.

'Come along, Mr Brown, we mustn't catch cold now, must we? And doctor did say no more pipes. You've been very naughty.'

The old man said nothing, but put the smoking pipe into his dressing-gown pocket, whence it was competently removed by the young nurse. She put a strong arm under his elbow, heaved him up and led him away.

David laughed.

'Poor old boy! Still, she's probably right to protect him from himself.' He swivelled sideways to look at George Mayford: 'Yes. That was what I meant, and I must say I'm

367

glad . . . not that hers . . . I think I'd better start this sentence again. I am extremely glad that yours are serious and I wish you the best of luck. Flixe is a rare woman.'

'As I have often told her.'

'And she took an appalling knock over Peter's death. Forgive the impertinence. It's just that I think she's badly muddled just now, what with not having got over that yet and now this throwing up of her parliamentary seat and battling with her bank manager over loans to extend the party-planning business.'

'I beg your pardon?'

'Oh, hadn't she told you?'

George thought that David looked peculiarly worried.

'Well, it's not so long since she decided. What do you think of young Andrew?'

George leaned back and crossed his long legs. Unlike David, who had been gardening and was still dressed casually in battered corduroy trousers and an old checked shirt with the sleeves rolled up to expose his powerful forearms, George was wearing a lightweight grey suit and highly polished black shoes.

'I think he has enormous potential,' he said, while his mind was still thinking about the implications of what David had told him. He was touched that the MP should have bothered to change the subject to avoid rubbing it in. 'But it's too soon to say how it'll develop. I gather he's besotted with your girl. She's very good-looking, of course.'

David looked sideways again with a quick grin.

'Isn't she? But it is a mess. They'd be disastrous for each other and they've already hurt each other. God knows how this will affect it. Oh, there's Flixe.'

'And Andrew.' George stood up and waited for them. Andrew came straight over, nodded to David and then held out his hand.

'It was good of you to bring my mother, Doctor Mayford. Thank you.'

'Call me George,' he said. 'It was a pleasure. Can I give you a lift home?'

'In a minute. I need to have a word with Amanda's father first.'

George nodded, thinking that the boy was showing remarkable dignity in what must be an excruciatingly painful – and embarrassing – moment, and took Flixe out to the car.

'Well?' he said when they were sitting side by side.

'I don't know. It's too early to say what'll happen. Cruel though it's been for her, the miscarriage has obviously got rid of some of the practical problems for poor Amanda. Would you see her if she needs it? Professionally, I mean. I think you could probably do a lot to help.'

'Certainly, but she mustn't be forced into talking to anyone.'

'No,' said Flixe just as Andrew appeared on the steps of the hospital under the imposing pedimented portico. David was beside him and they watched as the older man put his arm around Andrew's shoulders for a second.

'He seems a good man.'

'David? Oh, he is. And it can't be easy for him either. Come on, Andrew. Let's go home.'

He slid into the back seat and pulled the door shut. Flixe half turned, planning to say something, but she saw that he had closed his eyes and let his head fall against the padded back of the seat. He looked appallingly tired and the scratches and bruises on his face made her want to weep. Sitting straight again, she saw that George had been watching Andrew in the driving mirror. He put a hand briefly on hers before changing gear.

When they got back to Kensington, Andrew announced that he was going to have a bath and left the others to themselves.

'Cup of tea?' suggested Flixe with her hand on the kitchen doorknob.

'Don't you want to see to Andrew's hurts?'

'No. He'll be better presently and then he'll come down. I try not to invade his room. He's always preferred dealing with his own troubles in his own way, and he knows where the witch-hazel and plasters are kept.' She filled the kettle and made the tea, wondering why George was so quiet.

'Are you all right?' she eventually asked while fetching two mugs from the cupboard behind him. She noticed that his shoulders stiffened inside the impeccably cut coat of his suit.

'I'm perfectly all right,' he said in his usual detached voice. 'I was merely wondering what persuaded you to throw up all you've worked for in the constituency, but perhaps it's not a fair moment to ask you.'

'Ah,' said Flixe, standing quite still behind him. 'Did David tell you?'

'Yes, and I suppose I was . . . not that I have – or think I should have – any rights to know what you're doing. It's merely that we've become such friends, it seems a little odd that you've never mentioned it. After all, it's quite a dramatic move. Is it something very new?'

'Not altogether.' Flixe poured the tea and added milk. She handed George his cup and sat down opposite him. 'I didn't want to bother you with it.'

'Why not? We've talked about almost everything else, exchanged confidences of the utmost intimacy. We've discussed the most gruesome details of ourselves and our pasts. You must have known that I'd be interested.' Despite his good intentions, he sounded as hurt as he was.

'I see.' Flixe pushed the hair away from her eyes in an irritable gesture. 'I hadn't looked at it like that. Please don't be unhappy about it, George.'

She saw that her words had not touched him and so she added painfully: 'I didn't tell you about it because when I told my elder sister what I was planning, she said I was . . . Well, it amounted to an accusation of gold-digging and throwing up what she considered my only chance of a paying

career in favour of exploiting you, which is the last thing I
want – or intend – to do.'

George got up, leaving his tea untouched, and stood
behind her chair, with his arms crossed over her chest and his
chin resting on her hair.

'Don't worry so much about that, Felicity. I am old enough
to take care of myself – and, as it happens, rich enough to
take care of you, if you'd let me.'

'George.'

'Yes?'

'I must make some money for myself. I must. That sounds
ungracious after generosity like yours, and I'm sorry. But I
must learn to make my own living. It's . . . important.'

'I know it is. But I would love to help.'

At that she took his hands and kissed each one in turn. He
straightened up and she twisted round to look at him.

'You are the most generous man, and you can help.'

'I mistrust that wicked smile,' he said, bending once more
to kiss her properly. 'What are you about to say?'

'You can recommend my party-planning services to colleagues and professional organisations and even to rich
patients if your medical etiquette allows it.'

'It doesn't, as you very well know,' he said, returning to his
chair. 'But for the rest? Yes, I know you were joking, but I'll
certainly recommend you. What else did your sister tell you?'

Flixe's smile faded as she remembered the horrible
argument they had had. She shrugged.

'Nothing much.'

'Felicity, come on. You know that I love you for your
honesty; don't spoil that for me.'

'Do you?' she asked distracted into amusement. 'My
honesty? Golly.'

'Yes,' he answered seriously and then added with a little
wickedness of his own. 'And for your wonderful ability to
puncture pomposity. It's that talent that used to make me
wonder how you'd fare in the House of Commons. It was

always obvious that you'd charm any constituent you came into contact with, but your wickedness – as well as your anarchist tendencies – make you an unlikely Tory.'

'Anarchist?' There was a mixture of laughter and outrage in her face. Her lips curved into a glorious smile and her sparkling eyes looked directly at him, demanding that he answer her.

'Yes. Your late husband may have been a revolutionary in his youth, but I suspect Andrew gets a lot of his dislike of authority from his mother. You hide it well from your acquaintances, but it's there, isn't it? And strong, too.'

When Flixe said nothing, her face growing more serious, he went on: 'Don't you yearn to do precisely the opposite of what anyone instructs you to do?'

'Since you've commended my honesty so kindly,' said Flixe with tremendous – if completely spurious – dignity, 'I feel it only courteous to admit that there may perhaps be a grain of truth in what you have said.' As he laughed, she reached for his hand across the table, knocking her tea cup flying.

'Oh dear!' She rushed for a cloth. 'So much for romantic gestures, George. You're right, of course, and yet I'm surprised you've noticed my anarchic tendencies. I seem to have been suppressing them for ages.'

'I know and I want so much to give you the freedom to let them rip again.'

She squeezed all the milky tea out of the cloth and dumped it in the sink. Staring down at its unattractive greyness, she said much more seriously: 'I think you are the kindest, most perceptive man I have ever met.'

'Then will you think about it?'

He was sitting down again nursing his tea cup. Flixe turned, her back pressed hard into the sink unit. Her face was completely serious once more.

'Think about what exactly?'

His lips twisted into a self-mocking smile and he shrugged. 'Marrying me?'

'Oh, George.'

'You sound dismayed. Is it so ghastly a prospect?'

'You know it's not. But I hadn't . . . It never occurred to me that you'd want that. I haven't . . . I mean, I don't know. Isn't that feeble?'

'No. Perfectly sensible. And I didn't actually mean to say anything about it yet. Somehow you got under my defences this afternoon and it just popped out.'

Flixe laughed again, enchanted that he could treat even the prospect of their marrying so lightly. She stood beside him, touching his face with her fingertips until she remembered that they were wet with the tea-clogged cloth.

'You see how you've thrown me,' she said as she fetched a clean towel to dry his face. 'I don't usually put dishwater over the faces of people I love.'

'Do you?' He was serious again and she simply nodded.

'But . . .'

'But you want to keep some doors shut. It's all right, Felicity, I remember everything you've said to me and that is not a problem as far as I'm concerned. Don't worry about any of it, but if you could see your way to it, I should very much like you to marry me.'

She put her arms around him.

'I must think. Will you give me time, as they always say in historical novels?'

'Yes. As much as you need, provided that if the answer's to be "No" you promise to tell me as soon as you've decided.'

'That's fair. I promise. And you, too: if you find us all too much when you've got us under your roof in Dorset, you must tell me.'

He looked a little self-conscious then.

'It is true,' he said carefully, 'that I had intended to wait until after the holiday before putting my proposition to you.'

'I'm sure you were,' she said, laughing again. 'You're too practical not to have considered what we might be like *en masse.*'

The kitchen door opened noisily and Andrew came in, looking the better for his bath and clean clothes.

'Is that tea?' he asked, politely pretending that he had neither heard any of their conversation nor seen his mother removing her arms from George Mayford's neck.

374

CHAPTER 25

The hospital released Amanda the following day with instructions to rest and to remove the dressing from her hands in two days' time. Her mother had an important case and so her father came to collect her just before noon. He drove her to Kennington, saw her safely upstairs to her bedroom, kissed her, demanded no explanations or apologies, sat with her for half an hour as she lay on top of her bed in case she wanted to talk and then left for the House of Commons.

When he had gone, Amanda undressed and got into bed. Janice had already arranged three big vases of roses from the garden and had made up Amanda's narrow bed with the fine, unmended linen sheets that were usually kept for important guests. The family slept in linen sheets that had been turned sides-to-middle or in coarser cotton. Julia had talked wistfully about switching to nylon, which would not have to be sent to the laundry, but David and Amanda had refused to contemplate it. As soon as Amanda slid into bed, she noticed.

'What would my mother say, Janice? Giving the best sheets to one of the children!'

'She'd be the first to say it was right,' said Janice, leaning down to kiss the girl. 'You look very washed out, but I'll soon feed you up. Do you want anything now?'

Amanda shook her head.

'It's just lovely to be home and quiet,' she said, surprised to notice that it was true. Her familiar room embraced her with easy memories and its silence soothed her aching head.

'I'll leave you be,' said Janice. 'What about visitors? If they come, shall I let them in?'

'Yes, please,' said Amanda, assuming that only Andrew or his mother would come. She slid down the bed, shivering as her warm skin touched the cold smoothness of the delicate linen, and closed her eyes. Fragile though she felt, her most pressing problem was gone and she could sleep again in the blessed freedom of her own room.

She woke some hours later to see Janice standing with a white wicker tray in her hands. There was a doubtful expression in her eyes, which disappeared into a smile as she saw Amanda's eyes open.

'I've brought you a cheese soufflé,' she said, 'and some fruit.'

'And a glass of wine, I see,' trying not to cry as she recognised Janice's attempt to remind her of childhood. Little soufflés had been as much a part of chickenpox and measles as spots, a high fever and a bottle of Lucozade.

'Just to cheer you up a bit. There's a lady downstairs, come to see you, but when I told her about the soufflé, she said she'd wait.'

Amanda was pushing herself up the bed, scooping her long hair back behind her ears with hands that were still painful under their reduced strapping. Janice laid the tray across Amanda's legs.

'Miss Gillingham, she said she was.'

'Oh no! I don't want to see her,' said Amanda at once, shrinking back against the pillows.

Janice thought she had never seen the girl look so pathetic as she did with her bare thin arms sticking out of the white lace that edged her lawn nightie and her black hair hanging untidily down her back. Amanda remembered something someone had once told her about looking fear in the face and conquering it. Whatever she imagined Comfort had done to her in the studio, there was nothing else she could do.

'But I suppose we can't turn her away, Janice. How long has she been here?'

'Not much more than five minutes. I'm surprised her ringing the bell didn't wake you.'

'I'd better see her. Could you bring another glass of wine for her when you show her up?'

'I'll do that. Now you eat your soufflé before it sinks. You always used to like them when you'd been ill.'

'I still do. Nothing to chew and lots to taste. Thank you, Janice.'

Amanda had already scooped the last of the light cheese foam from the middle of the soufflé and its crunchy brown edges from the little fluted dish by the time the housekeeper ushered Comfort Gillingham into the room.

'Hello, Amanda,' she said, standing in the doorway of the flowery attic bedroom, looking almost like a stranger from an unknown country. 'You have been knocked about, haven't you?'

Her short slate-grey linen dress was the acme of understated elegance and the fat creamy pearls she wore in a long loop knotted at the breast added an old-fashioned luxury to its distinction. The pearls were obviously as real as the ones in her elaborately set earrings.

'Good afternoon.' Amanda felt at a shocking disadvantage in her childish nightdress with no make-up and dirty hair and the remains of her lunch in front of her.

Janice swooped over to remove the tray, putting the untouched glass of wine on Amanda's bedside table. Having put the tray on a stool, she pulled forward a chair for the visitor, handed her the second glass of wine and removed the tray to the kitchen.

'I was so sorry to hear what happened to you.'

'How do you know what happened to me?' Amanda felt cold.

'I heard it on the news. Daughter of an MP in hospital after a riot in Grosvenor Square. A famous model. You didn't really think the journalists would fail to get hold of it, do you?'

'I can't imagine why they should be interested.' Amanda was almost dizzy with relief at the limits of Comfort's knowledge, but she was determined to conceal it.

Comfort shrugged. 'Revolting students are always news and any opportunity to embarrass this Government would be seized on.'

'My father is not a member of the Government. Why are you here?'

'Shouldn't I be? You sound very hostile. I came to see how you are and to tell you I'm sorry you were hurt. I've brought you some grapes.' Comfort took a bunch of spherical purple grapes from the carrier bag and laid them in their tissue-paper bag on the bedside table.

'Thank you,' said Amanda, looking at them. 'If I sound hostile it's not because I'm not grateful for the fruit, but because I don't trust you.'

'That's an extraordinarily hurtful thing to say.' Sitting back, Comfort crossed her slender legs. The hem of her impeccable dress just cleared her knees. She looked completely untroubled, despite what she had said.

Amanda rolled sideways to open the drawer in her bedside table. She took out the battered leather box with the mermaid pin in it.

'I've been wondering how best to get this safely back to you. I didn't think I should trust the post. Please take it.'

Comfort sat in her chair unmoving, her slate-grey eyes intent.

'Neither me nor the post. Now why? Because I told you about your real parentage? I wasn't surprised you fled that night. Perhaps it was unfair of me to tell you so abruptly, but I had assumed you knew. I can see that it might have been a shock, but you must have come to terms with it by now.'

'You knew perfectly well that it wasn't true. My father is, as I have always thought, David Wallington.'

'Did Julia tell you that?'

'Yes.'

'And you believed her?' There was such patronising surprise in Comfort's question that Amanda almost lost her temper. Only one certainty kept her calm.

'Yes.'

'But why? She has clearly kept a great deal of her past from you.'

Amanda suddenly remembered how snakelike Comfort could look when her eyes were narrowed and her chin thrust forwards like that.

'Because,' Amanda said slowly and very distinctly, 'whatever I might believe or disbelieve about my mother, I cannot believe that Anthony Gillingham would have made love to me if I had been his child.'

She watched Comfort's face, believing she could identify shock, anger, satisfaction and curiosity before her expression changed to one of theatrical doubt.

'Don't bother to pretend surprise,' said Amanda coldly. 'You'll get wrinkles if you scrunch up your face like that. You must have known what he and I did the day you rushed off to your friend. You engineered it, after all, didn't you?'

'Amanda, what is this? What are you talking about?'

'"Goe, and catch a falling starre,"' she quoted deliberately, '"Get with child a mandrake roote" and so on. Just how much of the disaster did you plan?' She drank a gulp of wine, hardly noticing that it was an important claret and that Janice must have raided one of her employer's best bottles.

Comfort shook her remarkable head slowly from side to side, her eyebrows still touching over her sharp nose as she frowned, but the horizontal wrinkles smoothed away.

'I see you've taken Robertson's imaginative review to heart,' she said. 'All I did was paint the best portrait of you that I could. I told you on the first day that I saw you as a mermaid – indeed that Anthony had suggested it – and you and I swapped stories of mermaids enticing men to their deaths. Betraying them, if you like. To that extent Robertson was right: the painting was supposed to symbolise betrayal. You didn't seem to mind that at the time; in fact you were positively titillated at the idea. Is it only the review that has upset you?'

Amanda looked at the older woman, trying to think rationally about what had happened.

'Not entirely,' she said, fighting to keep her emotions from showing. 'Somehow you persuaded me into your brother's bed. Looking back, I don't know why I was so stupid as to fall in with your plans, but I was. Why did you do it? Did you see me as the mandrake root to be impregnated? Is that why you put purple flowers round my neck in the painting?'

Amanda realised that hysteria was not far away and clamped her lips shut. Comfort said nothing, her eyes staring at the opposite wall but obviously seeing nothing.

'I think you must have a more vivid imagination than I suspected,' she said slowly. 'My brother does not bed children.'

'Don't pretend you didn't know about it or want it,' said Amanda, pleased to hear how bitter she sounded. 'You set me up. As you've just said, you titillated me with all that talk of my attractions, my potential for power and all that mermaid lore, then you teased me with stories of his misery and subtly made it clear you thought I could save him. You made me take most of my clothes off, wet my hair and then engineered the telephone call that took you away, leaving me practically in his arms. Did you expect me to get pregnant, too? The picture looks as though you did. Well if so, you are out of luck, because the child is dead.'

Amanda took a remarkable, primitive satisfaction from watching Comfort's face whiten. Her eyes looked very dark and her sharp, bony nose seemed even bigger than usual.

'What are you talking about?' she whispered. 'A child? There was a child?'

'Yes. But it's dead now, thrown down the sluice at the hospital.' Amanda's voice quivered and she bit part of her upper lip to control herself, adding her hand when she could not stop her teeth clattering together and her jaw wobbling. Even that did not help and she put the other hand over her eyes. Her whole body shook. Her eyes and nose ran with disgusting fluids. 'Are you pleased?' she added when at last she could control her breathing again.

'Here, take these.' Comfort thrust a box of paper handkerchiefs on to Amanda's knees and watched as the girl blotted her face and slowly brought her body under control. 'Look at me.'

Amanda swivelled, knowing that she must look terrible and beaten and not caring about it any longer.

'How can you imagine that I should want any of the things you have said? And even if I had wanted them for some peculiar reason, how could I have achieved them?'

Amanda simply shook her head.

'You know it,' she said. 'I know it. I simply don't know why. I should like to understand you but not enough to listen to your stories. I think you'd better go, don't you?'

'Perhaps. These paranoid delusions are very sad. I liked you and found you interesting. Your face was paintable and as I worked I enjoyed your colossal vanity: it was so different from Julia's way of considering herself. It never occurred to me that you would be slut enough to sleep with my brother or idiotic enough not to take precautions against conception.'

381

Amanda, who had taken a tight grip on her feelings again, produced something very like a smile.

'You're a fine painter, but you'll never match Tibor Smith until you learn not to hate,' she said, hoping for the satisfaction of hurting Comfort.

'Sentimentality has no place in art criticism,' said the painter as she stood up. She looked down at Amanda with bitter eyes, her nose looking even sharper than usual and her mouth flattened. 'Good luck with your degree.'

With that last piece of sarcastic politeness, Comfort left the room.

Amanda lay back in bed with her eyes closed, more tears seeping out from under her lashes. Whether she was crying for herself or the baby, she did not know. She felt smirched.

Andrew came later in the afternoon and Janice brought them up a tray of tea as she escorted him upstairs.

'You've been crying,' he said when they were alone. Amanda nodded and then shrugged.

'I suppose it's only to be expected.'

'I am sorry, my darling; I should never have taken you on the march. If I'd known . . .'

Amanda put one of her bandaged hands on his. He slipped off the low chair and knelt by her bed, stroking the black hair back from her forehead.

'There are so many things I'd have done differently if I'd known or thought properly.'

'Me too,' she said.

'But we can salvage things,' said Andrew, still stroking. 'When you've got your degree we can start again. I'll have accumulated some money by then and found us a flat and we can get married – if you like.'

'I don't know,' she said, but she was smiling as he had not seen her smile for a long time. There was no glitter in her eyes and no mocking twist to her lips.

With that smile and without her make-up, with her eyes reddened and swollen, she looked fragile and gentle.

Andrew put his arms under her body and lifted her so that her head lay on his shoulder. He stroked her thin back through the delicate white cotton of her nightdress and felt the weight of her against him.

'I know you don't,' he said, 'but it doesn't matter. We've got time. There's no hurry.'

Much later that evening Amanda woke to hear heavy masculine footsteps climbing the stairs. They stopped two floors below her bedroom. She heard voices and then the sound of a door opening and then shutting again. Hurt that her father should have gone straight to bed without coming to see how she was, Amanda got out of bed and padded downstairs in her bare feet. When she reached the first floor, where her parents' rooms were, she saw that the only light was under the door of her mother's study. Sinking down on to the bottom stair, she decided to wait until her father emerged.

Slowly as she listened to the voices in the room, without even trying to hear the words, she realised that the new arrival was someone else, a stranger. She began to listen more carefully.

'All right. What is it that is so important that you had to come and tell me in person?' Her mother's voice was sharp. Despite herself, Amanda shivered at the harshness of it. She crossed her bare arms across her chest and hugged herself.

'Don't, Julia.' The voice was familiar but Amanda did not identify it until Anthony Gillingham added: 'It is not only important but painful. Don't make it harder for me.'

Amanda edged nearer to the door, straining to hear.

'So?'

'Comfort has told me about the child. I came to say . . . I came to tell you how sorry I am for my part in it.'

'I don't think that I am the person to whom your apologies should be directed.' Julia's voice was very cold then as well as sharp. 'It is surely my daughter who ought to hear them.'

Amanda recognised in the precise articulation and formality of phrasing that her mother was keeping her temper with difficulty.

'I have already apologised to her for what happened,' said Anthony mildly, 'and I think the less contact she has with me the better.'

'That is certainly true.'

'I came to say that and to tell you that I am leaving Comfort. After this last performance of hers I can no longer pretend that I . . .'

'What good do you think that will do?' There was real fury now in Julia's voice. Amanda leaned her head against the dado rail and waited.

'Perhaps none, but I find I can no longer bear the thought of living with her.'

There was a long pause before Julia, sounding slightly kinder, said: 'Anthony, it's too late for that. All you would achieve by leaving her is loneliness – for both of you. And what do you think Comfort would feel about me and my child then? If she hated me for the past while she had you to herself, what would that make her do?'

'So: I'm to live on beside her, loathing her in order to protect you?'

'Don't sound so dramatic. Leave her if you want to, for goodness' sake, but not in expiation for what happened to Amanda. Don't add any more selfish folly to that disaster.'

'I suppose you're right. God, I'm tired.'

'Are you? I'm sorry. Would you like a drink?'

For a moment Amanda thought that she was about to be discovered, but then she remembered her mother kept a bottle of whisky and some glasses on a side-table in her study. She could hear the clink of glass.

'You don't want ice, do you?'

'No, this is fine. Thank you. Do you think it was deliberate?'

'What? Your sister forcing you to seduce my daughter? Sorry, that may not have been fair. I do know what you mean, but I have no idea. I don't know enough of what happened.'

'I'm not sure that I do either. All I know is that she was there and willing and beautiful and like you.'

There was another silence while three-quarters of Amanda shrieked denial and rebellion at his identification of her with her mother.

'But what I don't understand is why she wanted me. Comfort can hardly have engineered that.'

Julia laughed then. 'You're an attractive man and Amanda's been searching for something for a long time. Perhaps it was simply that the things Comfort told her about you suggested that you could offer it.'

'I don't suppose she found it.'

'No, Anthony, I don't suppose she did.'

'You sound less angry.' His voice was surprised.

'Perhaps because I'm wondering how much of this has been my fault too.'

Amanda moved. The roughness of the red stair carpet rasped the skin of her thighs and she held her breath in case the noise had made them suspect a listener.

'What do you mean "too"?' Anthony's voice was interested but not suspicious.

'She's frequently accused me of disliking her, which I have always dismissed automatically. I love her. I always have.' Neither of them said anything for a while. Amanda found that she was biting her sore lip again and released it, feeling the blood flow painfully back into it.

'There's a but in there somewhere, isn't there?' said Anthony quite kindly.

'Over the last few days I've begun to think so. She's right; I did resent her arriving when she did. Not because it forced the break between you and me. That was overdue and necessary. But my pregnancy did make that break more violent and it

385

meant that we had no hope of salvaging anything from all those years we'd been married – and friends before that.'

'I'm not sure we could have salvaged much anyway. As far as I can remember things had gone too far.'

'Perhaps. But her arrival smashed so much. You and David had been friends all through the war in Italy. Comfort and I . . . Well, never mind that now. And perhaps worst of all it made my coming together with David shabby and hurried. We never had time alone with each other to feel free and happy after the divorce.'

'That could have been to do with your work as much as your child.'

Amanda, who had been sitting with yet more tears rolling down her face, picked up the hem of her nightdress to wipe her face. She could not blow her nose because of the noise it would make and breathing was becoming difficult.

'I'm not quite sure why I'm telling you this, Anthony. I've never managed to say anything of it to David or to Amanda.'

There was the sound of a chair scraping against the polished wood floor.

'I suspect that's because you care what they think of you. My opinion hasn't mattered to you for many years.' He sounded bitterly sad and for a moment Amanda managed to think of someone else's pain. 'I must go. Don't cry, Julia. You never did that, however bad things were. You'll have time with David yet. He's a very loyal man and he's always loved you. He'll wait if you can. Don't get up. I'll see myself out. Good-night.'

The door of the study opened and Anthony appeared. He stopped the moment he saw Amanda, crouching on the stairs in her sleeveless white nightdress, her face helplessly sodden. She put a finger to her lips. Carefully he closed the study door behind him and stood, looking down at her.

'I'm sorry,' he whispered. Amanda just shook her head and the tears poured out of her eyes again. Anthony reached forwards, but withdrew his hand before it could touch her.

He turned abruptly and went down the stairs. Amanda hauled herself up and, leaning on the banisters, climbed back up to her room.

CHAPTER 26

The following morning, Flixe was sitting breakfasting in the kitchen alone for the last time before her younger children's summer holidays began. She was revelling in the things George had said to her and yet his proposal had worried her and she could not stop thinking about what his feelings might be if she turned him down, and about the effect he might have on her younger children if she did not.

The thought of getting them away from London and being able to devote some time to them in peace seemed wonderful. George had suggested that she should take them to his country house a week early to give them a chance to get to know the place without having to worry about who he was or what part he played in their mother's life. Flixe had been touched by his thoughtfulness and also relieved to realise how much cheaper it would be to entertain the three of them near the Dorset coast than in the middle of London.

George had formally invited Andrew to stay as well, but he had said that he must wait in London until Amanda was well enough to go to Fiesole to work on her dissertation. That was likely to be towards the end of August and he had said that, unless she wanted him to go with her, he would like to stay

388

in Dorset for a long weekend over the bank holiday.

Pouring herself another cup of coffee, Flixe thought how pleasant it was that Andrew seemed so at ease with George and untroubled about the implications of his frequent presence in the house. She hoped that the younger children would be as easy when they eventually met him.

She heard the telephone ring and was about to get up and answer it when the bell stopped. Five minutes later, Andrew burst into the kitchen, looking transfigured with happiness.

'She says she will. Oh, Mama, thank God!'

Feeling cold to the very centre of her being, Flixe tried to summon up the right responses.

'Amanda?' she said as brightly as she could.

'Yes, yes.' Andrew sounded impatient. 'She's agreed to marry me.'

Suppressing her instinctive 'Why?', Flixe got up and opened her arms. Andrew walked into her embrace, topping her head by at least seven inches.

'I'm glad,' she said.

He pulled away, putting a hand under her pointed chin and staring into her blue eyes.

'Really?'

'I so much want you to be happy.'

He kissed her cheek and then let her go. 'I know you still don't like her properly, but you will. If you could have seen her yesterday, stripped of all the affectations and all the nonsense, you'd understand. The core of her is what matters and it's that core that's turned to me now.'

'Yes, I'm sure it is. Coffee? Excitement makes one awfully faint.'

Andrew laughed.

'Father was right: you are the most practical of women.'

'Am I? When did he say that?' Flixe felt the bulging side of the coffee pot and decided to make a new, hotter, brew for her son.

'Oh, years ago.' Andrew looked surprised at the response

389

to his casual compliment. 'I can't quite remember. It was a time when I was furious because there was something I badly wanted to do and you wouldn't let me. I'd gone to him assuming he'd override you, but he wouldn't. He said that you were practical and kind so that if you forbade something I ought to listen.'

She poured the boiling water on to the fine grounds, breathing in the richly bitter scent that for her was the best part of any pot of coffee. Peter had never told her that Andrew saw him as a final court of appeal or that they had had private talks about her. She could not think why she should find the idea comforting. The reverse ought to have been more likely.

'He also told me that your advice would never be grounded in malice or delivered to satisfy any of your own feelings. He said that was rare, and so it is.'

Flixe put the pot down on the bare wooden table in front of Andrew and returned to her chair. Her eyes were soft and her mouth curved into a reminiscent smile.

'I loved him very much, you know,' she said.

'I know you did.' Andrew poured out a cupful of coffee and added milk from the blue jug in front of her. He reached for the sugar bowl. 'I did, too. Will you go and see Amanda?'

'What?' Flixe, who had been back in the past once more, ran her fingers through her hair. 'This needs washing. Yes, if you think she'd like it.'

'I'm sure she would. She's very shaky after what happened.'

Flixe looked at her watch.

'The girls' train is due at twelve and Nicky's at half past two. If I'm to see her, I'd better go now. Are you coming?'

'No. I'll go later. Is there anything I can do? I could meet the girls, if you like.'

Flixe was filled with sudden delight, the loneliness of her efforts to support the family eased by his simple offer.

'That would be heaven. Will you really? You are the dearest

boy. Thank you. Platform six at five past twelve. They tend to panic if one's late.'

'I won't be. You'll find us all here when you get back from Kennington.'

'Wonderful. Lunch is cold meat and salad if any of you feel like getting it ready. It's all in the fridge. I'd better ring Amanda first to make sure she wants to see me.'

'I shouldn't worry. When she rang this morning to say she'd marry me, she asked if I thought you might have time to visit.'

'Right. I'll see you later. Do you want to take the car? They'll both have suitcases.'

'No. The tube will be easier. You take it. We'll be all right. Don't worry.'

Flixe went upstairs to fetch her jacket, a bright yellow linen affair that Ming had handed on, saying that it did not suit her at all. Flixe wore it with a yellow-and-white printed skirt and a plain white T-shirt of her elder daughter's. It was not fashionable, and the colour made her look washed-out, but it would do, she thought.

She still had no idea what she would say to Amanda when she reached the blackened brick house in Kennington with its impeccable Georgian proportions and its gaily planted window-boxes. Janice greeted her with real welcome and confided that Amanda was out of bed and lying in the garden.

'It's so lovely and warm, Mrs Suvarov. She'll do better out of doors than lying up there brooding in bed,' she said. 'Will you go on through?'

'Thank you.' Flixe walked through the immaculate emerald-and-white kitchen to the garden steps, pausing at the top to look down on the astonishing oasis that Julia and David had built up during their years in South London.

There was none of the paving that floored so many city gardens; no neat flowerbeds or wheelbarrows full of geraniums. Instead, a roughly mown, daisy-strewn lawn was bordered by loose masses of flowering shrubs, underplante◄ with everything from violas to creeping thyme. Productiv◄ apple trees formed the supports for a large hammock, i◄ which Amanda was lying oblivious of her visitor, dressed a◄ fashionably and expensively as usual in a thick white line◄ dress. Beyond her a sloppily clipped hedge half hid a clutc◄ of white beehives. The bees danced around their entrance◄ and multifarious butterflies flipped from one nectar-heav◄ flower to the next. Roses and honeysuckle tumbled aroun◄ the iron staircase that led down into the garden, their head◄ scents making Flixe feel almost dizzy.

She called out a greeting, not wanting to creep up o◄ Amanda and give her a shock. Having received a beckonin◄ smile, Flixe walked down the steps. There were severa◄ striped canvas chairs set up around the hammock and sh◄ chose a blue one.

'You must feel awful,' she said, putting a hand on Aman◄ da's wrist.

The girl's face was gleaming with sweat and there were ugl◄ swellings around her eyes. She looked mutinous and yet ful◄ of pathetic appeal.

'I do. Are you cross with me?'

'Why should I be cross?' Flixe sat down in the lo◄ deckchair, looking up into Amanda's face.

'Because I've said I'd marry Andrew.'

Flixe shook her head. 'He's wanted that very much for ◄ long time.'

'I know.' Amanda's voice quivered and she rolled her hea◄ away.

'Don't you? Amanda,' Flixe made her voice very sof◄ 'what's the trouble?'

'I don't know.' The words came out in a kind of wai◄ Amanda took a deep breath and tried to regain some of he◄ sophistication. 'I thought I was sure I wanted to marry hir◄ when I rang this morning, but ever since I've been getting i◄ more and more of a state.'

'Why?'

'Because having said I would it'll be even worse if I . . .'

'No.' Flixe interrupted quickly. 'I wasn't asking why you're in a state, but why you thought you wanted him.'

Amanda's face crumpled, but she did not cry. She was past tears.

'Because he's so kind and I need kindness. I never thought I did, but now I seem to need inordinate amounts.'

Flixe sat in silence, thinking. It was clear to her that whatever she said would have a huge influence over the girl while she was in such a vulnerable mood. Andrew wanted her terribly and yet Flixe was almost certain that he would not only grow out of that wanting but also suffer worse unhappiness if he got her. Amanda was of secondary importance but she still mattered and Flixe was just as certain that Andrew would never satisfy her.

If it had not been for his report of what Peter had said about her advice, Flixe might have kept her views to herself and hoped that the two of them would change their minds before they actually married. As it was, she felt that she could not shirk. Damaging or not, she had to say what she believed

'You won't always, you know.' She smiled as she saw Amanda's expression of outrage. 'I mean it, Amanda. Think back before all this horror and remember what you're really like. He annoyed you terribly in those days, didn't he?'

'Sometimes.' Amanda's lower lip was pushed out like an obstinate six-year-old's. 'But that was then. I've changed.'

'A poultice is wonderful when you're wounded,' said Flixe carefully, 'but it becomes irksome and smelly and downright dangerous when the wound has healed.'

'It's not like that.' Amanda's protest sounded sulky. When Flixe looked at her, she saw that the girl was close to tears again. Making her voice very gentle, she said: 'You've had a horrible time recently, but you will get better, and I think you'll find that a lot of the changes you feel in yourself are temporary.'

Flixe thought of George Mayford's description of hi
assumptions about his first wife and forced herself on.

'Andrew has often talked about "the real Amanda" an
"the core" of you, as though things like your pleasure in fam
and success aren't real. But they are, aren't they?'

Amanda moved suddenly, sending the hammock rockin
from side to side. A half-rotten apple fell heavily on to he
thigh, staining the pristine white linen with squashy brow
fruit.

'Ugh,' she said, frantically brushing the mess away.

Flixe silently held out a handkerchief and watched a
Amanda cleaned her dress. She then handed back th
handkerchief. That gesture in itself seem to express muc
about her character. Just as Peter Suvarov had always neede
to prove something to himself by persuading women to lov
him, so Amanda needed people to admire and serve her. Th
fact that she came to despise the admirers when they ha
abased themselves in front of her was unfortunate, bu
apparently inescapable. One day, thought Flixe, when sh
had learned enough about herself, it might change, but b
then Andrew, too, would have changed.

'I think,' she went on, 'that the things in you that used to fin
Andrew tiresome and possessive and difficult and boring wi
return when you've recovered physically and emotionally, an
then if you're married to him you'll both be unhappy.'

'How do you know he made me think all that? I've neve
told him about it in so many words.'

'It wasn't very difficult to see,' said Flixe mildly enough.

'Does he know?'

Flixe laughed and hoped that the sound was amuse
rather than mocking.

'I've never talked to him about it, but he's not stupid; h
probably saw it for himself.'

'So you don't think I ought to marry him.' The word
might have seemed sulky if it had not been for the pleadin
sound of Amanda's voice.

Flixe thought of her son's face as he told her his news at breakfast. She considered his unexpressed grief for his father, his probable – if concealed – disturbance over her friendship with George Mayford, his inevitable unhappiness Amanda were to retract her acceptance, and his no less inevitable fury at his mother's intervention.

'I can't help thinking,' she said, striving for absolute honesty, 'that neither of you would be happy for very long. The one thing of which I am completely certain is that one can never be happy – or make anyone else happy – by pretending to be something one is not.'

'But he makes me feel so safe.' The childish wail was back in Amanda's protest.

'Perhaps because you want so badly to feel that.'

An arrested expression in Amanda's blue eyes showed Flixe that she had at last said something useful, but she was surprised when the girl said bleakly: 'How is one ever to know?'

'Know what?'

Amanda brushed a cruising wasp away from her glistening forehead and tucked her hair away behind her neck. Flixe looked up at the tree over the hammock and noticed that most of the apples had been half-eaten, their cores squashy and their edges brown with rot. Lots were still crawling with wasps that tumbled over each other in their eagerness to get at the fruit.

'Whether what one feels is real? Whether it's self-deception or self-discipline to persuade oneself out of crossness or dislike?'

'I don't know,' said Flixe, touched by the honesty of Amanda's question. She seemed not to have heard her godmother's helpless answer for she went on: 'Is it love one feels when someone makes one feel comfortable and happy or is it just wanting to be loved? Is it cowardice when you don't do something difficult or sensible caution? Is it foolhardiness or generosity when you give more than you can

afford? Does refusing to let someone else in to your life mea[
selfishness or a reasonable effort to protect yourself?'

'There you have me.' Flixe sighed. Memories of her effor[
to banish jealousy and fear of the consequences of Peter[
amours flooded back to mix with her guilt about giving u[
the work she had hated. 'Those are questions I've rare[
stopped asking myself.'

'Don't you ever know?' Once again Amanda sounded yea[
younger than she was and all Flixe's maternal instincts urge[
her to comfort the girl.

'No. As far as I can see you just have to go on trying [
decide, getting it wrong sometimes and trying not to min[
too much.'

'You mean never feeling safe?'

'Often,' said Flixe with a smile, 'but never for very long [
a time. Do you see what I mean?'

'Yes.' There was a pause and then Amanda asked: 'Woul[
he hate me if I changed my mind?'

Flixe shrugged.

'He'd be unhappy. Of the two of us, I suspect it'd be m[
he'd hate more. But listen, Amanda, the last thing yo[
should ever do is commit yourself to someone out of pity
or fear. You both seem to me to be far too young to kno[
what you want or even who you are.'

'You sound as though we were still at school. I am twent[
you know.'

Flixe smiled again at the pettishness of Amanda's inte[
jection.

'Yes, I know that. I remember so well when you were bor[
But you're too muddled now to make a decision. Not ju[
about Andrew, but about everything.'

For a moment Amanda looked outraged. Then her fac[
went blank as memories of the last few months chase[
themselves through her mind: hating her mother and year[
ing for her; contemptuous of so many people and yet longin[
to be part of someone else; admiring Comfort and discoverin[

her to be loathsome; loving her father and understanding how much she had hurt him; furious with him for being hurt when it was she who needed solace. Aware that her godmother was talking, Amanda tried to concentrate.

'Neither of you has much idea what it's like out there.' Flixe pointed over the wall at the back of the flower-filled garden. 'And you haven't a clue about what it'll do to you or make you want. Andrew may well turn out to be right for you, but if I were you I'd leave it for a few years until you've had a chance to find out.'

'By doing what?'

'Find work you enjoy and get yourself some useful, professional qualification,' she said drily. 'Safety is more likely to come from that than from any man, however kind.'

'Hell!' Amanda swung her legs over the side of the hammock and stood up, holding on to the rough bark of one of the apple trees as dizziness overtook her. 'You sound just like my bloody mother. Have you been talking to her?'

'No. I'm talking out of my own experience and what I wish I had done before I married. That's all.'

'I'm sorry, Auntie Flixe,' said Amanda quickly. 'That wasn't fair. I didn't mean to sound so rude.'

'It's all right. You're in a turmoil. This is not the time to be making important decisions. Go to Fiesole when you can; talk to your grandmother, and don't do anything until you feel as strong and angry as you once were.'

A glinting smile narrowed Amanda's eyes and she bent her head briefly in acquiescence.

'And Andrew?'

Once again Flixe was torn between her aching wish to protect him from immediate hurt and her determination not to shirk saying things that might save him from something worse.

'I think it would be only fair to tell him that you're having doubts. To string him along would be unkind. I think,' she added in sudden doubt.

Amanda's smile came again, making her beautiful once more.

'I'll think about it. What will you say to him if he asks you?'

'That I saw you and you didn't seem quite yourself.'

'True enough. Thank you, Auntie Flixe. I wish ... Oh, I wish that I was one of those people who don't mind about things.'

Flixe got up and walked through the flowery grass to kiss the girl her son thought he loved.

'Don't wish that. It may be painful but it's far, far better to hurt than to be numb. I'm sure of that at least. Come and see me or ring me up if you need me. I'll be in Dorset for most of August. Here's the number.'

She fished in her handbag for the notebook she always carried, copied the address and telephone number George had given her and handed it to Amanda, who looked down at it and scrumpled it into her fist.

'Thank you,' she said, her lips quivering again. Flixe kissed her once more and then left the garden.

Flixe waited through the next week for a change in Andrew but it did not come. The only indication she had that her talk with Amanda had borne any fruit at all was a tiny letter in Julia's handwriting:

Dearest Flixe,
Thank you. Not many mothers would have done it.
Love, Julia

By the time Flixe was ready to drive her three younger children down to Dorset, she was no better informed about Andrew's state of mind. He helped her load the car with luggage and then took her in his arms.

'Will you be all right?' she asked, stroking his face and feeling it tauten under her fingers as he smiled.

'Undomesticated though I am, I can open a tin of beans, Mama. Besides, George is dining me at his club tonight.'

'How good of him!' Flixe was genuinely surprised.

'I like him, you know. Quite apart from his making you happy. He's a great guy.'

'Andrew, you . . . will come and see us, won't you? I hate the thought of your sweltering in London with nothing much to do.'

'I won't get into mischief. It's a relief to have nothing to fight for now that schools are over. I can catch up on sleep while I wait for Amanda's recovery. The poor little thing needs some company while she recuperates and – and I like to sit with her.'

Flixe wanted to warn him, to protect him, but there was nothing she could do.

'Now, drive carefully,' he said, sounding just like his father. He bent down to look into the back seat of the car. 'Take care of her, you lot.'

'We will,' called Sophie and Nicholas in chorus. Fiona looked cross. Seeing it, Andrew put his hand through the open window to hold her cheek for a moment.

'I'll miss you, Fee. Don't run off with any brawny yokels before I get down there, will you?'

Her face lit suddenly with her rare smile and she rubbed her pathetically pock-marked cheek against his hand. Flixe watched them in the mirror and did not switch on the engine until their moment was over.

CHAPTER 27

It was a terrible journey: a long, hot crawl out of London and westwards down the A30, stopping twice to let Nicholas be sick and then later so that Flixe could deal with the overheating engine; waiting at the bottlenecks at the end of each short stretch of dual carriageway and held up by roadworks just after they had first managed to get up a bit of speed. Sophie started to torment her elder sister about her spots and then wept bitterly when Fiona rounded on her in cutting fury. Things improved only when they turned off the main road outside Bridport four and half hours after leaving London.

Flixe stopped in a minute lay-by at the edge of the one-track road, which seemed to have been tunnelled out of one enormous hedge, to check the instructions George had written out for her. She handed the paper to Fiona, saying: 'Will you look out for the turn?'

'Yes.'

Flixe edged the car back on to the tiny road and, driving at a cautious ten miles an hour, crept up the steep incline, desperately hoping she was not about to meet a tractor. She did a few minutes later, just as Nicholas shrieked that he had seen the sea, and had to back, lurching from side to side, until she reached the same lay-by. The driver, a swarthy, sweating young man with a face as red as the spotted handkerchief he had tied round his neck, raised a hand and grinned at them. Fiona privately thought that the smile was for her in acknowledgement of the sympathy she had directed at him for putting up so patiently with her mother's erratic reversing. He had, she noticed, very white teeth and his eyes flashed in the sun.

They set off again and succeeded in reaching the sharp turn into the even narrower road that appeared to lead to George's farmhouse. There was no metalled surface to the road and the car bumped and slithered over the boulders, but Flixe managed to ease it up the hill until they saw the house, tucked into the hill that must protect it from the sea gales in winter. Built around three sides of the original farmyard, the house faced the sloping valley and looked as solid as the day it had been built four hundred years earlier. Its yellowish stone glowed in the evening light, as though it had absorbed the sun itself all day.

Nicholas got out of the car to open the gate that barred their way and waited as Flixe parked in what must once have been a cowshed. She switched off the engine with a sigh and arched her back to ease her cramped muscles, before getting out the car and pulling her skirt away from the damp backs of her legs.

'Let's leave the luggage until we've explored a bit,' she said, rocking her head from side to side against the stiffness of her neck. 'Doctor Mayford said there'd be someone to meet us with the key.'

'There he is,' called Nicholas, dancing through another gate and pointing at the figure of a man who was standing waiting for them.

Flixe followed her youngest child into the old farmyard and saw that it had been transformed into a garden. Perfectly espaliered fruit trees were pinned against the old walls of the house, catching the sun that poured into the courtyard. The ground had been cut into four square beds, each divided from the rest by immaculately mown grass paths, edged with herbs. In the centre of each bed stood a short standard apple tree and around it grew flowers and vegetables in glorious and muddled profusion. The mixture of discipline and generosity seemed so characteristic of George that it was a while before she remembered the man who was waiting for them.

'I am so sorry,' she said, turning towards him. 'I was quite lost in all this. It's lovely.'

'I'm glad you like it,' he said. 'George designed it, I put it into practice for him and my chaps keep it tidy while he's away. How was the journey, Mrs Suvarov?'

'Awful,' she said with a laugh. 'But what is even more awful is that he didn't tell me who would be here.'

'Mark Mayford. I'm a cousin of his. I farm across the valley. There are lots of us around here, I'm afraid. You'll probably be swamped by Mayfords.' He shook her hand. 'Would you like to come in and see the house first, or shall we fetch your kit?'

'I think we'd like to see it, wouldn't we? These are my daughters, Fiona and Sophie, and this is Nicholas. This is Mr Mayford.'

'Hello, kids. You lead the way.'

Despite his orders, they hung back, embarrassed and at a loss. Laughing, he ruffled Nicholas's hair and grinned at the girls. Once he had gone through the front door they all followed him into a low-ceilinged, rather dark hall. Its stone floor made it instantly cool and Flixe sighed in relief as her eyes adjusted to its dimness. She had a vague impression of old oak chests and a wide rush mat before Mark led the way upstairs.

'All the beds are made up,' he said over his shoulder, 'because George thought you'd like a choice of rooms.'

'Me first,' shrieked Sophie, hurtling past him before her

siblings could get at the best room. They fought it out between them, leaving Flixe and Mark to walk around the rest of the house in relative peace. She said very little as she took in all the differences between its old, shabby charm and the luxury of George's Harley Street flat. She liked the wide windowsills and the faded chintz curtains, the deep fireplaces and the pale pinks and yellows of the colour-washed walls, but she saw with regret that many of the beams had signs of worm and most of the floors were warped and sloping.

Mark Mayford showed her how the often temperamental hot-water system worked and what she had to do if the electric pump stopped producing water from the well. He told her where she would find telephone numbers for the local doctor and for his house, assured her that he would come to her assistance whenever she needed him and that she was to look on him as George's deputy.

'You are kind,' she said with a smile, wondering how much he knew about her and George. 'But I expect we'll be all right.'

'I'm sure you will. Now, I'll give you a hand with the bags.'

When everything had been unloaded from the back of the car and the roof rack, Flixe insisted that he stay to tea with them and unpacked a huge fruit cake she had cooked a week earlier.

'It ought really to have a week or two longer to mature, but it seems quite squishy,' she said.

'It looks wonderful. My wife loathes cooking and so we make do with stuff from the WI stall at the local market. They're pretty good as a rule, but this is a treat. By the way, she hopes you'll come over to dinner and wondered if tomorrow would suit – after you've had a chance to settle in.'

'How kind,' said Flixe, looking doubtfully at the children.

'Them too. If you were to come about six, they could meet mine and see the ponies and decide whether they want to have a go.'

Flixe gave the Mayford family a silent blessing and tried

not to think what it would be like to sink into their generosity and care for the rest of her life.

Nicholas woke her at exactly seven o'clock the next morning, quietly closing the old-fashioned latch on her bedroom door and sidling to the edge of her bed. Without a word, she lifted up the bedclothes and he slid under them, shivering.

'Golly, you've got cold feet,' said Flixe. 'What have you been doing?'

'Exploring,' he said, hugging her and rubbing his toes against her warm legs. 'Can we go to the beach today?'

'Good idea; but it's a bit early yet.'

'Sophie's up, but Fee's sleeping like a pig.'

'Nicky!'

'Well, she is. Like a fat, snoring, spotty pig.'

Flixe released his arms from her waist and turned him on his back, tickling him as she used to do when he was an infant.

'A fat, snoring pig,' he repeated through gritted teeth, determined not to squeal. In the end he had to succumb.

'There. Like a scrawny, squealing pig,' said his mother with some satisfaction. 'You're a dreadful boy and you must remember that Fiona is particularly sensitive at the moment.'

'When isn't she? Girls! I mean to say.'

'And Sophie?' asked Flixe, laughing. 'What's she up to?'

'She's found a footpath and she's seeing where it goes.' That sounded all right and Flixe lay back, smiling at the bright yellow light that reached through the old curtains and promised hours of blissful heat. 'She's wearing her nightie and her gumboots,' added Nicholas, deliberately watching for his mother's reaction.

Flixe groaned and covered her eyes. 'You children.'

'So will you get up now? You are awake.' He was twisting her earlobes between finger and thumb.

'It's so early, Nicky,' said Flixe, pushing his hands away.

'Too bad. Come on, Mum. It's a waste of the summer to lie in bed.'

'Snoring like a pig. I know. All right. Shoo while I get dressed. Don't forget to clean your teeth and if you're ready before I am you can start laying the breakfast table.'

Ignoring his look of outraged dignity, Flixe hustled him out, washed in the basin in the corner of the room and dressed in a cotton frock so old and well washed that the material felt soft and silky. She pushed her feet into a pair of sloppy, rope-soled canvas shoes and went down to the kitchen, tucking her unset hair behind her ears.

Sophie was already there, still dressed only in a torn nightdress and muddy wellington boots, pouring milk into a flat cereal bowl on the floor.

'What's that for?'

'The cat. It's called Murgatroyd. It belongs here.'

'How on earth do you know?'

'Mr Mayford told me when he brought us the milk. He said he didn't expect any of us to be up yet and he was just going to leave it on the step. It came in a churn.' She pointed to a small aluminium can that would have held about four pints. 'He says that one of the men will bring some every morning. I like him.'

'I liked him, too,' said Flixe. 'Did he say anything about your clothes?'

'No.' Sophie looked surprised and Flixe could only feel thankful that she still had some of her childhood lack of inhibition. It could not last much longer and then she would join Fiona in the almost permanent torment of embarrassment and anger about her body and its infuriating manifestations of growing up.

'Oh, yes, and he says we have to riddle the Aga.'

'He told me that last night. I'll do it after breakfast.'

'And then we'll go to the sea,' said Nicky from the doorway. 'Sophie says the footpath has a sign there, so we can walk.'

'Yes, Nicky.' Flixe was thankful that she would not have to take the big car up those minute lanes. 'Now, who wants bacon?'

By the time George Mayford was expected a week later, they had become completely at home. They knew the walk to the sea with its stiff pull up the hill amid the mingled smells of cow dung and blackberry leaves, hot mown grass and the sea itself. After the first few terrifying bathes, they had learned about the heavy undertow and the excitement of the tumbling waves it produced. The mysteries of the Aga and the well were mysteries no longer; the horses and the farm dogs were still frightening to the London-based Suvarovs, but the Mayford children had become allies.

Flixe herself had made friends with the house more than with any of George's relations, kind though they had all been. It seemed to offer her clues to a part of him that she had sensed but never confronted and she had spent much of the week longing to see him again to test her ideas against the reality. Lying in the baking sun on the beach or pitting herself against the freezing waves, she let the children run wild and herself ignore all the constraints of real life.

She spent the Friday of his expected arrival cooking, which her children thought, and said, was idiotic when she could have bought all the raised pies, cakes and loaves at the WI stall in the market. Having pointed out that it was a small return for the loan of the house, they sobered slightly and even agreed to tidy up some of the rooms they had turned into chaos.

Fiona shyly produced three glass vases she had found in an unused scullery and asked whether she might pick some of the flowers in the courtyard garden. Flixe kissed the top of her head.

'Good idea, darling.'

'Is he like Mr Mayford?'

Flixe put her head on one side.

'Yes, I think he is, quite. He's a little bit older and he's a doctor, as you know. But they look quite alike.'

'Does he make jokes like Mr Mayford?'

'I'm not sure. I expect so.'

'Oh. D'you know him well, Mum?'

'Quite well. I saw him at a lot of the dances I arranged this summer because his daughter was a deb.'

'And you went to Rome with him, didn't you?'

'That's right.'

'Oh. Are you in love with him?'

Flixe wiped her hot face on her apron and sat down at the kitchen table. Fiona stood opposite her, fiddling with the vases and looking miserable.

'I'm not absolutely sure yet. But I am very fond of him. Why do you ask?'

Fiona fiddled some more.

'I heard Mrs Mayford telling Mr Mayford that she thought you'd be perfect for him.'

Flixe laughed.

'And that we'd stop him getting too arrogant with our antics.'

'Oh, darling.' Flixe walked round the table to hug her daughter. 'That shows how much she must like you.'

Fiona pulled away.

'Your biscuits are burning,' she said coolly and disappeared with her vases.

Flixe fished the tray of blackened biscuits out of the top oven of the Aga and shot them straight into the rubbish bin.

'By the way.' Fiona had put her head round the top half of the stable door that led from the kitchen to the garden.

'Yes?'

'She's asked us three over to supper tonight so you can have him to yourself. They'll bring us back.'

Flixe did not know whether to bless Anne Mayford or curse her for alerting Fiona to the possibilities of her mother's friendship, but when George arrived, irritable and tired after

407

a wretched journey, she was glad the children were out of the way. She sat him down in the old rocking chair in his kitchen with a drink and *The Times* while she cooked a stew of fish in cream and saffron with rice, trying to be as quiet as possible.

He had recovered his temper and finished the drink long before she had reached the last tricky stage of beating the cream into the hot saffron-flavoured fish stock.

'Hello, darling,' he said. Flixe turned, the whisk in her hand, to smile at him.

'Hello. Better?'

'Much. Where are your brood?'

'Your cousin Anne's got them over at Manor Farm to give us a chance to be on our own.'

George was standing behind her with his arms round her waist and his face in her neck.

'This is going to curdle in a minute,' said Flixe, leaning happily back against him.

'Sorry. I'll get out of your way. It just seems an age since I hugged you.'

'You're telling me.'

As soon as the fish was ready they ate it quickly, enjoying its subtleties and the luxuriously smooth sauce, but wanting it out of the way. When they had stacked the dishes in the sink and put the remains of the fish out for the utterly rapacious Murgatroyd, they went upstairs to the big bedroom that Fiona had filled with flowers.

'I have missed you,' said George later, his head lying on her breasts and his hand tracing the dim blue lines of the veins in her thigh.

Flixe pulled his head closer and stroked his hair. 'Good.'

'I saw Andrew yesterday,' he said, suddenly sitting up. 'I should have told you before. He seemed fine and that girl of his has been given a clean bill of health. Apparently she keeps bursting into tears, but she's off to her Italian grandmother next week and he says he'll join us then.'

'Thank you, George. You have been good to him.'

'I like him, Felicity. Quite independently of you. It would have been nice if he and Gina could have seen how well they'd suit.'

'They yet may.'

'The pass has been sold, though, hasn't it? Amanda's agreed to marry him – unlike you, my dear. Have you had more thoughts on the subject?'

Flixe moved closer to him.

'You haven't yet seen the brood at close quarters,' she said. 'You may well withdraw your most obliging offer.'

He laughed.

'Unlikely, Miss Austen. As far as I can see, anything and anyone would be worth taking on if I could get you as well, but I know you're still doubtful.'

'It's so tempting, George. While I've been here, I've been wondering why on earth I ever questioned that I wanted it.'

'But?'

'But I want to be sure that it's you and not the circumstances,' she said frankly, remembering that he had said he liked her honesty.

'Ah. I see. Your sister again. You know, Felicity, wanting something that will make you more comfortable doesn't mean that that is why you want it – or even that wanting it is wrong.'

'No, I know,' she said, thinking of Amanda's despairing question: how does one ever know?

As the days passed and she watched him romping with her children – there was no other word for the exuberance of their expeditions to the sea and the hills – losing more of his smoothness every day, she remembered that conversation and all the others they had had.

Towards the end of the month Andrew came with the news of his first-class degree and a bundle of letters for his mother that had arrived at the house in Kensington so recently that it had not been worth forwarding them to Dorset before he left. She did not open them until she had congratulated him on his first and listened to everything he wanted to tell her. Then she sent him out to find George and the children, who were late for lunch, and quickly ran through the pile of envelopes.

Seeing one with the name of her bank embossed along the top left-hand corner, she opened that first.

Dear Mrs Suvarov,

Now that my colleagues and I have had a chance to discuss your revised plans, I am happy to be able to tell you that we have approved the loan you requested. The facilities will be available forthwith.

As I explained at our last meeting, we shall need monthly management accounts so that we can keep an eye on the progress of your business. I look forward to our future dealings.

Yours sincerely,

A.B. Smith,
Branch Manager

'I am free,' thought Flixe, rereading the letter several times to make sure she had not missed a negative somewhere.

She was still dazed with the magnitude of what had happened when her noisy brood and her rumpled lover returned from their morning by the sea. Their hair was caked with salt and their skins were tanned to a smooth, pale gold that made Andrew's London complexion look unhealthy. All four of them were wearing shorts and scuffed sandals that poured sand and bits of grass all over the kitchen floor.

Fiona went straight to the Aga, where her mother was standing.

'Are you all right, Mum? You must be boiling.'

'What, darling? Yes, I suppose I am. But the most wonderful thing has happened.'

'What?'

She looked around the room.

'The bank has promised to back my new business.'

Her three younger children looked puzzled, but Andrew kissed her and George stood with his back to the sink, his face blazing with happiness.

'Then you're free and able to choose. Will you?' he said.

She waited a moment, testing her feelings against her doubts. Then, across the heads of her four children, she nodded.

'Excellent,' he said, his voice nearly calm but his smile like a beacon of excitement. 'Come along, children, time to wash. Not in the sink, Nicky. Goodness me. It's full of saucepans. Hurry up and I'll follow you.'

The children left the kitchen. Andrew, who had been watching his mother with eyes like a judge, suddenly smiled.

'Welcome to the family, George,' he said, holding out his hand.

For the first time George Mayford saw that although the boy was dark and exactly like photographs of his father, he could also look very like his mother. George took his hand and shook it formally. Flixe went to put her arm around her son's waist, leaning her head against his shoulder.

'Thank you, my darling child,' she said.

CHAPTER 28

The next day at breakfast they were listening to the wireless as they always did, because the newspapers were not delivered until much later in the day. After hearing the home news, they listened to the stern voice of the newsreader announcing that the Russian tanks that had been threatening Czechoslovakia's borders for weeks had invaded.

Alexander Dubček, who had done everything he could to free his country from the tyranny of Russian Communism, had been kidnapped and flown to Moscow. All his reforms, the freedom of the press, the rights of citizens to fair trials and to leave the country whenever they wanted, had been reversed.

There were tears in Andrew's eyes as he listened to what amounted to the obituary of freedom behind the Iron Curtain.

'I am so sorry,' said his mother, understanding exactly why his emotions were so near the surface and how little the tears had to do with the politics of Eastern Europe. He blew his nose.

'Papa would have hated it.'

'I know.'

'Why?' said twelve-year-old Nicholas. Andrew looked down at him and sighed.

'Because he hated the way the ideals of the revolution had been warped in Russia,' he said simply. 'And the injustice of what the Russians were doing to their satellites.'

'He once said to me,' Fiona added, 'that there were times when he even thought that the old days he'd loathed so much, when it was a serious offence even to teach a peasant to read, had been better than now. Then at least some of the people were free.'

Flixe looked at her children and then at George. He was watching them with approval and, she thought, a certain measure of love.

'Did he know Anastasia? Would he have been able to tell if that woman in America is her?' asked Sophie, looking disgustedly at the soft yolk of her fried egg as it ran out over her plate. 'Ugh. I hate soft eggs.'

'Then you can cook them tomorrow, Sophie,' said George, 'to make sure they'll be exactly right.'

She laughed at him and nodded, acknowledging both the reproof and the encouragement, and his right to deliver them. Once more Flixe felt passionately grateful for his adoption of her family.

'No, he didn't,' she said. 'His father was in trade and had nothing to do with the Tsar, although the family was quite rich.'

'Then why aren't we?'

'Because he had to leave it all behind in the revolution, dumb-bell,' said Nicky. Then he blinked rapidly several times and coughed, muttering: 'I wish he wasn't dead. Why did he have to die?'

'So do I, Nicky,' said Flixe. 'But he was very tired at the end. An illness like that just wears you out. Don't you remember how exhausted he looked the last time you saw him?'

The boy nodded, his face very red and his chin clenched to stop it wobbling.

'He said something to me but I didn't understand it.' He burst into tears. 'He said something and I think it was Russian. I don't know what it was. He didn't hear me when I asked. He didn't say anything else. And then he died before I saw him again.'

Flixe cradled him in her arms, ignoring all the others, concentrating everything on Nicholas. From behind her she heard Andrew's voice.

'Did it sound like this? "*Spokoini nochi, malchik, nye ispugai*".'

Nicky pulled away from his mother.

'Yes, I think so. I don't know. It could have been. Why do you think it was?'

'It was what he said to me, too. It just means: Good-night, my son. Sleep well. Don't be frightened.'

Flixe felt tears in her own eyes then and looked across the head of her youngest child to George, who smiled at her with absolute openness. She felt as though he had agreed that the memory of Peter would always be with them and was necessary to their well-being.

'That sounds like the post,' said Fiona, leaping up from her chair and taking the opportunity to wipe her eyes as soon as she was in the passage that led to the front door. She came back with a bundle of envelopes, which she distributed.

Flixe looked at her single letter and recognised Amanda Wallington's writing. She put the envelope face down beside her plate and offered everyone more coffee. Andrew pushed his cup forwards and ripped open the envelope of his letter. Flixe filled his cup but before she had had a chance to hand it back to him he stood up, the letter in his hands and a blind, desperate look in his eyes.

'I'm going for a walk,' he said.

'Let me come too,' said Sophie, but George grabbed her sleeve as she passed him and kept her back.

414

'Let him go alone,' he whispered as she tried to pull away. 'I think he needs time to himself.'

When he had gone Flixe opened her own letter and when she had read it passed it across the table to George. It said:

Dear Auntie Flixe,

You were right. I can't marry him. I didn't ever love him, although I like him very much. I always have, but it isn't enough, is it? I know it was cowardly to wait until I was in Italy and then write, but I didn't want to hurt him face to face.

Will you look after him for me?

Love, Amanda

PS That's a silly question; I know you will. But I hate hurting him.

PPS I haven't told him any of the things you said to me that day. I've just told him that I can't marry him.

PPPS One good thing has come out of it all: my mother is pleased with me. What a miracle!

George made no comment, simply folding the letter up and putting it in his trouser pocket. When the three children had finished their breakfast and departed out of doors, he lit his pipe and came to sit on one of the old wheelback chairs beside Flixe, saying, 'I'm sorry.'

'It's my fault,' she said. 'I went to see her and the minute she expressed the slightest doubt about marrying him, I told her I thought it was a bad idea. I hope I did the right thing. Perhaps I was merely putting my doubts about us on to her. Perhaps . . .'

'Felicity.' George took her hands away from the linen napkin she was attempting to shred as though it were paper. 'Don't torment yourself. You did what was best at the time. From what I've seen of the young woman, I'd have said anyone's intervention was more likely to persuade her to do the opposite of what she was advised. It sounds as though you merely reinforced her own real doubts. She'd have come to

415

the same conclusion off her own bat.'

She got up and walked about the kitchen, gripping her hands together.

'My dear,' he said quietly. Flixe turned back to him. Her eyes, which had been so peaceful since she had agreed to marry him, looked tormented again.

'I must go and find him.'

'Yes, I know,' said George. 'I'll wait here in case you need me.' He hesitated for a moment and then added: 'Don't be too hurt if he can't accept help yet.'

'No, I won't,' she said, 'but I have to try. It must underline it so badly for him to see us together.'

'We are together, aren't we?' he said, asking for reassurance he ought not to have needed. He knew that it was her sudden switch from him to complete absorption in her son's needs that had roused his own insecurities. Much as he disliked being reminded of them, he trusted her enough – and loved her enough – to give them expression. Flixe looked at him seriously and nodded.

'Yes. This doesn't change anything for us, except that we'll have to be there when he needs us. I must go.'

Walking up on to the top of the cliff, she tried to make out which of the diminutive figures ahead of her might be her son. When none of them looked right, she set off for the path that led down to the beach, but again she was unlucky.

Eventually she found him, sitting in a small hollow of the cliff itself, just below the edge, surrounded by the drying leaves of *iris foetida* and the barbed ropes of brambles. He had his hands around his knees, gripping a handkerchief, and he was staring fiercely out to sea.

There was just enough space on the little ledge for her to sit beside him. As she went down, she ripped a long scratch in one brown leg. The blood bubbled out, just the same brilliant red as the iris seeds. Andrew offered her his handkerchief without saying anything.

Flixe mopped the blood.

'It's curious how much more a small scratch hurts than an actual cut.'

'That's because fewer nerves are damaged and so there are more left to carry pain messages to the brain,' he said impatiently.

'I am sorry,' said his mother after a long, difficult pause. 'I know how much you wanted her.'

'How do you know what's happened?'

'She wrote to me, too, to tell me she was sorry and to ask me to look after you.'

'Why should she care?'

His beautiful lips quivered and he tucked one corner of the lower between his teeth. Frowning, he looked away out to sea again. Flixe was not sure whether to touch him or not. Eventually she compromised by leaning her shoulder against his.

'I think she cares for you a great deal, but was afraid of committing herself to something she does not understand, because she doesn't yet understand herself.'

'But I understand her,' he shouted. 'Isn't that enough?'

At that Flixe did touch him. She edged round on her precarious perch and unlaced his hands from around his knees, holding them between her own.

'No, I don't think that it is,' she said, forebearing to add that she thought he had very little idea of the real Amanda. 'I have come to value her far more highly these last few weeks than I used to do, and I understand why you love her, but I don't think that either of you would have been happy for long.'

He pulled his hands back and turned his face away.

'I know it doesn't help now,' said Flixe sadly, 'and it must sound as though I'm rubbing salt into the wound, but I want you to be really happy one day, Andrew, not just making the best of something painful.'

She watched him struggling until at last he produced a faint reflection of his father's old, mocking smile.

'It doesn't seem very likely at the moment,' he said.

'Perhaps not, but that's not to say it's not possible.'

'Does it come back, Mum? Really?' He was looking at her again, searching her face for something, some certainty.

'Happiness?' she said, trying to give him the faith that had only recently come back to her. 'Yes, Andrew, if you wait patiently enough it does come back.'

NEVER SUCH INNOCENCE

Daphne Wright

V.E. night, 1945: the sky is glittering with fireworks as jubilant Londoners celebrate the end of the war. But for Julia Gillingham, a new ordeal is only just beginning . . .

Her husband Anthony, a doctor in the army, has been missing for two years. Captured in North Africa, taken to prison camp, he then vanished, leaving Julia with only a faint hope that faded as the months went by. And then a letter arrives. Anthony is alive, well, and in Italy – with no intention of returning to her.

Baffled, hurt and yet bent on finding out more, Julia sets off for the enigmatic, haunting city of Venice. There she lives through Europe's struggle to emerge from the devastation of war, and through her own conflict with the forces of danger, tragedy, loyalty and love . . .

FICTION
0 7515 0502 1

DREAMS OF ANOTHER DAY

Daphne Wright

Ten years after the end of the Second World War, and
Mary Alderbrook – known to family and friends as Ming
– feels life is passing her by. Although her sisters are all
happily married and settled, Ming shies away from
commitment and the attentions of Mark Sudley make her
feel uneasy. Is it friendship she wants from him – or
something deeper?

When her friend Connie Wroughton offers Ming the
chance to write for her new magazine, she gladly accepts,
discovering a true flair for writing. But before she knows
it, trouble is stalking her again – anonymous, threatening
letters arrive – and Ming knows she must finally face up
to tests that will change her life.

FICTION
0 7515 0191 3

☐	The Longest Winter	Daphne Wright	£4.99
☐	The Distant Kingdom	Daphne Wright	£4.99
☐	The Parrot Cage	Daphne Wright	£4.99
☐	Never Such Innocence	Daphne Wright	£4.99
☐	Dreams of Another Day	Daphne Wright	£4.99
☐	Voices in Summer	Rosamunde Pilcher	£4.50
☐	The Carousel	Rosamunde Pilcher	£4.50
☐	A Thread of Gold	Helen Cannam	£3.99
☐	The Last Ballad	Helen Cannam	£4.99

Warner Books now offers an exciting range of quality titles by both established and new authors. All of the books in this series are available from:

Little, Brown and Company (UK) Limited,
P.O. Box 11,
Falmouth,
Cornwall TR10 9EN.

Alternatively you may fax your order to the above address.
Fax No. 0326 376423.

Payments can be made as follows: cheque, postal order (payable to Little, Brown and Company) or by credit cards, Visa/Access. Do not send cash or currency. UK customers and B.F.P.O. please allow £1.00 for postage and packing for the first book, plus 50p for the second book, plus 30p for each additional book up to a maximum charge of £3.00 (7 books plus).

Overseas customers including Ireland, please allow £2.00 for the first book plus £1.00 for the second book, plus 50p for each additional book.

NAME (Block Letters) ....

....

ADDRESS ....

....

....

☐ I enclose my remittance for _____

☐ I wish to pay by Access/Visa Card

Number | | | | | | | | | | | | | | | | | |

Card Expiry Date | | | | |